Piece of My Heart

PETER ROBINSON

Piece of My Heart

HODDER &
STOUGHTON

First published in Great Britain in 2006 by Hodder & Stoughton
A division of Hodder Headline

The right of Peter Robinson to be identified as the Author
of the Work has been asserted by him in accordance
with the Copyright, Designs and Patents Act 1988.

A Hodder & Stoughton Book

2

A CIP catalogue record for this title is available from the British Library

Hardback ISBN 0 340 83686 5
Trade Paperback ISBN 0 340 83687 3

Typeset in Plantin by Hewer Text UK Ltd, Edinburgh
Printed and bound by Mackays of Chatham plc, Chatham, Kent

Hodder Headline's policy is to use papers that are natural, renewable and
recyclable products and made from wood grown in sustainable forests.
The logging and manufacturing processes are expected to conform to
the environmental regulations of the country of origin.

Hodder & Stoughton Ltd
A division of Hodder Headline
338 Euston Road
London NW1 3BH

For Sheila

'Imagination abandoned by reason produces impossible monsters; united with it, she is the mother of the arts and the source of its marvels.'

Francisco Goya, 1799

'The road of excess leads to the palace of wisdom.'

William Blake, *The Marriage of Heaven and Hell*, 1790–93

I

To an observer looking down from the peak of Brimleigh Beacon early that Monday morning, the scene below might have resembled the aftermath of a battle. It had rained briefly during the night, and the pale sun coaxed tendrils of mist from the damp earth. They swirled over fields dotted with motionless shapes, mingling here and there with the darker smoke of smouldering embers. Human scavengers picked their way through the carnage as if collecting discarded weapons, occasionally bending to extract an object of value from a dead man's pocket. Others appeared to be shovelling soil or quicklime into large open graves. The light wind carried a whiff of rotting flesh.

And over the whole scene a terrible stillness reigned.

But to Dave Sampson, down on the field, there had been no battle, only a peaceful gathering, and Dave had the worm's-eye view. It was just after eight a.m., and he had been up half the night along with everyone else, listening to Pink Floyd, Fleetwood Mac and Led Zeppelin. Now the crowd had gone home, and he was moving among the motionless shapes – litter left by the vanished hordes – helping to clean up after the very first Brimleigh festival. Here he was, bent over, back aching like hell, eyes burning with tiredness, plodding across the muddy field picking up rubbish. The eerie sounds of Jimmy Page playing his electric guitar with a violin bow still echoed in his mind as he shoved Cellophane wrappers and half-eaten Mars bars into his plastic bag.

Ants and beetles crawled over the remains of sandwiches and half-empty tins of baked beans. Flies buzzed around the faeces and wasps hovered about the necks of empty pop bottles. More than once, Dave had to manoeuvre sharply to avoid being stung. He couldn't believe some of the stuff people left behind. Food wrappers, soggy newspapers and magazines, used Durex, tampons, cigarette ends, knickers, empty beer cans and roaches you'd expect, but what on earth had the person who left the Underwood typewriter been thinking of? Or the wooden crutch? Had a cripple, suddenly healed by the music, run off and left it behind?

There were other things, too, things best avoided. The makeshift toilets set over the open cess-pit had been uninviting, as well as few and far between, and the queues had been long, encouraging more than one desperate person to find a quiet spot elsewhere in the field. Dave glanced towards the craters and felt glad that he wasn't one of the volunteers assigned to fill them with earth.

In an otherwise isolated spot at the southern edge of the field, where the land rose gently towards the fringes of Brimleigh Woods, Dave noticed an abandoned sleeping-bag. The closer he got, the more it looked to be occupied. Had someone passed out or simply gone to sleep? More likely, Dave thought, it was drugs. All night the medical tent had been open to people suffering hallucinations from bad acid, and there had been enough Mandrax and opiated hash around to knock out an army.

Dave prodded the bag with his foot. It felt soft and heavy. He prodded it again, harder this time. Still nothing. It definitely *felt* as if someone was inside. Finally, he bent and pulled the zip, and when he saw what was there, he wished he hadn't.

Monday, 8 September 1969

Detective Inspector Stanley Chadwick was at his desk in Brotherton House before eight o'clock on Monday morning, as usual, with every intention of finishing off the paperwork that had piled up during his two weeks' annual leave at the end of August. The caravan at Primrose Valley, with Janet and Yvonne, had made a nice haven for a while, but Yvonne was obviously restless, as only a sixteen-year-old on holiday with her parents can be, and crime didn't stop while he was away from Leeds. Nor, apparently, did the paperwork.

It had been a good weekend. Yorkshire beat Derbyshire in the Gillette Cup Final, and if Leeds United, coming off a season as league champions, hadn't managed to beat Manchester United at home, at least they had come out of it with a 2–2 draw, and Billy Bremner had scored.

The only blot on the landscape was that Yvonne had stayed out most of the night on Sunday, and it wasn't the first time. Chadwick had lain awake until he heard her come in at about half past six, and by then it was time for him to get up and get ready for work. Yvonne had gone straight to her room and closed the door, so he had put off the inevitable confrontation until later, but now it was gnawing at him. He didn't know what was happening to his daughter, what she was up to, but whatever it was, it frightened him. It seemed that the younger generation had been getting stranger and stranger over the past few years, more out of control, and Chadwick seemed unable to find any point of connection with them any more. Most seemed like members of another species to him now. Especially his own daughter.

Chadwick tried to shake off his worries about Yvonne and glanced over the crime sheets: trouble with squatters in a Leeds city-centre office building; a big drugs bust in Chapeltown; an assault on a woman with a stone in a sock in

Bradford. Manningham Lane, he noticed, and everyone knew what kind of women you found on Manningham Lane. Still, poor cow, nobody deserved to be hit with a stone in a sock. Just over the county border, in the North Riding, the Brimleigh festival had gone off peacefully enough, with only a few arrests for drunkenness and drug-dealing – only to be expected at such an event – and a bit of bother with some skinheads at one of the fences.

At about half past nine, Chadwick reached for the next file. He had just opened it when Karen popped her head round his door and told him Detective Chief Superintendent McCullen wanted to see him. Chadwick put the folder back on to the pile. If McCullen wanted to see him, it had to be something pretty big. Whatever it was, it was bound to be a lot more interesting than paperwork.

McCullen sat in his spacious office puffing at his pipe and enjoying the panoramic view. Brotherton House perched at the western edge of the city centre, adjacent to the university and Leeds General Infirmary, and looked out west over the new Inner Ring Road towards Park Lane College. All the old mills and factories in the area, blackened by a century or more of soot, had been demolished over the last two or three years, and it seemed that a whole new city was rising from the ruins of its Victorian past: the international swimming pool, Leeds Playhouse, Leeds Polytechnic, the *Yorkshire Post* building. Cranes criss-crossed on the horizon and the sound of pneumatic drills filled the air. Was it just Chadwick's imagination, or was there a building site no matter where you looked in the city, these days?

He wasn't sure that the future was better than the past it was replacing any more than he was sure that the emerging world order was better than the old one. There seemed a monotonous sterility to many of the new buildings, concrete and glass tower blocks for the most part, along with terraces of red-brick council houses. Their Victorian predecessors, like Benjamin Gott's Bean Ing Mills, might have looked a bit more grimy and shabby, but at least they had character. Or perhaps, Chadwick thought, he was just becoming an old fogey about architecture, the same way he was about young people. And at forty-eight he was too young for that. He made a mental note to try to be more tolerant of hippies and architects.

'Stan, sit down,' said McCullen, gesturing to the seat opposite his desk. He was a hard, compact man, one of the old school, and fast nearing retirement. Grey hair in a severe crew-cut, sharp, square features, an intimidating gleam in his narrowed eyes. People said he had no sense of humour, but Chadwick thought it was just so dark and buried so deep that nobody recognised it, or wanted to find it. McCullen had served as a commando during the war, and Chadwick himself had seen more than enough active duty. He liked to think it created a bond between them, something in common that they never spoke about. They also shared a Scottish background. Chadwick's mother was a Scot, and his father had worked in the Clydebank shipyards. Chadwick had grown up in Glasgow, drifting down to Yorkshire only after the war.

He sat.

'I won't beat about the bush,' McCullen began, knocking his pipe on the heavy glass ashtray, 'but there's been a body discovered at Brimleigh Glen, the big field where they held the festival this weekend. I don't have many details yet. The report has just this minute come in. All we know is that the victim is a young woman.'

'Oh,' said Chadwick, aware of that cold, sinking feeling deep in his belly. 'I thought Brimleigh was in the North Riding?'

McCullen refilled his pipe. 'Strictly speaking, it is,' he said finally, releasing clouds of aromatic blue smoke. 'Just over the border. But they're country coppers. They don't get many murders, just a bit of sheep-shagging now and then. They've certainly got no one capable of handling an investigation of this magnitude, given how many people must have been attending that festival, and they're asking for our help. I thought, perhaps, with your recent successes . . .'

'The locals still won't like it,' Chadwick said. 'Perhaps it's not as bad as having Scotland Yard tramping all over your provincial toes, but—'

'It's already cleared,' said McCullen, turning his gaze back to the window. 'There's a local detective sergeant, name of Keith Enderby. You'll be working with him. He's already at the scene.' McCullen glanced at his wristwatch. 'Better get out there, Stan. DC Bradley's waiting with the car. The doc'll be there soon, wanting to get the body back to the mortuary for the post-mortem.'

Chadwick knew when he was being dismissed. Solve two murders so far this year and you get lumbered with a case like this. Bloody hippies. Paperwork suddenly didn't look so bad, after all. *Tolerance*, he told himself. He stood up and headed for the door.

Monday, 8 September 1969

There was no easy access to the body in the field, not without getting his shoes muddy. Chadwick cursed under his breath as he saw his lovingly polished black brogues and the bottoms of his suit trousers daubed with brown mud. If he'd been a rural copper, he'd have kept a pair of wellies in the boot of his car, but you don't expect mud when you're used to working the streets of Leeds. If anything, DC Bradley complained even more.

Brimleigh Glen looked like a vast tip. A natural amphi-theatre cupped between low hills to the east and north and Brimleigh Woods to the west and south, it was a popular spot for picnics and brass-band concerts in summer. Not this weekend, though. A stage had been erected at the western end of the field, abutting the woods, and the audience had sprawled as far back as the hills on the eastern and northern sides to a distance where, Chadwick guessed, nobody would have been able to see very much at all, except little dots.

The small knot of people surrounding the body stood at the southern edge of the field, about a hundred yards back from the stage, near the edge of the woods. When Chadwick and Bradley arrived, a man with long greasy hair, bell-bottomed jeans and an Afghan waistcoat turned and said, with far more aggression than Chadwick would have expected of someone who was supposed to embrace peace and love, 'Who the fuck are you?'

Chadwick feigned a surprised expression and looked around. Then he pointed his thumb at his own chest. 'Who, me?'

'Yes, you.'

A clearly embarrassed young man hurried over to them. 'Er . . . I think that's probably the detective inspector from Leeds. Am I right, sir?'

Chadwick nodded.

'How d'you do, sir? I'm Detective Sergeant Enderby, North Yorkshire Constabulary. This is Rick Hayes, the festival promoter.'

'You must have been up all night,' said Chadwick. 'I'd have thought you'd be long tucked up in bed by now.'

'There's still a lot to see to,' Hayes said, gesturing behind him. 'That scaffolding, for a start. It's rented and it all has to be accounted for. I'm sorry, by the way.' He glanced in the direction of the sleeping-bag. 'This has all been very upsetting.'

'I'm sure,' said Chadwick, making his way forward. There were four people, besides himself and DC Bradley, at the

scene, only one a uniformed policeman, and most were
standing far too close to the body. They were also very
casually dressed. Even DS Enderby's hair, Chadwick noticed,
was dangerously close to touching his jacket collar, and his
sideboards needed trimming. His black winklepickers looked
as if they had been dirty even before he crossed the field. 'Were
you the first officer to arrive at the scene?' Chadwick asked the
young police constable, trying to move people back and clear a
little space round the sleeping-bag.

'Yes, sir. PC Jacobs. I was on patrol when the call came in.'

'Who called it in?'

One of the others stepped forward. 'I did. Steve Naylor. I was
working on the scaffolding when Dave here shouted me over.
There's a phone box on the road on the other side of the hill.'

'Did you find the body?' Chadwick asked Dave Sampson.

'Yes.'

Sampson looked pale, as well he might, Chadwick thought.
His own war service and eighteen years on the force had
hardened him to the sight of violent death, but he hadn't
forgotten his first time, and he never forgot how devastating it
could be to someone who had never witnessed it before. He
looked around. 'Any chance someone might rustle up a pot of
tea?'

Everyone stared at him, dumbfounded, then Naylor, the
stage worker, said, 'We've got a Primus and a billycan back
there. I'll see what I can do.'

'Good lad.'

Naylor headed for the stage.

Chadwick turned back to Sampson. 'Touch anything?' he
asked.

'Only the zip. I mean, I didn't know . . . I thought . . .'

'What did you think?'

'It felt like there was someone inside. I thought they might be
asleep or . . .'

'On drugs?'

'Possibly. Yes.'

'After you opened the zip and saw what it was, what did you do?'

'I called over to the stage.'

Chadwick glanced at the speckled mess on the grass about a yard away. 'Before or after you were sick?'

Sampson swallowed. 'After.'

'Did you touch the body at all?'

'No.'

'Good. Now, go over and give your statement to Detective Sergeant Enderby. We'll probably want to talk to you again, so stick around.'

Sampson nodded.

Chadwick crouched by the blue sleeping-bag, keeping his hands in his pockets so that he didn't touch anything, even by accident. Only the upper half of the girl's body was exposed, but it was enough. She was wearing a smocked white dress with a scooped neck, and the area under the left breast was a mess – knifework, by the look of it. Also, her dress was bunched up round her waist, as if she hadn't had time to smooth it down when she got into the bag – or as if someone had shoved her in quickly *after* he'd killed her. The long dress might also have been raised for sexual purposes, if she had been sharing the sleeping-bag with her boyfriend, Chadwick realised, but he would have to wait for the pathologist to find out any more about that.

She was a very pretty girl, with long blonde hair, an oval face and full lips. She looked so innocent. Not unlike Yvonne, he thought, with a sudden shudder, and Yvonne had been out all last night, too. But she had come home. Not this girl. She was perhaps a year or two older than Yvonne, and her eye-shadow emphasised the colour of her big blue eyes. The mascara stood out in stark contrast to the paleness of her skin. She wore several strings of cheap coloured beads around her neck, and a cornflower had been painted on her right cheek.

There was nothing more that Chadwick could do until the Home Office pathologist arrived – which should be very soon, McCullen had given him to understand. Standing, he scanned the ground nearby but saw only rubbish: KitKat wrappers, a soggy *International Times*, an empty pouch of Old Holborn rolling tobacco, an orange pack of Rizla cigarette papers. It would all have to be bagged and checked, of course. He sniffed the air – moist but warm enough for the time of year – and glanced at his watch. Half past eleven. It looked like being another fine day, and a long one.

He turned back to the others. 'Anybody recognise her?'

They all shook their heads. Chadwick thought he noticed a little hesitation in Rick Hayes's reaction.

'Mr Hayes?'

'No,' said Hayes. 'Never seen her before.'

Chadwick thought he was lying, but it would keep. He noticed a movement by the stage, then Naylor was coming back with a tray and, following shortly behind him, a nattily dressed man who seemed to be about as happy to find himself walking across a muddy field as Chadwick had been. But this man was carrying a black bag. The pathologist had arrived at last.

Detective Chief Inspector Alan Banks hit the play button, and after the heartbeats, the glorious sound of 'Breathe' from Pink Floyd's *Dark Side of the Moon* filled the room. He still hadn't got the hang of the new equipment yet, but he was finding his way round it slowly. He had inherited a state-of-the-art sound system along with a DVD-player, forty-two-inch plasma TV, 40G iPod and a Porsche 911 from his brother Roy. The estate had gone to Banks's parents, but they were set in their ways and had no use for a Porsche or a large-screen TV. The first wouldn't last five minutes parked outside their Peterborough council house, and the second wouldn't fit in their living room. They had sold Roy's London house, which had set them both up nicely for the rest of their lives, and passed on the things they couldn't use to Banks.

As for Roy's iPod, Banks's father had taken one look at it and been about to drop it in the waste-bin before Banks rescued it. Now it had become as essential to him, when he went out, as his wallet and his mobile. He had been able to download the software and buy new chargers and cables, along with an adaptor that allowed him to play it through his car radio, and while he had kept a great deal of his brother's music library on it, he had managed to clear a good fifteen hours' worth of space by deleting the complete *Ring* cycle – more than enough to accommodate his meagre collection.

Banks headed into the kitchen to see how dinner was getting along. All he'd had to do was remove the packaging and put the foil tray into the oven, but he didn't want to burn it. It was Friday evening, and Annie Cabbot was coming for dinner – just as a friend. The evening was to be a sort of unofficial house-warming, although that was a term Banks hesitated to use these days. He had been back in the restored cottage for less than a month, and tonight would be Annie's first visit.

It was a wild October night. Banks could hear the wind screaming and moaning and see the dark shadows of branches tossing and thrashing beyond the kitchen window. He hoped Annie would make the drive all right, that there were no trees down. There was a spare bed if she wanted to stay, but he doubted that she would. Too much history for that to be comfortable for either of them, although there had been moments over the summer when he'd thought it wouldn't take much to brush all the objections aside. Best not think about that, he told himself.

Banks poured himself the last of the Amarone. His parents

had inherited Roy's wine cellar, and they had passed this on to him, too. As far as Arthur Banks was concerned, white wine was for sissies and red wine tasted like vinegar. His mother preferred sweet sherry. Their loss was Banks's gain, and while it lasted, he got to enjoy the high life of first-growth Bordeaux and Sauterne, white and red Burgundy from major growers, Chianti Classico, Barolo and Amarone. When it was gone, of course, he would be back to boxes of Simply Chilean and Big Aussie Red, but for the moment he was enjoying himself.

Whenever he opened a bottle, though, he missed Roy, which was strange because they had never been close, and Banks felt he'd only got to know his brother after his death. He would just have to learn to live with it. It was the same with the other things – the TV, stereo, car, music: they all made him think of the brother he had never really known.

Part of the way through 'Us and Them' the doorbell rang. Annie, half past seven, right on time. He walked through and opened the front door, flinching at the gust of wind that almost blew her into his arms. She edged back, giggling, trying to hold down her hair as Banks pushed the door shut, but even in the short trip from her car to his front door it had become a tangled mess.

'Quite a night out there,' Banks said. 'I hope you didn't have any problems getting here.'

Annie smiled. 'Nothing I couldn't handle.' She handed Banks a bottle of wine – Tesco's Chilean Merlot, he noticed – and took out a hairbrush. As she attacked her hair, she wandered round the front room. 'This is certainly different from what I expected,' she said. 'It looks really cosy. I see you did go for the dark wood, after all.'

The wood for the desk had been one of the things they had talked about, and Annie had favoured the darker colour over light pine. What had been Banks's main living room was now a small study complete with bookcases, a reproduction Georgian writing-table for the laptop computer under the window, and a couple of comfortable brown leather armchairs arranged round the fire, perfect for reading. A door beside the fireplace led into the new entertainment room, which ran the length of the house. Annie walked up and down and admired it, then added that it was a bit of a bloke's den.

The TV hung on the wall at the front and the speakers were spread about in strategic positions round the deep plum sofa and armchairs. Storage racks on the side walls held CDs and DVDs, mostly Roy's, apart from the few Banks had bought over the past couple of months. At the back, French windows led to the new conservatory.

They wandered into the kitchen, which had been completely remodelled. Banks had tried to make sure it was as close to the original as possible, with the pine cupboards, copper-bottomed pans on wall hooks and the breakfast nook whose bench and table matched the cupboards, but that strange, benign presence he had felt there before had gone for good, or so it seemed. Now it was a fine kitchen, but only a kitchen. The builders had run the conservatory along the entire back of the house, and there was also a door leading to it from the kitchen.

'Impressive,' Annie said. 'All this and a Porsche parked outside, too. You'll be pulling the birds like nobody's business.'

'Some hope,' said Banks. 'I might even sell the Porsche.'

'Why?'

'It feels so strange, having all Roy's stuff. I mean, the TV, the movies and CDs are OK, I suppose, not quite as personal, but the car . . . I don't know. Roy loved that car.'

'Give it a chance. You might get to love it, too.'

'I like it well enough. It's just . . . Oh, never mind.'

'Mmm, it smells good in here. What's for dinner?'

'Roast beef and Yorkshire pudding.'

Annie gave him a look.

'Vegetarian lasagne,' he said. 'Marks and Spencer's best.'
'That'll do fine.'

Banks threw together a simple salad with an oil-and-vinegar dressing while Annie sat on the bench and opened the wine. Pink Floyd finished, so he went and put some Mozart wind quintets on the stereo. He'd had speakers wired into the kitchen, and the sound was good. When everything was ready, they sat opposite one another and Banks served the food. Annie was looking good, he thought. Her flowing chestnut hair still fell about her shoulders in disarray, but that only heightened her attraction for him. As for the rest, she was dressed in her usual casual style, just a touch of makeup, lightweight linen jacket, a green T-shirt and close-fitting black jeans, bead necklace and several thin silver bracelets which jingled when she moved her hand.

They had hardly got beyond the first mouthful when Banks's telephone rang. He muttered an apology to Annie and went to answer it.

'Sir?'

It was DC Winsome Jackman. 'Yes, Winsome,' Banks said. 'This had better be important. I've been slaving over a hot oven all day.'

'Sir?'

'Never mind. Go on.'

'There's been a murder, sir.'

'Are you certain?'

'I wouldn't be disturbing you if I wasn't, sir,' Winsome said. 'I'm at the scene right now. Moorview Cottage in Fordham, just outside Lyndgarth. I'm standing about six feet away from him, and the back of his head's caved in. Looks like someone bashed him with the poker. Kev's here, too, and he agrees. Sorry, Detective Sergeant Templeton. The local bobby called it in.'

Banks knew Fordham. It was nothing but a hamlet, really, a

cluster of cottages, a pub and a church. 'Christ,' he said. 'OK, Winsome, I'll get there as soon as I can. In the meantime, you can call in the SOCOs and Dr Glendenning, if he's available.'

'Right you are, sir. Should I ring DI Cabbot?'

'I'll deal with that. Keep the scene clear. We'll be there. Half an hour at the most.'

Banks hung up and went back into the kitchen. 'Sorry to spoil your dinner, Annie, but we've got to go out. Suspicious death. Winsome's certain it's murder.'

'Your car or mine?'

'Yours, I think. The Porsche is a bit pretentious for a crime scene, don't you think?'

Monday, 8 September 1969

As the day progressed, the scene around Brimleigh Glen became busy with the arrival of various medical and scientific experts and the incident van, a temporary operational head-quarters with telephone communications and, more impor-tantly, tea-making facilities. The immediate crime scene was taped off and a constable posted at the entrance to log the names of those who came and went. All work on rubbish disposal, stage-dismantling and cess-pit filling was suspended until further notice, much to the chagrin of Rick Hayes, who complained that every minute more spent at the field was costing him money.

Chadwick hadn't forgotten Hayes's possible lie earlier about not recognising the victim, and he looked forward to the pleasure of a more in-depth interview. In fact, Hayes was high on his list of priorities. For the moment, though, it was important to get the investigation organised, the mechanics in place and the right men appointed to the right jobs.

On first impression Detective Sergeant Enderby seemed capable enough, despite the length of his hair, and Chadwick already knew that Simon Bradley, his driver, was a bright young copper with a good future ahead of him. He also demonstrated the same sort of military neatness and precision in his demeanour that Chadwick appreciated. As for the rest of the team, they would come mostly from the North Riding, people he didn't know, and he would have to learn their strengths and weaknesses on the hoof. He preferred to enter into an investigation on more certain ground, but it couldn't be helped. Officially, this was North Yorkshire's case, and he was simply helping out.

The doctor had pronounced the victim dead and turned over the body to the coroner's officer, in this case a local constable specially appointed to the task, who arranged for its transportation to the mortuary in Leeds. During his brief examination at the scene, Dr O'Neill had been able to tell Chadwick only that the wounds had been inflicted almost certainly by a thin-bladed knife and that she had been dead less than ten hours and more than six before the time of his examination, which meant she had been killed some time between half past one and half past five in the morning. Her body had been moved after death, he added, and she had not been in the sleeping-bag when she died. Though stab wounds, even to the heart, often don't bleed a great deal, the doctor said, he would have expected more blood on the inside of the sleeping-bag, had she been stabbed there.

How long she had lain elsewhere before she had been moved, or where she had lain, he couldn't say, only that the post-mortem lividity indicated that she had been on her back for some hours. From an external examination, it didn't look as if she had been raped – she was still wearing her white cotton knickers, and they looked clean – but only a complete post-mortem would reveal details of any sexual activity prior to death. There were no defensive wounds on her hands, which meant most likely that she had been taken by surprise, and that the first stab had pierced her heart, incapacitating her immediately. There was light bruising on the front left side of her neck, which Dr O'Neill said could be an indication that someone, the killer probably, had restrained her from behind.

So, Chadwick thought, the killer had attempted clumsily to make it look as if the girl had been killed in the bag on the field, and clumsy attempts to mislead often yielded clues. Before doing anything else, Chadwick commissioned Enderby to get together a team with a police dog to comb Brimleigh Woods.

The photographer did his stuff and the specialists searched the scene, then bagged everything for scientific analysis. They got some partial footprints, but there was no guarantee that any of these were the killer's. Even so, they patiently made plaster-of-Paris casts. There was no weapon in the immediate vicinity, hardly surprising as the victim hadn't died there; nor was there anything in the sleeping-bag or near her body to indicate who she was. Lack of dragmarks indicated that she might have been moved there before it rained. The beads she wore were common enough, although Chadwick imagined it might be possible to track down a supplier.

No doubt some poor mother and father would be wringing their hands with worry about now, as he had been wringing his about Yvonne. Had she been at the festival? he wondered. It would be just like her, the kind of music she listened to, her rebellious spirit, the clothes she wore. He remembered the fuss she had made when he and Janet wouldn't let her go to the Isle of Wight festival the weekend before. The *Isle of Wight*, for crying out loud. It was three hundred miles away. Anything could happen. What on earth had she been thinking of?

For the time being, the best course of action was to check all missing-persons reports for someone matching the victim's description. Failing that, they would have to get a decent enough photograph of her to put in the papers and show on television, along with a plea for information from anyone in the crowd who might have seen or heard anything. However they did it, they needed to know who she was as soon as possible. Only then could they attempt to fathom out who had done this to her, and why.

The darkness deepened the closer Banks and Annie got to Lyndgarth. It looked as if the wind had taken down an electricity cable somewhere and caused a power cut. The silhouettes of branches jerked in the beam of the car's head-lights, while all around was dark, not even the light of a distant farmhouse to guide them. In Lyndgarth, houses, pubs, church and village green were all in darkness. Annie drove slowly as the road curved out of town, over the narrow stone bridge and round the bend another half a mile or so to Fordham. Even in the surrounding darkness it was easy to see where all the fuss was as they came over the second bridge shortly after half past eight.

The main road veered sharp left at the pub, opposite the church, towards Eastvale, but straight ahead, on a rough track that continued up the hill past the youth hostel and over the wild moorland, a police patrol car blocked the way, along with Winsome's unmarked Vectra. Annie pulled up behind them, and got out, the wind whipping at her clothes. The trouble was in the last cottage on the left. Opposite Moorview Cottage, a narrow lane ran west between the side of the church and a row of cottages until it was swallowed up in the dark countryside.

'Not much of a place, is it?' said Banks.

'Depends on what you want,' said Annie. 'It's quiet enough, I suppose.'

'And there is a pub.' Looking back across the main road, Banks fancied he could see the glow of candlelight through its windows and hear the muffled tones of conversation from inside. A little thing like a power cut clearly wasn't going to deprive the locals of their hand-pumped ale.

The light of a torch dazzled them, and Banks heard Winsome's voice: 'Sir? DI Cabbot? This way. I took the liberty of asking the SOCOs to bring some lighting with them, but for the moment this is all we've got.'

They followed the trail the torch lit up through a high wooden gate and a conservatory. The local PC was waiting inside the door, talking to newly promoted Detective Sergeant Kevin Templeton; the light from his torch improved visibility quite a bit but even so, they were limited to what they could see within the beams – the rest of the place was shrouded in darkness.

Treading carefully across the stone flags, Banks and Annie followed the lights to the edge of the living room. They weren't wearing protective clothing, so they had to keep their distance until the experts had finished. There, sprawled on the floor near the fireplace, lay the body of a man. He was lying on his face, so Banks couldn't tell how old he was, but his clothing – jeans and a dark green sweatshirt – suggested he was youngish. And Winsome was right: there was no doubt about this one. He could see even from a few feet away that the back of his head was a bloody mess and a long trail of dark, coagulating blood gleamed in the torchlight, ending in a puddle that was soaking into the rug. Winsome moved her torchbeam and Banks saw a poker lying on the floor not far from the victim, and a pair of glasses with one lens broken.

'Do you notice any signs of a struggle?' Banks asked.

'No,' said Annie.

The beam picked out a packet of Dunhill and a cheap disposable lighter on the table beside the armchair, towards which the victim's head was pointing. 'Say he was going for his cigarettes,' Banks said.

'And someone took him by surprise?'

'Yes. But someone he had no reason to think would kill him.' Banks pointed to the rack by the fireplace. 'The poker would most likely have been there on the hearth with the other implements.'

'Blood-spatter analysis should give us a better idea of how it happened,' Annie said.

Banks nodded and turned to Winsome. 'First thing we do is seal off this room completely,' he said. 'It's out of bounds to anyone who doesn't need to be in it.'

'Right, sir,' said Winsome.

'And organise a house-to-house as soon as possible. Ask for reinforcements, if necessary.'

'Sir.'

'Do we know who he is?'

'We don't know anything yet,' Winsome said. 'PC Travers here lives down the road and tells me he doesn't know him. Apparently it's a holiday cottage.'

'Then presumably there's an owner somewhere.'

'She's in here, sir.' It was the PC who spoke, and he pointed his torch into the dining room where a woman sat in the dark on a hardback chair staring into space. 'I didn't know what else to do with her, sir,' he went on. 'I mean, I couldn't let her go until she'd spoken with you, and she needed to sit down. She was feeling a bit faint.'

'You did the right thing,' said Banks.

'Anyway, this is Mrs Tanner.'

'I'm not the owner,' said Mrs Tanner. 'I just look after it for them. They live in London.'

'OK,' said Banks, sitting down opposite her. 'We'll get those details later.'

PC Travers shone his torch along the table between them, so that neither was dazzled and each could at least see the other. From what Banks could tell, she was a stout woman in her early fifties, with short, greying hair and a double chin.

'Are you all right, Mrs Tanner?' he asked.

She put a hand to her breast. 'I'm better now, thank you. It was just a shock. In the dark and all . . . It's not that I've never seen a dead body before. Just family, like, you know, but this . . .' She took a sip from the steaming mug in front of her. It looked as if Travers had had the good sense to make some tea, which meant there must be a gas cooker.

'Are you up to answering a few questions?' Banks asked her.

'I don't know that I can tell you anything.'

'Leave that to me to decide. How did you come to find the body?'

'He was just lying there, like he is now. I didn't touch anything.'

'Good. But what I meant was, why did you come here?'

'It was the power cut. I live just down the road, see, the other side of the pub, and I wanted to show him where the emergency candles were. There's a big torch, too.'

'What time was this?'

'Just before eight o'clock.'

'Did you see or hear anything unusual?'

'No.'

'See anyone?'

'Not a soul.'

'No cars?'

'No.'

'Was the door open?'

'No. It was shut.'

'So what did you do?'

'First, I knocked.'

'And then?'

'Well, there was no answer, see, and it was all dark inside.'

'Didn't you think he might be out?'

'His car's still here. Who'd go out walking on a night like this?'

'What about the pub?'

'I looked in, but he wasn't there, and nobody had seen him, so I came here. I've got the keys. I thought maybe he'd had an accident or something, fallen down the stairs in the dark, and all because I'd forgotten to show him where the candles and the torch were.'

'Where are they?' Banks asked.

'In a box on the shelf under the stairs.' She shook her head slowly. 'Sorry. As soon as I saw him just . . . lying there . . . it went out of my head completely, why I'd come.'

'That's all right.'

Banks sent PC Travers to find the candles. He came back a few moments later. 'There were matches in the kitchen by the cooker, sir,' he said, and proceeded to set candles in saucers and place them on the dining table.

'That's better,' said Banks. He turned back to Mrs Tanner. 'Do you know who your guest was? His name?'

'Nick.'

'That's all?'

'When he arrived last Saturday and introduced himself, he just said his name was Nick.'

'He didn't give you a cheque with his full name on it?'

'He paid cash.'

'Is that normal?'

'Some people prefer it that way.'

'How long was he staying?'

'He paid for two weeks.'

Two weeks in the Yorkshire Dales in late October seemed like an odd holiday choice to Banks, but there was no accounting for taste. Maybe this Nick was a keen rambler. 'How did he find the place?'

'The owners have a website, but don't ask me owt about that. I only see to the cleaning and general maintenance.'

'I understand,' said Banks. 'Any idea where Nick came from?'

'No. He didn't have any sort of foreign accent, but he wasn't from around here. Down south, I'd say.'

'Is there anything else you can tell me about him?'

'I only ever saw him the once,' Mrs Tanner said. 'He seemed like a nice enough lad.'

'How old would you say he was?'

'Not old. Mid-thirties, maybe. I'm not very good at ages.'

Car headlights shone through the window and soon the small house was filled with SOCOs. Peter Darby, the photographer, and Dr Glendenning, the Home Office pathologist, arrived at about the same time, Glendenning complaining that Banks thought he had nothing better to do than hang around dead bodies on a Friday evening. Banks asked PC Travers to take Mrs Tanner home and stay with her. Her husband was out at a darts match in Eastvale, she said, but he would soon be back, and she assured Banks she would be fine on her own. The SOCOs quickly set up lights in the living room, and while Peter Darby photographed the cottage with his Pentax and digital camcorder, Banks watched Dr Glendenning examine the body, turning it slightly to examine the eyes.

'Anything you can tell us, Doc?' Banks asked, after a few minutes.

Dr Glendenning got to his feet and sighed theatrically. 'I've told you about that before, Banks. Don't call me "Doc". It's disrespectful.'

'Sorry,' said Banks. He peered at the corpse. 'Anyway, he spoiled my Friday evening, too, so anything you can tell me would help.'

'Well, for a start, he's dead. You can write that down in your little notebook.'

'I suspected as much,' said Banks.

'And don't be so bloody sarcastic. You realise I was supposed to be at the Lord Mayor's banquet by now, drinking Country Manor and munching vol-au-vents?'

'Sounds bad for your health,' Banks said. 'You're better off here.'

Glendenning favoured him with a sly smile. 'Maybe you're right at that, laddie.' He smoothed down his silvery hair. 'Anyway, it was almost certainly the blow to the back of the head that killed him. I'll know better when I get him on the table, of course, but that'll have to do for now.'

'Time of death?'

'Not more than two or three hours. Rigor hasn't started yet.'

Banks looked at his watch. Five past nine. Mrs Tanner had probably been there about an hour or so, which narrowed it down even more, between six and eight, say. She couldn't have missed the killer by long, which made her a very lucky woman. 'Any chance he got drunk, fell and hit his head?' Banks knew it was unlikely, but he had to ask. You didn't waste valuable police time and resources on a domestic accident.

'Almost certainly not,' said Glendenning, glancing at the poker. 'For a start, if it had happened that way, he would most likely be lying on his back, and second, judging by the shape of the wound and the blood and hair on that poker over there, I'd say your murder weapon's pretty obvious this time. Maybe you'll find a nice clean set of fingerprints and be home by bedtime.'

'Some hope,' said Banks, seeing yet another weekend slip away. Why couldn't murderers commit their crimes on Monday? It wasn't only the prospect of working all weekend that made Friday murders such a pain in the arse but that people tended to make themselves scarce. Offices closed, workers visited relatives, everything slowed down. And the first forty-eight hours were crucial in any investigation. 'Anyway,' he said, 'the poker was close to hand, which probably means that whoever did it didn't come prepared to kill. Or wanted to make it look that way.'

'I'll leave the speculation to you. As far as I'm concerned, he belongs to the coroner now. You can remove the body whenever Cartier-Bresson here has finished.'

Banks smiled. He noticed Peter Darby stick out his tongue at Glendenning behind the doctor's back. They always seemed to be getting in one another's way at crime scenes, the only places they ever met.

By now it was impossible to ignore the activity in the rest of the house, which was swarming with SOCOs. Thick cables snaked through the conservatory, attached to bright lights, which cast shadows of men in protective clothing on the walls. The place resembled a film set. Feeling very much in the way, Banks edged out towards the conservatory. The wind was still raging, and at times it felt strong enough to blow away the whole frail structure. It didn't help that they had had to leave the door open to let the cables in.

Detective Sergeant Stefan Nowak, the crime-scene co-ordinator, arrived next, and after a brief hello to Banks and Annie, he set to work. It was his job to liaise between the scientists and the detectives, if necessary translating the jargon into comprehensible English, and he did it very well. His degrees in physics and chemistry certainly helped.

There are people who will stand for hours watching others work, Banks had noticed. You see them at building sites, eyes against the knotholes in the high wooden fences as the mechanical diggers claw at the earth and men in hard hats yell orders over the din. Or standing in the street looking up as someone on scaffolding sandblasts the front of an old building. Banks wasn't one of them. That kind of thing was a perverse form of voyeurism as far as he was concerned. Besides, there was nothing much more he could do at the house now until the team had finished, and his thoughts moved pleasantly to the candlelit pub not more than thirty yards away. The people in there would have to be interviewed. Someone might have seen or heard something, perhaps even have done it. Best talk to them now, while they were still in there and their memories were fresh. He told Winsome and Templeton to stay with Stefan and the SOCOs and to come and get him if anything important came up, then called to Annie, and they headed for the gate.

2

When Chadwick was satisfied that things were running smoothly, he called Rick Hayes over and suggested they talk in the van. It was set up so that one end was a self-contained cubicle, just about big enough for an interview, though at six foot two, Chadwick felt more than a little claustrophobic. Still, he could put up with it, and a bit of discomfort never did any harm when someone had something to hide.

Close up, Hayes looked older than Chadwick would have expected. Perhaps it was the stress of the weekend, but he had lines round his eyes and his jaw was tense. Chadwick put him in his late thirties, but with the hairstyle and the clothes, he could probably pass for ten years younger. He had three or four days' stubble on his face, his fingernails were bitten down to the quick, and the first two fingers of his left hand were stained yellow with nicotine.

'Mr Hayes,' Chadwick began, 'maybe you can help me. I need some background here. How many people attended the festival?'

'About twenty-five thousand.'

'Quite a lot.'

'Not really. There were a hundred and fifty thousand at the Isle of Wight last weekend. Mind you, they had Dylan and the Who. And we had competition. Crosby, Stills and Nash and Jefferson Airplane were playing in Hyde Park on Saturday.'

'And you had?'

'Biggest draws? Pink Floyd. Led Zeppelin.'

Chadwick, who had never heard of either, dutifully made a note of the names after checking the spelling with Hayes. 'Who else?'

'A couple of local groups. Jan Dukes de Grey. The Mad Hatters. The Hatters especially have been getting really big these past few months. Their first LP is already in the charts.'

'What do you mean local?' Chadwick asked, making a note of the names.

'Leeds. General area, at any rate.'

'How many groups in all?'

'Thirty. I can give you a full list, if you like.'

'Much appreciated.' Chadwick wasn't sure where that information would get him but every little helped. 'Something like that must require a lot of organisation.'

'You're telling me. Not only do you have to book the groups well in advance and arrange for concessions, parking, camping and toilet facilities, you've also got to supply generators, transport and a fair bit of sound equipment. Then there's security.'

'Who did you use?'

'My own people.'

'You've done this sort of thing before?'

'On a smaller scale. It's what I do. I'm a promoter.'

Chadwick scribbled something on his pad, shielding it from Hayes in the curve of his hand. Not that it meant anything; he just wanted Hayes to think it did. Hayes lit a cigarette. Chadwick opened the window. 'The festival lasted three days, is that correct?'

'Yes. We started late Friday afternoon and wrapped up today in the wee hours.'

'What time?'

'Led Zeppelin played last. They came on shortly after one

o'clock this morning, and they must have finished about three. We were supposed to wind up earlier, but there were the inevitable delays – equipment malfunctions, that sort of thing.'

'What happened at three?'

'People started drifting home.'

'In the middle of the night?'

'There was nothing to keep them here. The ones who had pitched tents probably went back to the campground to grab a few hours' sleep, but the rest left. The field was pretty much empty for the clean-up crew to start by dawn. The rain helped.'

'What time did it start?'

'Must have been about half two in the morning. Just a brief shower, like.'

'So it was mostly dry while this Led Zeppelin was playing?'

'Mostly. Yes.'

Yvonne had arrived home at six thirty, Chadwick thought, so she'd had more than enough time to get back from Brimleigh, if she'd been there. What had she been doing between three and six thirty? Chadwick decided he had better leave that well alone until he had established whether she had been there or not.

Given a time of death between one thirty and five thirty, the victim might have been killed while the band was playing, or while everyone was heading home. Most likely the former, he decided, as there would have been less chance of witnesses. And possibly before the rain, as there was no obvious trail. 'Are there any other gates,' he asked, 'in addition to where I came in?'

'No. Only to the north. But there are plenty of exits.'

'I assume there's fencing all round the site?'

'Yes. It wasn't a free concert, you know.'

'But no one would have had any real reason to go through the woods?'

'No. There are no exits on that side. It doesn't lead any-where. The parking, camping and gates are all on the north side, and that's where the nearest road is, too.'

'I understand you had a bit of trouble with skinheads.'

'Nothing my men couldn't handle. A gang of them tried to break through the fence and we saw them off.'

'North or south?

'East, actually.'

'When was this?'

'Saturday night.'

'Did they come back?'

'Not as far as I know. If they did, they were quiet about it.'

'Did people actually sleep in the field over the weekend?'

'Some did. Like I said, we had a couple of fields for parking and camping just over the hill there. A lot of people pitched tents and came back and forth. Others just brought sleeping-bags. Look, why does all this matter? I'd have thought it was obvious what happened.'

Chadwick raised his eyebrows. 'Oh? I must be missing something. Tell me.'

'Well, she must have got into an argument with her boy-friend or something, and he killed her. She was a bit away from the crowds, there by the edge of the woods, and if everyone was listening to Led Zeppelin, they probably wouldn't notice if the world ended.'

'Loud, are they, this Led Zeppelin?'

'You could say that. You should have a listen.'

'Maybe I will. Anyway, it's a good point you've raised. The music might have helped the killer. But why assume it was her boyfriend? Do boyfriends usually stab their girlfriends?'

'I don't know. It's just . . . I mean . . . who else?'

'Could have been a homicidal maniac, perhaps?'

'You'd know more about that than I do.'

'Or a passing tramp?'

'Now you're taking the piss.'

'I assure you, Mr Hayes, I'm taking this very seriously indeed. But in order to find out who might have done this, boyfriend or whatever, we need to know who she is.' He made a note, then looked directly at Hayes. 'Maybe you can help me there?'

'I've never seen her before in my life.'

'Oh, come off it, laddie.' Chadwick stared at him.

'I don't know who she is.'

'Ah, but you *did* see her somewhere?'

Hayes looked down at his clasped hands. 'Maybe.'

'And where, perhaps, might you have seen her?'

'She may have been backstage at some point.'

'*Now* we're getting somewhere. How does a person get to go backstage?'

'Well, usually, you need a pass.'

'And who hands them out?'

'Security.'

'But?'

Hayes wriggled in his chair. 'Well, you know, sometimes . . . a good-looking girl . . . What can I say?'

'How many people were backstage?'

'Dozens. It was chaos back there. We had a VIP area roped off with a beer tent and lounges. Then there were the performers' caravans, dressing rooms, toilets. We also had a press enclosure in front of the stage. Some of the performers hung around to listen to others, you know, then maybe they'd jam backstage and . . . you know . . .'

'Who were the last groups to play on Sunday?'

'We kicked off the evening session with the Mad Hatters just after dark, then Fleetwood Mac, Pink Floyd and Led Zeppelin.'

'Were they all backstage?'

'At one time or another, if they weren't onstage, yes.'

'With guests?'

'There were a lot of people.'

'How many?'

'I don't know . . . maybe fifty or so. More. That's including roadies, managers, publicists, disc jockeys, record-company people, agents, friends of the musicians, hangers-on and what-have-you.'

'Did you keep guest lists?'

'You must be joking.'

'Lists of those who were given passes?'

'No.'

'Anyone keep track of comings and goings?'

'Someone checked passes at the entrance to the backstage area. That's all.'

'And let in beautiful girls without passes?'

'Only if they were with someone who did have a pass.'

'Ah, I see. So our victim might not have been issued a pass for herself. In addition to beer, were there any other substances contributing to that general sense of well-being backstage?'

'I wouldn't know about that. Most of the time I was running around like a blue-arsed fly, making sure everything was running smoothly, keeping everyone happy.'

'Were they?'

'For the most part. You got the occasional pillock complaining his caravan was too small but on the whole it was OK.'

Chadwick jotted something down. He could tell that Hayes was craning his neck, trying to read it, so he rested his hand over the words when he had finished. 'Perhaps if we were to narrow down the time of death do you think you'd be able to give us a better idea of who might have been backstage?'

'Maybe. I dunno. Like I said, it was a bit of a zoo.'

'I can imagine. Did you see her with anyone in particular?'

'No. It might have been her or it might not. I only got a

fleeting glance. There were a lot of people. A lot of good-looking birds.' His expression brightened. 'Maybe it wasn't even her.'

'Let's remain optimistic, shall we, and assume that it was? Did the girl you saw have a flower painted on her right cheek?'

'I don't know. Like I said, I'm not even sure it *was* her. Lots of girls had painted flowers.'

'Perhaps your security team might be able to help us?'

'Maybe. If they remember.'

'Was the press around?'

'On and off.'

'What do you mean?'

'It's a matter of give and take, isn't it? I mean, the publicity's always useful and you don't want to piss off the press, but at the same time you don't want someone filming your every move or writing about you every time you go to the toilet, do you? We tried to strike a balance.'

'How did that work?'

'A big press conference before the event, scheduled interviews with specific artists at specific times.'

'Where?'

'In the press enclosure.'

'So the press weren't allowed backstage?'

'You must be joking.'

'Photographers?'

'Only in the press enclosure.'

'Can you give me their names?'

'I can't remember them all. You can ask Mick Lawton. He was press liaison officer for the event. I'll give you his number.'

'What about television?'

'They were here on Saturday and Sunday.'

'Let me guess, press enclosure?'

'For the most part, they filmed crowd scenes and the bands

performing, within strict copyright guidelines, with permission and everything.'

'I'll need the names of television companies involved.'

'Sure. The usual suspects.' Hayes named them. It wasn't as if there were that many to choose from, and Yorkshire Television and BBC North would have been Chadwick's first guesses anyway. Chadwick stood up, stooping so he didn't bang his head on the ceiling. 'We'll have a chat with them later, see if we can have a look at their footage. And we'll be talking with your security people, too. Thanks for your time.'

Hayes shuffled to his feet, looking surprised. 'That's it?'

Chadwick smiled. 'For now.'

It was like a scene out of Dickens painted with Rembrandt's sense of light and shade. There were two distinct groups in the low-beamed lounge, one playing cards, the other in the midst of an animated conversation: gnarled, weather-beaten faces with lined cheeks and potato noses lit by candles and the wood fire that crackled in the hearth. The two people behind the bar were younger. One was a local girl Banks was sure he had seen before, a pale, willowy blonde of nineteen or twenty. The other was a young man about ten years older, with curly hair and a wispy goatee.

Everyone stopped what they were doing and looked towards the door when Banks and Annie walked in, then the card-players resumed their game and the other group muttered quietly.

'Nasty night out there,' said the young man behind the bar. 'What can I get for you?'

'I'll have a pint of Black Sheep,' said Banks, showing his warrant card, 'and DI Cabbot here will have a Slimline bitter lemon, no ice.'

Annie raised an eyebrow at Banks but accepted the drink when it came and took out her notebook.

'Thought it wouldn't be long before you lot came sniffing around, all that activity going on out there,' said the young man. His biceps bulged as he pulled Banks's pint.

'And you'll be?'

'Cameron Clarke. Landlord. Everyone calls me CC.'

Banks paid for the drinks, against CC's protests, and took a sip of his beer. 'Well, Cameron,' he said, 'this is a nice pint you keep, I must say.'

'Thanks.'

Banks turned to the girl. 'And you are?'

'Kelly,' she said, shifting from foot to foot and twirling her hair. 'Kelly Soames. I just work here.'

Like CC, Kelly wore a white T-shirt with 'The Cross Keys Inn' emblazoned across her chest. There was enough candle-light behind the bar to see that it came to a stop about three inches above her low-rise jeans and broad studded belt, exposing a flat strip of pale white skin and a belly-button from which hung a short silver chain. As far as Banks was concerned, the bare-midriff trend had turned every male over forty into a dirty old man.

He looked around. A middle-aged couple he hadn't noticed when he came in sat on the bench below the bay-window, tourists from the anoraks and the expensive camera bag on the seat beside them. Several people were smoking, and Banks suppressed a sudden urge for a cigarette. He addressed the whole pub. 'Does anyone know what's happened up the road?'

They all shook their heads and muttered, 'No.'

'Anyone leave here during the last couple of hours?'

'One or two,' CC answered. 'I'll need their names,' CC told him.

'When did the electricity go off?'

'About two hours ago. There's a line down on the Eastvale road. It could take an hour or two more, or so they said.'

It was half past nine now, Banks noted, so the power cut had occurred at half past seven. It would be easy enough to check the exact time with Yorkshire Electricity, but that would do to be going on with. If Nick, the victim, had been killed between six and eight, had the killer seized the opportunity of the cover offered by extra darkness, or had he acted sooner, between six and half past seven? It probably didn't matter, except that the power cut had brought Mrs Tanner to check on her tenant, and the body had been discovered perhaps quite a bit sooner than the killer had hoped.

'Anyone arrive *after* the electricity went off?'

'We arrived at about a quarter to eight,' said the man in the bay-window seat. 'Isn't that right, darling?'

The woman beside him nodded.

'We were on our way to Eastvale, back to the hotel,' he went on, 'and this is the first place we saw that was open. I don't like driving after dark at the best of times.'

'I don't blame you,' Banks said. 'Did you see anyone else on the road?'

'No. I mean, there might have been a car or two earlier, but we didn't see anyone after the lights went out.'

'Where were you coming from?'

'Swainshead.'

'Did you see anyone when you parked here?'

'No – I mean, I don't think so. The wind was so loud and the branches . . .'

'You might have seen someone?'

'I thought I saw the tail-lights of a car,' the man's wife said.

'Where?'

'Heading up the hill. Straight on. I don't know where the road goes. But I can't be certain. As my husband says, it was a bit like a hurricane out there. It could have been something else flashing in the dark, a lantern or a torch or something.'

'You didn't see or hear anything else?'

They both shook their heads.

A possible sighting of a car heading up the unfenced road over the moors, then: that was the sum of it. They would make inquiries at the youth hostel, of course, but it was hardly likely their murderer was conveniently staying there. Still, someone might have seen something.

Banks turned back to CC. 'We'll need statements from everyone in here. Names and addresses, when they arrived, that sort of thing. I'll send someone over. For the moment, though, did anyone leave and come back between six and eight?'

'I did,' said one of the card-players.

'What time would that be?'

'About seven o'clock.'

'How long were you gone.'

'About fifteen minutes. As long as it takes to drive to Lyndgarth and back.'

'Why did you drive to Lyndgarth and back?'

'I live there,' he said. 'I thought I might have forgotten to turn the gas ring off after I had my tea, so I went back to check.'

'And had you?'

'What?'

'Turned the gas ring off?'

'Oh, aye.'

'Wasted journey, then.'

'Not if I *hadn't* turned it off.'

That raised a titter from his cronies. Banks didn't want to get mired any deeper in Yorkshire logic.

'You still haven't told us what's happened,' another card-player piped up. 'Why are you asking all these questions?' A candle guttered on the table and went out, leaving his gnarled face in shadow.

'This is just the beginning,' said Banks, thinking he might as well tell them. They would find out soon enough. 'It looks very much as if we have a murder on our hands.'

A collective gasp rose from the drinkers, followed by more muted muttering. 'Who was it, if I might ask?' said CC.

'I wish I knew,' said Banks. 'Maybe you can help me there. All I know is that his name was Nick and he was staying at Moorview Cottage.'

'Mrs Tanner's young lad, then,' said CC. 'She was in here looking for him not so long ago.'

'I know,' said Banks. 'She found him.'

'Poor woman. Tell her there's a drink on the house for her, whatever she wants.'

'Have you seen her husband tonight?' Banks asked, remembering that Mrs Tanner had told him her husband was at a darts match.

'Jack Tanner? No. He's not welcome here.'

'Why's that?'

'I'm sorry to say it, but he's a trouble-maker. Ask anyone. Soon as he's got three or four pints into him he's picking on someone.'

'I see,' said Banks. 'That's interesting to know.'

'Now, wait a minute,' protested CC. 'I'm not saying he's capable of owt like that.'

'Like what?'

'You know. What you said. Murdering someone.'

'Do you know anything about the young man?' Annie asked.

CC was so distracted by her breaking her silence that he stopped spluttering. 'He came in a couple of times,' he said.

'Did he talk to anyone?'

'Only to ask for a drink, like. And food. He had a bar snack here once, didn't he, Kelly?'

Kelly was on the verge of tears, Banks noticed. 'Anything to add?' he asked her.

Even in the candlelight, Banks could see that she blushed. 'No,' she said. 'Why should I?'

'Just asking.'

'Look, he was just a normal bloke,' CC said. 'You know, said hello, smiled, put his glass back on the bar when he left. Not like some.'

'Did he smoke?'

'CC seemed puzzled by the question. Then he said, 'Yes, he did.'

'Did he stand at the bar and chat?' Annie asked.

'He wasn't the chatty sort,' said CC. 'He'd take his drink and sit over there with the newspaper.' He gestured towards the hearth.

'Which newspaper?' Banks asked.

CC frowned. 'The *Independent*,' he said. 'I think he liked to do the crossword. Too hard for me, that one. I can barely manage the *Daily Mirror*. Why? Does it matter?'

Banks favoured him with a tight smile. 'Maybe it doesn't,' he said, 'but I like to know these things. It tells me he was intelligent, at any rate.'

'If you call doing crossword puzzles intelligent, I suppose it does. I think they're a bit of a waste of time, myself.'

'Ah, but you can't do them, can you?'

'Does either of you have any idea what he did for a living?' Annie asked, glancing from CC to Kelly and back.

'I told you,' said CC. 'He wasn't chatty, and I'm not the nosy type. Man wants to come in here and have a quiet drink, he's more than welcome, as far as I'm concerned.'

'So it never came up?' Annie said.

'No. Maybe he was a writer or a reviewer or something.'

'Why do you say that?'

'Well, if he didn't have the newspaper, he always had a book with him.' He glanced towards Banks. 'And don't ask me what book he was reading, because I didn't spot the title.'

'Any idea what he was doing here, this time of year?' Banks asked.

'None. Look, we often get people staying at Moorview Cottage dropping by for a pint or a meal, and we don't know any more or less about them than we did about him. You don't get to know people that quickly, especially if they're quiet.'

'Point taken,' said Banks. He knew how long it took the locals to accept newcomers in a place like Fordham, and no holidaying cottager could ever stay long enough. 'That just about wraps it up for now.' He looked at Annie. 'Anything else you can think of?'

'No,' said Annie, putting away her notebook.

Banks drained his pint. 'Right, then, we'll be off, and someone will be over to take your statements.'

Kelly Soames was chewing her plump, pink lower lip Banks saw, as he followed Annie out of the pub.

Monday, 8 September 1969

The newshounds had sniffed out a crime at about the same time that the incident van arrived, and the first on the scene was a *Yorkshire Evening Post* reporter, shortly followed by local radio and television, the same people who had, no doubt, been reporting on the festival. Chadwick knew that his relationship with them was held in a delicate balance. They were after a sensational story, one that would make people buy their newspapers or tune in to their channel, and Chadwick needed them on his side. They could be of invaluable help in identifying a victim, for example, or even in staging a reconstruction. In this case, there wasn't much he could tell them. He didn't go into details about the wounds, or mention the flower painted on the victim's cheek, though he knew that that was the sort of sensationalist information they wanted. The more he could keep out of the public domain, the better when it came to court. He did, however, get them to agree to let police look at the weekend's footage. It would probably be a waste of time, but it had to be done.

It was afternoon when Chadwick had finished at the field, and he realised he was hungry. He had DC Bradley drive him to the nearest village, Denleigh, about a mile to the north-east. It had turned into a fine day, and only a thin gauze of cloud hung in the sky to filter a little of the sun's heat. The village had a sort of stunned appearance, and Chadwick noticed that it was unusually messy, the streets littered with waste-paper and empty cigarette packets.

At first it seemed there was nobody about, but then they saw a man walking by the village green and pulled up beside him. He was a tweedy sort with a stiff-brush moustache and a pipe. He looked to Chadwick like a retired military officer – reminded him of a colonel he'd had in Burma during the war. 'Anywhere to eat around here?' Chadwick asked, winding down the window.

'Fish-and-chip shop, just round the corner,' the man said. 'Should still be open.' Then he peered more closely at Chadwick. 'Do I know you?'

'I don't think so,' Chadwick said. 'I'm a policeman.'

'Huh. We could have done with a few more of your lot this weekend,' the man went on. 'By the way, Forbes is the name. Archie Forbes.'

They shook hands through the window. 'Unfortunately, we can't be everywhere, Mr Forbes,' said Chadwick. 'Was there any damage?'

'One of them broke the newsagent's window when Ted told them he'd run out of cigarette papers. Some even slept in Mrs Wrigley's back garden. Scared her half to death. I suppose you're here about that girl they found dead in a sleeping-bag.'

'News travels fast.'

'It does in these parts. Communism. You mark my words, that's what's behind it. Communism.'

'Probably,' said Chadwick, moving to wind up the window.

Forbes kept talking. 'I still have one or two contacts in the intelligence services, if you catch my drift,' he said, putting a crooked finger to the side of his nose, 'and there's no doubt in my mind, and in the minds of many other right-thinking people, I might add, that this is a lot more than just youthful high spirits. Behind it all you'll find those French and German student anarchist groups, and behind them you'll find Communism. Need I spell it out, sir? The Russians.' He puffed at his pipe. 'There's no doubt in my mind that some very unscrupulous people are directing events behind the scenes, unscrupulous *foreigners*, for the most part, and their goal is the overthrow of democratic government everywhere. Drugs are only a part of their master plan. These are frightening times we live in.'

'Yes,' said Chadwick. 'Well, thanks very much, Mr Forbes. We'll be off for those fish and chips now.' He signalled for Bradley to drive off as he wound up the window, leaving Forbes staring after them. They had a laugh about Forbes, although Chadwick believed there might be something in what he'd said about foreign students fomenting dissent. They soon found the fish-and-chip shop and sat in the car eating.

When Chadwick had finished, he screwed up the newspaper, then excused himself, got out of the car and put it into the rubbish bin. Next he went into the telephone booth beside the fish-and-chip shop and dialled home.

Janet answered on the third ring. 'Hello, darling,' she said. 'Is anything wrong?'

'No, nothing's wrong,' said Chadwick. 'I was wondering about Yvonne. How is she today?'

'Back to normal, it seems.'

'Did she say anything about last night?'

'No. We didn't talk. She left for school at the usual time and gave me a peck on the cheek on her way out. Look, let's just leave it at that for the time being, darling.'

'If she's sleeping with someone, I want to know who it is.'

'And what good would that do you? What would you do if you knew? Go over and beat him up? Arrest him? Be sensible, Stan. She'll tell us in her own time.'

'Or when it's too late.'

'What do you mean?'

'Oh, never mind,' said Chadwick. 'Look, I have to go. Don't bother keeping dinner warm tonight. I'll probably be late.'

'How late?'

'I don't know. Don't wait up.'

'What is it?'

'Murder. A nasty one. You'll hear all about it on the evening news.'

'Be careful, Stan.'

'Don't worry, I'll be fine.'

Chadwick hung up and went back to the car.

'Everything all right, sir?' Bradley asked, window down, half-way through his post fish-and-chips cigarette. The car's interior smelt of lard, vinegar and warm newsprint.

'Yes,' said Chadwick. 'Right now, I think we'd better head back to Brimleigh Glen and see what's been happening there, don't you?'

Monday, 8 September 1969

The search team had fastened tape to the four trees that surrounded the little grove deep in Brimleigh Woods, about two hundred yards from where the body had been found. The woods were dense enough that, from there, you couldn't see as far as the field, and any noise would certainly have been drowned by the music.

The police dog had found the spot easily enough by following the smell of the victim's blood. Officers had also marked off the route the dog had taken and painted little crosses on the trees. Every inch of the path would have to be searched. For the moment, though, Chadwick, Enderby and Bradley stood behind the tape gazing down at the bloodstained ground.

'This where it happened?' Chadwick asked.

'So the experts tell me,' said Enderby, pointing to blood-stains on the leaves and undergrowth. 'There's some blood here, consistent with the wounds the victim received.'

'Wouldn't the killer have been covered in blood?' Bradley asked.

'Not necessarily,' said Enderby. 'Peculiar things, stab wounds. Certainly with a slashed neck artery or vein, or a head wound, there's quite a lot of spatter, but with the heart, oddly enough, the edges of the wound close and most of the bleeding is internal. It doesn't spurt the way many people think it does. There's quite a bit of seepage, of course – that's what you're seeing here and in the sleeping-bag – and I doubt he'd have got away with his hands completely clean. After all, it looks as if he stabbed her five or six times and twisted the blade.' He gestured to the edge of the copse. 'If you look over there, though, by the stream, you can see that little pile of leaves. They've got traces of blood on them, too. I reckon he tried to wipe it off with the leaves first, then washed his hands in the running water.'

'Get it all collected and sent to the lab,' said Chadwick, turning away. He wasn't usually sentimental about victims, but he couldn't get the image of the innocent-looking girl in the bloodstained white dress out of his mind, and he couldn't help thinking of his daughter. 'When did the doctor say he'd get round to the post-mortem?'

'He said he'd try for later this afternoon, sir,' said Enderby.

'Good.'

'We've interviewed most of the people on security duty,' Enderby added.

'And?'

'Nothing, I'm afraid, sir. They all agree there was so much coming and going, so much pandemonium, that nobody knows who was where when. I've a good suspicion most of them were partaking of the same substances as the musicians and guests, which doesn't help their memories much. Lots of people were wandering around in a daze.'

'Hmm,' said Chadwick. 'I didn't think we could expect too much from them. What about the girl?'

'No one admits definitely to seeing her, but we've got a couple of cautious maybes.'

'Push a bit harder.'

'Will do, sir.'

Chadwick sighed. 'I suppose we'd better arrange to talk to the groups who were backstage at the time, get statements, for what they're worth.'

'Sir?' said Enderby.

'What?'

'You might find that a bit difficult, sir. I mean . . . they'll have all gone home now, and these people . . . well, they're not readily accessible.'

'They're no different from you and me, are they, Enderby? Not royalty or anything?'

'No, sir, more like film stars. But—'

'Well, then, I'll deal with the two local groups, but as far as the rest are concerned, arrange to have them interviewed. Get someone to help you.'

'Yes, sir,' Enderby replied tightly, and turned away.

'And, Enderby . . .'

'Sir?'

'I don't know what the standards are in North Yorkshire,

but while you're working for me I'd prefer it if you got your hair cut.'

Enderby reddened. 'Yes, sir.'

'Bit hard on him, weren't you, sir?' said Bradley, when Enderby had gone.

'He's a scruff.'

'No, sir. I mean about questioning the groups. He's right, you know. Some of these pop stars are a bit high and mighty.'

'What would you have me do, Simon? Ignore the fifty or so people who might have seen the victim with her killer?'

'No, sir.'

'Come on. Let's head home. I should be in time for Dr O'Neill's post-mortem if I'm lucky, and I want you to go to Yorkshire Television and the BBC and watch the footage they shot of the festival.'

'What am I looking for, sir?'

'Right now, anything. The girl, anyone she might have been with. Any odd or unusual behaviour.' Chadwick paused. 'On second thoughts, don't worry about that last bit. It's all bound to be odd and unusual, given the people we're dealing with.'

Bradley laughed. 'Yes, sir.'

'Just use your initiative, laddie. At least you won't have to watch the doctor open the poor girl up.'

Before they walked away, Chadwick turned back to the bloodstained ground.

'What is it, sir?' Bradley asked.

'Something that's been bothering me all morning. The sleeping-bag.'

'Sleeping-bag?'

'Aye. Who did it belong to?'

'Her, I suppose,' said Bradley.

'Perhaps,' Chadwick said. 'But why would she carry it into the woods with her? It just seems odd, that's all.'

3

It was after midnight when the lights came back on, and the wind was still raging, now lashing torrents of rain against the windows and lichen-stained roofs of Fordham. The coroner's van had taken the body away, and Dr Glendenning had said he would try to get the post-mortem done the following day, even though it was a Saturday. The SOCOs worked on in the new light, collecting samples, labelling and storing everything carefully. So far, they had discovered nothing of immediate importance. One or two members of the local media had arrived, and the police press officer, David Whitney, was on the scene keeping them back and feeding them titbits of information.

Banks used the newly restored electric light to have a good look round the rest of the cottage, and it didn't take him very long to realise that any personal items Nick might have had with him were gone, except for his clothes, toiletries and a few books. There was no wallet, for example, no mobile, nothing with his name on it. The clothes didn't tell him much. Nothing fancy, just casual Gap-style shirts, a grey pinstripe jacket, cargos and Levi's for the most part. All the toiletries told him was that Nick suffered from, or worried that he might suffer from, heartburn and indigestion, judging by the variety of antacids he had brought with him. Winsome reported that his car was a Renault Mégane, and to open it you needed a card, not a key. There wasn't one in sight, so she had phoned the police garage in Eastvale, who said they would send someone out as soon as possible.

There was nothing relating to the car on the Police National Computer, Winsome added, so she would have to get the details from the Driver and Vehicle Licensing Agency in Swansea as soon as she could raise someone, which wouldn't be easy at a weekend. If necessary, they could check the National DNA Database, which held samples of the DNA not only of convicted criminals but of anyone who had been arrested, even if they had been acquitted. The public railed about its attacks on freedom, but the database had come in useful more than once for identifying a body, among other things.

They would find out who Nick was soon enough, but someone was making it difficult for them, and Banks wondered why. Would knowing the victim's identity point the police quickly in the direction of the killer? Did he need time to make his escape?

It was clear that only one of the two bedrooms had been used. The beds weren't even made up in the other. From what Banks could see at a cursory glance, it looked as if both sides of the double bed had been slept on, but Nick might have been a restless sleeper. Peter Darby had already photographed the room, and the SOCOs would bag the sheets for testing. There was no sign of condoms in the bedside drawers, or anywhere else, for that matter, and nothing at all to show who, or what, the mysterious Nick had been, except for the paperback copy of Ian McEwan's *Atonement* on the bedside table.

According to the Waterstone's bookmark, Nick had got to page sixty-eight. Banks picked up the book and flipped through it. On the back endpaper, someone had written in faint pencil six uneven rows of figures, some of them circled. He turned to the front and saw the price of the book, £3.50, also in pencil, but in a different hand, at the top right of the first inside page. A second-hand copy, then. Which meant that any number of people might have owned it and written the figures in the back. Still, it might mean something. Banks called up a SOCO to bag it and told him to be sure to make a photocopy of the page in question.

Frustrated by this early lack of knowledge of the victim, Banks went back downstairs. Usually he had a person's books or CD collection to go on, not to mention the opinions of others, but this time all he knew was that Nick did the *Independent* crossword, was reading *Atonement,* was polite but not particularly chatty, favoured casual clothing, perhaps suffered from indigestion, smoked Dunhill and wore glasses. It wasn't anywhere near enough to start figuring out who might have wanted him dead and why. Patience, he told himself, early days yet, but he didn't feel patient.

By half past twelve, he'd had enough. Time to go home. Just as he was about to get PC Travers to fix up a lift for him, Annie edged over and said, 'There's not a lot more we can achieve hanging around here, is there?'

'Nothing,' said Banks. 'The mechanics are all in motion and Stefan will get in touch with us if anything important comes up, but I doubt we'll get any further tonight. Why?'

Annie smiled at him. 'Well, I don't know about you, but I'm starving and, as I remember, Marks and Spencer's vegetarian lasagne heats up a treat. You know what they say about an army marching on its stomach and all that . . .'

Monday, 8 September 1969

Yvonne Chadwick accepted the joint that Steve passed her and drew deeply. She liked getting high. Not the hard stuff, no pills or needles, only dope. Sex was all right, too – she liked that well enough with Steve – but most of all she liked getting high, and the two usually went together really well. Music, too. They were listening to Hendrix's *Electric Ladyland,* and it sounded out of this world.

Take now. She was supposed to be at school, but she had taken the afternoon off. It was only games and free periods, anyway; the new term hadn't really got under way yet. There was a house just up the road from her school, on Springfield Mount, where a group of hippies lived: Steve, Todd, Jacqui, American Charlie, and others who came and went. She had become friendly with them after she'd met Steve upstairs at the Peel, on Boar Lane, one night in April when she'd gone there with her friend Lorraine from school. She had turned sixteen the month before, but she could pass for eighteen easily enough, with a bit of makeup and high heels. Steve was the handsome, sensitive sort of boy, and she had fancied him straight away. He'd read her some of his poetry, and while she didn't really understand it, it sounded important.

There were other houses she visited where people were into the same things, too – one on Carberry Place and another on Bayswater Terrace. Yvonne felt that she could turn up at either of them at any time and feel as if she belonged there. Everyone accepted her as she was. Someone was always around to welcome her, maybe with a joint and a pot of jasmine tea. They all liked the same music, too, and agreed about society and the evils of the war and stuff. But Springfield Mount was the closest, and Steve lived there.

The air smelt of sandalwood incense, and there were posters on the walls: Jimi Hendrix, Janis Joplin, a creepy Salvador Dali print and, even creepier, Goya's etching, *The Sleep of Reason Brings Forth Monsters*. Sometimes, when she was smoking really good dope, Yvonne would lose herself in that one, the sleeping artist surrounded by creatures of the night.

Mostly they all just sat around and talked about the terrible shape the world was in and how they hoped to change it, end the war in Vietnam, free the universities from the establishment and their professor lackeys, put a stop to imperialism and capitalist oppression. Yvonne couldn't wait to go to university: as far as she was concerned, that was where life got really exciting, not like boring old school, where they still treated you like a kid and weren't interested in what you thought about the world. At university you were a *student*, and you went to demos and things. Steve was a second-year English student, but the term wasn't due to start for a couple of weeks yet. He'd told her he would get her into all the great concerts at the university refectory next term, and she could hardly wait. The Moody Blues were coming, and Family and Tyrannosaurus Rex. There were even rumours of the Who coming to record a live concert.

They had already seen a lot of great local gigs together that summer: Thunderclap Newman at the town hall; Pink Floyd, Colosseum and Eire Apparent at Selby Abbey. She regretted missing the Isle of Wight – *Dylan* had been there, after all – but her parents wouldn't let her go that far. She had two years to wait to go to university, *and* she had to get good A levels. Right now, that didn't look like a strong possibility, but she'd worry about it later: she had just started in the lower sixth, so there was plenty of time to catch up. After all, she had managed to get seven good O levels.

She had to admit, as she grinned through the haze of smoke, that things were pretty good. Sunday had been great. They had gone to the Brimleigh festival – she, Steve, Todd, Charlie and Jacqui – and they had stayed up all night on the field, sharing joints, food and drink with their fellow revellers. Steve had dropped acid, but Yvonne hadn't wanted to because there were too many people around and she worried about getting paranoid. But Steve had seemed OK, though she'd got worried when he disappeared for more than an hour. When it was all over, they went to Springfield Mount to come down with a couple of joints, and then she went home to get ready for school, narrowly avoiding bumping into her father.

She hadn't dared tell her parents where she was going.

Christ, why did she have to have a father who was a *pig*, for crying out loud? It just wasn't fair. If she told her new friends what her old man did for a living they'd drop her like a hot coal. And if it wasn't for her parents she could have gone to Brimleigh on Saturday, too. Steve and the others had been there both nights. But if she'd done that, she realised, they wouldn't have let her out on Sunday.

They were sitting on the living-room floor propped up against the sofa. Just her and Steve this time – the others were all out. Some of the people who came and went she wasn't too sure about. Magic Jack was scary with his beard and wild eyes, although she had never seen him behave in any other way than gently, but the most frightening of all – and thank God he didn't turn up very often – was McGarrity, the mad poet.

There was something about McGarrity that really worried Yvonne. Older than the rest, he had a thin, lined, parchment face and black eyes. He always wore a black hat and a matching cape, and he had a flick-knife with a tortoiseshell handle. He never really talked to anyone, never joined in the discussions. Sometimes he would pace up and down tapping the blade against his palm, muttering to himself, reciting poetry. T. S. Eliot mostly, *The Waste Land*. Yvonne only recognised it because Steve had loaned her a copy to read not so long ago, and had explained it to her.

Some people found McGarrity OK, but he gave Yvonne the creeps. She had asked Steve once why they let him hang around, but all Steve said was that McGarrity was harmless, really; it was just that his mind had been damaged a bit by the electric-shock treatment they'd given him at the mental home when he deserted from the army. Besides, if they wanted a free and open society, how could they justify excluding people? There wasn't much to say after that, although Yvonne thought there were probably a few people they wouldn't like to have in the house: her dad, for example. McGarrity had been at Brimleigh, too, but luckily he'd wandered off and left them alone.

Yvonne could feel Steve's hand on her thigh, stroking, and she turned to smile at him. It was all right – really, it was all right. Her parents didn't know it, but she was on the pill, had been since she'd turned sixteen. It wasn't easy to get, and there was no way she would have asked old Cuthbertson, the family doctor. But her friend Maggie had told her about a new family-planning clinic on Woodhouse Lane where they were very concerned about teenage pregnancies and very obliging if you were over the age of consent.

Steve kissed her and put his hand on her breast. The dope they were smoking wasn't especially strong, but it heightened her sense of touch as it did her hearing, and she felt herself responding to his caresses, getting wet. He undid the buttons on her school blouse and then she felt his hand moving up over her bare thighs. Jimi Hendrix was singing '1983' when Steve and Yvonne toppled on to the floor, pulling at one another's clothing.

Monday, 8 September 1969

Chadwick leaned back against the cool tiles of the mortuary wall and watched Dr O'Neill and his assistant at work under the bright light. Post-mortems had never bothered him, and this one was no exception, even though the victim had re-minded him earlier of Yvonne. Now she was just an unfortu-nate dead girl on the porcelain slab. Her life was gone, drained out of her, and all that remained were flesh, muscle, blood, bone and organs. And, possibly, clues.

The painted cornflower looked even more incongruous in this harsh steel and porcelain environment, blooming on her dead cheek. Chadwick found himself wondering, not for the first time, whether it had been painted by the girl herself, by a friend or by her killer. And if the latter, what was its significance?

After matching the holes in the material to the wounds Dr O'Neill had carefully removed the dress, and set it aside with the sleeping-bag for further forensic testing. So far they had discovered that the sleeping-bag was a cheap, popular brand sold mainly through Woolworth's.

The doctor bent over the pale naked body to examine the stab wounds. There were five in all, he noted, and one had been so hard and gone so deep that it had bruised the surrounding skin. If the hilt of the knife had caused the bruising, as Dr O'Neill believed it had, they were dealing with a single-edged four-inch blade. A very thin, stiletto-type blade, too, allowing that it was a bit bigger than the actual wounds, owing to the elasticity of the skin. One strong possibility, he suggested, was a flick-knife. They were illegal in Britain but easy enough to pick up on the Continent.

Judging by the angles of the wounds, Dr O'Neill concluded that the victim had been stabbed by a strong, left-handed person standing behind her. The complete lack of defence wounds on her hands indicated that she had been so taken by surprise that she had either died or gone into shock before she knew what was happening.

'She may not have seen her killer, then,' said Chadwick, 'unless it was someone she knew well enough to let them so close?'

'I can't speculate on that. You can see as well as I can, though, that there appear to be no other injuries to the surface of the body apart from that light bruising on the neck, which tells me someone had her in a stranglehold with his right arm while he stabbed her with the left. We'll be testing for drugs, too, of course – it's possible she was slipped something that immobilised her: Nembutal, Tuinal, something like that. But she was standing when she was stabbed – the angles tell us that much – so she must have been conscious.'

Chadwick looked down at the body. Dr O'Neill was right. Apart from the faint discoloration on her neck and the mess round her left breast, she was in almost pristine condition: no cuts, no rope burns, nothing.

'Was he taller than her?' Chadwick asked.

'Yes – judging by the shape and position of the bruises and the angle of the cuts, I'd estimate by a good six inches. She was five foot four, which makes him at least five foot ten.'

'Would you say the bruising indicates a struggle?'

'Not necessarily. As you can see, it's fairly mild. He could simply have had his arm loosely round her neck, then tightened it when he stabbed her. It probably all happened so quickly he didn't need to restrain her. We already know there are no defensive wounds to the hands, which indicates she was taken by surprise. If that's the case, she would have slumped as she died, and his arm could have caused the bruising then.'

'I thought bodies didn't bruise after death.'

'This would have been the moment before death, or at the moment of death.' Dr O'Neill turned his attention to the golden hair between the girl's legs and Chadwick felt himself tense. So like Yvonne's when he had seen her naked by accident that time at the caravan. How embarrassed they had both felt.

'Again,' said Dr O'Neill, 'we'll have to do swabs and further tests, but there doesn't appear to be any sign of sexual activity. There's no bruising around the vaginal area or the anus.'

'So you're saying she wasn't raped, she didn't have sex?'

'I'm not committing myself to anything yet,' said Dr O'Neill, sharply. 'Not until I've done an internal examination and the samples have been analysed. All I'm saying is there are no obvious superficial signs of forced or rough sexual activity.

One thing we did find was a tampon. It looks as if our victim was menstruating at the time of the murder.'

'Which still doesn't rule out sexual activity altogether?'

'Not at all. But if she did have sex, she had time to put another tampon in before she was killed.'

Chadwick thought for a moment. If sex had been the reason for her death, then surely there would have been more signs of violence, unless they had been lovers to begin with. Had they made love first, then dressed, and while she was leaning back on him in the afterglow he killed her? But why, if sex had been consensual? Had she, perhaps, refused, said she was having her period, and had that somehow angered her attacker? Were they really dealing with a nutcase?

As often as not, Chadwick knew, investigations, including the medical kind, threw up more questions than answers, and it was only through answering them that you made progress.

Chadwick watched as O'Neill and his assistant made the Y incision and peeled back the skin, muscle and soft tissues from the chest wall, then pulled the chest flap up over her face and cut through the ribcage with an electric saw. The smell was overwhelming. Raw meat. Lamb, mostly, Chadwick thought.

'Hmm, it's as I suspected,' said Dr O'Neill. 'The chest cavity is filled with blood, as are all the other cavities. Massive internal bleeding.'

'Would she have died quickly?'

Dr O'Neill probed around and remained silent a few minutes, then he said, 'From the state of her, seconds at most. Look here – he twisted the knife so sharply he actually cut off a piece of her heart.'

Chadwick looked. As usual, he wished he could see what Dr O'Neill saw, but all he saw was a mass of glistening, bloody organ tissue. 'I'll take your word for it,' he said.

Dr O'Neill's assistant carefully started removing the inner organs for sectioning, further testing and examination. Barring any glaring anomalies, Chadwick knew it would be a few days before he received the results of all this. There was no real reason to stick around, and he had more than enough to do. He left as Dr O'Neill started up the saw to cut through the victim's skull and remove her brain.

Saturday morning dawned fresh and clear, and Helmthorpe had that rinsed and scoured look, the streets, limestone buildings and flagstone roofs still dark with rain but the sun out, the sky blue and a cool wind to rattle the bare branches.

Banks fiddled with the attachment that let him play the iPod through the car stereo and was rewarded by Judy Collins singing 'Who Knows Where The Time Goes?' in a voice of such aching beauty and clarity that it made him want to laugh and cry at the same time. Sandy Denny's lyrics had never seemed so doom-laden: they made him think about his brother, Roy. Almost as a rebuke, it seemed, the Porsche coursed smoothly and powerfully through the late autumn landscape.

After she had eaten the lasagne and drunk one small glass of wine, Annie had driven off to Harkside and left Banks to his own devices. It was after two in the morning, but he had poured himself a glass of Amarone and listened to Fischer-Dieskau's 1962 *Winterreise* in the dark before heading for bed, his head full of gloomy thoughts. Even then he hadn't been able to sleep. It was partly heartburn from eating so late – he wished he had taken one of Nick's antacids as he had none in the house – and partly disturbing dreams during those brief moments when he did nod off. Several times he awoke abruptly with his heart pounding and a vague, terrifying image skittering away down the slippery slopes of his subconscious. He had lain there taking slow, deep breaths until he had fallen asleep about an hour before the alarm went off.

The team gathered in the boardroom, crime-scene photos pinned to the corkboard, but the whiteboard was conspicuously empty apart from the name 'Nick'. An incident van had been dispatched to Fordham earlier in the morning, fitted out with phones and computers. Information collected there would be collated and passed on to Headquarters. Banks was officially the Senior Investigating Officer, appointed by Assistant Chief Constable Ron McLaughlin, and Annie was his deputy. Other tasks would be assigned to various officers according to their skills.

Since Detective Superintendent Gristhorpe had retired two months ago, they had been given a temporary replacement in Catherine Gervaise. There were those who muttered that Banks should have got the job, but he knew it had never been on the cards. He had got on well enough with ACC McLaughlin, 'Red Ron', and with the chief constable himself, on those rare occasions when they met, but he was too much of a loose cannon. If nothing else, running off to London to look for his brother, and getting involved in all that followed from that, had put several nails in the coffin of his career. Besides, he didn't want the responsibility, or the paperwork. Gristhorpe had always left him alone to work cases the way he wanted, which meant he ended up doing a lot of the legwork and streetwork himself, because that was the way he liked it.

Catherine Gervaise was cool and distant, not a mentor and friend the way Gristhorpe had been, and under her rule he found he had to fight harder for his privileges. She was an administrator through and through, an ambitious woman who had risen quickly through the ranks via accelerated-promotion schemes, management and computer courses and, some said, by affirmative action. This would be her first major investigation at Western Area Headquarters, so it would be interesting to see how she handled it. At least she wasn't stupid, Banks thought, and she should know best how to use her resources.

Some were put off by her posh accent and Cheltenham Ladies' College background, but Banks was inclined to give her the benefit of the doubt, as long as she left him alone. The one thing they had in common, he discovered, was that she also had season tickets to Opera North, and he had seen her at a performance of *Lucia di Lammermoor* with her husband. He didn't think she had noticed him. At least, she hadn't let on. In appearance, she wore little makeup and was rather severe, with short blonde hair, rather unexpected Cupid's-bow lips and a trim figure. In dress she was conservative, favouring navy suits and white blouses, and in manner she was no-nonsense, remaining aloof and either not getting the squad-room humour or not wishing to show that she did.

The superintendent asked for a summary of what they had so far, which wasn't much. The blood-spatter analysis was consistent with the theory that Nick had been bashed over the back of the head with a poker as he had been turning away from his killer, perhaps walking towards his cigarettes. After that, he had been hit once or twice more – they wouldn't know until Dr Glendenning performed the post-mortem – no doubt to make sure he was dead.

'Have we got any further identifying the victim?' Superintendent Gervaise asked next.

'A little, ma'am,' said Winsome. 'At least, the local memory tag on his licence-plate number indicates the car was registered in London.'

'It's not hired?'

'No. We finally got a look inside with the help of the garage. Unfortunately there was nothing to indicate who he was.'

'So someone really wanted to throw sand in our eyes.'

'Well, ma'am, it's a fairly new car, and he might not have been the kind of person who lives out of it, but it certainly looks that way. Whoever did it must have known he could only have slowed the investigation down, though.' Winsome looked to Banks, who nodded for her to go on. 'Which probably means

that he wanted to give himself a bit of time to get far enough
away and arrange an alibi.'

'Interesting theory, DC Jackman,' said Gervaise. 'But that's
all it is, isn't it, a theory?'

'Yes, ma'am. For the moment.'

'And we need facts.'

That was pretty much self-evident in any investigation,
Banks thought. Of course you wanted facts, but until you
got them you played around with theories, you used what you
did have, then you applied a bit of imagination, and as often as
not you came up with an approximation of the truth, which was
what he thought Winsome was doing. So Ms Gervaise wanted
to establish herself as a just-the-facts-no-fancy-theories kind of
superintendent. Well, so be it. The squad would soon learn to
keep their theories to themselves, but Banks hoped her attitude
wouldn't crush their creativity, and wouldn't stop them from
confiding their theories in him. It was all very well to come in
with an attitude, but it was something else if that attitude
destroyed the delicate balance that had been achieved over
time.

They were drastically short of DCs, having recently lost
Gavin Rickerd, their best office manager, to the new neigh-
bourhood-policing initiative, where he was working with com-
munity-support officers and specials to tackle the antisocial
behaviour that was becoming increasingly the norm all over
the country, especially on a Saturday night in Eastvale. He
hadn't been replaced yet, and in his absence the job this time
had gone to one of the uniformed constables, hardly the ideal
choice but the best they could do right now.

Banks wanted Winsome Jackman and Kevin Templeton
doing what they did best – tracking down information and
following leads – and when it came to that, DS Hatchley had
always been a bit slow and lazy. His physical presence had
once helped intimidate the odd suspect or two but, these days,

the ex-rugby-player's muscle had gone mostly to fat, and the police weren't allowed to intimidate villains any more. Villains' Rights had put paid to that, or so it sometimes seemed, especially since a burglar had fallen off the roof of a warehouse he'd broken into last summer, then sued the owner for damages and won.

'I'm trying to get in touch with the D.VLA in Swansea,' Winsome said, 'but it's Saturday. They're closed and I can't seem to track down my contact.'

'Keep trying,' said Superintendent Gervaise. 'Is there anything else?'

Winsome consulted her notes. 'DS Templeton and I interviewed the people in the Cross Keys and took statements. Nothing new there. And when the lights came on we made a quick check of their outer clothing for signs of blood. There were none.'

'What's your take on this?' Gervaise asked Banks.

'I don't have enough facts yet to form an opinion,' Banks said.

The irony wasn't lost on Superintendent Gervaise, who pursed her lips. She looked as if she had just bitten into a particularly vinegary pickle. Banks noticed Annie look away and smile to herself, pen against her lips, shaking her head slowly.

'I understand you entered licensed premises during the early stages of the investigation yesterday evening,' Gervaise said.

'That's right.' Banks wondered who had been talking, and why.

'I suppose you know there are regulations governing drinking while on duty?'

'With all due respect,' Banks said, 'I didn't go there for a drink. I went to question possible witnesses.'

'But you did have a drink?'

'While I was there, yes. I find it puts people at ease. They see you as more like they are, not as the enemy.'

'Duly noted,' said Gervaise, drily. 'And did you find any co-operative witnesses?'

'Nobody seemed to know very much about the victim,' Banks said. 'He was renting a cottage, not a local.'

'On holiday at this time of year?'

'That's what I wondered about.'

'Find out what he was doing there. That might help us get to the bottom of this.' Quite the one for dishing out obvious orders, was Superintendent Gervaise, Banks thought. He'd had bosses like her before: state the obvious, the things your team would do anyway, without being asked, and take the credit for the results. 'Of course,' he said. 'We're working on it. One of the staff might know a bit more than she's letting on.'

'What makes you think that?'

'Her manner, body language.'

'All right. Question her. Bring her in, if necessary.'

Banks could tell by Superintendent Gervaise's clipped tone and the way her hand strayed to her short, layered locks that she was bored with the meeting and anxious to get away, no doubt to send out a memo on drinking while on duty, or the ten most obvious courses to pursue during a murder inquiry.

'If that's all for now, ladies and gentlemen,' she went on, stuffing her papers into her briefcase, 'I suggest we get down to work.'

To a muttered chorus of 'Yes, ma'am', she left the room, heels clicking against the hardwood floor. Only after she'd gone did Banks realise that he had forgotten to tell her about the figures in the book.

Monday, 8 September 1969

Janet was watching the *News at Ten* when Chadwick got home that evening, and Reginald Bosanquet was talking about ITA's exciting new UHF colour transmissions from the Crystal

Palace transmitter, which was all very well, Chadwick thought, if you happened to own a colour TV. He didn't. Not on a DI's pay of a little over two thousand pounds per year. Janet walked towards him.

'Hard day?' she asked.

Chadwick nodded, kissed her and sat down in his favourite armchair.

'Drink?'

'A small whisky would go down nicely. Yvonne not home yet?' He glanced at the clock. Twenty past ten.

'Not yet.'

'Know where she is?'

Janet turned from pouring the whisky. 'Out with friends was all she said.'

'She shouldn't go out so often on school nights. She knows that.'

Janet handed him the drink. 'She's sixteen. We can't expect her to do everything the way we'd like it. Things are different these days. Teenagers have a lot more freedom.'

'Freedom? As long as she's under this roof we've a right to expect some degree of honesty and respect from her, haven't we?' Chadwick argued. 'The next thing you know she'll be dropping out and running off to live in a hippie commune. *Freedom.*'

'Oh, give it a rest, Stan. She's going through a stage, that's all.' Janet softened her tone. 'She'll get over it. Weren't you just a bit rebellious when you were sixteen?'

Chadwick tried to remember. He didn't think so. It was 1937 when he was sixteen, before 'teenagers' had been invented, when youth was simply an unfortunate period one had to pass through on the route from childhood to maturity. Another world. George VI was crowned king that year, Neville Chamberlain became prime minister and looked likely to get along well with Hitler, and the Spanish Civil War was at its bloodiest. But Chadwick had paid only scant attention to world affairs. He was at grammar school then, on a scholarship, playing rugby with the first fifteen, and all set for a university career that was interrupted by the war and was somehow never resurrected.

He had volunteered for the Green Howards in 1940 because his father had served with them in the first war, and spent the next five years killing first Japanese, then Germans, while trying to stay alive himself. After it was all over and he was back on Civvy Street in his demob suit, it took him six years to get over it. Six years of dead-end jobs, bouts of depression, loneliness and hunger. He nearly died of cold in the bitter winter of 1947. Then it was as if the weight suddenly lifted and the lights came on. He joined the West Riding constabulary in 1951. The following year he met Janet at a dance. They were married only three months later, and a year after that, in March 1953, Yvonne was born.

Rebellious? He didn't think so. It seemed to be a young person's lot in life to go off to war back then, just like the generation before him, and in the army you obeyed orders. He'd got into minor mischief, like all the other kids, smoking before he was old enough, the odd bit of shoplifting, sneaking drinks from his father's whisky bottle, replacing what he'd drunk with water. He also got into the occasional scrap. But one thing he didn't dare do was disobey his parents. If he had stayed out all night without permission, his father would have beaten him black and blue.

Chadwick grunted. He didn't suppose Janet really wanted an answer: she was just trying to ease the way for Yvonne's arrival home, which he hoped would be soon.

The news finished at ten forty-five and the late-night X film came on. Normally Chadwick wouldn't bother watching such rubbish, but this week it was *Saturday Night and Sunday Morning*, which he and Janet had seen at the Lyric about eight years ago, and he didn't mind watching it again. At least it was the sort of life he could understand, *real life*, not long-haired kids listening to loud music and taking drugs.

It was about a quarter past eleven when he heard the front door open and shut. By that time, his anger had edged into concern, but in a parent the two are often so intermingled as to be indistinguishable.

'Where have you been?' he asked Yvonne, when she walked into the living room in her pale blue bell-bottomed jeans and red cheesecloth top with white and blue embroidery down the gathered front. Her eyes looked a little bleary, but other than that she seemed all right.

'That's a nice welcome,' she said.

'Are you going to answer me?'

'If you must know, I've been to the Grove.'

'Where's that?'

'Down past the station, by the canal.'

'And what goes on there?'

'Nothing goes on. It's folk night on Mondays. People sing folk songs and read poetry.'

'You know you're not old enough to drink.'

'I wasn't drinking. Not alcohol anyway.'

'You smell of smoke.'

'It's a pub, Dad. People were smoking. Look, if all you're going to do is go on at me, I'm off to bed. It's a school day tomorrow, or didn't you know?'

'Enough of your cheek! You're too young to be hanging around pubs in town. God knows who—'

'If it was up to you I wouldn't have any friends at all, would I? And I'd never go anywhere. You make me sick!'

And with that Yvonne stormed upstairs to her room.

Chadwick made to follow her, but Janet grabbed his arm. 'No, Stan. Not now. Let's not have another flaming row. Not tonight.'

Furious as he felt, Chadwick realised she was right. Besides, he was exhausted. Not the best time to get into a long argument with his daughter. But he'd have it out with her tomorrow. Find out what she was up to, where she had been all Sunday night, exactly what crowd she was hanging around with. Even if he had to follow her.

He could hear her banging about upstairs, using the toilet and the bathroom, slamming her bedroom door, making a point of it. It was impossible to get back into the film now. Impossible to go to sleep, too, no matter how tired he felt. If he'd had a dog he would have taken it for a walk. Instead he poured himself another small whisky, and while Janet pretended to read her *Woman's Weekly* he pretended to watch *Saturday Night and Sunday Morning* until all was silent upstairs and it was safe to go to bed.

4

Annie took a chance that Kelly Soames would turn up for work on Saturday morning so she parked behind the incident van in Fordham and adjusted her rear-view mirror so that she could see the pub and the road behind her. Banks had told her he thought Kelly didn't want to talk last night because there were people around and she might have a personal secret; therefore, it would be a good idea to get her alone, take her somewhere. He also thought a woman might have more chance of getting whatever it was out of her, hence Annie.

Just before eleven o'clock, Annie saw Kelly get out of a car. She recognised the driver as one of the men in the pub the previous evening, a card-player. As soon as he had driven off and turned the bend, Annie backed up and intercepted Kelly. 'A word with you, please,' she said.

Kelly made towards the pub door. 'I can't. I'll be late for work.'

Annie opened her passenger door. 'You'll be a lot later if you don't come with me now.'

Kelly chewed her lip, then muttered something under her breath and got into the old purple Astra. It was long past time for a new car, Annie realized, but she'd had neither the time nor the money lately. Banks had offered her his Renault when he got the Porsche, but she had declined. It wasn't her kind of car, for a start, and there was something rather shabby, she'd thought, about taking Banks's castoffs. She'd buy something new soon, but for now, the Astra still got her where she wanted to go.

Annie set off up the hill, past the youth hostel, where a couple of uniforms were still making inquiries, on to the wild moorland beyond. She pulled over into a lay-by next to a stile. It was the start of a walk to an old lead mine, Annie knew, as Banks had taken her there to show her where someone had once found a body in the flue. That morning, no one was around and the wind whistled round the car, plucking at the purple heather and rough sere grass. Kelly took a packet of Embassy Regal out of her handbag, but Annie pushed her hand down and said, 'Not in here. I don't like the smell of smoke, and I'm not opening the windows. It's too cold.'

Kelly put away the cigarettes and pouted.

'Last night, when we were talking in the pub,' Annie said, 'you reacted in a rather extreme way to what happened.'

'Well, someone got killed. I mean, it might be normal for you, but not round here. It was a shock, that's all.'

'It seemed like a personal shock.'

'What do you mean?'

'Do I have to spell it out, Kelly?'

'I'm not thick.'

'Then stop playing games. What was your relationship with the deceased?'

'I didn't have a relationship. He came in the pub, that's all. He had a nice smile, said, "Have one for yourself." Isn't that enough?'

'Enough for what?'

'Enough to be upset that he's dead.'

'Look, I'm sorry if this is hard for you,' Annie went on, 'but we're only doing this because we care, too.'

Kelly shot her a glance. 'You never even saw him when he was alive. You didn't even know he existed.'

True, it was one of the things about Annie's job that more

often than not she found herself investigating the deaths of strangers. But Banks had taught her that, during the course of such investigations, they don't remain strangers. You get to know the dead, become their voice, in a way, because they can no longer speak for themselves. She couldn't explain this to Kelly, though.

'He'd been in the cottage a week,' said Annie, 'and you're telling me you only saw him when he came into the pub and said hello.'

'So?'

'If that was all he meant to you, you seemed more upset than it warranted.'

Kelly folded her arms. 'I don't know what you're talking about.'

Annie faced her. 'I think you do, Kelly,'

They sat silently cocooned in the car, Kelly stiff, facing the front, Annie turned sideways in her seat, looking at her profile. A few spots of acne stood out on the girl's right cheek and she had a little white scar at the outer edge of an eyebrow. Outside, the wind continued to rage through the moorland grass and to rock the car a little with unexpected gusts and buffets. The sky was a vast expanse of blue with small, high, fast-moving white clouds casting brief shadows on the moor. It must have been three, maybe four minutes, an awful long time in that sort of situation, anyway, before Kelly started to shiver a little, and before long she was shaking like a leaf in Annie's arms, tears streaming down her face. 'You mustn't tell my father,' she kept saying, through the tears. 'You mustn't tell my father.'

Tuesday, 9 September 1969

On Tuesday evening, Yvonne was in her room reading Mark Knopfler's column in the *Yorkshire Evening Post*. He wrote about the music scene, as well as jamming sometimes with local bands at the Peel and the Guildford, and she thought he might have something to say about Brimleigh, but this week's column was about a series of forthcoming concerts at the Harrogate Theatre – the Nice, the Who, Yes, Fairport Convention. It sounded great, *if* her father would let her go to Harrogate.

She heard a knock at her door and was surprised to see her father standing there – and even more so that he didn't appear angry with her. Her mother must have put in a good word for her. Even so, she braced herself for the worst: accusations, the cutting of pocket money and limitation of freedom, but they didn't come. Instead, he and she came to a compromise. She would be allowed to go to the Grove on Mondays, but had to be home by eleven o'clock and must not drink any alcohol. Then she had to stop in and do her homework every other school night. She could also go out Friday and Saturday. But *not* all night. He tried to get her to tell him where she'd been on Sunday, but all she said was she'd spent the night listening to music with friends and had lost track of the time. Somehow she got the impression that he didn't believe her, but instead of pushing it, he asked, 'Have you got anything by Led Zeppelin?'

'Led Zeppelin? Yes. Why?' They had released only one LP so far, and Yvonne had bought it with the record token her aunt Moira had given her for her sixteenth birthday back in March. It said in *Melody Maker* that they had a new album coming out next month, and Robert Plant had mentioned it at Brimleigh, when they had played songs from it, like 'Heartbreaker'. Yvonne could hardly wait. Robert Plant was so sexy.

'Would you say they're loud?'

Yvonne laughed. 'Pretty loud, yes.'

'Mind if I give them a listen?'

Still confused, Yvonne said, 'No, not at all. Go ahead.' She picked it out of her pile and handed it to him, the LP with the big Zeppelin touching the edge of the Eiffel Tower and bursting into flames.

The Dansette record-player that her father had got for five thousand Embassy coupons before he stopped smoking was downstairs in the living room. It was a bone of contention, as Yvonne maintained that she was the only one who bought records and really cared about music, apart from the occasional Johnny Mathis and Jim Reeves her mother put on, and her father's few big-band LPs. She thought it should be in her room, but her father insisted that it was the *family* record-player.

At least he had bought her, for her birthday, an extra speaker unit that you could plug in and create a real stereo effect, and she had the little transistor radio she kept on her bedside table, but she still had to wait until her parents were out before she could listen to her own records properly, at the right volume.

She went down with him and turned it on. He didn't even seem to know how to operate the thing, so Yvonne took over. Soon 'Good Times, Bad Times' was blasting out loudly enough to bring Janet dashing in from the kitchen to see what was going on.

After listening to less than half of the song, Chadwick turned down the volume and asked, 'Are they all like that?'

'You'd probably think so,' Yvonne said, 'but every song is different. Why?'

'Nothing, really. Just something I was wondering about.' He rejected the LP and switched off the record-player. 'Thanks. You can have it back now.'

Still puzzled, Yvonne put it back into its sleeve and went up to her room.

Banks looked out of his office window. It was market day and the wooden stalls, canvas covers flapping in the wind, spread out over the cobbled square selling everything from cheap shirts and flat caps to used books, bootleg CDs and DVDs. The monthly farmers' market extended further across the square, selling locally grown vegetables, Wensleydale and Swaledale cheese, organic beef and pork. Banks thought all beef and pork – not to mention wine, fruit and vegetables – was organic, but someone had told him it really meant 'organically raised' without pesticides or chemicals. He wondered why didn't they say that.

Locals and tourists mingled and sampled the wares. When they had finished there, Banks knew, many would move on to the big car-boot sale at Catterick, where they would agonise over dodgy mobile phones for a couple of quid and dubious 50p inkjet refills.

It was half past twelve. Banks had spent the rest of the morning after the meeting going over the SOCO exhibits lists and talking with Stefan Nowak and Vic Manson about fingerprints and possible DNA samples from the bedding at Moorview Cottage. What they would prove, he didn't know, but he needed everything he could get. And these were probably the kind of 'facts' over which Detective Superintendent Gervaise salivated. That wasn't fair, he realised, especially as he had decided to give her the benefit of the doubt, but that remark about going to the pub had stung. He had felt like a schoolboy on the headmaster's carpet again.

Martha Argerich was playing a Beethoven piano concerto on Radio 3 in the background. It was a live recording, and in the quiet bits Banks could hear the audience coughing. He thought again about seeing Catherine Gervaise and her husband at Opera North. They had had much better seats than he had, closer to the front. They'd have been able to see the sweat and spittle at close hand. Rumour had it that Superintendent Gervaise was after a commander's job at Scotland Yard, but until something came up, they were stuck with her in Eastvale.

Banks sat down and picked up the book again. It looked well thumbed. He had never read any Ian McEwan, but the name was on his list. One day. He liked the opening well enough.

The book gave no clue as to where it had been bought. Some second-hand bookshops, Banks knew, had little stamps on the inside cover with their name and address on, but not this one. He would check the local shops and see if the victim had bought it in Eastvale, where there were two possible suppliers, and a number of charity shops that sold used books.

Nick hadn't written his name on the inside, the way some people do. All it said was '£3.50'. There was a sticker on the back, and Banks realised it was from Border's; he'd seen it before. There looked to be enough coded information on there to locate the branch, but he very much doubted that that would lead him to the customer who had bought it originally. And who knew how many people had owned it since then?

Once again he turned to the neat pencilled figures in the back:

6 8 9 21 22 25
1 2 3 16 17 18 22 23
10 (12) 13
8 9 10 11 12 15 16 17 19 22 23 25 26 30
17 18 (19)
2 5 6 7 8 11 13 14 16 18 (19) 21 22 23

They meant nothing to him but, then, he had never been any good at codes – if that was what it was supposed to be – or numbers at all, really. He couldn't even tackle sudokus. It might be the most obvious sequence of prime negative ordinals in the world, and he wouldn't know it from a betting slip. He racked his brains to think of someone who was good at stuff like that. Not Annie or Kev Templeton, that was for sure.

Winsome was good with computers, so maybe she had a strong mathematical brain. Then it came to him. Of course! How could he have forgotten so soon? He grabbed his internal telephone directory, but before he could find the number he wanted, the phone rang.

'Sir?'

'Yes, Winsome.'

'We've got him. I mean, we know who he is. The victim.'

'That's great.'

'Sorry it took so long, but my contact at the DVLA was at a wedding this morning. That's why I couldn't get in touch with her. She had her mobile turned off.'

'Who is he?'

'His name was Nicholas Barber, and he lived in Chiswick.' Winsome gave Banks an address.

'Bloody hell,' said Banks. 'That's the second Londoner killed up here this year. If they get wind of that down south, the tourists will think there's a conspiracy and stop coming.'

'A lot of people might think that wouldn't be such a bad idea, sir,' said Winsome. 'Maybe then some of the locals could afford to live here.'

'Don't you believe it. Estate agents would find some other way to gouge the buyers. Anyway, now we know who he is, we can see about checking his phone records. I can't believe he didn't have a mobile.'

'Even if he had, he couldn't have used it in Fordham. No coverage.'

'Yes, but he might have gone to Eastvale or somewhere to make calls.'

'But what network?'

'Check with all the majors.'

'But, sir—'

'I know. It's Saturday. Just do the best you can, Winsome. If you have to wait until Monday morning, so be it. Nick

Barber's not going anywhere, and his killer's already long gone.'

'Will do, sir.'

Banks thought for a moment. *Nick Barber.* There was something familiar about that name, but he couldn't for the life of him remember what it was. He reached for the directory again and carried on with what he had been doing.

Annie let Kelly Soames collect herself and dry her eyes, trying to minimise the embarrassment the girl obviously felt at her outburst of emotion.

'I'm sorry,' Kelly said eventually. 'I'm not usually like this. It's the shock.'

'You knew him well?'

Kelly blushed. 'No, not at all. We only . . . I mean, it was just a shag, that's all.'

'Still . . .' said Annie, thinking that shagging was pretty intimate, even if there was no love involved, and that, by speaking of it as she had, Kelly was trying to diminish what had happened so she wouldn't feel it so painfully. If someone was naked with you one minute, caressing you, entering you and giving you pleasure, and at the next lying on the floor with his head bashed in, it didn't make you a softie if you shed a tear or two. 'Care to tell me about it?'

'You mustn't tell my dad. He'll go spare. Promise?'

'Kelly, I'm after information about the . . . about Nick. Unless you were involved in some way with his murder, you've got nothing to worry about.'

'I won't have to go to court or anything?'

'I can't imagine why.'

Kelly thought for a moment. 'There wasn't much to it, really,' she said. Then she looked at Annie. 'It's not something I do all the time, you know. I'm not a slag.'

'Nobody's saying you are.'

'My dad would if he found out.'

'What about your mother?'

'She died when I was sixteen. Dad's never remarried. She . . . They weren't very happy together.'

'I'm sorry,' said Annie. 'But there's no reason for your father to find out.'

'As long as you promise.'

Annie hadn't promised, and she wasn't going to. As things stood, she couldn't see why Kelly's secret should come out, and she would do her best to protect it, but the situation might change. 'How did it happen?' she asked.

'Like I said, he was nice. In the pub, you know. Lots of people treat you like dirt because you're a barmaid, but not Nick.'

'Did you know his second name?'

'No, sorry.'

The wind moaned and rocked the car. Kelly hugged herself. She wasn't wearing much more than she had been the previous evening. 'Cold?' Annie asked. 'I'll turn the heater on.' She started the car and soon the windows were misty with condensation. 'That's better. Go on. You got chatting in the pub.'

'No. That's just it. My dad's always there, isn't he? He was there last night. That's why I . . . Anyway, at work he watches me like a hawk. He's like the rest, thinks a barmaid's no better than a whore. You should have heard the arguments we had about me taking the job.'

'Why did he let you, then?'

'Money. He was sick of me living at home and not having a job.'

'That'll do it. So you didn't meet Nick in the pub?'

'Well, we did meet there. I mean, that's where we first saw each other, but he was like any other customer. He was a fit-looking lad. I'll admit I fancied him, and I think maybe he could see that.'

'But he wasn't a lad, Kelly. He was much older than you.'

Kelly stiffened. 'He was only thirty-eight. That's not old. And I'm twenty-one. Besides, I like older men. They're not always pawing you like kids my age. They understand. They listen. And they know about things. All the kids my age talk about is football and beer, but Nick knew everything about music, all the bands, everything. The stories he told me – he was sophisticated.'

Annie made a mental note of that and wondered how long it had taken this Nick to start 'pawing' Kelly. 'How *did* you meet him, then?' she asked.

'In town. Eastvale. Wednesday's my day off, see, and I was out shopping. He was just coming out of that second-hand-book shop down by the side of the church, and I almost bumped into him. Talk about blush. Anyway, he recognised me, and we got chatting, went for a drink in the Queen's Arms. He was funny.'

'What happened?'

'He gave me a lift back – I'd come on the bus – and we arranged to meet later.'

'Where?'

'At the cottage. He invited me for a meal. I told my dad I was going out with some girlfriends.'

'And what happened?'

'What do you think? He made a curry – he wasn't a bad cook – and we listened to some music and . . . you know . . .'

'You went to bed together.'

'Yes.'

'Only that once?'

Kelly looked away.

'Kelly?'

'We did it again on Friday, all right? I got two hours off in the afternoon to go to the dentist but I rearranged my appointment for next Wednesday.'

'What time on Friday?'

'Between two and four.'

That was the afternoon of the murder. In all likelihood, Nick had been killed only two or three hours after Kelly had left. 'And those were the only occasions you spent with him? Wednesday night and Friday afternoon?'

'We didn't spend the night together – not that I wouldn't have, mind you – just the evening. Had to be home by eleven. My father's a bit Victorian when it comes to matters of freedom and discipline.'

Yes, and you were off shagging some older bloke you'd just laid eyes on for the first time, Annie thought. Maybe Kelly's father had a point. Anyway, it was none of her business. She was surprised at herself for being so judgemental. 'What does he do for a living?'

'He's a farmer. Can you imagine anything more naff?'

'Plenty of things.'

'Huh. Well, I can't.'

'Do you know someone called Jack Tanner?'

Kelly seemed surprised at the question. 'Yes,' she said. 'He lives down the road from the pub.'

'What do you think of him?'

'I can't say I do very much – think of him, that is. He always seems a bit of a miserable sod, to me. And he's a total lech.'

'What do you mean?'

'He's always looking at my tits. He thinks I don't know, but it's well obvious. He does it with all us girls.'

'Have you ever seen him in the pub?'

'No. CC barred him before I started working there. He can't hold his drink. He's always picking fights.'

Annie made a note to look further into Jack Tanner and went on: 'What do you remember about the cottage?'

'It just looked like a cottage. You know, old furniture and stuff, a creaky bed, toilet with a wonky seat.'

'What about Nick's personal things?'

'You must know. You were in there.'

'Everything's gone, Kelly.'

Kelly gave her a startled look. 'Somebody stole it? Is that why they killed him? But there was hardly anything there, unless he was hiding money under the mattress, and I don't think he was. You could have felt a pea under that thing.'

'What did he have?'

'Just a few books, a portable CD-player with a couple of those small speakers you can set up. Not great sound, but OK. Mostly he liked old stuff, but he had some more modern bands, Doves, Franz Ferdinand, Kaiser Chiefs. And a computer.'

'Laptop?'

'Yes. A little one. Toshiba, I think. He said he used it mostly for watching DVDs, but he did some work on it, too.'

'What kind of work?'

'He was a writer.'

'What sort of writer?'

'I don't know. He never told me about it and I never asked. None of my business, was it? Maybe he was writing his autobiography.'

That would be a bit presumptuous at thirty-eight, Annie thought, but people younger than that had written autobiographies. 'But he definitely said he was a writer?'

'I asked him what he was doing up here at such a miserable time of year, and he said he wanted a bit of peace and quiet to do some writing. I could tell he was being a bit shy and secretive about it so I didn't push. I wasn't after his life story, anyway.'

'Did he ever show you anything he'd written?'

'No. All we did was have a curry, a chat and a shag. I didn't go searching through his stuff or anything. What do you think I am?'

'All right, Kelly, don't get your knickers in a twist.'

Kelly managed a brief smile. 'Bit late for that, isn't it?'

'What did you use for contraception?'

'Condoms. What do you think?'

'We didn't find any in the house.'

'We used them all. On Friday, like, he wanted to, you know, do it again, but we couldn't. There weren't any left, and it was too late to go into Eastvale. I had to be at work. And there's no way I was going to do it without. I'm not totally stupid.'

'OK,' said Annie. Once she had got Kelly talking, she had proved far less shy and reticent than she appeared in public. So that explained the rumpled bed and lack of condoms. But robbery hardly seemed a motive. Obviously if Nick had had something of great value there he wouldn't have told some local scrubber he'd picked up in a pub, but why cart anything of value up here in the first place? Unless he was blackmailing somebody. Or making a pay-off.

'Did he have a mobile?'

'He did. A fancy Nokia. Fat lot of good it did him, though. They don't work around here. You have to go to Eastvale or Helmthorpe. It's a real drag.'

That was a problem in the Dales, Annie knew. They'd put up some new towers, but coverage was still patchy in places because of the hills. There wasn't a landline at the cottage – most rental places don't include one for obvious reasons – so both Mrs Tanner and Winsome had used the telephone box across the road by the church. 'How did he seem when you were with him?' she asked.

'He was fine.'

'He didn't seem upset, depressed or worried about anything?'

'No, not at all.'

'What about drugs?'

Kelly paused. 'We smoked a couple of joints. I'd never do anything harder than that.'

'Did he have a lot of gear?'

'No, just enough for himself. At least, that's all I saw. Look, he wasn't a drug-dealer, if that's what you're getting at.'

'I'm not getting at anything,' said Annie. 'I just want to establish some idea of Nick's state of mind. Was he any different on Friday afternoon?'

'No, not so's I noticed.'

'He wasn't nervous or edgy, as if he was expecting someone?'

'No.'

'Did you make any plans for the future?'

'Well, he didn't ask me to marry him, if that's what you're thinking.'

Annie laughed. 'I don't suppose he did, but were you going to see one another again?'

'Sure. He was up here for another week, and I said I could get away a few times – if he got some more condoms. He said I could come and see him in London, too, if I wanted. He gets lots of free tickets and he said he'd take me to concerts.' She pouted. 'My dad would never let me go, though. He thinks London's some sort of den of iniquity.'

'Did Nick give you his address?'

'We didn't get that far. We thought . . . you know . . . we'd see one another again up here. Oh, shit! Sorry.' She dabbed at her face again. Crying had made her skin blotchy. Other than that, she was a beautiful young woman, and Annie could see why any man would be attracted to her. She wasn't stupid, either, as she had pointed out, and there was a forthrightness about her attitude to sex that many might envy. But now she was an upset, confused kid, and her skin was breaking out.

When she'd pulled herself together, she laughed and said,

'You must think I'm well daft, crying over some bloke I just met.'

'No, I don't,' said Annie. 'You felt close to him, and now he's dead. That must be terrible. It must hurt.'

Kelly looked at her. 'You understand, don't you? You're not like the rest. Not like that sourpuss you had with you last night.'

Annie smiled at the description of Banks, not one she would have used herself. 'Oh, he's all right,' she said. 'He's been going through a rough time lately, too.'

'No, I mean it. You're all right, you are. What's it like being a copper?'

'It has its moments,' Annie said.

'Do you think they'd have me, if I applied, like?'

'I'm sure it would be worth a try,' Annie said. 'We're always looking for bright, motivated people.'

'That's me,' Kelly said, with a crooked smile. 'Bright and motivated. My dad would approve.'

'I wouldn't be too sure about that,' Annie said, thinking of what Banks had told her about the way his parents had reacted to his chosen profession. 'But don't let it stop you.'

Kelly frowned, then she said, 'Look, I've got to get to work. I'm already late. CC'll go spare.'

'OK,' said Annie. 'I think I'm about done for now.'

'Can you give me a minute before we go?' said Kelly, pulling down the mirror and taking a small pink container from her handbag. 'I've got to put my face on.'

'Of course.' Annie watched with amusement while Kelly applied eye-shadow, mascara, various powders and potions to hide the acne and blotchiness, then drove down the hill to drop the girl at the Cross Keys before heading back up to see what was happening at the youth hostel.

5

Over the next few days, Chadwick's investigation proceeded with a frustrating lack of progress. The two essential questions – who was the victim, and who was with her at the time of her death? – remained unanswered. Surely, Chadwick thought, someone, somewhere, must be missing her? Unless she was a runaway.

Things had been quiet on the home front since he and Yvonne had come to their compromise. He was convinced now that she *had* been at the Brimleigh festival on Sunday night – she wasn't a very good liar – but there seemed little point in pursuing the issue. It was over. The important thing was to try to head off anything along the same lines in the future, and Janet was right; he wouldn't achieve that by ranting at her.

On Wednesday, though, Chadwick had paid a quick visit to the Grove, just to see the kind of place where his daughter was spending her time. It was a small, scruffy, old-fashioned pub by the canal, with one dingy room set aside for the young crowd. He checked with his friend Geoff Broome on the Drugs Squad and found it didn't have a particularly bad reputation, which was good news. God only knew what Yvonne saw in the dump.

Dr O'Neill – whose full post-mortem report had yielded nothing to dispute the cause of death – had estimated the victim's age at between seventeen and twenty-one, so it was conceivable that she had left home and was living by herself at the time of her murder. In which case, what about her friends, boyfriends, colleagues at work? Either they didn't know what had happened, or they hadn't missed her yet. Did she even have a job? Hippies didn't like work, Chadwick knew. Perhaps she was a student, or on holiday. One interesting point that Dr O'Neill had included in his report was that there was a parturition scar on the pelvic bone, which meant that she had given birth to a baby.

DC Bradley had viewed all the television footage of the festival and spoken with newspaper reporters who had attended the event. He had learned precisely nothing. The victim was nowhere to be seen on the film, which, more often than not, panned over a sea of idealistic young faces, and cut back and forth from the gymnastic displays of the bands on stage to close-shot interviews with individual musicians and revellers. Perhaps it might be of some use in the future, when they had a suspect or needed to pick someone out of the crowd, but for the moment it was useless.

Bradley had also contacted the festival's press officer, Mick Lawton, and made a start phoning the photographers. Most were co-operative; they had no objection to the police examining their photographs and would be happy to send prints. After all, they had been taken for public consumption. How different it was from asking reporters to name sources.

The experts were still combing the area where the victim had been killed and the spot she had been moved to, collecting all the trace evidence for later analysis. If nothing else, it might provide useful forensic evidence in a trial. The lab had already reported back on the painted cornflower on the victim's cheek, informing Chadwick that it was simple greasepaint, available in any number of outlets. The flower was still one small detail the police had not yet made public.

When it came to questioning the stars, Enderby's original doubts proved remarkably prophetic. It had been done, mostly, but in a perfunctory and unsatisfactory way, as far as Chadwick was concerned, usually by the local forces who had had only minimal briefing in the case. More than one provincial DI was dying to have a crack at his local rock star, bring in the dogs and the drugs search team, despite the fiasco of the Rolling Stones bust a couple of years ago, but asking a few questions about a poxy festival up north hardly excited anyone's interest. These long-haired idiots may be stoned and anarchic, the thinking went, but they're hardly likely to be bloody murderers, are they?

Chadwick preferred to keep an open mind. He thought of the murders in Los Angeles, a story he had been following in the newspapers and on television, like everyone else. According to the reports, someone had broken into a house in Benedict Canyon, cut the telephone wires and murdered five people, including the actress Sharon Tate, who had been eight and a half months pregnant when she was stabbed to death. Later that night, another house had been broken into and a wealthy couple had been killed in a similar way. There was much speculation about drug orgies, as the male victims had been wearing hippie-type clothing and drugs were found in one of their cars. There was also talk about a 'ritualistic' aspect to the murders: the word PIG had been written in blood on the front door of Sharon Tate's house, and DEATH TO PIGS had been written on the living-room wall of the other house, also in blood, and HEALTHER SKELTER inside the fridge door, which the authorities took to be a misspelling of 'Helter Skelter' a Beatles song from the *White Album*. What little inside knowledge Chadwick had been able to pick up on the grapevine indicated that the police were looking for members of some obscure hippie cult.

It had not occurred to Chadwick that the crimes had anything in common with the Brimleigh festival murder. Los Angeles was a long way from Yorkshire. Still, if people who listened to Beatles songs and called the police 'pigs' could do something like that in Los Angeles, then why not in England?

Chadwick would have interviewed the musicians himself, but they lived as far afield as London, Buckinghamshire, Sussex, Ireland and Glasgow, some in small flats and bedsits, but a surprising number owned country estates with swimming-pools or large detached houses in nice areas. He would have spent half his life on the motorway and the rest on country roads.

He had hoped that one of the interviewers might at least have sniffed out a half-truth or a full-blown lie, whereupon he would have conducted a follow-up interview himself, however far he had to travel, but everything came back routine: no further action.

A lot of the bands whose names he had seen in connection with Brimleigh were playing at another festival, in Rugby, that weekend: Pink Floyd, the Nice, Roy Harper, the Edgar Broughton Band and the Third Ear Band. He sent Enderby to Rugby to see if he could come up with anything. Enderby seemed in his element at the prospect of meeting such heroes.

Two of the bands at Brimleigh had been local. During the week Chadwick had already spoken briefly with Jan Dukes de Grey in Leeds. Derek and Mick seemed pleasant enough lads, beneath the long hair and unusual clothes, and they had left the festival well before the time of the murder. The Mad Hatters were in London at the moment but were expected back up north early the following week to stay at Swainsview Lodge, Lord Jessop's residence near Eastvale, where they were to rehearse for a forthcoming tour and album. He would talk to them then.

It was half past two in the afternoon by the time DC Gavin Rickerd made it over to Western Area Headquarters in

Eastvale. Banks was due to sit in on the Nicholas Barber post-mortem at three, but he wanted to get this out of the way first. He had rung Annie at Fordham, and they had given one another a quick update, then agreed to meet in the Queen's Arms at six o'clock.

'Come in, Gavin,' said Banks. 'How are things going in Neighbourhood Policing? Teething troubles?'

'Busy. You know how things are with a new job, sir. But it's fine, really. I like it.' Rickerd adjusted his glasses. He was still wearing old-fashioned National Health specs held together at the bridge with sticking plaster. It had to be a fashion statement of some sort, Banks thought, as even a poor DC could afford new ones. The words 'fashion statement' and Gavin Rickerd hardly seemed a match made in heaven, so maybe it was an anti-fashion statement. He wore a bottle-green corduroy jacket, with leather elbow patches, and brown corduroy trousers a bit worse for wear. His tie was awkwardly fastened and his shirt collar bent up on the left side. An array of pens and pencils poked from the top pocket of his jacket. His face had the pasty look of someone who didn't get outside very much. Banks remembered how Kevin Templeton used to take the piss out of him mercilessly. He had a cruel streak, did Templeton.

'Miss the thrust and parry of policing on the edge?' Banks asked.

'Not really, sir. I'm quite happy where I am.'

'Ah, right.' Banks had never known how to talk to Rickerd. Rumour had it that he was a bona-fide train-spotter, that he actually stood at the end of cold station platforms in Darlington, Leeds or York, come rain or shine, scanning the horizon for the Royal Scotsman, the Mallard, or whatever they called it, these days. Nobody had actually seen him, but the rumour persisted. He also had a bachelor's degree in mathematics and was reputed to be a whiz at puzzles and computer games.

Banks thought he was probably wasted in Eastvale and should have been recruited by MI5 years ago, but their loss was his gain.

One thing Banks knew for certain was that Gavin Rickerd was a fanatical cricket fan, so he chatted briefly about England's recent Ashes victory, then said, 'Got a little job for you, Gavin.'

'But, sir, you know I'm Neighbourhood Policing now, not CID or Major Crimes.'

'Yes,' said Banks. 'But what's in a name?'

'It's not just the name, sir, it's a serious job.'

'I'm sure it is. That's not in dispute.'

'The superintendent won't like it, sir.' Rickerd was starting to look decidedly nervous, glancing over his shoulder at the door.

'Been warned off, have you?'

Rickerd adjusted his glasses again.

'OK,' Banks said. 'I understand. I wouldn't want to get you into trouble. You can go. It's just that I've got this puzzle I thought you might be interested in. At least, I think it could be a puzzle. Whatever it is, though, we need to know.'

'Puzzle?' said Rickerd, licking his lips. 'What sort of puzzle?'

'Well, I was thinking maybe you could have a look at it in your spare time. That way the super can't complain, can she?'

'I don't know, sir.'

'Like a little peek?'

'Well, maybe just a quick one.'

'Good lad.' Banks handed him a photocopy of the page from Nick Barber's copy of *Atonement* he had got from the SOCOs.

Rickerd squinted at it, turned it this way and that, and put it down on the desk. 'Interesting,' he said.

'I was thinking . . . You like mathematical puzzles and

things, know a bit about them. Maybe you could take it away with you and play around with it.'

'I can take it away?'

'Of course. It's only a photocopy.'

'All right, then,' said Rickerd, evidently charged with a new sense of importance. He folded the piece of paper carefully into a square and slipped it into the inside pocket of his corduroy jacket.

'You'll get back to me?' said Banks.

'Soon as I've got something. I can't promise, mind you. It might be just random gibberish.'

'I understand,' said Banks. 'Do your best.'

Rickerd left the office, pausing to glance both ways down the corridor before he dashed off towards the Neighbourhood Policing offices. Banks glanced at his watch and pulled a face. Time to go to the post-mortem.

Saturday, 13 September 1969

Chadwick was hoping to get away early as he and Geoff Broome had tickets for Leeds United's away game with Sheffield Wednesday. At about ten o'clock, though, a woman who said she lived on the Raynville estate rang to say she thought she recognised the victim. She didn't want to commit herself, saying the sketch in the paper wasn't a very good likeness, but she thought she knew who it was. Out of respect to the victim, the newspapers hadn't published a photograph of the dead girl, only an artist's impression, but Chadwick had a photo in his briefcase.

This wasn't the kind of interview he could delegate to an underling, like the inexperienced Simon Bradley, let alone the scruffy Keith Enderby, so before he left he rang Geoff Broome with his apologies. There would be no problem getting rid of the ticket somewhere in Brotherton House, Geoff told him.

After that, Chadwick went down to his ageing Vauxhall Victor and drove out to Armley, rain streaking his windscreen.

The Raynville estate was not among the best of the newer Leeds council estates, and it looked even worse in the rain. Built only a few years ago, it had quickly gone to seed, and those who could afford to avoided it. Chadwick and Janet had lived nearby, on the Astons, until they'd saved up to buy their semi just off Church Road, in the shadow of St Bartholomew's, Armley, when Chadwick was promoted to detective inspector four years ago.

The caller, who had given her name as Carol Wilkinson, lived in a second-storey maisonette on Raynville Walk. The stairs smelt of urine and the walls were covered with filthy graffiti, a phenomenon that was starting to spring up in places like this. It was just another sign of the degeneracy of modern youth, as far as Chadwick was concerned: no respect for property. When he knocked on the faded green door, a young woman holding a baby in one arm opened it, the chain still on.

'Are you the policeman?'

'Detective Inspector Chadwick.' He showed his warrant card.

She glanced at it, looked Chadwick up and down, then unfastened the chain. 'Come in. You'll have to excuse the mess.'

And he did. She deposited the baby in a wooden playpen in a living room untidy with toys, discarded clothing and magazines. It – he couldn't tell whether it was a girl or a boy – stood and gawped at him briefly, then started rattling the bars and crying. The cream carpet was stained with only God knew what, and the room smelt of unwashed nappies and warm milk. A television set stood in one corner, and a radio was playing somewhere: Kenny Everett. Chadwick only knew who it was because Yvonne liked to listen to him, and he recognised the inane patter and the clumsy attempts at humour. When it came to radio, Chadwick preferred quiz programmes and the news.

He took the chair the woman offered, first giving it a quick once over to make sure it was clean, and plucking at the crease in his trousers before he sat. The maisonette had a small balcony, but there were no chairs outside. Chadwick imagined the woman had to be careful because of her baby. More than once a young child had crawled on to a balcony and fallen off, despite the guard-rail.

Trying to distance himself from the noise, the smell and the mess, Chadwick focused on the woman as she sat down opposite him and lit a cigarette. She was pale and careworn, wearing a baggy fawn cardigan and shapeless checked slacks. Dirty blonde hair hung down to her shoulders. She might have been fifteen or thirty.

'You said on the phone that you think you know the woman whose picture was in the paper?'

'I think so,' she said. 'I just wasn't sure. That's why I took so long to ring you. I had to think about it.'

'Are you sure now?'

'Well, no, not really. I mean, her hair was different and everything. It's just . . .'

'What?'

'Something about her, that's all.'

Chadwick opened his briefcase and took out the photograph of the dead girl, head and shoulders. He warned Carol what to expect, and she seemed to brace herself, drawing an exceptionally deep lungful of smoke. When she looked at the photo, she put her hand to her chest. Slowly, she let the smoke out. 'I've never seen a dead person before,' she said.

'Do you recognise her?'

She passed the photo back and nodded. 'Funnily enough, this looks more like her than the drawing, even though she's dead.'

'Do you know who she is?'

'Yes. I think it's Linda. Linda Lofthouse.'

'How did you know her?'

'We went to school together.' She jerked her head in a generally northern direction. 'Sandford Girls'. She was in the same class as me.'

At least the victim was local, then, which made the investigation a lot easier. Still, it made perfect sense. While many young people would have made the pilgrimage from all parts of the country to the Brimleigh festival, Chadwick guessed that the majority of those attending would have been from a bit closer to home – Leeds, Bradford, York, Harrogate and the surrounding areas: the event had been practically on their doorstep. 'When was this?'

'I left school two years ago last July, when I was sixteen. Linda left the same year. We were almost the same age.'

Eighteen and one kid already. Chadwick wondered if she had a husband. She wasn't wearing a wedding ring, which didn't mean much in itself, but there didn't seem to be any evidence of a male presence, as far as he could see. Anyway, the age was about right for the victim. 'Were you friends?'

Carol paused. 'I thought so,' she said, 'but after we'd left school we didn't see much of one another.'

'Why not?'

'Linda got pregnant after Christmas in her final year, just before she turned sixteen.' She looked at her own child and gave a harsh laugh. 'At least I waited until I'd left school and got married.'

'The father?'

'He's at work. Tom's not a bad bloke, really.'

So she was married. In a way, Chadwick felt relieved. 'I meant the father of Linda's child.'

'Oh, him. She was going out with Donald Hughes at the time. I just assumed, you know, like . . .'

'Did they marry, live together?'

'Not that I know of. Linda . . . Well, she was getting a bit weird that last year at school.'

'In what way?'

'The way she dressed, like she didn't care any more. And she was more in her own world, wherever that was. She kept getting into trouble for not paying attention in class, but it wasn't as if she was stupid or anything – she even did OK in her O levels, despite being pregnant. She was just . . .'

'In her own world?'

'Yes. The teachers didn't know what to do with her. If they said anything, she'd give them a right clever answer. She had some nerve. And that last year she stopped hanging around with us – you know, there were a few of us. Me, Linda, Julie and Anita used to go down the Locarno on a Saturday night, have a good dance and see if there were any decent lads around.' She blushed. 'Sometimes we'd go to Le Phonograph later if we could get in. Most of us could pass for eighteen, but sometimes they got a bit picky on the door. You know what it's like.'

'So Linda became a bit of a loner?'

'Yes. And this was before she got pregnant. Quiet. Liked to read. Not school books. Poetry and stuff. And she loved Bob Dylan.'

'Didn't the rest of you?'

'He's all right, I suppose, but you can't dance to him, can you? And I can't understand a word he's singing about, if you can call it singing.'

Chadwick didn't know whether he had ever heard Bob Dylan, though he did know the name, so he was thankful the question was rhetorical. Dancing had never been a skill he possessed in any great measure, although he had met Janet at a dance and that had seemed to go well enough. 'Did she have any enemies, anyone who disliked her?'

'No, nothing like that. You couldn't *hate* Linda. You'd know what I mean if you'd met her.'

'Did she ever get into any fights or serious disagreements with anyone?'

'No, never.'

'Do you know if she was taking drugs?'

'She never said so, and I never saw her do anything like that. Not that I'd have known, I suppose.'

'Where did she live?'

'On the Sandford estate with her mum and dad – though I heard her dad died a short while ago. In the spring. Sudden. Heart-attack.'

'Can you give me her mother's address?'

Carol told him.

'Do you know if she had the child?'

'About two years ago.'

'That would be September 1967?'

'Around that time, yes. But I never saw her after school broke up that July. I got married and Tom and me set up house here and all. Then little Andy came along.'

'Have you bumped into her since then?'

'No. I heard she'd moved away down south after the baby was born. London.'

Maybe she had, Chadwick thought. That would explain why she hadn't been immediately missed. As Carol had said, the likeness in the newspaper wasn't a particularly good one, and a lot of people don't pay attention to the papers anyway. 'Have you any idea what happened to the baby, or the father?'

'I've seen Don around. He's been going out with Pamela Davis for about a year now. I think they might be engaged. He works in a garage on Kirkstall Road, near the viaduct. I remember Linda talking about having the baby adopted. I don't think she planned on keeping it.'

The mother would probably know, not that it mattered.

Whoever had killed Linda Lofthouse, it wasn't a two-year-old. 'Is there anything else you can tell me about Linda?' he asked.

'Not really,' said Carol. 'I mean, I don't know what you want to hear. We *were* best friends, but we drifted apart, as you do. I don't know what she got up to the last two years. I'm sorry to hear she was killed, though. That's terrible. Why would somebody do a thing like that?'

'That's what we're trying to find out,' said Chadwick, trying to sound as reassuring as he could. He didn't think it came over very well. He stood up. 'Thanks for your time, and for the information.'

'You'll let me know when you find out?'

'I'll let you know,' said Chadwick, standing up. 'Please, stay here with the baby. I'll let myself out.'

'What's up with you, then?' asked Cyril, the landlord of the Queen's Arms, as Banks ordered a bitter lemon and ice late that afternoon. 'Doctor's orders?'

'More like boss's orders,' Banks grumbled. 'We've got a new super. She's dead keen and seems to have eyes in the back of her bloody head.'

'She'll get nowt out of me,' said Cyril. 'My lips are sealed.'

Banks laughed. 'Cheers, mate. Maybe another time.'

'Bad for business, this new boss of yours.'

'Give us time,' said Banks, with a wink. 'We'll get her trained.'

He took his glass over to a dimpled, copper-topped table by the window and contemplated its unappetising contents gloomily. The ashtray was half full of crushed filters. Banks pushed it as far away as he could. Now that he no longer smoked, he'd come to loathe the smell of cigarettes. As a smoker, he'd never noticed it but now when he got home from the pub he had to put his clothes straight into the laundry basket because they stank. Which would be fine if he got round to doing his laundry more often.

Annie turned up at six o'clock, as arranged. She'd been at Fordham earlier, Banks knew, and had talked to Kelly Soames. She got herself a Britvic Orange and joined him. 'Christ,' she said, when she saw Banks's drink. 'They'll be thinking we're all on the wagon.'

'Too true. Good day?'

'Not bad, I suppose. You?'

Banks swirled the liquid in his glass. Ice clinked against the sides. 'I've had better,' he said. 'Just come from the post-mortem.'

'Ah.'

'No picnic. Never is. Even after all these years you never get quite used to it.'

'I know,' said Annie.

'Anyway,' Banks went on, 'we weren't far wrong in our original suspicions. Nick Barber was in generally good health apart from being bashed on the back of the head with a poker. It fits the wound, and Dr Glendenning says he was hit four times, once when he was standing up, which accounts for most of the blood-spatter, and three times when he was on the floor.'

Annie raised an eyebrow. 'Overkill?'

'Not necessarily. The doc said it needn't have been a frenzied attack, just that whoever did it wanted to make sure his victim was dead. In all likelihood he'd have got a bit of blood on him, too, so that might give us something we can use in court if we ever catch the bastard. Anyway, there were no prints on the poker, so our killer obviously wiped it clean.'

'What do you make of it all?'

'I don't know,' said Banks, sipping bitter lemon and pulling a face. 'It certainly doesn't look professional, and it wasn't frenzied enough to look like a lovers' quarrel, not that we can rule that out.'

'I doubt if the motive was robbery, either.' Annie told Banks more detail than she had given him over the phone about her conversation with Kelly Soames and what little she had discovered about Barber from her.

'And the timing is interesting,' Banks added.

'What do you mean?'

'Was he killed before or after the power cut? All the doc can tell us is that it probably happened between six and eight. One bloke left the pub at seven and came back around quarter past. The others bear this out, but nobody saw him in Lyndgarth.' Banks consulted his notes. 'Name of Calvin Soames.'

'Soames?' said Annie. 'That's the barmaid's name. Kelly Soames. He must be her father. I recognised him when he dropped her off.'

'That's right,' said Banks.

'She said he's always in the pub when she's working. I know she was terrified about him finding out about her and Nick.'

'I'll have a talk with him tomorrow.'

'Go carefully, Alan. He didn't know about her and Nick Barber. Apparently he's a very strict father.'

'That's not such a terrible thing, is it? Anyway, I'll do my best. But if he really *did* know . . .'

'I understand,' said Annie.

'And don't forget Jack Tanner,' said Banks. 'We don't know what motive he might have had, but he had a connection with the victim through his wife. We'd better check his alibi thoroughly.'

'It's being done,' said Annie. 'Ought to be easy enough to check with his darts cronies. And I've got Kev following up on all the blokes who left the pub between the relevant times.'

'Good. Now, the tourist couple, the Browns, say they arrived at about a quarter to eight and thought they saw a car heading up the hill, right?'

Annie consulted the notes she had taken in the incident van. 'Someone from the youth hostel, a New Zealander called

Vanessa Napier, told PC Travers that she saw a car going by at about half past seven or a quarter to eight on Friday evening, shortly after the lights went off. She was looking out of her window at the storm.'

'Did she get any details?'

'No. It was dark, and she doesn't know a Honda from a Fiat.'

'Doesn't help us much, does it?'

'It's all we've got. They questioned everyone in the hostel and Vanessa's the only one who saw anything.'

'She's not been shagging our Nick too, has she?'

Annie laughed. 'I shouldn't think so.'

'Hmm,' Banks said. 'There seem to have been more comings and goings between half past seven and eight than there were earlier.'

'Yorkshire Electricity confirms the power went off at seven twenty-eight p.m.'

'The problem is,' Banks went on, 'that if the killer came from some distance away and timed his arrival for half seven or a quarter to eight, he can't have known there would be a power cut, so it's not a factor.'

'Maybe it gave him an opportunity,' Annie said. 'He and Nick are arguing, the lights go out, Nick turns to reach for his cigarette lighter and the killer seizes the moment to lash out.'

'Possibly,' said Banks. 'Though the darkness would have made it a bit harder for him to search the cottage and be certain he took away everything he needed to. Also, your eyes need time to adjust. Look at the timing. Mrs Tanner showed up at eight. That didn't give him much time to search in the dark and check Barber's car.'

'He could have had a torch in his own vehicle.'

'He'd still have had to go and get it. There would've been no reason for him to be carrying one if he arrived *before* the power cut.'

'Does the electricity failure really matter, then?'

'I think we can assume that the killer would have done what he came to do anyway, and if the lights went out, that just gave him a better opportunity.'

'What about the Browns? Their timing is interesting.'

'Yes,' said Banks. 'But do they strike you as the type to kill someone, then drop by the local pub for a pint?'

'It was dark. There was no electricity. Maybe the local was as good a place to hide as any.'

'What about blood?'

'Winsome checked after the lights came back on,' Annie said. 'She didn't see any signs, but they'd hardly have hung around till the lights came back on if they were hiding blood-stains. We could hardly strip-search everyone.'

'True,' said Banks. 'Look, we've still got a long way to go. You mentioned that Nick Barber was a writer?'

'That's what Kelly said he told her.'

'Who'd want to kill a writer?'

'There were plenty I wanted to kill when I was at school doing English,' said Annie, 'but they were dead already.'

Banks laughed. 'But seriously.'

'Well, it depends what kind of writer he was, doesn't it?' Annie said. 'I mean, if he was an investigative journalist on to something big, someone might have had a reason to get rid of him.'

'But what was he doing up here?'

'There are plenty of cupboards full of skeletons in North Yorkshire.'

'Yes, but where to begin? That's the problem.'

'Google?' suggested Annie.

'It'd be a start.'

'And shouldn't we be going to London?'

'Monday morning,' said Banks. 'Then we'll be able to talk to his employer, if we can find out who it is. You know how useless Sundays are for finding anything out. I've asked the locals to keep an eye on the place until then to make sure no one tries to get in.'

'What about next of kin?'

'Winsome sorted that, too. They live just outside Sheffield. They've been informed. I thought you and Winsome could go and talk to them tomorrow.'

'Fine,' said Annie. 'I was only going to wash my hair, anyway. Oh, there's one more thing. About that book.'

'Yes?'

'It looks as if he might have bought it over the road here. Kelly said she met him coming out of the second-hand-book shop.'

Banks consulted his watch. 'Damn, it'll be closed now.'

'Is it important?'

'Could be. It didn't look as if the figures were written in the same hand as the price, but you never know.'

'We can ring the owner at home, I suppose.'

'Good idea,' said Banks.

'From the way you're still sitting there, I assume you're expecting me to do it?'

'If you would. Look, I'm sick of this bloody bitter lemon. As far as I'm concerned we're off duty, working on our own time, and if Lady Gervaise wants to make something of it, then good luck to her. I'm having a pint. You?'

Annie smiled. 'Spoken like a true rebel. I'll have the same. And while you're getting them in . . .' She took her mobile phone from her briefcase and waved it in the air.

Banks had to wait until a party of six tourists, who couldn't make up their minds what they wanted to drink, had been served, and when he got back with two foaming pints of Black Sheep, Annie had finished. 'Well, he certainly didn't do it,' she said. 'Fair bristled at the idea of anyone writing anything but the price in books, even the blank pages at the back. Sacrilege, he said. Anyway, he remembers the book. It only came in the day before Nick Barber bought it last Wednesday, and he checks them all thoroughly. There was nothing written in the back then.'

'Interesting,' said Banks. 'Very interesting indeed. We'll just have to wait and see what young Gavin makes of it, won't we?'

Saturday, 13 September 1969

Yvonne sat upstairs at the front of a number sixteen bus heading for the city centre chewing her fingernails and wondering what to do. Some clever sod had taken a marker to the NO SPITTING sign and altered it to read NO SHITTING. Yvonne lit a cigarette and pondered her dilemma. If she was right, it could be serious.

It had happened the previous evening, when her father came home late from work, as usual. He'd been taking something out of his briefcase when a photograph had slipped on to the floor. He'd put it back quickly and obviously thought she hadn't seen it, but she had. It was a picture of the dead girl, the one who had been stabbed on Sunday at the Brimleigh festival and, with a shock, Yvonne had realised she recognised her: *Linda.*

She didn't know Linda well, had only met her once and hadn't talked to her much, but the local hippie community was so small that if you hung around the right places long enough you'd come across pretty much everyone in the scene – at the Grove, the Adelphi, the Peel or one of the student pubs on Woodhouse Lane, in Hyde Park or Headingley. Even as far away as the Farmer's Inn, where they had blues bands like Savoy Brown, Chicken Shack, Free and Jethro Tull on a Sunday night. You could also be damned sure that they'd beg, borrow or steal to get to an event with a line-up like the Brimleigh festival. So, when you thought about it, Linda being there wasn't quite such a coincidence as it appeared on the surface. The thing was, you didn't expect to be killed there; it was supposed to be a peaceful event, a gathering of the tribe and a celebration of unity.

The bus lumbered down Tong Road, past the Lyric, which was advertising a double bill of last year's *Carry On Up the Khyber* and *Carry On Camping*. What crap, Yvonne thought. It was a grey day, and light rain pattered against the windows. Rows of grim back-to-back terraces sloped up the hill towards Hall Lane, all dark slate roofs and dirty red brick. A couple of kids got on at the junction with Wellington Road, behind the Crown, by the flats, and took the other front seat.

They'd filmed part of *Billy Liar* there a few years ago, Yvonne remembered, while it was a wasteland of demolished houses before the flats were built. Yvonne had been about eight, and her father had brought her down to watch. She had ended up in one of the crowd scenes waving a little flag as Tom Courtenay drove through in his tank, but when she'd watched the film, she couldn't see herself anywhere.

The kids lit cigarettes, kept looking over at her and making cheeky remarks. Yvonne ignored them.

She had met Linda at Bayswater Terrace one evening during the summer holidays. She'd got the impression that Linda was on a flying visit, that she had lived there for a while but had moved to London. Linda was fantastic, she remembered. She actually knew some of the bands and hung around with lots of rock stars at clubs and other 'in' places. She wasn't a groupie – she'd made that clear – just liked the music and the guys who played it. Someone had said that one of the Mad Hatters was Linda's cousin, but Yvonne couldn't remember which.

Linda even played a bit of guitar herself. She had sat down that evening with an acoustic and played 'As Tears Go By' and 'Both Sides Now'. Not a bad voice, either, Yvonne had thought, a little in awe of her and the sort of luminous haze her long blonde hair and the full-length white dress she wore created round her pale features. The guys were all in love with her, you could tell, but she wasn't interested in them. Linda didn't belong to anyone. She was her own person. She also had a great throaty laugh, which surprised Yvonne in one who looked so demure, like Marianne Faithfull.

McGarrity had been there that night, Yvonne remembered, and even he had seemed subdued, keeping his knife in his pocket for once and refraining from muttering T. S. Eliot all evening. The guy they said was organising the Brimleigh festival, Rick Hayes, had also been present, which was how they'd managed to score some free tickets. He knew Linda from down in London and seemed to know Dennis, too, whose house it was. Yvonne hadn't liked Hayes. He had tried to get her to go upstairs with him and got a bit stroppy when she wouldn't.

That was the only time Yvonne and Linda had met, but Linda had made an impression. Yvonne was waiting for her O-level results, and Linda had said something about exams not proving anything and the real truth of what you were was inside you. That had made sense to Yvonne. Now Linda was dead. Stabbed. Yvonne felt tears prick her eyes. She could hardly believe it. One of her own. She hadn't seen her during the festival, but that wasn't surprising.

The bus carried on past the gasworks, over the canal and river and past the huge building site where they were putting up the new *Yorkshire Post* building at the corner of Wellington Street, then past the dark, high Victorian buildings to City Square, where Yvonne got off. There were a couple of new boutiques she wanted to visit, and that little record shop down the ginnel off Albion Street might still have a copy of the *Blind Faith* LP. Her parents hadn't let her go to the free concert in London's Hyde Park last June, but at least she could enjoy the music on record. Later she was going over to Carberry Place to meet up with Steve and have a few tokes. A bunch of them were going to the Peel that night to see Jan Dukes de Grey. Derek and Mick were quite the local celebrities and they were like real people: they'd talk to you and sign their first LP cover, *Sorcerers*, not hide away backstage like rock stars.

Yvonne's problem persisted, though: whether or not to tell her father about Linda. If she did, the police would be at Bayswater Terrace like a shot. Maybe Dennis and Martin and Julie and the others would get busted. And it would be *her* fault. If they found out, they'd never speak to her again. She was sure that none of them could have had anything to do with what happened to Linda, so why bring grief on them? Rick Hayes was a creep and McGarrity was weird, but neither man would kill one of their own. How could knowing about Linda being at Bayswater Terrace in July possibly help the police investigation? Her father would find out who Linda was eventually – he was good at finding things out – but it wouldn't be from her, and nobody would be able to blame her for what happened.

That was what she decided in the end, turning the corner into the wet cobbled ginnel; she would keep it to herself. There was no way she was going to the pigs, even if the chief pig was her father.

6

There were some advantages to being a DCI, Banks thought, on Sunday morning as he lingered over a second cup of coffee in the conservatory and read his way through the Sunday papers. Outside, the wind had dropped over the past couple of hours, the sun was shining and the weather had turned a little milder, though there was an unmistakable edge of autumn in the air, the smell of the musty leaves and a whiff of acrid smoke from a distant peat fire.

He was still senior investigating officer, of course, and in a short while he would go to interview Calvin Soames. At some point he would also drop by at the station and the incident van to make his presence felt and get up to date with developments, if there were any. In an investigation like this, he could never be far away from the action for any length of time, but the team had enough to occupy itself for the moment, and the SOCOs had plenty of trace evidence to sift through. He was always only a phone call away so, barring a major breakthrough, there was no reason for him to appear at the office at the crack of dawn every day: he would only get lumbered with paperwork. First thing tomorrow morning, he and Annie would be on the train to London, and perhaps there they would find out more about Nick Barber. All Annie had been able to find out on Google was that he had written for *MOJO* magazine and had penned a couple of quickie rock-star biographies. It was interesting, and Banks thought he recognised the name now he saw it in context, but it still wasn't much to go on.

Just as Banks thought it was time to tidy up and set off for Soames's farm, he heard a knock at the door. It couldn't be Annie, he thought, because she had gone to see Nick Barber's parents near Sheffield. Puzzled, he ambled through to the front room and answered it. He was stunned to see his son, Brian, standing there.

'Oh, great, Dad, you're in.'

'So it would appear,' said Banks. 'You didn't ring.'

'Battery's dead and the car charger's fucked. Sorry. It *is* OK, isn't it?'

'Of course,' Banks said, smiling, putting his hand on Brian's shoulder and stepping back. 'Come on in. It's always good to see you.'

Banks heard rather than saw a movement behind Brian, then a young woman came into view. 'This is Emilia,' said Brian. 'Emilia, my dad.'

'Hi, Mr Banks,' said Emilia, holding out a soft hand with long, tapered fingers and a bangled wrist. 'It's really nice to meet you.'

'Can we bring the stuff in from the car?' Brian asked.

Still puzzled, Banks said OK and stood there while Brian and Emilia pulled a couple of holdalls from the boot of a red Honda that looked as if it had seen better days, then walked back to the cottage.

'We're going to stay for a few days, if that's OK with you,' Brian said, as Banks gestured them into the cottage. 'Only I've got some time off before rehearsals for the next tour, and Emilia's never been to the Dales before. I thought I'd show her around. We'll do a bit of walking, you know, country stuff.'

Brian and Emilia put their bags down, then Brian took his mobile phone from his pocket and searched for the lead in the side pouch of his holdall. 'OK if I charge up the phone?' he asked.

'Of course,' said Banks, pointing to the nearest plug socket.

'Can I get you something?' He looked at his watch. 'I have to go out soon, but we could have some coffee first.'

'Great,' said Brian.

Emilia nodded in agreement. She looked terribly familiar, Banks thought.

'Come through to the conservatory, then,' said Banks.

'Conservatory. Lah-di-dah,' said Brian.

'Enough of your lip,' Banks joked. 'There's something very relaxing about conservatories. They're like an escape from the real world.'

But Brian was already poking his nose into the entertainment room. 'Jesus Christ!' he said. 'Look at this stuff. Is this what you told me you got from Uncle Roy?'

'Yes,' said Banks. 'Your grandparents didn't want it, so . . .'

'Fantastic,' said Brian. 'I mean, it's sad about Uncle Roy, but look at that plasma screen, all those movies. That Porsche out there is yours, too, isn't it?'

'It was Roy's, yes,' said Banks, feeling a bit guilty about it now. He left Brian and Emilia nosing around the growing CD collection and headed for the kitchen, where he put the coffee-maker on. Then he picked up the scattered newspapers in the conservatory and set them aside on a spare chair. Brian and Emilia came through via the doors from the entertainment room. 'I wouldn't have had you down for a Streets fan, Dad,' he said.

'Just shows how little you know me,' said Banks.

'Yeah, but hip-hop?'

'Research,' said Banks. 'Have to get to know the criminal mind, don't I? Besides, it's not really hip-hop, is it? And the kid tells a great story. Sit down, both of you. I'll fetch the coffee. Milk? Sugar?'

They both said yes. Banks brought the coffee and sat on his usual white wicker chair opposite Brian and Emilia. He knew it was unlikely – Brian was in his twenties, after all – but his son seemed to have grown another couple of inches since he'd last seen him. He was about six foot two and skinny, wearing a green T-shirt with the band's logo, the Blue Lamps, and cream cargos. He had also had his hair cut really short and gelled. Banks thought it made him look older, which in turn made Banks *feel* older.

Emilia looked like a model. Only a couple of inches shorter than Brian, slender as a reed, wearing tight blue low-rise jeans and a skimpy belly-top, with the requisite wide gap between the two, and a green jewel gracing her navel, she moved with languorous grace and economy. Her streaky brown-blonde hair hung over her shoulders and half-way down her back, framing and almost obscuring an oval face with an exquisite complexion, full lips, small nose and high cheekbones. Her violet eyes were unnaturally bright, but Banks suspected contact lenses rather than drugs. He'd seen her somewhere before: he knew it. 'It really is good to see you again,' he said to Brian, 'and nice to meet you, Emilia. I'm sorry you caught me unawares.'

'Don't tell me, there's no food in the house,' Brian said, 'or, worse, no booze?'

'There's wine, and a few cans of beer. But that's about it. Oh, there's also some leftover vegetarian lasagne.'

'You've gone veggy?'

'No. Annie was over the other evening.'

'Aha,' said Brian. 'You two an item again?'

Banks felt himself redden. 'Don't be cheeky. And, no, we're not. Can't a couple of colleagues have a quiet dinner together?'

Brian held his hands up, grinning. 'OK. OK.'

'Why don't we eat out later? Pub lunch, if I can make it. If not, dinner. On me.'

'OK,' said Brian. 'That all right with you, Emmy?'

'Of course,' said Emilia. 'I can hardly wait to try some of this famous Yorkshire pudding.'

'You've never had Yorkshire pudding before?' said Banks. Emilia blushed. 'I've led a sheltered life.'

'Well, I think that can be arranged,' said Banks. He glanced at his watch. 'Right now, I'd better be off. I'll phone.'

'Cool,' said Brian. 'If you tell us which room we can have, we'll take our stuff up while you're out.'

Saturday, 13 September 1969

The Sandford estate was older than the Raynville, and it hadn't improved with age. Mrs Lofthouse lived right at the heart of things in a semi-detached house with a postage-stamp garden and a privet hedge. Across the street, a rusty Hillman Minx without tyres was parked on a neighbour's overgrown lawn, and three windows were boarded up in the house next door. It was that kind of estate.

Mrs Lofthouse, though, had done as much as she could to brighten the place up with a vase of chrysanthemums on the windowsill and a colourful painting of a Cornish fishing village over the mantelpiece. She was a small, slight woman in her early forties, her dyed brown hair recently permed. Chadwick could read the grief in the lines round her eyes and mouth. She had just lost her husband and now he was here to burden her with the death of her daughter.

'It's a nice house you have,' said Chadwick, sitting on the flower-patterned armchair with lace antimacassars.

'Thank you,' said Mrs Lofthouse. 'It's a rough estate, but I do my best. And there are some good people here. Anyway, now Jim's gone I don't need all this room. I've put my name down for a bungalow out Sherbourne-in-Elmet way.'

'That should be a bit quieter.'

'It's about Linda, isn't it?'

'You know?'

Mrs Lofthouse bit her lip. 'I saw the sketch in the paper.

Ever since then I just . . . I've been denying it, convincing myself it's not her, it's a mistake, but it *is* her, isn't it?' Her accent was noticeably Yorkshire, but not as broad as Carol Wilkinson's.

'We think so.' Chadwick slipped the photograph from his briefcase. 'I'm afraid this won't be very pleasant,' he said, 'but it is important.' He showed her the photograph. 'Is this Linda?'

After a sharp intake of breath, Mrs Lofthouse said, 'Yes.'

'You'll have to make a formal identification down at the mortuary.'

'I will?'

'I'm afraid so. We'll make it as easy for you as we can, though. Please don't worry.'

'When can I . . . you know, the funeral?'

'Soon,' said Chadwick. 'When the coroner releases the body for burial. I'll let you know. I'm very sorry, Mrs Lofthouse, but I must ask you some questions. The sooner the better.'

'Of course. I'll be all right. And it's Margaret, please. Shall I make some tea? Would that be OK?'

'I could do with a cuppa right now,' said Chadwick, with a smile.

'Won't be a moment.'

Margaret Lofthouse disappeared into the kitchen, no doubt to give private expression to her grief as she boiled the kettle and filled the teapot in the time-honoured, comforting ritual. A clock ticked on the mantel beside a framed photograph. Twenty-five to one. Broome and his pal would be well on their way to Sheffield by now, if they weren't there already. Chadwick got up to examine the photograph. It showed a younger Margaret Lofthouse, and the man beside her with his arm round her waist was, no doubt, her husband. Also in the picture, which looked as if it had been taken outside in the country, a young girl with short blonde hair was staring into the camera.

Margaret Lofthouse came back with a tray and caught him looking at it. 'That was taken at Garstang Farm, near Hawes in Wensleydale,' she said. 'We used to go for summer holidays up there a few years ago, when Linda was little. My uncle owned the place. He's dead now and strangers have bought it, but I have some wonderful memories. Linda was such a beautiful child.'

Chadwick watched the tears well in her eyes. She dabbed at them with a tissue. 'Sorry,' she said. 'I get all choked up when I remember how things were, when we were a happy family.'

'I understand,' said Chadwick. 'What happened?'

Margaret Lofthouse didn't seem surprised at the question. 'What always seems to happen, these days,' she said, with a sniffle. 'She grew up into a teenager. They expect the world at the age of sixteen these days, don't they? Well, what she got was a baby.'

'What did she do with the child?'

'Put him up for adoption – it's a boy. What else could she do? She couldn't look after him, and Jim and I were too old to start caring for another child. I'm sure he's gone to a good home.'

'I'm sure,' agreed Chadwick. 'But it's not the baby I'm here to talk about, it's Linda.'

'Yes, of course. Milk and sugar?'

'Please.'

She poured tea from a Royal Doulton teapot into fragile-looking cups with gold-painted rims and handles. 'This was my grandmother's tea-set,' she said. 'It's the only thing of value I own. There's nobody left to pass it on to now. Linda was an only child.'

'When did she leave home?'

'Shortly after the baby was born. The winter of 1967.'

'Where did she go?'

'London. At least, that's what she told me.'

'Where in London?'

'I don't know. She never said.'

'You didn't have her address?'

'No.'

'Did she know people down there?'

'She must have done, mustn't she? But I never met or heard of any of them.'

'Did she never come back and visit you?'

'Yes. Several times. We were quite friendly, but in a distant sort of way. She never talked about her life down there, just said she was all right and not to worry, and I must say, she always *looked* all right. I mean, she was clean and sober and nicely dressed, if you can call them sort of clothes nice, and she looked well fed.'

'Hippie-style clothing?'

'Yes. Long, flowing dresses. Bell-bottomed jeans with flowers embroidered on them. That sort of thing. But as I said, they was always clean and they always looked good quality.'

'Do you know how she earned a living?'

'I have no idea.'

'What *did* you talk about?'

'She told me about London, the parks, the buildings, the art galleries – I've never been there, you see. She was interested in art and music and poetry. She said all she wanted was peace in the world and for people to be happy.' She reached for the tissues again.

'So you got along OK?'

'I suppose so. On the surface. She knew I disapproved of her life, even though I didn't know much about it. She talked about Buddhism and Hindus and Sufis and goodness knows what, but she never once mentioned our Lord Jesus Christ, and I brought her up to be a good Christian.' She gave her head a little shake. 'I don't know. Maybe I could have tried harder to understand. She just seemed so far away from me and anything I've ever believed in.'

'What did you talk to her about?'

'Just local gossip, what her old schoolfriends were up to, that sort of thing. She never stopped long.'

'Did you know any of her friends?'

'I knew the kids she'd played with around the estate and from school, but I don't know who she spent her time with after she left home.'

'She never mentioned any names?'

'Well, she might have done, but I don't remember any.'

'Did she ever tell you if anything or anyone was bothering her?'

'No. She always seemed happy, as if she hadn't a care in the world.'

'You don't know of any enemies she might have had?'

'No. I can't imagine her having any.'

'When did you last see her?'

'In the summer. July it would be, not long after Jim . . .'

'Was she at the funeral?'

'Oh, yes. She came home for that in May. She loved her father. She was a great support. I don't want to give you the impression that we'd fallen out or anything, Mr Chadwick. I still loved Linda and I know she loved me. It was just that we couldn't really talk any more, not about anything important. She'd got secretive. In the end I gave up trying. But this was a couple of months after Jim's death, just a flying visit to see how I was getting on.'

'What *did* she talk about on that visit?'

'We watched that man walk on the moon. Neil Armstrong. Linda was all excited about it, said it marked the beginning of a new age, but I don't know. We stayed up watching till after three in the morning.'

'Anything else?'

'I'm sorry. Nothing else really stood out, except the moon landing. Some pop star she liked had died and she'd been to see the Rolling Stones play a free concert for him in Hyde Park. London, that is. And I remember her talking about the war, Vietnam. About how immoral it was. She always talked about the war. I tried to tell her that sometimes wars have to be fought, but she'd have none of it. To her all war was evil. You should have heard it when Linda and her dad went at it – he was in the navy in the last war, towards the end, like.'

'But you say Linda loved her father?'

'Oh, yes. Don't get me wrong. But they didn't see eye to eye about everything. I mean, he tried to discipline her, got on at her for staying out till all hours, but she was a handful. They fought like cat and dog sometimes, but they still loved one another.'

It all sounded so familiar to Chadwick that the thought depressed him. Surely all children weren't like this, didn't cause their parents such grief? Was he taking the wrong approach with Yvonne? Was there another way? He felt such a failure as a parent, but short of locking her in her room, what could he do? When Yvonne went on about the evils of war, he always tensed inside; he could never even enter into a rational argument about it for fear he would lose his temper, lash out and say something he would regret. What did she know about war? Evil? Yes. Necessary? Well, how else were you going to stop someone like Hitler? He didn't know much about Vietnam, but he assumed the Americans were there for a good reason, and the sight of all these unruly long-haired youngsters burning the flag and chanting anti-war slogans made his blood boil.

'What about the boyfriend, Donald Hughes?'

'What about him?'

'Is he the father?'

'That's what Linda said, and she wasn't . . . you know . . . some sort of trollop.'

'What did you think of him?'

'He's all right, I suppose. Not much gumption, mind. The Hugheses aren't one of the best families on the estate, but they're not one of the worst either. And you can't blame poor Eileen Hughes. She's had six kids to bring up, mostly on her own. She tries hard.'

'Do you know if Donald kept in touch after Linda left?'

'I doubt it. He made himself scarce after he found out our Linda was pregnant. Just after the baby was born, though, he was all concerned, said they should get married and keep it, that it wasn't right to give his child up for adoption. That's how he put it. *His child.*'

'What did Linda say?'

'She gave him his marching orders and not long after that she was gone to London.'

'Do you know if he ever bothered her at all?'

'I don't think so. She never mentioned him or the baby.'

'Did he ever come here asking about her?'

'Just once, about three weeks after she'd left. Wanted to know her address.'

'What did you tell him?'

'That I didn't know. Of course, he didn't believe me, and he made a bit of a fuss on the doorstep.'

'What did you do?'

'I sent him packing. Told him I'd set Jim on him if he came back again and shut the door in his face. He left us alone after that. Surely you don't think Donald could have . . . ?'

'We don't know what to think yet, Mrs Lofthouse. We have to look at all possibilities.'

'He's a bit of a hothead, anyone will tell you that, but I doubt he's a murderer.' She dabbed at her eyes again. 'I'm sorry,' she said. 'I still can't seem to take it in.'

'I understand,' said Chadwick. 'Is there anyone you'd like me to get to stay with you? Relative? Neighbour?'

'Mrs Bennett next door. She's always been a good friend. She's a widow, like me. She understands what it's like.'

Chadwick stood up to leave. 'I'll let her know you want her to come over. Look, before I go, do you have a recent photograph of Linda I could borrow?'

'I might have,' she said. 'Just a minute.' She went to the sideboard and rummaged through one of the drawers. 'This was taken last year when she came home for her birthday. Her father was a bit of an amateur photographer.'

She handed Chadwick the colour photograph. It was the girl in the sleeping-bag, only she was alive, a half-smile on her lips, a faraway look in her big blue eyes, wavy blonde hair tumbling over her shoulders. 'Thank you,' he said. 'I'll let you have it back.'

'And you'll keep in touch, won't you? About the arrangements?'

'Of course. I'll also send someone to drive you to the hospital and back to make the formal identification.'

'Thank you,' she said, and stood with him at the door, holding a damp tissue to her eyes. 'How can something like this happen to me, Mr Chadwick?' she said. 'I've been a devout Christian woman all my life. I've never hurt a soul and I've always served the Lord to the best of my ability. How can He do this to me? A husband *and* a daughter, both in the same year.'

All Chadwick could do was shake his head. 'I wish I knew the answer,' he said.

'Just outside Sheffield' turned out to be a quaint village on the edge of the Peak District National Park, and the house was a detached limestone cottage with a fair-sized, well-tended garden, central door, symmetrical up and down mullioned windows, garage and outbuildings. In the Dales, Annie guessed, it would be valued at about half a million, but she had no idea what prices were like in the Peak District. Probably not much different. There were many similarities between the two areas, with their limestone hills and valleys, and both drew hordes of tourists, ramblers and climbers almost year round.

Winsome parked by the gate and they made their way down the garden path. A few birds twittered in the nearby trees, completing the rural idyll. The woman who opened the door to them had clearly been crying. Annie felt grateful she hadn't been the one to break the news. She hated that. The last time she had told someone about the death of a friend, the woman had fainted.

'Annie Cabbot and Winsome Jackman from North Yorkshire Major Crimes,' she said.

'Yes, come in,' said the woman. 'We've been expecting you.' If the sight of a six-foot black woman surprised her, she didn't show it. Perhaps, like many others, she watched crime programmes on TV and had got used to the idea of a multiracial police force, even in such a 'white' enclave as the Peaks.

She led them through a dim hallway, where coats hung on pegs, and boots and shoes were neatly aligned on a low, slatted rack, then into an airy living room with french windows that led to the back garden, a neatly manicured lawn with a stone birdbath, white plastic table and chairs, and herbaceous borders. Plane trees framed a magnificent view over the fields to the limestone peaks beyond. The sky was mostly light grey, with a hint of sun hiding behind clouds somewhere in the north.

'We've just got back from church,' the woman said. 'We go every week, and it seemed especially important today.'

'Of course,' said Annie, whose religious background had been agnostic, and whose own spiritual dabbling in yoga and meditation had never brought her to any sort of organised religion. 'We're very sorry about your son, Mrs Barber.'

'Please,' she said, 'call me Louise. My husband, Ross, is making tea. I hope that will be all right?'

'Perfect,' said Annie.

'You'd better sit down.'

The chintz-covered armchairs all had spotless lace antimacassars, and Annie sat carefully, not quite daring to let the back of her head touch the material. In a few moments a tall, rangy man with unruly white hair, wearing a grey V-neck pullover and baggy cords, brought in a tray and placed it on the low glass table between the chairs and the fireplace. He looked a bit like a sort of mad-scientist character who could do complex equations in his head but had trouble fastening his shoelaces. Annie admired the framed print of Seurat's *Sunday Afternoon on The Island of La Grande Jatte* over the mantelpiece.

Once tea had been served and everyone was settled, Winsome took out her notebook and Annie began, 'I know this is a difficult time for you, but anything you can tell us about your son would be helpful right now.'

'Do you have any suspects?' Mr Barber asked.

'I'm afraid not. It's early days yet. We're just trying to piece together what happened.'

'I can't imagine why anyone would want to harm our Nicholas. He wouldn't have hurt a fly.'

'It's often the innocent who suffer,' said Annie.

'But Nicholas . . .' He let the sentence trail off.

'Did he have any enemies?'

Ross and Louise Barber looked at one another. 'No,' Louise said. 'I mean, he never mentioned anyone. And, like Ross says, he was a gentle person. He loved music, books and films. And his writing, of course.'

'He wasn't married, was he?' They had found no record of a wife, but Annie thought it best to make sure. If a jealous wife had caught wind of what Barber was up to with Kelly Soames, she might easily have lost it.

'No. He was engaged once, ten years ago,' said Ross Barber. 'Nice girl. Local. But they drifted apart when he moved to London. More tea?'

Annie and Winsome said yes, please. Barber topped up their cups.

'We understand that your son was a music journalist,' Annie went on.

'Yes,' said Louise. 'It was what he always wanted. Even when he was at school, he was editor of the magazine, and he wrote most of the articles himself.'

'We found out from the Internet that he's done some articles for *MOJO* and written a couple of biographies. Can you tell us anything else about his work? Does he write for anyone in particular, for example?'

'No. He was a freelancer,' Ross Barber answered. 'He did some writing for the newspapers, reviews and such, and feature pieces for that magazine sometimes, as you said. I'm afraid that sort of music isn't exactly to my taste.' He smiled indulgently. 'But he loved it, and apparently he made a decent living.'

Annie liked pop music, but she hadn't heard of *MOJO*, though she knew she must have seen it in W. H. Smith's when she was picking up *Now*, *Star* or *Heat*, the trashy celebrity-gossip magazines she liked to read in the bath, her one secret vice. 'You didn't approve of your son's interest in rock music?' she asked.

'It's not that we're against it, you understand,' said Ross Barber, 'just that we've always been a bit more inclined towards classical – Louise sings with the local operatic society – but we're happy that Nicholas seemed to pick up a love of music at an early age, along with the writing. He loved classical music, too, of course, but writing about rock was how he made his living.'

'He was lucky, then,' said Annie, 'being able to combine his two loves.'

'Yes,' Louise agreed, wiping away a tear with a lacy hand-kerchief.

'Do you have copies of his articles? You must be proud of him. A scrapbook, perhaps?'

'I'm afraid not,' said Louise. 'It never really entered our heads, did it, darling?'

Her husband agreed. 'It wouldn't mean anything to us, you see, what he was writing about. The names. The records. We would never have heard of them.'

Annie wanted to tell them that wasn't the point, but it would clearly do no good. 'How long had he been doing this for a living?' she asked.

'About eight years now,' Ross answered.

'And before that?'

'He got a BA in English at Nottingham, then did an MA in film studies, I think, at Leicester. After that he did a bit of teaching and wrote reviews, then he got a feature accepted, and after that . . .'

'He never studied journalism?'

'No. I suppose you might say he got in through the back door.'

'What's your profession, if you don't mind my asking?'

'I was a university professor,' said Ross Barber. 'Classics and ancient history. Rather dull, I'm afraid. I'm retired now.'

Annie was trying frantically to puzzle out why anyone would want to kill a music journalist, but she couldn't come up with anything. Except drugs. Kelly Soames had said that she and Nick smoked a joint, but that meant nothing. Annie had smoked a few joints in her time, even while she was a copper. Even Banks had smoked joints. She wondered about Winsome, and Kevin Templeton. Kev's drug of choice was probably E washed down with liberal amounts of Red Bull, but she didn't know about Winsome. She seemed a clean-living girl, with her passion for the outdoors and potholing, but surely there had to be something. Anyway, it didn't help much to know that Nick Barber had smoked marijuana occasionally. She imagined it was par for the course in the rock business, whichever end of it you were in.

'Can you tell us anything about Nick's life?' she asked. 'We have so little to go on.'

'I can't see how any of it would help you,' said Louise, 'but we'll do our best.'

'Did you see him often?'

'You know what it's like when they leave home,' Louise said. 'They phone and visit when they can. Our Nick was no better or worse than anyone else in that regard, I shouldn't think.'

'So he was in touch regularly?'

'He phoned us once a week and dropped in whenever he could.'

'When was the last time you saw him?'

Her eyes filled with tears again. 'Just the week before last. Friday. He was on his way up to Yorkshire, and he stopped over for the night. We always keep his old room ready for him, just in case.'

'Was there anything different about him?'

'Different? What do you mean?'

'Did he seem fearful?'

'No, not at all.'

'Was he depressed?'

The Barbers looked at one another, then Louise replied, 'No. Maybe a little preoccupied, but certainly not depressed. He seemed quite cheerful, as a matter of fact. Nick was never the most demonstrative of children, but he was generally even-tempered. He was no different this time from any other time he called in.'

'He didn't seem anxious?'

'Not as far as we could tell. If anything, he was a bit more excited than usual.'

'Excited? About what?'

'He didn't say. I think it might have been a story he was working on.'

'What was it about?'

'He never told us details like that. Not that we weren't interested in his work but I think he realised it would mean nothing to us. Besides, it was probably a "scoop". He'd learned to become secretive in his business.'

'Even from you?'

'The walls have ears. He'd developed an instinct. I don't think it really mattered to whom he was talking.'

'So he didn't mention any names?'

'No. I'm sorry.'

'Did he tell you why he was going to Yorkshire?'

'He said he'd found what sounded like a quiet place to write, and I think there was someone he wanted to see who lives up there.'

'Who?'

Mrs Barber spread her hands. 'I had the impression it was to do with what he was working on.'

Annie cursed under her breath. If only Nick had named names. If he'd thought his parents had the least interest in his passion, he probably would have, despite his journalistic instinct to protect his scoop. 'Is that what he was excited about?'

'I think so.'

'Can you add anything, Mr Barber?'

Ross Barber shook his head. 'No. As Louise said, the names of these groups and singers mean nothing to us. I think he'd learned there was no point in mentioning them. I'm afraid I glaze over in discussions like that. No doubt members of his own generation would be very impressed, but they went right over our heads.'

'I can understand that,' said Annie. 'What do you know about Nick's life in London?'

'He had a nice flat,' said Louise, 'didn't he, Ross? Just off the Great West Road. We stayed there not so long ago on our way to Heathrow. He slept on the sofa and let us have his bedroom. Spotless, it was.'

'He didn't live or share with anyone?'

'No. It was all his own.'

'Did you meet a girlfriend or a close friend? Anyone?'

'No. He took us out for dinner somewhere in the West End. The next day we flew to New York. Ross and I have old friends there, and they invited us for our fortieth wedding anniversary.'

'That's nice,' said Annie. 'So you don't really know much about Nick's life in London?'

'He worked all the hours God sent. He didn't have time for girlfriends and relationships. I'm sure he would have settled down eventually.'

In Annie's admittedly limited experience, if someone had reached the age of thirty-eight without 'settling down', you were a fool if you held your breath and waited for him to do so, but she also knew that many more people held off committing to relationships now, herself included. 'I know this is a rather delicate question,' she said, 'and I don't want it to upset you, but did Nick ever have anything to do with drugs?'

'Well,' said Ross, 'we assumed he experimented, of course, like so many young people today, but we never saw him under the influence of anything more than a couple of pints of bitter, or perhaps a small whisky. We're fairly liberal about things like that. You can't teach in a university for as long as I did and not have some knowledge of marijuana. But if he did use drugs, they didn't interfere with his job or his health, and we certainly never noticed any signs, did we?'

'No,' Louise agreed.

It was a fair answer, if not entirely what Annie had expected.

She sensed that Ross Barber was being as honest as he could be. The Barbers clearly loved their son and were distraught over his death, but there seemed to have been some sort of communication gap between them. They were proud of his achievements, but not interested in the achievements themselves. Nick might well have interviewed Coldplay or Oasis, but Annie could imagine Ross Barber saying, 'That's very nice, son,' as he pored over his ancient tomes. She couldn't think of anything else to ask and glanced at Winsome, who shrugged. Perhaps Banks would have done better. Perhaps she wasn't asking the right questions, but she couldn't think of any more. They would have a quick look in Nick's room, just in case he had left anything of interest, then maybe catch a pub lunch somewhere on the way back. After that, Annie would check in at the incident van and give Banks a ring. He'd want to know what she had found out, no matter how little it was.

Saturday, 13 September 1969

The young man in the greasy overalls was standing with a spanner in his hand surrounded by pieces of a dismantled motorbike when Chadwick arrived at the garage later that afternoon. According to the car radio, Leeds were 1–0 up.

'Vincent Black Lightning, 1952,' the young man said. 'Lovely machine. How can I help you?'

Chadwick showed his warrant card. 'Are you Donald Hughes?'

Immediately Hughes looked cagey, put down the spanner and wiped his hands on his greasy overalls. 'Maybe,' he said. 'Depends why you want to know.'

Chadwick's immediate inclination was to tell the kid to stop messing about and come up with some answers, but he realised that Hughes might not know yet about Linda's murder, and that his reaction to the news could reveal a lot. Perhaps a softer approach would be best, at least to start with.

'Maybe you'd better sit down, laddie,' he said.

'Why?'

There were two fold-up chairs in the garage. Instead of answering, Chadwick sat on one. A little dazed, Hughes followed suit. The dim garage smelt of oil, petrol and warm metal. It was still raining outside and he could hear the steady dripping of water from the gutters.

'What is it?' Hughes said. 'Has something happened to Mum?'

'Not as far as I know,' said Chadwick. 'Read the papers much?'

'Nah. Nothing but bad news.'

'Hear about the festival up at Brimleigh Glen last weekend?'

'Hard not to.'

'Were you there?'

'Nah. Not my cup of tea. Look, why are you asking all these questions?'

'A young girl was killed there,' he said. 'Stabbed.' When Hughes said nothing, he continued, 'We've good reason to believe that she was Linda Lofthouse.'

'Linda? But . . . she . . . Bloody hell . . .' Hughes turned pale.

'She what?'

'She went off to live in London.'

'She was at Brimleigh for the festival.'

'I should have known. Look,' he said, 'I'm really sorry to hear about what happened. It was a long time ago, though, me and Linda. Another lifetime, it seems.'

'Two years isn't very long. People have held grudges longer.'

'What do you mean?'

'Revenge is a dish that's best eaten cold.'

'I don't know what you're on about.'

'Suppose we start at the beginning,' said Chadwick. 'You and Linda.'

'We went out together for a couple of years when we were fifteen and sixteen, that's all.'

'And she had your baby.'

Hughes looked down at his oily hands in his lap. 'Yeah, well . . . I tried to make it right, asked her to marry me and all.'

'That's not the way I hear it.'

'Look, all right. At first I was scared. Wouldn't you be? I was only sixteen, I didn't have no job, nothing. We left school. Linda stayed at home with her mum and dad that summer and had the baby, and I . . . I don't know, I suppose I brooded about it. Anyway, I decided in the end we should make a go of it. I had a job here at the garage by then and I thought . . . we might have had a chance, after all.'

'But?'

'She didn't want to know, did she? By then she'd got her head full of this hippie rubbish. Bob Dylan and his stupid songs and all the rest of it.'

'When did this start?'

'Before we split up. Just little things. Always correcting me when I said something wrong, like she was a bloody grammar expert. Talking about poets and singers I'd never heard of, reincarnation and karma and I don't know what else. Always arguing. It was like she wasn't interested in a normal life.'

'What about her new friends?'

'Long-haired pillocks and poxy birds. I hadn't time for any of them.'

'Did she chuck you?'

'You could say that.'

'And when you came back, cap in hand, she wanted nothing more to do with you?'

'I suppose so. Then she buggered off to London soon as she'd had the kid. Put him up for adoption. *My* son.'

'Did you follow her down there?'

'I'd had enough by then. Let her go with her poncy new friends and take all the drugs she wanted.'

'Did she take drugs when she was with you?'

'No, not that I knew of. I wouldn't have stood for it. But that's what they do, isn't it?'

'So they stole her from you, did they? The hippies?'

He looked away. 'I suppose you could say that.'

'Made you angry enough to do her harm?'

Hughes stood so violently that his chair tipped over. 'What are you getting at? Are you trying to say I killed her?'

'Calm down, laddie. I have to ask these questions. It's a murder investigation.'

'Yeah. Well, I'm not your murderer.'

'Got a bit of a quick temper, though, haven't you?'

Hughes said nothing. He picked up the chair and sat again, folding his arms across his chest.

'Did you ever meet any of Linda's new friends?'

Hughes rubbed the back of his hand across his upper lip and nose. 'She took me to this house once,' he said. 'I think she wanted me to be like her, and she thought maybe she'd convince me by introducing me to her new friends.'

'When was this?'

'Just after she left school. That summer.'

'1967? When she was pregnant?'

'Yes.'

'Go on.'

'We weren't getting along well at all. Like I said before, she was weird, into all sorts of things I didn't understand, like tarot cards and astrology and all that crap. This one time she was going to see some friends and I didn't want her to go – I wanted her to come to the pictures with me to see *You Only*

Live Twice, but she said she didn't want to see some stupid James Bond film, and if I wanted to be with her I could come along. If I didn't . . . Well, she made it clear I didn't have much choice. So I thought, What the hell? Let's see what's going on here.'

'Do you remember *where* she took you?'

'I dunno. It was off Roundhay Road, near that big pub at the junction with Spenser Place.'

'The Gaiety?'

'That's the one.'

Chadwick knew it. There weren't many coppers in Leeds, plainclothes or uniformed, who didn't. 'Do you remember the name of the street?'

'No, but it was just over Roundhay Road.'

'One of the Bayswaters?' Chadwick knew the area, a densely packed triangle of streets full of small terraced houses between Roundhay Road, Bayswater Road and Harehills Road. It didn't have a particularly bad reputation, but quite a few of the houses had been rented to students, and where there were students there were probably drugs.

'That's the place.'

'Do you know which one?'

'I can't say for sure, but I think it was the terrace. Or maybe the crescent.'

'Remember where the house was?'

'About half-way.'

'Which side of the street?'

'Don't remember.'

'Was there anything odd about the place from the outside?'

'No. It looked like all the others.'

'What colour was the door?'

'I don't remember.'

'OK. Thanks,' said Chadwick. Maybe he could find it. It was frustrating to be so close but still so far. Even so, it was probably a cold lead. The students who had been there two years ago might have graduated and left town by now. If they *were* students.

'What happened?'

'Nothing, really. There were these people, about five of them, hippies, like, in funny clothes. Freaks.'

'Were they students?'

'Maybe some of them. I don't know. They didn't say. The place smelt like a tart's window-box.'

'That bad?'

'Some sort of perfume smell, anyway. I think it was something they were smoking. One or two of them were definitely on *something*. You could tell by their eyes and the rubbish they were spouting.'

'Like what?'

'I don't remember but it was all cosmic this and cosmic that, and there was this droning music in the background, like someone rubbing a hacksaw on a metal railing.'

'Do you remember any names?'

'I think one was called Dennis. It seemed to be his place. And there was a girl called Julie. She was blowing bubbles and giggling, like a little kid. Linda had been there before, I could tell. She knew her way around and didn't have to ask anyone, you know, like where the kettle or the toilet was.'

'What happened?'

'I wanted to go. I mean, I knew they were taking the mickey because I didn't talk the same language or like the same music. Even Linda. In the end I said we should leave but she wouldn't.'

'So what did you do?'

'I left. I couldn't stick any more of it. I went to see *You Only Live Twice* by myself.'

There couldn't have been that many hippies in Leeds during the summer of 1967. It might have been the Summer of Love in San Francisco, but Leeds was still a northern provincial backwater in many ways, always a little behind the times, and it was only over the past two years or so that the numbers had grown everywhere. The Leeds Drugs Squad hadn't even been formed until 1967. Anyway, if there was a Dennis still living on Bayswater Terrace, it shouldn't be too hard to find him.

'How often did you see her again?'

'A couple of times, and after the baby was born, when I tried to make things up between us. Then she went down south and her mother wouldn't even give me an address.'

'And finally?'

'I got over her. I've been going out with someone else for a while now. Might get engaged at Christmas.'

'Congratulations,' said Chadwick, standing up.

'I'm really sorry about Linda,' Hughes said, 'but it was nothing to do with me. Honest. I was here working all last weekend. Ask the boss. He'll tell you.'

Chadwick said he would, then left. When he turned on the car radio he found that Leeds had beaten Sheffield Wednesday 2–1, Allan Clarke and Eddie Grey scoring. Still, he hadn't missed the game for nothing; he now knew who the victim was and had a lead on some of the people she'd knocked around with in Leeds, if only he could find them.

7

The Soames farm was about half a mile up a narrow walled lane off the main Lyndgarth to Eastvale road, and it boasted the usual collection of ramshackle outbuildings, built from local limestone, a muddy yard and a barking dog straining at its chain. It also presented the unmistakable bouquet of barnyard smells. Calvin Soames answered the door and, with a rather grudging good afternoon, let Banks in. The inside was dim with low, dark beams and gloomy corridors. The smell of roast beef still lurked somewhere in the depths.

'Our Kelly's in the kitchen,' he said, pointing with his thumb.

'That's all right,' said Banks. 'It's you I came to talk to, really.'

'Me? I told you everything I know the other night.'

'I'm sure you did,' said Banks, 'but sometimes, after a while, things come back, little things you'd forgotten. May I sit down?'

'Aye, go on, then.'

Banks sat in a deep armchair with a sagging seat. The whole place, once he could see it a bit better, was in some disrepair and lacked what they used to call a woman's touch. 'Is there a Mrs Soames?' he asked.

'The wife died five years ago. Complications of surgery.' Soames spat out these last words, making it clear that he blamed the doctors, the health system or both for his wife's untimely death.

'I'm sorry,' said Banks.

Soames grunted. He was a short, squat man, almost as broad as he was tall, but muscular and fit, Banks judged, wearing a tight waistcoat over his shirt, and a pair of baggy brown trousers. He probably wasn't more than about forty-five, but farming had aged him, and it showed in the deep lines and rough texture of his ruddy face.

'Look,' Banks went on, 'I want to go over what you told us in the pub on Friday.'

'It werc the truth.'

'Nobody doubts that. You said you left the Cross Keys at about seven o'clock because you thought you might have left the gas ring on.'

'That's right.'

'Have you done that before?'

'He has,' said a voice from the doorway. 'Twice he nearly burned the place down.'

Banks turned. Kelly Soames stood there, arms folded, one blue-jeaned hip cocked against the door jamb in a graceful curve, flat stomach exposed. She certainly was a lovely girl, Banks thought again; she was fit, and she knew it, as the Streets would say. He'd been spoiled for lovely girls this morning, what with Brian's Emilia turning up, too.

Should he have said something? Brian and Emilia had evidently assumed they would sleep together under his roof, but he wasn't sure how he felt about that. His own son. What if he *heard* them? But what else could he have done? Made an issue of it? His parents, of course, would never have stood for such a thing. But attitudes changed. When he was young, he had left home and got a flat in London so he could sleep with girls, stay out late and drink too much. These days, parents allowed their kids to do all that at home, so they never left, had no reason to: they could have all thc sex they wanted, come home drunk and still get fed and their washing done. But Brian was only visiting. Surely it would be best to let him and Emilia do what they usually did? Banks could imagine the atmosphere it would create if he came on all disciplinarian and said, 'Not under my roof you don't!' But the whole thing, the assumption, the reality, still made him uneasy.

Despite her cocky stance, Kelly Soames seemed nervous, Banks thought. After what Annie had told him about her exploits, he wasn't surprised. She must be worried that he was going to spill the beans to her father.

'Kelly,' said Soames, 'make a cup of tea for Mr Banks here. He might be a copper, but we still owe him our hospitality.'

'No, that's all right, thank you,' said Banks. 'I've already had far too much coffee this morning.'

'Please yourself. I'll have a cuppa, myself, though, lass.'

Kelly slouched off to make the tea, and Banks could imagine her straining her ears to hear what they were talking about. Calvin Soames took out a pipe and began puffing at some vile-smelling tobacco. Outside, the dog barked from time to time when a group of ramblers passed on the footpath that skirted the farm property.

'What did you think of Nick Barber?' Banks asked.

'Was that his name, poor sod?'

'Yes.'

'I can't say as I thought much, really. I didn't know him.'

'But he was a regular in your local.'

Soames laughed. 'Dropping by the Cross Keys for a pint every day or so for a week doesn't make anyone a regular round these parts. Tha should know that.'

'Even so,' said Banks, 'it was long enough at least to be on greeting terms, wasn't it?'

'I suppose so. But I can't say as I have much to do with visitors myself.'

'Why not?'

'Do you need it spelling out? Bloody Londoners come up

here buying properties, pushing prices up, and what do they do? They sit in poncy flats in Kensington and pull in the cash, that's what they do.'

'It brings tourism to the Dales, Mr Soames,' said Banks. 'They spend money.'

'Aye. Well, maybe it's all right for the shopkeepers,' Soames went on, 'but it doesn't do us farmers a lot of good, does it? People tramping over our land morning, noon and night, ruining good grazing pasture.'

As far as Banks had heard, absolutely nothing ever benefited the farmers. He knew they had a hard life, but he also felt that people might respect them more if they didn't whine so much. If it wasn't EU regulations or footpath access, it was something else. Of course, foot-and-mouth disease had taken a terrible toll on the Dales a few years ago, but the effects hadn't been limited to farmers, many of whom had been compensated handsomely. The pinch had also been felt by local businesses, particularly bed-and-breakfast establishments, cafés and tea-rooms, pubs, walking-gear shops and market-stall holders. And they hadn't been compensated. Banks also knew that the outbreak had driven more than one ruined local businessman to suicide. It wasn't that he had no sympathy for the farmers; it was that they often seemed to assume they were the only ones with any rights, or any serious grievances, and they had more than enough sympathy for themselves to make any from other sources seem superfluous. But Banks knew he had to tread carefully: this was marshy ground.

'I understand there's a problem,' he said, 'but it won't be solved by killing off tourists.'

'Do you think that's what happened?'

'I don't know what happened,' said Banks.

Kelly came back with the tea, and after she had handed it to her father, she lingered by the door again, biting her fingernail.

'Nobody round here would have murdered that lad, you can take it from me,' said Soames.

'How do you know?'

'Because most know you're right. CC benefits from the holidaymakers, and so do most of the others. Oh, people talk a tough game, that's Dalesmen for you. We've got our pride, if nowt else. But nobody'd go so far as to kill a bloke who's minding his own business and not doing anyone any harm.'

'Is that your impression of Nick Barber?'

'I didn't see much of him, like I said, but from what I did see he seemed like a harmless lad. Not mouthy, or full of himself, like some – and we didn't even murder them.'

'When you came home on Friday to check on the gas ring, did you notice anything out of the ordinary?'

'No,' said Soames. 'There were one or two cars on the road – this was before the power cut, remember – but not a lot. It was a nasty evening even by then, and most folks, given the choice, were stopping indoors.'

'Did you see anyone near the cottage where Nick Barber was staying?'

'No, but I live the other way so I wouldn't have.'

'What about you, Kelly?' Banks asked.

'I was in the pub all the time, working,' said Kelly. 'I never left the place. You can ask CC.'

'But what did you think about Nick Barber?'

This was clearly dangerous ground, and Kelly became even more nervous. She wouldn't look him in the eye. But Banks wasn't worried about her. She didn't know how far he would go, but without giving away Kelly's secret, he wanted to keep his eyes on Soames to see if there was any hint that he had known what was going on between his nubile daughter and Nick Barber.

'Don't know, really,' said Kelly. 'He seemed pleasant enough, like Dad says. He never really said much.' She examined her fingernails.

'So neither of you knew why he was here?'

'Holiday, I suppose,' said Soames. 'Though why anyone would want to come up here at this time of year is beyond me.'

'Would it surprise you to hear that he was a writer of some sort?'

'Can't say as I ever really thought about it,' said Soames.

'I think he was mostly just looking for a secluded place to work,' said Banks, 'but there might also be another reason why he was up here rather than, say, in Cornwall or Norfolk, for example.' Banks noticed Kelly tense up. 'I don't know if he was writing fiction or history, but it's possible that, either way, he might have been doing some research, and there might have been someone he wanted to see, someone he'd been looking for with some connection to the area, maybe to the past. Any ideas who that might be?'

Soames shook his head, and Kelly followed suit. Banks studied them. He thought himself a reasonable judge, and he was satisfied from the reactions and body language he had seen that Calvin Soames did not know about his daughter shagging Nick Barber, which gave him no real motive for the murder. No more than anyone else, anyway. Whether Kelly had a motive, he didn't know. True, she had been working at the time of the murder, but she admitted to seeing Barber in the afternoon, and if the doctor was wrong about the time of death, he could have been dead when she left him. But why? They'd only known one another a few days, according to Annie, and they'd both had a bit of fun without any expectation of a future.

It would be good to keep an open mind, as ever, Banks thought, but for now his thoughts moved towards London and what they might find out from Nick's flat.

Monday, 15 September 1969

One thing that disappointed Chadwick as he rifled through the stack of Brimleigh festival photographs on Monday morning was that they had all, except a few obviously posed ones, been taken in daylight. He should have expected that. Flash doesn't carry a great distance, and it would have been useless for shots of the crowd at night or of the bands performing.

One photographer seemed to have got backstage, though; at least, several of his photographs were taken there, candids. Linda Lofthouse showed up in three; the flowing white dress with the delicate embroidery was easy to spot. In one she was chatting casually with a mixed group of long-haired people, in another she was with two men he didn't recognise, and in the third she was sitting alone, staring into the distance. It was an exquisite photograph, head and shoulders in profile, perhaps taken with a telephoto lens. She looked beautiful and fragile, and there was *no* flower painted on her cheek.

'Someone to see you downstairs, sir,' said Karen, popping her head round his door and breaking the spell.

'Who?' Chadwick asked.

'Young couple. They just asked to see the man in charge of the Brimleigh festival murder.'

'Did they, indeed? Better have them sent up.'

Chadwick glanced out of his window as he waited, sipping his tepid coffee. He was high up at the back and looked out over British Insulated Callender's Cables Ltd up Westgate towards the majestic dome of the town hall, blackened like the other buildings by a century of industry. A steady flow of traffic headed west towards the Inner Ring Road.

Finally, there was a knock at his door and Karen showed in the young couple.

They looked a bit sheepish, the way most people would in the inner sanctum of police headquarters. Chadwick

introduced himself and asked them to sit down. Both were in
their early twenties, the young man with neatly cut short hair
and a dark suit, and the girl in a white blouse and a black
miniskirt, blonde hair pulled back and tied with a red ribbon.
Dressed for work. They introduced themselves as Ian Tilbrook and June Betts.

'You said it was about the Brimleigh festival murder,'
Chadwick began.

Ian Tilbrook's eyes looked anywhere but at Chadwick, and
June fidgeted with her handbag on her lap. But it was she who
spoke first. 'Yes,' she said, giving Tilbrook a sideways glance.
'I know we should have come forward sooner,' she said, 'but
we were there.'

'At the festival?'

'Yes.'

'So were thousands of others. Did you see something?'

'No, it's not that,' June went on. She glanced at Tilbrook,
who was staring out of the window, took a deep breath and
went on, 'Someone stole our sleeping-bag.'

'I see,' said Chadwick, suddenly interested.

'Well, the newspapers said to report anything odd, and it
was odd, wasn't it?'

'Why didn't you come forward earlier?'

June looked at Tilbrook again. 'He didn't want to get
involved,' she said. 'He's up for promotion at the Copper
Works, and he thinks it'll spoil his chances if they find out he's
been going to pop festivals. They'll think he's a drug-taking
hippie. *And* a murder suspect.'

'That's not fair!' said Tilbrook. 'I said it was probably
nothing, just a sleeping-bag pinched, but you kept going on
about it.' He glanced at his watch. 'And now I'm going to be
late for work.'

'Never mind about that, laddie,' said Chadwick. 'Just tell me
about it.'

Tilbrook sulked, but June took up the story. 'Well, the papers said she was found in a blue Woolworth's sleeping-bag and ours was blue and from Woolworth's. I just thought . . . you know.'

'Can you identify it?'

'I'm not sure. I don't think so. They're all the same, aren't they?'

'I suppose you both . . . er . . . it was big enough for the two of you . . . You spent some time in it over the weekend?'

June blushed. 'Yes.'

'There'll be evidence we can match. You'll still have to look at it.'

June cringed. 'I don't think I could. Is there . . . ? I mean, did she . . . ?'

'There's not a lot of blood, no, and you won't have to see it.'

'All right. I suppose.'

'But first give me a few details. Let's start with the time.'

'We weren't paying attention to time,' said Tilbrook, 'but it was late Sunday night.'

'How do you know?'

'Led Zeppelin were on,' said June. 'They were last to play, and we went to see if we could get anywhere closer to the stage. We left our stuff, thinking if we did find somewhere one of us could go back and get it while the other remained, but we couldn't find anywhere, it was so crowded near the front. When we got back it was gone.'

'Just the sleeping-bag?'

'Yes.'

'What else did you have?'

'A rucksack with some extra clothes, a bottle of pop and sandwiches.'

'And that remained untouched?'

'Yes.'

'Where were you sitting?'

'Right at the edge of the woods, about half-way down the field.'

It was close, Chadwick thought, with a surge of excitement, very close. So the killer had walked two hundred yards through the dense woods to the edge of the field and found a sleeping-bag. Had that been what he was looking for? He would certainly have known that plenty of people there had one. It had been dark by then. The crowd, for the most part, would have been entranced by the music, their attention focused on the stage, and it would have been easy enough for a dark figure to pick up a sleeping-bag, even if the owners had been sitting nearby, and slip back into the woods.

Putting it back on the field with a body in it would have been more difficult, of course, and Chadwick was willing to bet that someone had seen something, a figure dragging a bag of some sort, or carrying it over his shoulder. Why had no one come forward? Clearly they hadn't found what they saw suspicious, or they simply wanted to avoid contact with the police. Drugs might have played a part, too. Perhaps whoever saw it was too far gone to comprehend what he or she was seeing. On the other hand, the killer might have waited until Led Zeppelin had finished playing and people started wandering home. Then it would have been easy to plant the sleeping-bag. However it happened, the best thing the killer had in his favour was that not one of the twenty-five thousand people present would have expected to see someone dragging a body over the grass in a sleeping-bag.

There were risks, of course – there always are. Someone might also have seen him steal the bag, for example, and raised a hue and cry. But it was so dark that they wouldn't have been able to describe him, and those hippies, in Chadwick's experience, had a very cavalier attitude towards private property. Also, someone might have found the body while he was away. Even then, all he would have lost was the opportunity to try to disguise the crime, to make it look as if the girl had been killed in the sleeping-bag on the field.

It was clear they weren't dealing with a criminal genius here, but he had had luck on his side. Even if he hadn't disguised the crime scene and someone had found the body in the woods, there was still no evidence to link it to him, and the police would be exactly where they were now – or, at least, where they had been before June Betts and Ian Tilbrook had come forward. It hadn't taken long to debunk the misleading evidence about where the victim was killed, and now, as Chadwick had hoped, the attempt to mislead had yielded a clue. Now they had a much better idea of the time of the murder, if nothing else, but they still didn't know what had happened to the knife.

'Can you be a bit more specific about the time?' he asked. 'How long had the group been playing?'

'It's hard to say,' said June, looking at Tilbrook. 'They hadn't been on long.'

'They were playing "I Can't Quit You Baby" when we set off to see if we could find somewhere nearer the stage,' said Tilbrook, 'and they were still playing it when we got back. I think it was their second number of the set, and the first was pretty short.'

Chadwick had no idea how long these songs lasted, but he realised he could probably get a set list from Rick Hayes, whom he wanted to speak to again anyway. For now, this would have to do. 'Say between five past one and half past, then?'

'We didn't have watches,' said June, 'but if you say they started at one then, yes, it would have been about twenty minutes into the show, something like that.'

That would put the time at about one twenty, which meant that Linda must have been killed between about one, when the band started, and then. He showed them her photograph. 'Did you see this girl at any time?'

'No,' they said.

Then Chadwick showed them the pictures of Linda with others. 'Recognise anyone?'

'Isn't that . . . ?' June said.

'It could be, I suppose,' said Ian.

'Who?' Chadwick asked.

'They're from the Mad Hatters,' Ian explained. 'Terry Watson and Robin Merchant.'

Chadwick looked at the photograph again. He would be talking to the Mad Hatters that afternoon. 'OK,' he said, standing up. 'Now, if you'd like to come to the evidence room with me, you can see that sleeping-bag.'

Reluctantly, they followed him down.

'I know you have a train to catch,' said Detective Superintendent Catherine Gervaise early on Monday morning, 'but I wanted to have a quick word with you before you left.'

Banks sat across the desk from her in what used to be Gristhorpe's office. It was a lot more sparsely decorated now, and the bookcases held only books on law, criminology and management technique. Gone were the leatherbound volumes of Dickens, Hardy and Austen with which Gristhorpe had surrounded himself, and the books about fly-fishing and drystone-wall building. One shelf displayed a few of the superintendent's archery awards, alongside a framed photograph of her aiming a bow. The only true decorative effect was a poster for an old Covent Garden production of *Tosca* on the wall.

'As you probably know,' Superintendent Gervaise went on, 'this is my first murder investigation at this level, and I'm sure the boys and girls in the squad room have been having a good laugh at my expense.'

'Not at—'

She waved him down. 'It doesn't matter. That's not what

this is about.' She shuffled some papers on her desk. 'I know a lot about you, DCI Banks. I make a point of knowing as much as I can about the officers under my command.'

'A wise move,' said Banks, wondering if he was in for even more of the obvious.

She gave him a sharp glance. 'Including your penchant for cheap sarcasm,' she said. 'But that's not why we're here, either.' She leaned back in her executive chair and smiled, her Cupid's-bow lips turning up at the edges as if she was ready to fire an arrow. 'I'd like, if I may, to be completely frank with you, DCI Banks, on the understanding that nothing that's said in here this morning goes beyond you, me and these four walls. Is that clear?'

'Yes,' said Banks, wondering what the hell was coming next.

'I'm aware that you recently lost your brother in appalling circumstances, and you have my sincere commiserations. I am also aware that you lost your home, and almost your life, not too long ago. All in all, it's been quite an eventful year for you, hasn't it?'

'It has, but I hope none of that has affected my job.'

'Oh, but I think we can be quite sure that it has, don't you?' She was wearing oval glasses with silver frames, which she adjusted as she looked at the papers on her desk. 'Withholding information in a major investigation, assault on a suspect with an iron bar. Need I go on? But you don't need much encouragement to go a little bit over the top, do you, DCI Banks? You never did. Your record is a patchwork quilt of questionable decisions and downright insubordination. *Res ipso loquitor*, as the lawyers are fond of saying.'

So you can quote Latin, Banks thought. Big deal. 'Look,' he said, 'I've cut a few corners, I admit it. You have to in this job if you're to keep ahead of the villains. But I've never perjured myself, I've never faked evidence and I've never used force to get a confession. I admit I lost it in London last summer but, like you said, a personal tragedy. You're the new broom, I understand that. You want to make a clean sweep. Fair enough. If I'm a transfer waiting to happen, then let's get on with it.'

'What on earth makes you think that?'

'Maybe something you said?'

She regarded him through narrowed eyes. 'You got on very well with my predecessor Detective Superintendent Gristhorpe, didn't you?'

'He was a good copper.'

'What's that supposed to mean?'

'What I said. Mr Gristhorpe was an experienced officer.'

'And he gave you free rein.'

'He knew how to get the job done.'

'Right.' Superintendent Gervaise leaned forward and clasped her hands on the desk. 'Well, let me tell you something that may surprise you. I don't want you to change. I want you to get the job done, too.'

'What?' said Banks.

'I thought that might surprise you. Let me tell you something. I'm a woman in a man's world. Do you think I don't know that? Do you think I don't know how many people resent me because of it, how many are waiting in the wings to see me fail? But I'm also ambitious. I see no reason why I shouldn't make chief constable in a few years. Not here, necessarily, but somewhere. Maybe they'll give me the position *because* I'm a woman. I don't care. I've got nothing against positive discrimination. We've had it coming for centuries. It's well overdue. My predecessor wasn't ambitious. He didn't care. He was close to retirement. But I'm not, and I still see a career ahead of me, a long career, and a *great* one.'

'And my role in all this is?'

'You know as well as I do that we're judged by results, and one thing I've noticed as I've studied your chequered career is that you get results. Maybe not in the traditional ways, maybe not always in the legally prescribed ways, but you get them. And it may also interest you to know that there are relatively few black marks against you. That means you get away with it. Most of the time.' She sat back and smiled. 'When the doctor asks you how much you drink, what do you tell him?'

'Pardon?'

'Come on. This isn't about drinking. What do you tell him?'

'A couple of drinks a day, something like that.'

'And do you know what your doctor does?'

'Tell me.'

'He immediately doubles that figure.' She leaned forward again. 'My point is that we all lie about things like that, and this,' she tapped the folders in front of her, 'simply tells me that the number of times you've been caught out in something not exactly kosher is the tip of the iceberg. And that's good.'

'It is?'

'Yes. I want someone who gets away with it. I don't want black marks against you because they'll reflect on me, but I do want results. And, as I said, you get results. It looks good on me, and when I leave this Godforsaken wasteland of sheep-shaggers and Saturday-night pub brawlers, I want to take a shining record with me. And that might be sooner than we think, if the Home Office has its way. I assume you've been reading the newspapers?'

'Yes, ma'am,' said Banks. Many of the smaller county forces, such as North Yorkshire, had recently been deemed by the Home Office as not up to the task of policing the modern world. Consequently, there was talk of them being merged with larger neighbouring forces, which meant that the North Yorkshire Constabulary might be swallowed up by West Yorkshire. Nobody was saying what would happen to the present personnel if such a shake-up went ahead.

'You can give me that shining record,' Superintendent

Gervaise went on, 'and in return I can give you enough rope. Drink on duty, follow leads on your own, disappear for days without reporting in. I don't care. But all the while you're doing those things, they'd damn well better be for the sake of solving the case, and you'd damn well better solve it quick, and I'd damn well better get all the reflected glory. No slacking. Am I still making myself clear?'

'You are, ma'am,' said Banks, struck with admiration and awe for the spectacle of naked ambition unfolding before him, and working in his favour.

'And if you do anything over the top, make damn sure you don't get caught or you'll be out on your arse,' she said. Then she straightened the collar of her white silk blouse and leaned back in her chair. 'Now,' she said, 'don't you have a train to catch?'

Banks got up and walked to the door.

'DCI Banks?'

'Yes?'

'That Opera North production of *Lucia di Lammermoor*. Don't you think it was just a little lacklustre? And wasn't Lucia just a little too shrill?'

Monday, 15 September 1969

After a meeting with Bradley, Enderby and Chief Superintendent McCullen later on Monday morning, Chadwick invited Geoff Broome for a lunch-time sandwich and pint at the pub across from Park Lane College. Most of the students hung out in the slightly more posh lounge, but the public bar was Chadwick's domain, and that of a few pensioners who sat playing dominoes quietly over their halves of mild. With a couple of pints of Webster's Pennine Bitter beside them, and a plate each of roast-beef sandwiches Chadwick brought Broome up to date on the Linda Lofthouse murder.

'I don't know why you're telling me all this, Stan,' said Broome, finishing his sandwich and taking out a packet of ten Kensitas, tapping one on the table and lighting it. 'It doesn't sound like a drug-related killing to me.'

Chadwick watched Broome inhale and exhale and felt the familiar urge he thought he'd vanquished six years ago when the doctor found a shadow on his lung that turned out to be tuberculosis and cost him six months in a sanatorium.

'Smoke bothering you?' Broome asked.

'No, it's all right.' Chadwick sipped some beer. 'I'm not saying it's a drugs-related murder, but drugs might play a part in it, that's all. I was wondering whether you might be able to help me find out who the girl's contacts were in Leeds. You know that scene far better than I do.'

'Of course, if I can,' said Broome. As usual, his hair was dishevelled and his suit looked as if it had been slept in. All of which might have masked the fact that he was one of the best detectives in the county. Perhaps not good enough to detect that his wife had been having it off behind his back with a vacuum-cleaner salesman, but good enough to reduce significantly the amount of illegal drugs entering into the city. He also ran one of the most efficient networks of undercover officers, and his many paid informants within the drugs community knew they could depend on absolute anonymity.

Chadwick told him what Donald Hughes had said about visiting the house in one of the Bayswaters.

'I can't say anything springs immediately to mind,' said Broome, 'but we've had call to visit that neighbourhood once in a while. Let me do a bit of fishing.'

'Bloke called Dennis,' said Chadwick. 'And it's maybe Terrace or Crescent. That's all I know.'

Broome jotted the name and streets down. 'You really think it's not just some random nutcase?' he asked.

'I don't know,' Chadwick answered. 'If you look at the crime, what we know of it, that's certainly a possibility. Until we have more on the girl's background and movements and whether she was drugged or not, for example, we can't say much more. She was stabbed five times, so hard that the knife hilt bruised her chest and the blade cut off a piece of her heart. But there were no signs of any struggle in the surrounding grass, and the bruising round her neck is minimal.'

'Maybe it was a lovers' quarrel? Lovers kill each other all the time, Stan. You know that.'

'Yes, but they're usually a bit more obvious about it. Like I said, this has more deliberate elements. The killer stood behind her, for a start.'

'So she's leaning back on him. She felt safe. What about her boyfriend?'

'Didn't have one, as far as we know. She had an ex, Donald Hughes, but his alibi checks out. Most of the night he was on a rush job at the garage where he works, and he wouldn't have had time to go anywhere near Brimleigh.'

'Someone else close to her, then?'

'I suppose there's a chance she knew her killer,' Chadwick admitted, 'that it was someone familiar she felt comfortable with. Why he did it is another matter entirely. But to find out more we need to track down her friends.'

'Well, I can't promise anything but I'll see what I can do,' said Broome. 'Good Lord, is that the time? Must dash. I have to see a man about a shipment of Dexedrine.'

'All go, isn't it?'

'You can say that again. What's next on your agenda? Why so gloomy?'

'I've got an appointment with Their Majesties the Mad Hatters this afternoon,' Chadwick said.

'Lucky you. Maybe they'll give you a free LP.'

'They know what they can do with it.'

'Think of Yvonne, though, Stan. You'd be golden in her eyes, you met the Mad Hatters and got a signed LP.'

'Get away with you.'

'I'll come back to you about the house,' Broome said, then left.

Broome's cigarette butt still smouldered in the ashtray. Chadwick put it out. That made his fingers smell of smoke, so he went to the toilet and washed them, then sat down to finish his drink. He could hear a group of students in the lounge laughing over Stevie Wonder's 'My Cherie Amour' on the jukebox, a song Chadwick actually quite liked when he heard it on the radio. Maybe it wouldn't be such a bad idea to get a signed LP for Yvonne, he thought, then immediately dismissed the idea. A lot of good that would do for his authority, begging a bunch of drug-addled layabouts for their autographs.

Chadwick tried to picture the twenty-five thousand kids at the Brimleigh festival all sitting in the dark listening to a loud band on a distant lit-up stage. He knew he could narrow his range of suspects if he tried hard enough, especially now that he had a more accurate idea of the *time* of the murder. For a start, Rick Hayes was still holding something back, he was certain of it. The candid photographs proved that Linda Lofthouse had been in the backstage area, and that she had talked with two members of the Mad Hatters, among others. Hayes must have known this, but he didn't say anything. Why? Was he protecting someone? On the other hand, Chadwick remembered that Hayes himself was left-handed, like the killer, so if he knew more than he was telling . . .

Still, he admonished himself, no point in too much theorising ahead of the facts. Imagination had never been his forte, and he had seen enough to know that the details of the murder did not always give any clues as to the state of mind of the killer, or to his relationship with the victim. People were capable of strange and wondrous behaviour, and some of it was murderous. He finished his pint and went back to the station. He would get DC Bradley to give the boffins a gentle nudge while he went out to Swainsview Lodge with young Enderby.

8

Banks hadn't been to London since Roy's death, or since the terrible tube and bus suicide bombings that summer, and he was surprised, getting off the GNER InterCity at King's Cross that lunchtime, at how just being there brought a lump to his throat. It was partly Roy, of course, and partly some deep-rooted sense of outrage at what the place had suffered.

King's Cross station was the usual throng of travellers gazing up at the boards like people seeking alien spacecraft. There was nowhere to sit; that was the problem. The station authorities didn't want to encourage people to hang around the station: they had enough problems with terrorists, teenage prostitution and drugs as it was. So they let the poor buggers stand to wait for their trains.

A uniformed constable met Banks and Annie at the side exit, as arranged, and whisked them in a patrol car through the streets of central London to Cromwell Road and along the Great West Road, past the roadside graffiti-scored concrete and glass towers of Hammersmith to Nick Barber's Chiswick flat, not far from Fuller's Brewery. It was a modern brick low-rise building, three storeys in all, and Barber had lived at the top in one of the corner units. The police locksmith was waiting for them.

When the paperwork had been completed and handed over, the lock yielded so quickly to the smith's ministrations that Banks wondered whether he had once used his skills to less legitimate ends.

Banks and Annie found themselves standing in a room with purple walls on which hung a number of prints of famous psychedelic poster art: Jimi Hendrix and John Mayall at Winterland, 1 February 1968, Buffalo Springfield at the Fillmore Auditorium, 21 December 1967, the Mad Hatters at the Roundhouse, Chalk Farm, 6 October 1968. Mixed with these were a number of framed sixties album covers: *Cheap Thrills, Disraeli Gears, Blind Faith, Forever Changes* and Sir Peter Blake's infamous *Sgt. Pepper's Lonely Hearts Club Band.* Custom shelving held a formidable collection of CDs and LPs, and the stereo equipment was Bang & Olufsen top-of-the-range, as were the Bose headphones resting by the leather armchair.

There were far too many CDs to browse through, but on a cursory glance Banks noticed a prevalence of late-sixties to early-seventies rock, stopping around Bowie and Roxy Music, and including some bands he hadn't thought of in years, like Atomic Rooster, Quintessence, Dr Strangely Strange and Amazing Blondel. There was also a smattering of jazz, mostly Miles Davis, John Coltrane and Charles Mingus, along with a fair collection of J. S. Bach, Vivaldi and Mozart.

One shelf was devoted to magazines and newspapers in which Nick Barber had published reviews or features, and his quickie rock bios. Some recent correspondence, mostly bills and junk mail, sat on a small worktable under the window. There was no desktop computer, Banks noticed, which probably meant Barber did all his work on his laptop, which had been taken.

The bedroom was tidy and functional, with a neatly made double bed and a wardrobe full of clothes, much the same as what he'd had with him in Yorkshire: casual and not too expensive. There was nothing to indicate any interests other than music, apart from the bookshelves, which reflected a fairly catholic taste in modern fiction, from Amis to Wodehouse, with a few popular science-fiction, horror and crime novels mixed in – Philip K. Dick, Ramsey Campbell, Derek Raymond, James Herbert, Ursula K. Le Guin, James Elroy and George Pelecanos. The rest were books about rock and roll: Greil Marcus, Lester Bangs, Peter Guralnik.

A filing cabinet in a corner of the bedroom held copies of contracts, lists and reviews of concerts attended, expense sheets and drafts of articles, all of which would have to be taken away and examined in detail. For the moment, though, Banks found what he needed to know in a brief note in the 'Current' file referring to 'the matter we discussed' and urging Barber to go ahead and get started. It also reminded him that they didn't pay expenses up front. The notepaper was headed with the *MOJO* logo and an address at Mappin House, on Winsley Street in the West End. It was dated 1 October, just a couple of weeks before Nick Barber left for Yorkshire.

There were several messages on Nick's answering-machine: two from an anxious girlfriend, who left him her work number, said she hadn't seen him for a while and wanted to get together for a drink, another from a mate about tickets to a Kasabian concert, and one offering the deal of the century on double-glazing. As far as Banks could see, Nick Barber had kept his life clean and tidy and taken most of it with him on the road. Now it had disappeared.

'We'd better split up,' he said to Annie. 'I'll try the *MOJO* offices and you see if you can get any luck with the girl who left her work number. See if there's anything else you can find around the flat that might tell us anything about him, too, and arrange to have the files and stuff taken up to Eastvale. I'll take the tube and leave you the driver.'

'OK,' said Annie. 'Where shall we meet up?'

Banks named an Italian restaurant in Soho, one he was sure they hadn't been to together before so it held no memories for them. They'd have to take a taxi or the tube back to their hotel, which was some distance away, just off Cromwell Road, not too far from the magnificent Natural History Museum. It was clean, they had been assured, and unlikely to break the tight police budget. As Annie busied herself listening to Barber's phone messages again, Banks left the flat and headed for the Underground.

Melanie Wright dabbed at her cheeks and apologised to Annie for the second time. They were sitting in a Starbucks near the Embankment, not far from where Melanie worked as an estate agent. She said she could take a break when Annie called, but when she found out about Nick Barber's murder, she'd got upset and her boss told her she could have the rest of the afternoon off. If Nick had a 'type', then Annie was at a loss to know what it was. Kelly Soames was gamine, pale and rather naïve, while Melanie was shapely, tanned and sophisticated. They were similar only in that both were a few years younger than him, and both were blonde.

'Nick never let anyone get really close to him,' Melanie said, over a decaff Frappuccino, 'but that was OK. I mean, I'm only twenty-four. I'm not ready to get married yet. Or even to live with someone, for that matter. I've got a nice flat in Chelsea I share with a girlfriend, and we get on really well and give each other lots of space.'

'But you did go out with Nick?'

'Yes. We'd been seeing one another for a year or so, on and off. We weren't exclusive or anything. We weren't even what you'd call a couple, really. But we had fun. Nick was fun to be with, most of the time.'

'What do you mean, most of the time?'

'Oh, he could be a bit of a bore when he got on his hobby-horse. That's all. I mean, I wasn't even born when the bloody sixties happened. It wasn't my fault. Can't stand the music, either.'

'So you didn't share his enthusiasm?'

'Nobody could. It was more than an enthusiasm with him. I mean, I know this sounds weird, because he was really cool and I got to meet all sorts of bands and stuff – we even had a drink with Jimmy Page once at some awards do. Can you believe it? Jimmy Page! Even I know who he is. But even though it all sounds really cool and everything, being a rock writer and meeting famous people, when you get right down to it, it's a bit like having any kind of all-consuming hobby, isn't it? It could have been train-spotting, or computers or something.'

'Are you saying Nick was a bit of a nerd?'

'In some ways. Of course, there was more to him than that, or I wouldn't have hung around. Nerds aren't my type.'

'It wasn't just for the bands, then?'

She shot Annie a sharp, disapproving glance. 'No. I'm not like that, either. We really had fun, me and Nick. I can't believe he's gone. I'll miss him so much.' She dabbed at her eyes.

'I'm sorry, Melanie,' said Annie. 'I don't mean to be insensitive or anything, but in this job you tend to get a bit cynical. When was the last time you saw Nick?'

'It must have been about two weeks ago, a bit over.'

'What did you do?'

She gave Annie a look. 'What do you think we did?'

'Before that.'

'We had dinner.'

'At his place?'

'Yeah. He was a fair chef. Liked watching all those cooking programmes on TV. Can't stand them myself. You ask me what I can make, and I say, "Reservations."'

Annie had heard it before, but she laughed anyway. 'Was there anything different about him?'

Melanie thought for a moment, frowning. Then she said, 'It was just a feeling I got, really. I'd been around him before when he was pitching for a feature. It always mattered to him – he loved it – but this time he was sort of anxious. I don't think he'd got the green light yet.'

'Why do you think he was anxious? Because he wouldn't get the assignment?'

'Maybe it was partly that, but I think it was more that it was personal.'

'Personal?'

'Yeah. Don't ask me why. Nick was fanatical about all his projects, and secretive about the details, but I got the sense that this one was a little more personal for him.'

'Did he tell you what, or who, he was working on?'

'No. But he never did. I don't know if he thought I'd tell someone else who'd get to it first but, like I said, he was always secretive until he'd finished. Used to disappear for weeks on end. Never told me where he was going. Not that he had any obligation to, mind you. It's not like we were joined at the hip.'

'Did he say anything at all about it?'

'Just once, that last night.' She gave a little laugh. 'It was a funny sort of thing to say. He said it was a very juicy story and it had everything, including murder.'

'Murder? He actually said that?'

Melanie started crying again. 'Yes,' she said. 'But I don't think he meant his own.'

Monday, 15 September 1969

The Mad Hatters, Enderby explained, as he negotiated the winding country roads with seeming ease, consisted of five members: Terry Watson on rhythm guitar and vocals, Vic Greaves on keyboards and back-up vocals, Reg Cooper on lead guitar, Robin Merchant on bass and vocals and Adrian Pritchard on drums. They had formed about three years ago after they met at Leeds University, and were considered a local band, although only two of them – Greaves and Cooper – came from Yorkshire. For the first year or so they played only gigs around the West Riding, then a London promoter happened to catch one of their shows at a Bradford pub and decided they'd fill a niche in the London scene with their unique blend of psychedelic pastoral.

'Hold on a minute,' said a frustrated Chadwick. 'What on earth is "psychedelic pastoral" when it's at home?'

Enderby smiled indulgently. 'Think of *Alice in Wonderland* or *Winnie the Pooh* set to rock music.'

Chadwick winced. 'I'd rather not. Go on.'

'That's about all, sir. They caught on, got bigger and bigger, and now they've got a bestselling LP out, and they're hobnobbing with rock's élite. They're tipped for even bigger things. Roger Waters from Pink Floyd was telling me yesterday in Rugby that he thought they'd go far.'

Chadwick was getting tired of Enderby's name-dropping, which had been going on since the weekend, and he wondered if it had been a mistake to send him down to interview the Brimleigh festival groups who were appearing in Rugby. In two days he hadn't found out anything of interest, and reported that there had only been about three hundred people there. And he still hadn't had a haircut. 'What the hell does Lord Jessop have to do with this?' he asked, changing the subject. 'This place does belong to him, doesn't it?'

'Yes. He's young, rich, a bit of a long-hair himself. He likes the music, and he likes to be associated with that world. Bit of a swinger, you might say. Actually, he's away a lot of the time, and he lets them use his house and grounds for rest and rehearsals.'

'Simple as that?'

'Yes, sir.'

Chadwick gazed out at the landscape, the valley bottom to his left where the river Swain meandered between wooded banks, and the rising slope of the daleside opposite, a haphazard pattern of drystone walls and green fields until about half-way up, where the grass turned brown and the rise ended in grey limestone outcrops along the top, marking the start of the gorse and heather moorland.

It was a fine day with only a few high white clouds in the sky. Even so, Chadwick felt out of his element. It wasn't as if he had never visited the Dales before. He and Janet had had many rides out there when Yvonne was younger and he got his first car, a Reliant three-wheeler that rocked dangerously in even the slightest crosswind. He wasn't untouched by the beauty of nature, but he was still a city boy at heart. After a short while, the open country did nothing for him, except make him miss the damp pavements, the noise, bustle and crowds.

If he had his way, they would spend their holidays exploring new cities, but Janet liked the caravan. Yvonne wouldn't be coming with them for much longer, he thought, so he might be able to persuade Janet to take a trip to Paris or Amsterdam, if they could afford it, and broaden her horizons. Janet had never been abroad, and Chadwick himself had only been on the Continent during wartime. It would be interesting to revisit some of his old haunts. Not the beaches, battlefields or cemeteries – he had no interest in them – but the bars, cafés and homes, where people had opened their doors and hearts and shown their gratitude after liberation.

'Here we are, sir.'

Chadwick snapped out of his reverie as Enderby pulled off the narrow track on to the grass. 'Is this it?' he asked. 'It doesn't look much of a place.'

What he could see of the house beyond its high stone wall and wooden gate was an unremarkable building of limestone with a flagstone roof and three chimneys. It was long and low with few windows; all in all, a gloomy-looking place.

'This is just the back,' said Enderby, as they approached the gate. It opened into a flagged yard, and the path led to a heavy red door with a large brass knocker in the shape of a lion's head. 'Tradesmen's entrance.'

Enderby knocked on the door, and they waited. The silence was oppressive, Chadwick thought. No birds singing. Even the sound of a rock band rehearsing would have been preferable. Well, on second thoughts . . .

The door opened and a young man of about thirty in a Paisley shirt and flared black denim jeans greeted them. His chestnut hair wasn't as long as Chadwick had expected, but it hung over his collar. 'You must be the police,' he said. 'I'm Chris Adams, the band's manager. I don't see how we can help you but please come in.'

Enderby and Chadwick followed him into a broad, panelled hallway with doors leading off to left and right. The dark wood gleamed, and Chadwick caught a whiff of lemon-scented polish. At the far end, a set of French windows framed a stunning view of the opposite daleside, an asymmetrical jumble of fields and drystone walls, and below them, at the bottom of the slope, the river. The doors, Chadwick noticed as he got closer, led out to a terrace with stone balustrades. A table, complete with umbrella and six chairs, stood in front of the doors. 'Impressive,' he said.

'It's nice when the weather's good,' said Adams. 'Which I can't say is all that often in this part of the world.'

'Local?'

'I grew up in Leeds. Went to school with Vic, the keyboards player. It's down here.'

He led them down a flight of stone steps and Chadwick realised then that they had entered the house on its highest level and there was a whole other floor beneath. At least half of it, he noticed, as they walked in through the door, was taken up by one large room, at the moment full of guitars, drums, keyboard instruments, microphones, consoles, amplifiers, speakers and thick, snaking electrical cords: the rehearsal studio, mercifully silent, except for the all-pervading hum of electricity. More French windows, which stood open, led out to a patio area in the shadow of the terrace above. Just beyond that, across a short stretch of overgrown lawn, was a granite and marble swimming-pool. Why anyone would want an outdoor swimming-pool in Yorkshire was beyond Chadwick, but the rich had their tastes and the wherewithal to indulge them. Perhaps it was heated. Sunlight reflecting from the surface told him the pool was full of water.

Four young men sat around in the large room smoking cigarettes, chatting and laughing with three girls, and one lay on a sofa reading. On a table by a wall stood a variety of bottles – Coca-Cola, gin, vodka, whisky, brandy, beer and wine. Some of the others seemed to have drinks already, and Adams offered refreshments, but Chadwick declined. He didn't like to feel beholden in any way towards people who might very well be, or might soon become, suspects. Everyone was wearing casual clothes, mostly jeans and T-shirts, some tie-dyed in the most outrageous patterns and colours. Very long hair was the norm for both men and women, except Adams, who seemed a shade more conservative than the rest. Chadwick was wearing a dark suit and muted tie.

Now that he was here, Chadwick didn't know where to start. Adams introduced the band members, who all said hello politely, and the girls, who giggled and retreated to one of the other rooms.

Fortunately, one of the group members stepped forward and said, 'How can we help you, Mr Chadwick? We heard about what happened at Brimleigh. It's terrible.'

It was Robin Merchant, bass and vocals, and clearly the spokesman. He was tall and thin and wore jeans and a jacket made of some satiny blue material with zodiac signs embroidered on it.

'I don't know that you can,' said Chadwick, sitting down on a folding chair. 'It's just that we have information the girl was in the backstage area at some point on Sunday evening, and we're trying to find out if anyone saw her there or talked to her.'

'There were a lot of people around,' said Merchant.

'I know that. And I also know that things might have been . . . a wee bit chaotic, shall we say, back there?'

One of the others – Adrian Pritchard, the drummer, Chadwick thought – laughed. 'You can say that again. It was anarchy, man.'

They all laughed.

'Even so,' Chadwick said, 'one of you might have seen or heard something important. You might not know it, what it is, but it's possible.'

'Does a tree fall in the woods if no one is there to hear it?' chimed in the one on the sofa. Vic Greaves, keyboard player.

'Come again?' said Chadwick.

Greaves stared off into space. 'It's a matter of philosophy, isn't it? How can I know something if I don't know it? How can I know that something happens if I don't experience it?'

'What Vic means,' said Merchant, jumping to the rescue, 'is that we were all pretty much focused on what we were doing.'

'Which was?'

'Pardon?'

'What were you doing?'

'Well, you know,' said Merchant, 'just relaxing in the caravan, practising a few chord changes, or maybe having a drink, talking to guys in the other bands. Depends what time it was.'

Chadwick doubted it. Most likely, he thought, they were taking drugs and having sex with groupies, but none of them was going to admit that. 'What time did you perform?'

Merchant looked to the others for confirmation. 'We went on about eight, just after, right, and we played an hour set, so we were off again just after nine. After the roadies moved the equipment around and set up the lightshow, Pink Floyd came on about ten, then Fleetwood Mac, then Led Zep.'

'And after your set, what did you do?'

Merchant shrugged. 'We just hung around, you know. We were pretty wired, the adrenaline from performing and everything – I mean, it went *really* well, a great gig, and a big one for us – so we needed a couple of drinks to come down. I don't know, we just listened to the other bands, that sort of thing. I spent a bit of time in the caravan reading.'

'Reading what?'

'You wouldn't have heard of it.'

'Try me.'

'Aleister Crowley, *Magick in Theory and Practice*.'

'Never heard of it,' said Chadwick, with a smile.

Merchant gave him a sharp, penetrating glance. 'As I said, I didn't think you would have.'

'Did you stay until the end?'

'Yeah. Jesse said we could stay here for the night, so we didn't have too far to go.'

'Jesse?'

'Sorry. Lord Jessop. Everyone calls him Jesse.'

'I see. Is he here now?'

'No, he's in France. Spends quite a bit of his time in Antibes. We saw him last month when we were on a tour.'

'In France?'

'Yeah. The album's selling really well there.'

'Congratulations.'

'Thanks.'

'Was Lord Jessop at Brimleigh?'

'Sure. He went to Antibes maybe last Tuesday or Wednesday.'

All of a sudden a loud, violent buzzing noise cut like a chainsaw through Chadwick's head.

'Sorry,' a sheepish Reg Cooper, lead guitarist, said. 'Feedback.' He put his guitar down carefully. The noise ebbed slowly away.

'Boring you, am I, laddie?' said Chadwick.

'No,' Cooper muttered. 'Not at all. I said I was sorry. Accident.'

Chadwick held Cooper's gaze for a moment, then turned his attention back to Robin Merchant. 'Let's get back to the eighth of September,' he said. 'We think the girl was killed between about one o'clock and twenty past one in the morning, while Led Zeppelin were playing a song called "I Can't Quit You Baby".' Such language came only with difficulty from Chadwick's mouth, and he noticed some of the others smirk as he spoke the words. 'I understand that they're very loud,' he went on, ignoring them, 'so it's unlikely anybody heard anything, if there was anything to hear, but were any of you in Brimleigh Woods at that time?'

'The woods?' said Merchant. 'No, we didn't go there at all. We were backstage, up front in the press enclosure, or in the caravan.'

'All of you? All the time?' Chadwick scanned the others' faces. They all nodded.

' "If you go down to the woods today . . ." ' Vic Greaves intoned in the background.

'Why would we go to the woods, man?' said Adrian Pritchard. 'All the action was backstage.'

'What action?'

'You know, man . . . the birds . . . the—'

'Shut up, Adrian,' said Merchant. He turned back to Chadwick and folded his arms. 'Look, I know what preconceptions the police have of us, but we're clean. You can search the place if you like. Go on.'

'I'm sure you are,' said Chadwick. 'You knew we were coming. But I'm not interested in drugs. Not at the moment, anyway. I'm more interested in what you were doing when this girl died, and in whether any of you saw her or talked to her.'

'Well, I told you,' said Merchant. 'We never went near the woods, and how do we know if we saw her or not when none of us knows her name or what she looked like?'

'You didn't see the papers?'

'We never bother with them. Full of establishment lies.'

'Anyway,' Chadwick said, reaching for his briefcase, 'I was getting to that. As it happens I now have a fairly recent photograph. It should interest you.' He took out the photograph of Linda with the members of the Mad Hatters and passed it to Merchant, who gasped and stared, open-mouthed. 'Is that . . . Vic?' He passed it to Vic Greaves, who still lay sprawled on a sofa smoking and looking, to Chadwick, quite out of it. Greaves stirred and took the photo. 'Fuck,' he said. 'Fucking hell.' And the photo slipped out of his hands.

Chadwick went over and picked it up, standing over Greaves. 'Who is it?' he asked. 'You know her?'

'Sort of,' said Greaves. 'Look, I don't feel too good, Rob. My head, it's . . . like snakes and things coming back, you know, man . . . like I need . . .' He turned away.

Merchant stepped forward. 'Vic's not too well,' he said. 'The doctor says he's suffering from fatigue, and his emotional state is pretty fragile right now. This must be a hell of a shock for him.'

'Why?' asked Chadwick, sitting down again.

He gestured towards the photo. 'That girl. It's Linda. Linda Lofthouse. She's Vic's cousin.'

Cousin. Mrs Lofthouse had never mentioned that. But why should she? He hadn't asked her about the Mad Hatters, and she had probably been in shock. Still, this was a new development worth following. Chadwick looked at Vic Greaves

with more interest. By far the scruffiest of the bunch, he looked
as if he hadn't shaved in four or five days and his skin was
deathly pale, as if he never saw the sun, but dotted with angry
red spots. His dark hair stuck out in tufts as if he had slept on it
and not washed or combed it for a week. His clothes looked
rumpled, slept-in, too. There was a well-thumbed paperback
on the sofa beside him called *Meetings With Remarkable Men*.

'Were they particularly close?' Chadwick asked Robin
Merchant.

'No, not really, I don't think, just cousins. She grew up in
west Leeds, and Vic's family lived in Seacroft.'

'But we understand she was living in London,' Chadwick
said. 'Isn't that where you all live now?'

'It's a big place.'

Chadwick took a deep breath. 'Mr Merchant,' he said, 'I
appreciate that you lads are busy, not to mention famous, and
no doubt wealthy. But a young girl has been brutally murdered
at a festival in which you were taking part. She was seen
backstage talking to two of you, and now it appears that one of
you is also her cousin. Is there any particular reason Mr
Greaves over there is suffering from fatigue, that he is distressed? That's exactly the kind of thing that killing someone
might do to you.'

A stunned silence followed Chadwick's controlled tirade.
Greaves tossed on the sofa and his book fell to the floor. He
put his head into his hands and groaned. 'Talk to him, Rob,
talk to him,' he said. 'You tell him. I can't handle this.'

'Look,' said Merchant, 'why don't we take a walk outside,
Inspector? I'll answer all your questions as best I can. But can't
you see it's upsetting Vic?'

Upsetting Vic Greaves was not Chadwick's main concern,
but he thought he might be able to get a bit more information
out of Robin Merchant, who seemed the most level-headed of
the lot, if he did as requested. He gestured to Enderby to stay

with the others and accompanied Merchant out to the patio
and down the slope towards the swimming-pool.

'Ever use it?' Chadwick asked.

'Sometimes,' Merchant answered, with a smile. 'For midnight orgies on the two days in August when it's warm enough.
Jesse tries to keep it cleaned up, but it's difficult.'

'Lord Jessop isn't a relation, too, is he?'

'Jesse? Good Lord, no. He's a patron of the arts. A friend.'

They stood by the side of the pool looking out across the
dale. Chadwick could see a red tractor making its way across
one of the opposite fields towards a tiny farmhouse. The
hillside was dotted with sheep. He glanced down at the
swimming-pool. A few early autumn leaves floated on the
water's scummy surface, along with a dead sparrow.

'All right, Mr Merchant,' said Chadwick. 'Am I to take it
you're the leader of the group?'

'Spokesman. We don't believe in leaders.'

'Very well. *Spokesman.* That means you can speak for the
others?'

'To some extent, yes. It's not that they can't speak for
themselves. But Vic, as you can see, is not exactly a social
charmer, though he's a great creative force. Adrian and Reg
are OK but they're not especially articulate, and Terry is way
too hip to talk to the fuzz.'

'You sound educated.'

'I've got a degree, if that's what you mean. English literature.'

'I'm impressed.'

'You're not meant to be. It's just a piece of paper.' Merchant kicked a couple of loose pebbles with his foot. They
plopped into the swimming-pool. 'Can we get this over with? I
don't mean to be rude or anything, but we do have a tour to
rehearse for. Contrary to what a lot of people think, rock
musicians aren't just layabouts with minimal ability and loud

amplifiers. We take our music seriously, and we work hard at it.'

'I'm sure you do. If I ask you direct, simple questions and you answer them straightforwardly, we'll soon be done here. How about that?'

'Fine. Ask away.' Merchant lit a cigarette.

'Was it Mr Greaves who got the backstage pass for Linda Lofthouse?'

'It was me,' said Merchant.

'Why you?'

'Vic's not . . . As you can see, he doesn't deal well with rules, people in authority, things like that. It intimidates him. It was his cousin, but he asked me to do it for him.'

'So you did?'

'Yes.'

'She would have picked this up where?'

'At the entrance to the backstage area.'

'From security, I assume?'

'Yes.'

That meant either they'd missed out on questioning the guard who had given Linda the pass, or he had forgotten or lied about it. Well, Chadwick thought, people lie often enough to the police. They don't want to get involved. And there's always that little bit of guilt everybody carries around with them.

'Could she come and go as she pleased?'

'Yes.'

'What were you talking about when you were photographed with her?'

'Just asking if she was having a good time, that sort of thing. It was very casual. We only chatted for a couple of minutes. I didn't even know that someone had taken a photo of us.'

'Was she having a good time?'

'So she said.'

'Was anything bothering her?'

'Not as far as I could tell.'

'What was her state of mind?'

'Fine. Just, you know, normal.'

'Was she worried about anything, frightened by anything?'

'No.'

'Did you talk to her again after the photo was taken, later in the evening?'

'No.'

'See her?'

'Only around, you know, from a distance.'

'Did she have a flower painted on her cheek later?'

Merchant paused for a moment, then he said, 'As a matter of fact, she did. At least, I think it was her. There was some bird doing body art in the enclosure.'

Well, Chadwick thought, there went one theory. Still, it would be useful to track down the 'bird', if possible, and establish for certain whether she had painted the flower on Linda's cheek. 'How well did you know Linda?'

'Not well at all. I'd met her in London a couple of times. Once when we were doing the album she got in touch with Vic through his parents and asked if she could sit in on the studio sessions with a friend. She's interested in music – as a matter of fact we let her play a little acoustic guitar on one track, and she and her friend did some harmonies. They weren't bad at all.'

'What friend?'

'Just another bird. I didn't really talk to her.'

'Did Linda ever go out with anyone in the group?'

'No.'

'Come off it, Mr Merchant. Linda Lofthouse was an exceptionally attractive girl, or hadn't you noticed?'

'There's no shortage of attractive girls in our business. Anyway, she didn't strike me as the sort to take up with a rock musician.'

'What do you mean?'

'That she seemed like a decent, well-brought-up girl, just a little brighter than most and with broader interests than her friends.'

'She had a baby.'

'So?'

'You have to sleep with someone to get pregnant. She did it when she was fifteen, so how can you tell me that on the strength of two meetings she wasn't "that" sort of girl?'

'Call it gut instinct. I don't know. Maybe I'm wrong. She just seemed a nice girl, that's all. Didn't give off that kind of vibe. You get to recognise it, especially in this business. Take those three you saw when you came in.'

'So Linda wasn't going out with anyone in the group?'

'No.'

'What about the other groups at the festival?'

'She might have talked to people, but I didn't see her hanging around with anyone in particular for very long.'

'What about Rick Hayes?'

'The promoter? Yeah, I saw her with him. She said she knew him in London.'

'Was he her boyfriend?'

'I doubt it. I mean, Rick's a good guy, don't get me wrong, but he's a bit of a loser in that department, and they weren't acting that way towards one another.'

Chadwick made a mental note. Losers in love often found interesting and violent ways to express their dissatisfaction. 'Do you know if she had a boyfriend? Did she ever mention anyone?'

'Not that I recall. Look, have you ever thought that it was something else?'

'What do you mean?'

'They might have thought that it was something other than murder.'

'They?'

'Figure of speech. Whoever did it.'

'You've lost me.'

'So I see. I don't know. I'm just speculating. Not everyone sees the world the same way as you do.'

'I'm coming to realise that.'

'Well . . . you know . . . I mean, murder's just a word.'

'I can assure you it's more than that to me.'

'Sorry. Sorry. I didn't mean to be offensive. But that's you. I'm just trying to show you that other people think differently.'

Chadwick was beginning to wonder if he'd wandered into a *Wednesday Play*. Desperate to get back to more tenable ground, he asked, 'Do you know where she lived?'

Merchant seemed to come back from a long way off and gather his thoughts before answering in a tired voice, 'She had a room on Powis Terrace. Notting Hill Gate. That's what she said that time she came down to the studio, anyway.'

'You don't know the number?'

'No. I wouldn't even know the street except when she said Notting Hill I asked her about it, because it's a great neighbourhood. Everyone knows Notting Hill, Portobello Road, Powis Square and all that.'

Chadwick remembered Portobello Road from some leave he had spent in London during the war. 'Expensive?'

'Bloody hell, no. Not for London, at any rate. It's all cheap bedsits.'

'You said you met her a couple of times in London. When was the other time?'

'A gig at the Roundhouse last year. October, I think it was. One of the ones Rick Hayes promoted. Again, she asked Vic to get her and a friend backstage passes and he delegated it to me.'

'The same friend who sat in on the recording session with her?'

'Yeah. Sorry, but, like I said, I didn't talk to her. I can't remember her name.'

Chadwick stared out across the dale again. The tractor had disappeared. Cloud shadows raced across the fields and lime-stone outcrops as the breeze picked up. 'Not much of a memory, have you, laddie?' he said.

'Look, I'm sorry if I'm not sounding helpful,' said Merchant, 'but it's the truth. Linda was never part of the entourage, and she wasn't a groupie. She got in touch with Vic exactly three times over the past two years, just to ask for little favours. We didn't mind. It was no problem. She was family, after all. But that's all there was to it. None of us went out with her and none of us really knew her.'

'And that's it?'

'Yes.'

'Back to last Sunday. Where were you all between one and twenty past one that night?'

Merchant flicked his cigarette end into the swimming-pool. 'I don't really remember.'

'Were you with the others listening to Led Zeppelin?'

'Some of the time, yeah, but they're not really my thing. I might have been in the caravan reading, or in the beer tent.'

'That's not much of an alibi, is it?'

'I wasn't aware I'd need one.'

'What about the others?'

'They were around.'

'Your manager, Mr Adams. Was he there?'

'Chris? Yeah, he was somewhere around.'

'But you didn't see him?'

'I don't really remember seeing him at any particular time, no, but I did see him now and then in passing.'

'So any one of you could have gone out to the woods with Linda Lofthouse and stabbed her?'

'But nobody had any reason to,' Merchant said. 'We didn't hang out with her, didn't really know her. I just got the passes for her, that's all.'

'Passes?'

'Yeah, two.'

'You didn't say this before.'

'You didn't ask.'

'Who was the other pass for?'

'Her friend, the girl she was with.'

'The same one you saw her with at the Roundhouse and the recording session? The one whose name you can't remember?'

'That's the one.'

'Why didn't you say so earlier?'

Merchant shrugged.

'If you got her a pass, you must know her name.'

'I didn't *look* at it.'

'Did you see her later, at the festival?'

'Once or twice.'

'Were they together?'

'The first time I saw them, yes. Later on they weren't.'

'What do you know about this girl?'

'Nothing. She was a friend of Linda's and they sang together in clubs. I think they shared a pad or were neighbours.'

'What does she look like?'

'About the same age as Linda. Long dark hair, olive complexion. Nice figure.'

'What time did you last see her?'

'I don't know. When Pink Floyd were on. It must have been close to midnight.'

'And were the two of them together?'

'I didn't see Linda then, no.'

'What was this other girl doing?'

'Just standing around with a group of people drinking and chatting.'

'Who?'

'Just people. Nobody in particular.'

So who was she? Chadwick wondered. And why hadn't she reported her friend missing? Not for the first time, he wondered about the mental faculties of the world he was dealing with. Didn't these people care if someone stole their sleeping-bag or, worse, if someone close to them disappeared? He didn't expect them to see the world as he did, with danger at every turn, but surely it was simple common sense to worry? Unless something had happened to her friend, too. He wouldn't find that out by hanging around Swainsview Lodge, he decided, and the thought of trying to talk to any of the others again brought on a headache.

Chadwick thanked Robin Merchant for his time, said he would have to talk to Vic Greaves when he was feeling better, then they went back inside. Enderby, looking pleased with himself, held out a copy of the Mad Hatters LP and asked Merchant if he would sign it. He did. The others were slouching in their chairs, smoking and sipping drinks, Reg Cooper picking a quiet tune on his guitar, Vic Greaves apparently asleep on his sofa, tranquillised to the gills. The sound system was buzzing in the background. Chris Adams showed them out, apologising for Greaves and promising that if there was anything else they needed, they should get in touch with him. He gave them his phone number and left them at the door.

'Where did you get that?' Chadwick said in the car, pointing to the LP.

'He gave it to me. The manager. I got them all to sign it.'

'Better hand it over,' said Chadwick. 'You wouldn't want anyone to think you'd been accepting bribes, would you?'

'But, sir!'

Chadwick held his hand out. 'Come on, laddie. Give.'

Reluctantly, Enderby handed over the signed LP. Chadwick slipped it into his briefcase, suppressing a little smile as Enderby practically stripped the gears getting back to the road.

9

The *MOJO* office was a square, open-plan area on the same floor as *Q* and *Kerrang!* magazines, accommodating twenty or so people. There were two fairly large windows at one end, and two long desks equipped with Mac computers in various colours and stacked with CDs, reference books and file folders. Cluttered, but appealingly so. Filing cabinets fitted under the desks. Posters covered the walls, mostly blow-ups of old *MOJO* covers. The people Banks could see working there ran the whole gamut: short hair, long hair, grey hair, shaved heads. Dress was mostly casual, but some ties were in evidence.

Nobody paid Banks any attention as John Butler, the editor he had come to see, led him to a section of desk close to the window. An empty Prêt à Manger bag sat among the papers on his desk, and a whiff of bacon hung in the air, reminding Banks that it was mid-afternoon and he was starving. He could feel his stomach growling as he sat down.

John Butler looked to be in his late thirties and was one of the more casually dressed people in the office, wearing jeans and an old Hawkwind T-shirt. His shaved head gleamed under the strip-lighting. There was music playing, some sixties piece with jangling guitars and harmonies. Banks didn't recognise it, but he liked it. He could also hear the thumping bass of dance mix coming from round the corner. He thought it must be hard to concentrate on writing with all that noise going on.

'It's about Nick Barber,' said Banks. 'I understand he was working on an assignment for you?'

'Yes, that's right. Poor Nick.' Butler's brow crinkled. 'One of the best. Nobody, and I mean nobody, knew more about late-sixties and early-seventies music than Nick, especially the Mad Hatters. He's a great loss to the entire music community.'

'It's my job to find out who killed him,' said Banks.

'I understand. Any help I can give, of course . . . though I don't see how . . .'

'What was Nick Barber's assignment?'

'He was doing a big feature on the Mad Hatters,' said Butler. 'More specifically on Vic Greaves, the keyboards player. Next year is the fortieth anniversary of when the band was formed, and they're re-forming for a big concert tour.'

Banks had heard of the Mad Hatters. Not many people hadn't. They had rebuilt themselves from the ashes of the sixties in a way that few other bands had, except perhaps Fleetwood Mac after Peter Green, and Pink Floyd after Syd Barrett left. But not without tremendous cost, as Banks recalled. 'Where are they now?' he asked.

'All over the place. Most of them live in LA.'

'Vic Greaves disappeared years ago, didn't he?' Banks said.

'That's right. Nick had found him.'

'How did he manage that?'

'He protected his sources pretty well, but I'd say most likely through a rental agency or an estate agent. He had his contacts. Vic Greaves doesn't go to extraordinary lengths to stay anonymous, he's just a recluse and doesn't advertise his presence. He's been found before. The problem is that no one can ever get much out of him so they give up, except maybe some of the weirdoes who see him as a sort of cult figure, which is why he guards his privacy to the extent that he does – or Chris Adams does. Anyway, however Nick did it, you can guarantee it wouldn't be through Adams, the manager.'

'Why not?'

'Adams is very protective of Greaves. Has been ever since the breakdown. They're old friends, apparently, go back to schooldays.'

'Where did Nick find Greaves?'

'In North Yorkshire. The Hatters always had a strong connection with Yorkshire, through Lord Jessop and Swainsview Lodge. Besides, Vic and Reg Cooper, the lead guitarist, were both local lads. Met the others at the University of Leeds.'

'North Yorkshire? How long has he been living there?'

'Dunno,' said Butler. 'Nick didn't say.'

So the object of Nick Barber's pilgrimage had been right under his nose all the time, and he had never guessed. Well, why would he? If you wanted to live as a hermit in the Dales, it could be done. Now Banks had a glimmer of a memory. Something that he might have guessed brought Nick Barber to Swainsdale. 'Help me here,' he said. 'I didn't grow up in the area, and I wasn't there at the time, but as far as I can remember, there was some other connection with the group, wasn't there?'

'Robin Merchant, the bass player.'

'He drowned, didn't he?'

'Indeed he did. Drowned in a swimming-pool about a year after Brian Jones. June 1970. Tragic business.'

'And that swimming-pool was at Swainsview Lodge,' said Banks. 'Now I remember.' He was surprised at himself for not making the connection earlier, but when it came down to it, although he knew that Brian Jones had also died in a swimming-pool, he didn't know where that pool was either. To him, a swimming-pool was a swimming-pool. But Nick Barber would know things like that, just as sports fans knew their team's scores, statistics and greatest players going back years.

'Swainsview Lodge has been empty for a few years now,'

Banks said, 'ever since Lord Jessop died of Aids in 1997. There were no heirs.' And nobody wanted the old pile of stone, Banks remembered. It cost too much to keep up, for a start, and it needed a lot of work. A couple of hotel chains had shown a brief interest, but the foot-and-mouth business had soon scared them off. At one time there was talk of the Lodge being converted into a convention centre, but nothing had come of it. 'Tell me more about Nick Barber,' he said.

'Not much to tell, really,' said Butler.

'How did he get into the business? According to his parents, he had no training in journalism.'

'It might sound a bit odd to you, but in this line of work we don't encourage journalistic training. You pick up too many bad habits. Naturally, we require writing ability, but we judge that for ourselves. What counts most is love of the music.'

That would suit Banks right down to the ground, he thought, if only he could write. 'And Nick Barber had that?'

'In spades. And he had in-depth knowledge on all sorts of genres, too, including jazz and some classical. Like I said, a remarkable mind, and a tragic loss.'

'How long had he been writing for you?'

'Seven or eight years, on and off.'

'And his interest in the Mad Hatters?'

'The last five years or so.'

'He seemed to live quite frugally, from what I've seen.'

'Nobody said music journalism pays well, but there are a lot of fringe benefits.'

'Drugs?'

'I didn't mean that. Backstage passes to concerts, rubbing shoulders with the rock aristocracy, a bit of cachet with girls, that sort of thing.'

'I think I'd rather have an extra hundred quid a week,' said Banks.

'Well, I suppose that's one reason why this business isn't for you.'

'Fair enough. Why didn't he have a job on the staff?'

'Didn't want one. We'd have taken him on like a shot, as would the competition, but Nick wanted to keep his independence. He *liked* being a freelancer. To be quite frank, some people don't function at their best in an office environment, and I think Nick was one of them. He liked the freedom to roam, but he always delivered on deadline.'

Banks understood what Butler was talking about. Wasn't that pretty much what Detective Superintendent Gervaise had said about him that very morning? Stay out of the office, but bring me results.

'How did he get the assignment?'

'He pitched for it. Funnily enough, we'd just had our monthly meeting and decided we wanted to do something on the Hatters. Anniversaries, reunion tours and things like that are usually a good excuse for a reappraisal, or a new revelation.'

'So he rang you?'

'Yes. Just when we were about to ring him. He'd written about them before, only brief pieces and reviews but insightful. Look, I can give you a few back copies, if you'd like, so you can see the kind of thing he did.'

'I'd appreciate that,' said Banks, who knew that he had probably read some of Barber's pieces in the past. But he didn't keep his back issues of *MOJO*. The pile just got too high. 'What was the next step?'

'We had a couple of meetings to sharpen things up and came up with a tight brief, a focus for the piece.'

'Which was to be Vic Greaves?'

'Yes. He's always been the key figure, the mystery man. Troubled genius and all that. And the timing of his leaving couldn't have been worse for the band. Robin Merchant had just drowned, and they were falling apart. If it hadn't been for Chris Adams, they might have done. Nick was hoping to get an exclusive interview. That would have been a real scoop, if he could have got Greaves to talk. He also wanted to do something on their early gigs, before Merchant died and Greaves left, contrast their style with the later works.'

'How long would it take Barber to write a feature like that?'

'Anything from two to five months. There's a lot of background research, for a start, a lot of history to sift through, a lot of people to talk to, and it's not always easy. You also have to sort out the truth from the apocryphal, and that can be really difficult. You know what they say about the sixties and memory? What they don't say is that if people can't remember it, they make it up. But Nick was nothing if not thorough. He was a fine writer. He checked all his facts and sources. Twice. There's not a Mad Hatters gig he'd leave unexamined, not a university-newspaper review he wouldn't dig up, not an obscure B-side he wouldn't listen to a hundred times.'

'How far had he got?'

'Hardly begun. He'd spent a week or two driving around, making phone calls, checking out old venues, that sort of thing. I mean, a lot of the places the original Hatters played don't even exist any more. And he might have done a bit of general background – you know, browsed over a few old reviews in the newspaper archives at the British Library. But he planned to get started on the main story up in Yorkshire. He'd only been there a week when . . . Well, you know what happened.'

'Had he sent in any reports?'

'No. I'd spoken to him on the phone a couple of times, that's all. Apparently he had to go into a public phone box over the road to ring when he was in Yorkshire. He didn't have any mobile signal up there.'

'I know,' said Banks. 'How did he sound?'

'He was excited, but very cagey. A story like this – if Nick could really have got Vic Greaves to open up about the past and someone else got wind of it . . . you can imagine what that would mean. Ours can be a bit of a cut-throat business.'

'We really need to know where Vic Greaves lives,' said Banks.

'I understand that, and if I knew his address I'd tell you. Nick mentioned a village called Lyndgarth in North Yorkshire. I'd never heard of it, but apparently it's near Eastvale, if that's any help. That's all I know.'

Banks knew he ought to be able to find Vic Greaves in Lyndgarth easily enough. 'I know it,' he said. 'It's very close to where Nick was staying. Walking distance, in fact. Do you happen to know if he had already spoken to Greaves?'

'Once.'

'And?'

'It didn't go well. According to Nick, Greaves freaked out, refused to talk, as usual, sent him packing. To be honest, I very much doubt you'll get any sense out of him.'

'What's wrong with him?'

'Nobody knows. He went strange – has been for years.'

'When did Nick talk to him?'

'He didn't say. Some time last week.'

'What day did he phone you?'

'Friday – Friday morning.'

'What was he going to do?'

'Talk to Greaves again. Work out a different approach. Nick was good. He'd simply tested the waters. He'd have found something to catch Greaves's interest, some common ground, and he'd have taken it from there.'

'Have you any idea,' Banks asked, 'why this story should have cost Nick Barber his life?'

'None at all,' said Butler, spreading his hands. 'I still can't really believe it did. Maybe what happened was nothing to do with the Hatters. Have you considered that? Maybe it was an irate husband. Bit of a swordsman, was our Nick.'

'Any husband in particular might have wanted him dead recently?'

'Not that I know of. He never seemed to stick with anyone for long, especially if they started to get clingy. He liked his independence. And the music always got in the way. Most of our guys live alone in flats, when you get right down to it. They'd rather be ferreting out old vinyl on Berwick Street than go out with a girl. They're loners, obsessed.'

'So Nick Barber would love 'em and leave 'em?'

'Something like that.'

'Maybe it was an irate girlfriend, then?'

Butler laughed uneasily.

Banks thought of Kelly Soames again, but he didn't think she had killed Nick Barber, and not only because of the discrepancy in timing. There was still her father, though, Calvin Soames. He had disappeared from the pub for fifteen minutes, and nobody had seen him return to his farm in Lyndgarth to check the gas ring. Admittedly, it was a bad night, and the farm was off the beaten track, but it was still worth further consideration. The question was, had Soames been hiding that he knew about Barber and Kelly? Banks couldn't tell. And if he had done it, why take all Barber's stuff?

When it came right down to it, though, Banks had a gut feeling that the Mad Hatters story had got Barber killed. He had no idea why. Unless you were a soul or rap artist, music was generally a murder-free profession, and it was a bit of a stretch to imagine ageing hippies going around bashing people over the head with pokers. But there it was. Nick Barber had headed to Yorkshire in search of a reclusive ex-rock star, had found him, and within days he had turned up dead, his notes, mobile phone and laptop computer missing.

Banks thanked Butler for his time and said he might be back

with more questions. Butler accompanied him to the lift, stopping to pick out some back issues for him on the way. Banks walked out on to busy Oxford Street a little more enlightened than when he had entered Mappin House. He noticed that he was standing right outside HMV, so he went inside.

Monday, 15 September 1969

The mood in the Grove was subdued that Monday evening. Somebody had turned out all the electric lights and put candles on every table. Yvonne sat at the back of the small room, near the door, with Steve, Julie and a bunch of others. McGarrity was there, but thankfully not sitting with them. At one point he took the stage and recited a T. S. Eliot poem. That was typical of him, Yvonne thought. He dismissed everybody else's poetry, but didn't have the creativity to make up his own. There was a bit of talk about a concert in Toronto that Saturday, where John Lennon and Yoko had turned up to play with some legendary rock 'n' roll stars, and some desultory conversation about the Los Angeles murders, but mostly people seemed to have turned in on themselves. They had known the previous Monday that something had happened at Brimleigh, of course, but now it was all over the place – and the victim's name had been in that morning's paper and on the evening news. Many people had known her, at least by name or sight.

Yvonne was still stunned by the signed Mad Hatters LP her father had given her before she went out that evening. She couldn't imagine him even being in the same room as such a fantastic band, let alone asking them to sign a copy of their LP. But he was full of surprises, these days. Maybe there was hope for him yet.

McGarrity's Eliot travesty aside, most of the evening was

given over to local folk-singers. A plump, short-haired girl in jeans and a T-shirt sang 'She Walks Through The Fair' and 'Farewell, Farewell'. A curly-haired troubadour with a gap between his front teeth sang 'The Trees They Do Grow High' and 'Needle Of Death', followed by a clutch of early Bob Dylan songs.

There was a sombre tone to it all, and Yvonne knew, although it was never said, that this was a farewell concert for Linda. Other people in the place had known her far better than Yvonne had; in fact, she had sung there on more than one occasion when she visited her friends in Leeds. Everybody had looked forward to her visits. Yvonne wished she could be like that, the kind of person who had such a radiant, spiritual quality that people were drawn to her. But she also couldn't forget that someone had been drawn to kill her.

She remembered the photograph that had slipped out of her father's briefcase: Linda with an expressionless face and eyes. The pathetic little cornflower on her cheek; Linda not at home; dead Linda, just a shell, her spirit scared off into the light. She felt herself well up with tears as she thought her thoughts and listened to the sad songs of long ago, ballads of murder and betrayal, of supernatural lovers, metamorphoses, disasters at sea and wasted youth. She wasn't supposed to drink, but she could easily pass for eighteen in the Grove, and Steve brought her drinks like Babycham, Pony and Cherry B. After a while she started to feel light-headed and sick.

She made her way to the toilet and forced her finger down her throat. That helped. When she had finished, she rinsed her mouth, washed her face and lit a cigarette. She didn't look too bad. On her way out she had to squeeze past McGarrity in the narrow corridor, and the cruel amusement on his face at her obvious discomfort frightened her. He paused, pressed up against her breasts, ran one dirty, nail-bitten finger down her cheek and whispered her name. It made her shiver.

When she got back to Steve and the others it was the intermission. She hadn't brought up the subject of Linda with Steve yet, partly because she was afraid that she might feel jealous if he had slept with her. She shouldn't. Jealousy was a negative emotion, Steve always said, to be cast aside, but she couldn't help it. Linda was so perfect, and beside her Yvonne felt like a naïve, awkward schoolgirl. Finally, she made herself do it. 'Did you know Linda well?' she asked him, as casually as she could.

Steve rolled a cigarette from his Old Holborn tin before answering. 'Not really,' he said. 'She'd gone before I came on the scene. I only saw her a couple of times when she came up from London and stayed at Dennis's.'

'Bayswater Terrace? Is that where she lived?'

'Yeah. Before she went to London.'

'With Dennis?'

'No, not *with* him, just at his pad, man.' Steve gave her a puzzled look. 'What does it matter, anyway? She's dead now. We have to let go.'

Yvonne felt flustered. 'It doesn't. It . . . I mean . . . I only met her once, myself, and I liked her, that's all.'

'Everybody loved Linda.'

'Not everybody, obviously.'

'What do you mean?'

'Well, somebody murdered her.'

'That doesn't mean he didn't love her.'

'I don't understand.'

Steve stroked her arm. 'It's a complicated world, Von, and people do things for many reasons, often reasons we don't understand, reasons they don't understand themselves. All I'm saying is that whoever did it didn't necessarily do it from hatred or jealousy or envy or some other negative emotion. It might have been from love. Or an act of kindness. Sometimes you have to destroy the thing you love most. It's not for us to question.'

Yvonne hated it when he talked down to her like that, as if she were indeed a silly schoolgirl who just didn't get it. But she didn't get it. To her, Linda had been murdered. No amount of talk about killing for love or kindness made any sense. Perhaps it was because she was a policeman's daughter, she thought, in which case she had better stop sounding like one, or they would be on to her in a flash.

'You're right,' she said. 'It's not for us to question.'

And the second half of the evening started. She could see McGarrity through the crowds, a dark shadow hunched in the candlelight, just to the right of the stage area, and she thought he was staring at her. Then a young man with long blond hair climbed on to the tiny stage and began to sing 'Polly On The Shore'.

In a booth in a noisy and smoky Italian restaurant on Frith Street, Banks and Annie shared fizzy water and a bottle of the house red, as Banks tucked into his veal Marsala and Annie her pasta primavera. Outside, darkness had fallen and the streets and pubs and restaurants of Soho were filling as people finished work, or arrived in the West End for an evening out. Red and purple lights reflected in the sheen of rain on the pavements and road.

'You've got a lot of explaining to do,' Annie said, fixing her hair behind her ears so it didn't get into her mouth while she ate.

'About what?' said Banks.

'This Mad Hatters business. I hardly understood a word of what you were talking about before dinner.'

'It's not my fault if your cultural education is severely lacking,' said Banks.

'Put it down to my callow youth and explain in words of one syllable.'

'You've never heard of the Mad Hatters?'

'Of course I have. I've even seen them on Jonathan Ross. That's not the point. I just don't happen to know their entire bloody history.'

'They got big in the late sixties, around the same time as Led Zeppelin, a bit after Pink Floyd and the Who. Their music was different. It had elements of folk-rock, the Byrds and Fairport Convention, but they gave a sort of psychedelic twist to it, at first, anyway. Think 'Eight Miles High' meets 'Sir Patrick Spens'.'

Annie made a face. 'I would if I knew what either of those sounded like.'

'I give up,' said Banks. 'Anyway, a lot of their sound and style was down to the keyboards player, Vic Greaves, the bloke we were talking about, who now lives in Lyndgarth, and the lead guitarist, Reg Cooper, another Yorkshire lad.'

'Vic Greaves was the keyboards player?'

'Yeah. He was a bit of a Keith Emerson, got amazing sounds out of his organ.'

Annie raised her eyebrows. 'The mind boggles.'

'They had light shows, did long guitar solos, wore funny floppy hats and purple velvet trousers, gold kaftans, and they did all that other sixties psychedelic stuff. Anyway, in June 1970, not long after their second album hit the charts, the bass player Robin Merchant drowned in Lord Jessop's swimming-pool at Swainsview Lodge.'

'*Our* Swainsview Lodge?'

'The one and only.'

'Was there an investigation?'

'I should imagine so,' said Banks. 'That's something we'll have to dig up when we get back to Eastvale. There should be files in the basement somewhere.'

'Wonderful,' said Annie. 'Last time I went down there I was sneezing for a week.'

'Don't worry, we'll send Kev.'

Annie smiled. She could imagine Templeton's reaction to that, especially since he had become puffed up to an almost unbearable level since his promotion. 'Maybe your folk-singer friend will know something?' she asked.

'Penny Cartwright?' said Banks, remembering his last, unsatisfactory encounter with Penny on the banks of the river Swain one summer evening. 'It was all long before her time. Besides, she's gone away again. America, this time.'

'What happened to the Mad Hatters?'

'They got another bass player.'

'And what about Vic Greaves?'

'He'd been a problem for a long time. He was unpredictable. Sometimes he didn't show up for gigs. He'd walk off stage. He got violent with other band members, with his girlfriends. They say there were times he just sat staring into space, too stoned to play. Naturally, there were stories about the huge quantities of LSD he consumed, not to mention other drugs. He wrote a lot of their early songs and some of the lyrics are very . . . well, drug-induced, trippy, I suppose you'd say. The rest of the band were a bit more practical and ambitious, and they didn't know what to do about him, but in the end they didn't have to worry. He disappeared for a month late in 1970 – September, I think – and when they found him again, he was living rough in the country-side like a tramp. He wanted nothing more to do with the music business. Been a hermit ever since.'

'Did nobody do anything for him?'

'Like what?'

'Help him get psychiatric help, for a start.'

'Different times, Annie. There was a lot of distrust of conventional psychiatry at the time. You had weirdoes like R. D. Laing running around talking about the politics of insanity and quoting William Blake.'

'Blake was a visionary,' said Annie. 'A poet and an artist. He didn't take drugs.'

'I know that. I'm just trying to explain the prevalent attitudes as I understand them. Look, when everyone's weird, just how weird do you have to be to get noticed?'

'I'd say staring into space when you're supposed to be playing keyboards is a pretty good place to start, not to mention beating up your girlfriend.'

'I agree there's no excuse for violence, but people still turn a blind eye, even the victims themselves sometimes. And there was a lot of tolerance within the community for drug consumption, bad trips and suchlike. As for the rest, odd behaviour, especially on stage, might just have been regarded as nonconformist or avant garde theatrics. They say that Syd Barrett from Pink Floyd once put a whole jar of Brylcreem on his head before a performance, and during the show it melted and dripped down his face. People thought it was some sort of artistic statement, not a symptom of insanity. Don't forget, there were so many weird influences at play. Dadaism, surrealism, nihilism. If John Cage could write four minutes and thirty-three seconds of silence, who's to say Greaves wasn't doing something similar by not playing? You ought to know this, given your Bohemian background. Did nobody at your dad's place ever paint a blank canvas?'

'I was just a kid,' said Annie, 'but I do remember we had more than our fair share of freaks around. My dad used to protect me from them, though. You'd be surprised in some ways how conservative my upbringing was. They went out of their way to instil "normal" values in me. It was as if they didn't want me to be too different, like them.'

'They probably didn't want you to be singled out and picked on at school.'

'Ha! Then it didn't help. The other kids still thought I was a freak. How did the Mad Hatters survive all this?'

'Their manager Chris Adams pulled it all together. He

brought a replacement in, fiddled with the band's sound and image a bit and, wham, they were off.'

'How did he change them?'

'Instead of another keyboards player, he brought in a female vocalist. Their sound became more commercial, more pop, without losing its sixties edge entirely. They just got rid of that juvenile psychedelia. That's probably the way you remember them, the nice harmonies. Anyway, the rest is history. They conquered America, became a big stadium band, youth anthems and all that. By the time they released their fourth album in 1973 they were megastars. Not all their new fans were aware of their early roots, but then not everyone knows that Fleetwood Mac were a decent blues band before Stevie Nicks and "Rhiannon" and all that crap.'

'Hey, watch what you're calling crap! I happen to like "Rhiannon".'

Banks smiled. 'Sorry,' he said. 'I should have known.'

'Snob.'

'Anyway, that's the Mad Hatters' story. And you say the girlfriend—'

'Melanie Wright.'

'Melanie Wright said that Nick thought he'd got his teeth into a juicy story and that she felt it was somehow personal to him.'

'Yes. And he mentioned murder. Don't forget that.'

'I haven't,' said Banks. 'Whose murder did he mean?'

'At a guess, from what you've just told me, I'd say Robin Merchant's, wouldn't you?'

Tuesday, 16 September 1969

'I want to apologise to you about that Mad Hatters LP,' Chadwick said to DS Enderby, over a late breakfast in the canteen on Tuesday morning. Geoff Broome had come up with an address on Bayswater Terrace, Enderby had driven down from Brimleigh, and they were fortifying themselves with bacon and eggs before the visit.

'It's all right, sir,' said Enderby. 'I got Pink Floyd to sign my copy of *More* last weekend. As a matter of fact, the Mad Hatters and even Floyd aren't really my cup of tea. I'm more of a blues man, myself.'

'Blues?'

'Howlin' Wolf, Muddy Waters, Chicken Shack, John Mayall.'

'Right,' said Chadwick, still no wiser. 'Anyway, I'm sorry. It was wrong of me.'

'You were probably right, though, about not being seen accepting gifts.'

'Well, I'd feel a bit better about saying that if I hadn't gone and given it to my daughter.'

'You did what, sir?'

Chadwick looked away. 'I gave it to my daughter. A few bridges to build, you know.'

Enderby burst out laughing. 'I'm sorry, sir,' he said. 'What did she say?'

'She seemed a bit shocked, but she was very grateful.'

'I hope she enjoys it.'

'She will. She likes them. And again . . . you know . . .'

'Don't worry about it, sir. Probably the best use for it. I'm only glad I didn't get them to sign it to me.'

'Look, Enderby, about these young people. You seem to take them in your stride, but they stick in my craw.'

'I'd noticed that, sir. It's just a matter of perspective.'

'But I don't understand them at all.'

'They're just kids, mostly, having a good time. Some of them are political, and that can become violent if they mix with the wrong types, and now that unscrupulous dealers have moved in on the drugs trade, that can be dangerous, too. A lot of them are confused by the world, and they're looking for answers. Maybe we think they're looking in all the wrong places, but they're looking. What's so wrong with wanting peace in the world?'

'Nothing. But most of them come from decent homes, have parents who love them. Why on earth do they want to run off and live in filthy squats and squalid bedsits?'

'You really don't get it, do you, sir?'

'That's why I'm asking you, damnit.'

'Freedom. You know yourself how parents often disapprove of what their kids do and prevent them doing it. These kids don't mind a bit of dirt and mess as long as they can come and go as they please.'

'But what about the drugs, the sex?'

'That's what they want! I mean, they couldn't smoke pot and have sex if they lived with their parents, could they?'

Chadwick shook his head.

'It's more than that, though,' Enderby went on. 'Especially in the north. A lot of kids, girls like Linda Lofthouse, for example, they see a pretty bleak future waiting for them. Marriage, babies, dirty nappies, washing, cooking, a life of drudgery, slavery, even. It can look a lot like a prison, if you've got a bit of imagination and intelligence, as it seems she had. And it's not that much different for the blokes. Same boring job at the factory, day in day out, down at the same old pub with your same old cronies night after night. Footie on Saturdays, telly most nights. If they catch a glimpse of something else, if they've got a bit about them, you can see how it might appeal. An escape, perhaps. Something new. Something different.'

'But marriage and family are the cornerstones of our civilisation.'

'I know that, sir. I'm just trying to answer your question. Put myself in their shoes. Marriage and family are our traditional values. A lot of kids today argue against them, say that's why the world's in the trouble it's in. War. Famine. Greed. And girls, these days, think there ought to be more for them in life. They want to work, for example, and get paid as much as men for doing the same job.'

'They'll be after our jobs before long.'

'I wouldn't be too surprised, sir.'

'Freedom, eh?' said Chadwick. 'Is that what it's all about?'

'I think so, sir. A lot of it, at any rate. Freedom to think what you want and do what you want. The rest is just trappings, icing on the cake.'

'But what about responsibility? What about consequences?'

'They're young, sir. Indestructible and immortal. They don't worry too much about those sorts of things.'

'I thought freedom was what I was fighting for in the war.'

'It was, sir. And we won.'

'And this is the result?'

Enderby shrugged.

'All right,' said Chadwick. 'I take your point. We'll just have to live with it, then, won't we? Another fried slice?'

'Don't mind if I do, sir.'

10

It was raining when Chadwick and Enderby paid their visit to Bayswater Terrace, and the rows of slate-roofed, red-brick houses were suitably gloomy. DI Broome had found the number of the house they wanted easily enough. It wasn't known as a drug house especially, though Broome had no doubt that drugs were consumed there, but the police had been looking for a dealer who had slipped through their net a few months ago, and they had visited all his possible known haunts, including this house, rented by a Dennis Nokes since early 1967. According to their information, the occupancy turnover was pretty high and included students, hippies and general layabouts. Nokes described himself as a student and a musician, but as far as anyone knew he was on the dole.

After the previous day's exhausting session with the Mad Hatters, Chadwick wasn't looking forward to the interview. Also, he hadn't been certain when was the best time to call to find somebody home. In the end he decided it didn't matter so they went around lunch-time. Either these people didn't work or they were students, and the university term hadn't started yet, so the odds were that someone would be there at almost any time of the day or night.

Chadwick could hear the sound of a solo acoustic guitar coming from inside the house, which was encouraging. It stopped when Enderby knocked on the door, and they could hear someone shuffling down the hall. It turned out to be a young girl, surely no older than Yvonne, wearing only a long grubby white T-shirt with a target on the front, which hardly covered her bare thighs. The top did nothing much to hide her breasts, either, as she clearly wasn't wearing a bra.

'Police,' Enderby said. They showed their warrant cards and introduced themselves.

She didn't looked scared or nervous, merely puzzled. 'Police? Yeah. Right. OK. Come in, then.' And she stood aside. When they were all inside the hall, she reached her arms in the air, pulling up the T-shirt even higher, and yawned. As he averted his gaze, Chadwick could see that Enderby made no effort to do likewise, that he was gazing with open admiration at her exposed thighs and pubic hair.

'You woke me up,' the girl said. 'I was having a nice dream.'

'Who is it, Julie?' came a voice from upstairs, followed by a young man peering down from the landing, a guitar in his hand.

'Police,' said Julie.

'OK, right, just a minute.' There was a short pause while the young man disappeared back into his room, then visited the toilet. Chadwick thought he could hear a few quid's worth of marijuana flushing away. If he'd been Drugs Squad, the young lad wouldn't have stood a chance.

When he came down he was without his guitar. 'What can I do for you?' he asked.

'Are you Dennis Nokes?'

'Yes.'

'We'd like to talk to you. Is there somewhere we can go?'

Nokes gestured towards the rear. 'Kitchen. Julie's crashing in the front room. Go back to bed, Julie. It's OK. I'll take care of it.'

Chadwick could just about make out a sleeping-bag, or a pile of blankets, on the floor before the door closed.

The kitchen was cleaner than Chadwick would have expected, but Janet would definitely have turned up her nose and gone at it with the Ajax and Domestos. The chairs were covered with some sort of red plastic material that had cracked and lined like parchment over time, and the table with a red and white checked oilcloth. On it lay a magazine called *Oz* with a photograph of a white man embracing a naked black man on the cover. Beside that stood an open jar of marmalade, rim encrusted with dried syrup, a half-wrapped slab of Lurpak butter and some breadcrumbs. Nearby were a bottle of Camp coffee, salt and pepper shakers, a packet of Coco Krispies and a half-empty bottle of milk. Not to mention the overflowing ashtray to which Dennis Nokes, by the look of it, was soon to add.

They sat down and Enderby took out his notebook and pen.

'It's only tobacco,' Nokes said, as he rolled a cigarette. He had a tangle of curly dark hair and finely chiselled, almost pixieish, features, and wore an open-necked blue shirt with jeans and sandals. A necklace of tiny multi-coloured beads hung round his neck, while a silver bracelet engraved with various occult symbols encircled his left wrist.

'It had better be,' Chadwick said. 'Pity you had to flush everything you had down the toilet when that's not what I came about.'

It only lasted a moment, but Chadwick noticed the flash of annoyance before Nokes gave a practised shrug. 'I've got nothing to hide from the fuzz.'

'While we're talking,' said Chadwick, 'let's agree on a few ground rules. It's not "fuzz", or "pigs", it's DI Chadwick and DS Enderby. OK?'

'Whatever you want,' Nokes agreed, lighting the cigarette.

'Right. I'm glad we've got that out of the way. Now, let's get to the real subject of our visit. Linda Lofthouse.'

'Linda?'

'Yes. I assume you've heard the news?'

'Bummer, man,' said Nokes. 'I was trying to write a song for her when you guys arrived. It's OK, I mean, I'm not blaming you for interrupting me or anything. It wasn't going very well.'

'Sorry to hear that,' said Chadwick. 'I don't suppose you thought for a moment to come forward with information?'

'Why, man? I haven't seen Linda in a while.'

'When was the last time?'

'Summer. July, I think. Same time Rick was up.'

'Rick?'

'Rick Hayes, man. He put on the festival.'

'Was he with Linda Lofthouse in July?'

'Not *with* her, just here at the same time.'

'Did they know one another well?'

'They'd met, I think. Linda's cousin's Vic Greaves, you know, the keyboard player in the Mad Hatters, and Rick promoted some of their gigs in London.'

'Were they going out together?'

'No way, man.' Nokes laughed. 'Linda and Rick? You must be joking. She was way out of his league.'

'I thought he made plenty of money from the concerts.'

'It's not about money, man. Is that all you people ever think of?'

'So what was it about?'

'It was a spiritual thing. Linda was an old soul. Spiritually she was lifetimes ahead of Rick.'

'I see,' said Chadwick. 'But they *were* here at the same time?'

'Yes. That time. Linda crashed here but Rick was staying in a hotel in town. Didn't stop him trying to pick up some bird to take back with him, but he ended up going alone.'

'Why was he here?'

'I used to know him a few years ago when I lived in London. We're sort of old mates, I suppose. Anyway, he'd come up to check out something at Brimleigh Glen for the festival, so he dropped by to see me.'

Chadwick filed all that information away for his next talk with Rick Hayes, who was proving even more of a liar than he had at first appeared. 'You say Linda hasn't been here since July?'

'That's right.'

'Have you seen her since then?'

'No.'

'Were you at Brimleigh?'

'Of course. Rick scored us some free tickets.'

'Did you see her there?'

'No.'

'Where were you between one and one twenty on Sunday night?'

'How do you expect me to remember that?'

'Led Zeppelin had just started, if that refreshes your memory.'

'Yeah, right. I sat through the whole set in the same place. We were in the middle, quite near the front. We got there early on Friday and staked out a good space.'

'Who was with you?'

Nokes nodded towards the front room. 'Julie there, and the others from the house. There were five of us in all.'

'I'll need names.'

'Sure. There was me, Julie, Martin, Rob and Cathy.'

'Full names, please, sir,' DS Enderby interrupted. Nokes gave him a pitying look and told him.

'Are any of the others at home now?' Chadwick asked.

'Only Julie.'

'We'll send someone over later to take statements. Now, about Linda. Did she stay here around the time of the festival?'

'No. She knows she's welcome any time she wants, man. She doesn't have to ask, just turn up. But I don't know where she was staying. Maybe in a tent or out on the field or something. Maybe she was with someone. Maybe they had a car. I don't know, man. All I know is this is freaking me out.'

'Stay calm, Mr Nokes. Try a few deep breaths. I hear it works wonders.'

Nokes glared at him. 'You're taking the piss.'

'Not at all.'

'This is *very* upsetting.'

'What? That Linda was murdered or that you're being questioned?'

Nokes ran the end of his index figure over some grains of salt on the tablecloth. 'All of it, man. It's just so heavy. You're laying a real trip on us, and you're way off course. We're into making love, not killing.'

His whiny voice was starting to grate on Chadwick. 'Tell me about Linda.'

'What about her?'

'When did you first meet?'

'Couple of years ago. Not long after I moved here, May, June 1967, around then.'

'And you came up from London?'

'Yeah. I was living down there until early 'sixty-seven. I'd seen the sort of stuff that was happening, and thought I could make some of it happen up here. Those were really exciting times – great music, poetry readings, light shows, happenings. Revolution was in the air, man.'

'Back to Linda. How did you meet?'

'In town, in a record shop. We were both looking through the folk section, and we got talking. She was so alone. I mean, she was changing, but she didn't know it, trying to find herself, didn't know how to go about it. Like a caterpillar turning into a butterfly. Know what I mean?'

'So you helped her to find herself?'

'I invited her round here from time to time. I gave her a few books – Leary, Gurdjieff, Alan Watts. Played music for her. We talked a lot.'

'Did you sleep with her?'

'No way. She was six months pregnant.'

'Drugs?'

'Of course not.'

'How long did she stay here?'

'Not very long. After she'd had the baby she came here for a while, maybe a month or two the winter of 'sixty-seven, then she went to London early in 'sixty-eight. After that she'd crash here when she was up visiting.'

'What did she do?'

'What do you mean?'

'Work? Earn a living? Did she have a job?'

'Oh, that shit. Well, she didn't when I first met her, of course. She was still living with her parents. Then the baby . . . Anyway, she made really beautiful jewellery, but I don't think she got much money for it. Gave most of it away. Clothes, too. She could fix anything, and make a shirt from any old scraps of material. She was into fashion, did some of her own designs.'

'So how did she make money?'

'She worked in a shop. Biba. It's pretty well known. They just moved to Kensington High Street. Do a lot of thirties nostalgia stuff. You know the sort of thing – all floppy hats, ostrich feathers and long satin dresses in plum and pink.'

'Do you happen to know her address in London?'

Nokes gave him an address in Notting Hill.

'Did she live alone or share?'

'Alone. But she had a good friend living in the same house, across the hall. Came up here with Linda once or twice. American girl. Her name's Tania Hutchison.'

'What does she look like?'

'Like a dream. I mean, she's a negative image of Linda,

man, but just as beautiful in her own way. She's got long dark hair, really long, you know. And she has a dark complexion, like she's half Mexican or something. And white teeth. But all Americans have white teeth, don't they?'

It sounded like the girl Robin Merchant had described. So, what, if anything, did Tania Hutchison have to do with Linda Lofthouse's murder?

There was nothing more to be got from Dennis Nokes, so Chadwick gave Enderby the signal to wrap up the interview. He would send someone to talk to the others later. He didn't really think that Nokes and his pals had had anything to do with Linda Lofthouse's murder, but now at least he knew where she had been living, and this Tania woman might be able to tell him something about Linda's recent life. And death.

Before heading to interview Vic Greaves the following day, Banks first called at Swainsview Lodge out of curiosity, to soak up the atmosphere. He got the keys from the estate agent, who told him they had kept the place locked up tight since there had been reports from local farmers of someone breaking in. She thought it was probably just kids, but the last thing they needed, she said, was squatters or travellers occupying the place.

In the cold and draughty hallway, Banks felt as if he were venturing into one of those creepy mansions from the old Roger Corman films of Poe stories, the *Fall of the House of Usher*, or something. The long wainscoted hallway had panelled doors opening off each side, and there were obvious spaces on the walls where paintings had once hung. Banks tried some of the doors and found they opened to empty rooms in varied states of disrepair. Bits of ceiling had crumbled, and a veneer of plaster-dust lay over everything. Banks kicked up clouds of it as he walked, and it made him cough, dried his mouth.

At the end of the hall, a moth-eaten, dusty old curtain covered French windows. Banks fiddled for the key and opened them. They led out to a broad, empty balcony. Banks walked out and leaned against the cool stone of the balustrade to admire the view. Below him lay the empty granite and marble swimming-pool, its dark bottom clogged with weeds, lichen and rubbish. Lower down the hillside, the trees on the banks of the river Swain were red, brown and yellow. Some of the leaves blew off and swirled in the wind as Banks watched. Sheep grazed in the fields of the opposite daleside, dots of white on green among the irregular patterns of drystone walls. The clouds were so low they grazed the limestone outcrops along the top and shrouded the upper moorland in mist.

Wrapping his arms round himself against the autumn chill, Banks went back inside the building and headed downstairs to the lower level, where he found himself in a cavernous room that he guessed must have been used as the recording studio. So this was where the Mad Hatters had recorded their break-through second album during the winter of 1969–70, and several others over the years. There was no equipment left, of course, but there were still a few strips of wire lying around, along with a broken drumstick, and what looked like a guitar string. Banks strained but could hear no echoes of events or music long past.

He unlocked the doors and walked out to the edge of the swimming-pool. There was broken glass on the courtyard and bottles and cans at the bottom of the pool, where it sloped down to the deep end. Banks saw what the estate agent meant, and guessed that local kids must have climbed the wall and had a party. He wondered if they knew the house's history. Maybe they were celebrating Robin Merchant the way the kids flocked to Jim Morrison's tomb in the Père Lachaise cemetery in Paris. Banks doubted it. He thought he heard a sound behind him, in the abandoned recording studio, and turned in time to see a mouse skitter through the dust.

He tried to imagine the scene on that summer night thirty-five years ago. There would have been music, and probably lights strung up outside round the pool. Incense. Drugs, of course, and alcohol, too. By the early seventies booze was coming back into fashion among the younger generation. There would also have been girls, half undressed or more, perhaps, laughing, dancing, making love. And when everyone was sated, Robin Merchant had . . . Well, what *had* happened? Banks didn't know yet. Kevin Templeton was still in the basement of Western Area Headquarters going through the archives.

A gust of wind rattled the open door and Banks went back inside. There was nothing for him here except ghosts. Lord Jessop was dead of Aids, poor sod, and Robin Merchant had drowned in the swimming-pool. The rest of the Mad Hatters were still very much alive, though, and Vic Greaves was around somewhere. If he would talk. If he *could* talk. Banks didn't know exactly what the official diagnosis was, only that everyone claimed he'd taken too much acid and gone over the top. Well, in a short while, with a little skill and a little luck, he would find out.

Wednesday, 17 September 1969

It was a long time since Chadwick had walked along the Portobello Road. Wartime, in fact, once when he had been back on leave between assignments. He was sure the street had been narrower then. And there had been sandbags, blackout curtains, empty shop windows, rubble from bomb damage, the smell of ash, fractured gas lines and sewage pipes. Now the biggest mess was caused by construction on the Westway, an overhead motorway that was almost completed, and most of the smells were exotic spices that reminded him of his days in India and Burma.

Chadwick had taken the afternoon train down to King's Cross, a journey of about five hours. Now it was early evening. The market had closed for the day; the stall-holders had packed up their wares and gone to one of the many local pubs. Outside the Duke of Wellington, a fire-eater entertained a small crowd. The atmosphere was lively, the people young and colourful in brightly printed fabrics, flared jeans with flowers embroidered on them, or gold-lamé kaftans. Some of the girls were wearing old-fashioned, wide-brimmed hats and long dresses trailing round their ankles. There were quite a few West Indians wandering the street, too, some also in bright clothes, with beards and fuzzy hairdos. Chadwick was sure he could smell marijuana in the air. He was also sure he looked quite out of place in his navy-blue suit, although one or two business types mingled with the crowds.

According to his map, there were quicker ways of getting to Powis Terrace than from the Notting Hill Underground station, but out of interest he had wanted to wander up and down Portobello Road. He had heard so much about it, from the Notting Hill race riots of over ten years ago to the notorious slum landlord Peter Rachman, connected to both the Kray twins and the Profumo affair of 1963. The area had history.

Now the street was full of chic boutiques, hairdressers and antiques shops with bright-painted façades. There was even a local flea-pit called the Electric Cinema, showing a double-bill of *Easy Rider* and *Girl on a Motorcycle*. One shop, Alice's Antiques, sold Edwardian policemen's capes, and for a moment Chadwick was tempted to buy one. But he knew he wouldn't wear it: it would just hang at the back of his wardobe until the moths got at it.

Chadwick turned down Colville Terrace and finally found

the street he was looking for. At the end of the block someone had drawn graffiti depicting Che Guevara, and underneath the bearded face and beret were the words LONG LIVE THE REVOLUTION in red paint, imitating dripping blood. The terraced houses, once-majestic four-storey Georgian-style stucco, were now dirty white, with stained and graffiti-covered façades – THE ROAD OF EXCESS LEADS TO THE PALACE OF WISDOM and CRIME IS THE HIGHEST FORM OF SENSUALITY. Rubbish littered the street. Each house had a low black-metal railing and gate, which led down murky stone steps to the basement flat. The broad stairs leading up to the front door were flanked by two columns supporting a portico. Most of the doors looked badly in need of a paint job. Chadwick had heard that the houses were all divided into a warren of bedsits.

Several names were listed beside the intercom at the house he wanted. Chadwick had timed his visit for early evening, thinking that might be the best time to find Tania Hutchison at home. The problem was that he didn't want her to be warned of his visit. If she had had anything to do with Linda's murder, there was a chance she would scarper the minute she heard his voice. He needed another way in.

Tania's flat, he noted, was number eight. He wondered how security conscious the other tenants were. If drugs were involved, probably very, though if someone was under the influence . . . He decided to start with the ground floor and, after getting no answer, went on up the list. Finally he was rewarded by a bad connection with an incomprehensible young man in flat five, who buzzed the door open.

The smell of cats' piss and onions was almost overwhelming, the floor was covered with drab, cracked lino and the stair carpet was threadbare. If it had had a pattern once, it was indiscernible from the dull grey background now. The walls were also bare, apart from a few telephone numbers scribbled round the shared payphone. Out of habit, Chadwick made a note of them.

Now he just had to find number eight. It wasn't on the ground floor, or the first, but on the second floor, facing the front. That landing had another shared payphone, and again Chadwick copied down the numbers. It smelt a little better up here, mostly due to the burning incense coming from one of the rooms, but the bulb was bare and cast a thankfully weak light on the shabby décor. Chadwick could hear soft music coming from inside number eight, guitars and flutes and some sort of Oriental percussion. A good sign.

He tapped on the door. A few moments later, it opened on the chain. He wasn't in yet, but he was close. 'Are you Tania Hutchison?' he asked.

'I'm Tania,' she said. 'Who wants to know?'

Chadwick thought he detected an American accent. Only a thin strip of her face showed, but he could see what Dennis Nokes had meant about her good looks. 'I'm Detective Inspector Chadwick,' he said, holding up his warrant card. 'It's about Linda Lofthouse.'

'Linda? Of course.'

'Do you mind if I come in?'

She looked at him for a moment – he could see only one eye – and he sensed she was calculating what was her best option. In the end the door shut, then opened all the way. 'All right,' she said.

Chadwick followed her into an L-shaped room, the smaller part of which was taken up with a tiny kitchen. The rest was sparsely furnished, perhaps because there was so little space. There was no carpet on the floor. A mattress covered with red cheesecloth and scattered with cushions lay against one wall, and in front of that stood a low glass table holding a vase of flowers, a copy of the *Evening Standard*, an ashtray and a book called *The Glass Bead Game* by Hermann Hesse. Chadwick had never heard of Hermann Hesse, but he had the feeling he would be safer sticking to Dick Francis, Alistair

MacLean and Desmond Bagley. An acoustic guitar leaned against one wall.

Tania stretched out on the mattress, leaning against the wall, and Chadwick grabbed one of the hard-backed kitchen chairs. The room seemed clean and bright, with a colourful abstract painting on the wall and a little light coming in through the sash window, but there was no disguising the essential decrepitude of the house and neighbourhood.

The woman was as Dennis Nokes and Robin Merchant had described her, petite, attractive, with white teeth and glossy dark hair down to her waist. She was wearing flared jeans and a thin cotton blouse that left little to the imagination. She reached for a packet of Pall Mall filter-tipped and lit one. 'I just found out yesterday,' she said, blowing out smoke. 'About Linda.'

'How?'

'The newspaper. I've been away.'

'How long?'

'Nine days.'

It made sense. Chadwick had only discovered Linda Lofthouse's identity from Carol Wilkinson on Saturday, so it hadn't really hit the papers and other news media until Monday, and now it was Wednesday, ten days since the Brimleigh festival had ended and the body was discovered. Looking at Tania, he could see that she had been crying: the tears had dried and crusted on her flawless olive skin, and her big green eyes were glassy.

'Where were you?' Chadwick asked.

'In France with my boyfriend. He's studying in Paris. The Sorbonne. I got back yesterday.'

'I assume we could check that?'

'Go ahead.' She gave him a name and a telephone number in Paris. It wasn't of much use to Chadwick. The guy was her boyfriend, after all, and he would probably swear black was white for her. But he had to go through the motions.

'You *were* at Brimleigh, though?'

'Sure.'

'That's what I want to talk about.'

Tania blew out some smoke and reached for the ashtray on the table, cradling it on her lap between crossed legs.

'What happened there?' Chadwick went on.

'What do you mean, "What happened there"? Lots of things happened there. It was a festival, a celebration.'

'Of what?'

'Youth. Music. Life. Love. Peace. Things you wouldn't understand.'

'Oh, I don't know,' said Chadwick. 'I was young once.' He was getting used to being criticised by these people for being old and square, and as it didn't bother him in the least, it seemed easier to brush it aside with a glib comment, like water off a duck's back. What he still didn't understand, though, despite Enderby's explanation, was why intelligent young people from good homes wanted to come to places like this and live in squalor, probably hardly eating a healthy meal from one day to the next. Were all the sex and drugs you wanted worth such a miserable existence?

Tania managed a little smile. 'It was different then.'

'You can say that again. Swing. Jitterbug. Glenn Miller. Tommy Dorsey. Henry Hall. Harry Roy. Nat Gonella. Al Bowlly. Real music. And the war, of course.'

'We choose not to fight in wars.'

'It must be nice to believe that you have a choice,' said Chadwick, feeling the anger rise the way it did when he heard such pat comments. He was keen to steer back to the topic at hand. They'd sidetrack you, these people, put you on the defensive, and before you knew it you'd be arguing about war and revolution. 'Look, I'd just like to know the story of you and Linda, how you came to be at Brimleigh, why you didn't leave together, what happened. Is that so difficult?'

'Not at all. We drove up on Sunday morning. I've got an old Mini.'

'Just the two of you?'

'That's about all you can fit into a Mini if you want to be comfortable.'

'And you were only there for the one day?'

'Yes. The Mad Hatters said they could get backstage passes for us, but only for the day they were there. That was Sunday. To be honest, we didn't feel like sitting around in a muddy field in Yorkshire for three days.'

That was about the first sensible thing Chadwick had heard a young person say in a long time. 'When did you arrive?'

'Early afternoon.'

'Were the Mad Hatters there already?'

'They were around.'

'What did you do?'

'Well, it was great, really. We got to park where the bands parked, and we could come and go as we pleased.'

'What was going on back there?'

'Music, mostly, believe it or not. When the bands were playing you could get round the front, into the press enclosure, if there was room – it had got the best view in the entire place.'

'The rest of the time?'

'It's sort of like a garden party round the back. You know, a beer tent, food, tables and chairs, someone plucking at a guitar, conversation, jamming, dancing. Like a big club and a restaurant rolled into one. It was a bit chaotic at times, especially between bands when the roadies were running back and forth, but mostly it was great fun.'

'I understand there were caravans for some of the stars.'

'People need privacy. And, you know, if you wanted somewhere to go and . . . Well, I don't have to spell it out, do I?'

'Did you go to a caravan with anyone?'

Her eyes widened and she flushed. 'That's hardly a question a gentleman would ask of a lady. And I can't see that it has any bearing on what happened to Linda.'

'So, nobody needed to go into the woods for privacy?'

'No. It was like we had our own little community, and there was no one there to lay down the law, to tell us what to do. A perfect anarchist state.'

Chadwick thought that was something of a contradiction in terms, but he didn't bother pointing it out. He didn't want to get sidetracked again. 'Who did you spend your time with?' he asked.

'Lots of people. I suppose I was with Chris Adams a fair bit. He's the Hatters' manager. A nice guy. Smart *and* sensitive.' She smiled. 'And not too stoned to have a decent conversation with.'

Interesting, Chadwick thought, that Adams hadn't mentioned this. But why would he? It would only connect him with events from which he wanted to distance himself and his group. 'Were you with him during Led Zeppelin's performance?'

Tania frowned. 'No. I was out front, in the press enclosure. I suppose he might have been there, but it was really crowded and dark. I don't remember seeing him.'

'You're American, I understand,' Chadwick said.

'Canadian, actually, but a lot of people make that mistake. And don't worry, I'm here legally, work permit and all. My parents were born here. Scotland. Strathclyde – my father was a professor at the university.'

A professor's daughter, no less. And no doubt they had moved to Canada because he was better paid over there. Even less reason, then, for Tania to be spending her days in a tiny, shabby bedsit in Notting Hill. 'So what about Linda?' he asked. 'Did she disappear into any caravans?'

'Not that I saw. Look, Linda got a bit claustrophobic,

developed a headache, and when Led Zeppelin came on, she told me she was going for a walk in the woods. I said I'd probably head home as soon as they finished because I wanted to catch a bit of sleep before taking the ferry over to see my boyfriend Jeff. She told me not to worry about her, she had friends she could stay with. I knew that. I'd been up with her before and met them. It was a place in Leeds where she used to live before she moved to London.'

'Bayswater Terrace?'

'That sounds right.'

'So she told you she'd stay there?'

'Not in so many words. Only that she wasn't planning on heading back to London with me that night.'

'Any reason?'

'I guess there were people she wanted to see. I mean, it was where she came from. Home.'

'Did you see any of these people from the house with her at the festival?'

'No. Like I said, we had backstage passes. We were in with the bands. We didn't know anybody there apart from Vic, Robin, Chris and the rest. Didn't even know them very well. Look, as you can imagine, it got a bit wild at times, like all parties do. Linda slipped away. I didn't see her again.'

'Did she have a flower painted on her face when she left you?'

Tania looked puzzled. 'I don't think so. I don't know. It was dark. I don't remember.'

'Would you have noticed?'

'Maybe. I don't know. Lots of girls had flowers painted on their faces. Is it important?'

'It could be.' Chadwick remembered Robin Merchant saying that Linda *did* have the flower on her face when he had last seen her. 'How was she going to get to Leeds? It was the middle of the night.'

'Hitch a ride. Plenty of people were heading that way. Most of the crowd came from Leeds or Bradford. Stands to reason.'

'Was this your original plan? For her to stay in Leeds, hitch a ride?'

'We didn't have a plan. It was all pretty spontaneous. She knew I was going to Paris on Monday and I had to drive back Sunday night, but she also knew she could come back to London with me in the Mini if she wanted.'

'And what did you do?'

'After Zeppelin finished, I went round the back again, hung around a while and waited for her. There was still a party going on backstage, but people were leaving fast. I didn't see her, so I assumed she'd headed off to Bayswater Terrace. I got in my car and drove back down here. It was about four in the morning by the time I left and I got home about nine. I slept till two, then drove to Dover and took the ferry to Calais.'

'You must have been tired.'

'Not really.'

'Don't you have a job?'

'I'm between jobs. I'm a temp. I happened to be good at typing at school. I can choose my own hours now.'

'But what about education? You said your father was a professor. Surely he would want you to go to university?'

She gave him a curious, almost pitying look. 'What my father wants doesn't come into it,' she said. 'It's my life. I might go to university one day, but it'll be when I want to, not when someone else decides for me.' Tania shook back her hair and lit another cigarette.

Chadwick thought he saw a mouse scurry across the kitchen floor. He gave a little shudder. It wasn't that mice scared him, but the idea of living with them held no appeal. 'I'd like to know more about Linda,' he said. 'I understand she was a shop girl?'

Tania laughed. ' "Shop girl." How very quaint and English.

I suppose you could say that. She worked at Biba, but she wanted to be a designer. She was good, too.'

'Wouldn't they be worried about her not coming back?'

'She took the week off.'

'So there was a plan?'

'There were possibilities, that's all. There were some people in St Ives she wanted to see. Maybe she was going to stay in Leeds a few days, see her friends and her mother, then go down there. I don't know. She also had a friend living on Anglesey she wanted to visit. What can I say? Linda was a spontaneous sort of person. She just did things. That's why I wasn't worried about her. Besides, you don't think . . . I mean, we were with people who are into love and peace and all that, and you just don't expect . . .' Tears ran down her cheek. 'I'm sorry,' she said. 'This is all too much.'

Chadwick gave her a few minutes to compose herself and wipe away the tears, then he said, 'When Linda left the enclosure for the woods, did you see anyone follow her?'

Tania thought for a moment, sucked at her cigarette and flicked some ash. 'No,' she said.

'Did you see anyone else go out around that time?'

'Not that I remember. Most of us were excited about Led Zeppelin, getting ready to go round the front and get our minds blown.'

'Could she have arranged to meet someone? Could the headache have been an excuse?'

Tania gave him a blank look. 'Why would she? If she'd been going to meet someone, she'd have said so. It wasn't Linda's way to be sly and sneaky.'

Christ, Chadwick thought, it was a lot easier when you were dealing with ordinary folk, most of whom lied and cheated as easily as they breathed, rather than this lot with their fancy ideals and high-handed attitudes. 'Did you notice anyone paying her undue attention?' he asked.

'Linda's a beautiful girl. Of course there were people talking to her, maybe trying to make an impression, pick her up.'

'But nobody succeeded?'

Tania paused. 'Linda wasn't seeing anyone this past while,' she answered. 'Look, I've seen what you read in the newspapers about us. The *News of the World*, the *People*, trash like that. They paint us as a drug-addled, sex-crazed subculture, nothing but orgies and excess. Well, some people might be like that, but Linda was a spiritual person. She was into Buddhism, the caballa, yoga, astrology, tarot, all sorts of spiritual stuff, and sometimes she just . . . you know . . . sex wasn't always a part of it for her.'

'And drugs?'

'Out of the picture, too. I'm not saying she'd never smoked a joint or dropped a tab of acid, but not for a while. She was moving on, evolving.'

'I understand the two of you performed musical duets together?'

Tania looked at him as if she didn't understand, then managed a brief smile. '*Performed musical duets?* We sang together sometimes, if that's what you mean, in folk clubs and such.'

'Can I have a look at Linda's flat?'

Tania bit her lip. 'I don't know. I shouldn't. I mean . . .'

'You can come with me, keep an eye on me. It'll have to be done eventually. Officially.'

Finally, Tania said, 'OK. I've got a key. Come on.'

She led him across the hall. Linda's room was the same shape as Tania's, but like a mirror-image. It was more luxuriously furnished, with a couple of patterened rugs on the floor and a stylised painting of a man sitting cross-legged under a tree, surrounded by strange symbols on a wall. Chadwick recognised the signs of the zodiac from the newspaper horoscopes Janet read. There was also a small bookcase full of volumes on mysticism and the spiritual life, and packs of variously scented joss-sticks. An acoustic guitar, similar to the one in Tania's room, leaned against the wall.

Linda also had a record-player, and beside it a stack of LPs similar to those Yvonne had. There was nothing really personal in the room, at least not that Chadwick could find. One drawer held a couple of letters from her mother and some old photographs taken with her father. There were no diaries or notebooks – whatever she had been carrying with her at Brimleigh had disappeared – and very little else apart from her birth certificate and a post-office book showing that she had £123 13*s*. 5*d*. in her account, which seemed rather a lot to Chadwick. She had also set up a sewing-machine at a make-shift table, and a few bolts of printed fabric lay around. In her small wardrobe hung many long dresses and skirts in colourful fabrics.

He searched under the drawers and tried the cupboards and wardrobe for false bottoms but found nowhere that might have provided a good hiding-place for drugs. If Tania knew this was what he was doing, she didn't say anything. She just leaned against the door jamb with her arms folded.

As far as food was concerned, the pickings were slim. Linda had no oven, only a gas-burner beside the little sink, and the contents of her cupboard consisted of brown rice, chick peas, muesli, tahini, mung beans, herbs and spices. There was no refrigerator, either, and no sign of meat, vegetables or dairy products, except a bottle of sterilised milk on the table. Frugal living indeed.

Frustrated, Chadwick stood by the door and gave one last look around. Still nothing.

'What will happen to it now?' Tania asked.

'I suppose it'll be re-let eventually,' he said. 'For the moment I'll get the local police to come in and seal it off until we've done a thorough search. What do you know about Rick Hayes?'

Tania locked Linda's door and led Chadwick back to her room, where they resumed their previous positions.

'Rick Hayes, the promoter?'

'That's the one.'

'Nothing much. I chatted with him a couple of times. He's a bit of a creep. If you must know, he tried to pick me up, suggested we go to his caravan.'

'And?'

'I told him to get lost.'

'How did he react?'

'He laughed and said he liked a girl who spoke her mind. Look, Hayes is one of those men who asks every girl he meets to sleep with him. He thinks the odds are pretty good. If nine out of ten tell him what they think of him, or slap his face, there's always the tenth who might say yes.'

'He knew Linda, is that right?'

'They'd met before, yes. Once we went backstage at a Mad Hatters concert at the Roundhouse and Rick was there. He's harmless enough, really. To be honest, he's far too taken with himself to give much thought to anyone else.'

'But if someone he wanted turned him down, do you think he could get violent?'

Tania gave him a sharp look. 'I . . . I don't know,' she said. 'I've never really thought about it. He's got a bit of a temper. I saw him laying into one of the security guards, but that was just . . . I don't know, some sort of a power trip, I thought. You're not suggesting he might have killed Linda because she wouldn't let him fuck her?'

If the word was meant to shock Chadwick, it did. He wasn't used to such language coming from the mouths of lovely young women. He was damned if he was going to give her the satisfaction of a reaction, though. 'Did you see him leave the enclosure during the time you were there?'

'No. Mostly he was co-ordinating the performers and

roadies, making sure the equipment got set up right and everything went smoothly. There were a few problems with the PA system and so on that he also had to deal with. And he acted as MC, introducing the artists. He was pretty busy all the time. I don't think he'd have had a chance to slip away even if he'd wanted to.'

'So he was always in sight?'

'Pretty much – not always, but most of the time you'd see him out the corner of your eye here and there, running around. There was always somebody wanting him for something.'

'Where was he while Linda was in the woods?'

'I don't know. Like I told you, I went round to the front to get a good view.'

'Was he there?'

'No. He introduced the band, then left the stage.'

'Did you see him after that?'

'Come to think of it, no. But I don't believe it. I don't believe he could have had anything to do with what happened.'

'Probably not,' said Chadwick, standing to leave. 'It just pays to cover all the angles, that's all.' He lingered at the door. 'Before I leave, tell me how Linda was behaving these past few weeks.'

'What do you mean?'

'Did anything out of the ordinary happen?'

'No.'

'Was she upset, depressed or worried about anything?'

'No, she was her usual self. She was saving up to go to India. She was really excited about that.'

Chadwick, who had spent time in India before seeing action in Burma during the war, didn't understand what there was to get excited about. As far as he was concerned the place was filthy, hot and insanitary. Still, it explained the reason for the £123 13*s*. 5*d*. in her post-office account. 'Is that all?'

'As far as I know.'

'Had she fought or argued with anyone recently?'

'Not that I know. I doubt it, anyway.'

'Why's that?'

'Linda didn't like scenes or arguments. She was a peaceful person, easy-going.'

'Did anyone threaten her in any way?'

'Good Lord, no.'

'Was anybody bothering her?'

'No. The only thing that was at all upsetting her was Vic Greaves. They weren't close or anything, but they *were* family, and on the two or three occasions we saw the Mad Hatters, he seemed to be getting worse. She thought he ought to be getting treatment, but whenever she mentioned it to Chris, he just said shrinks were government brainwashers and mental hospitals were prisons for the true visionaries. I suppose he had a point.'

'Did either you or Linda try to do anything about Greaves?'

'What do you mean?'

'Persuade him to get treatment.'

'Linda did once, but he refused point blank.'

'Did you try to change Chris Adams's mind?'

'It wasn't his decision,' Tania said. 'Look, nobody was going to be party to getting Vic Greaves certified. Simple as that.'

'I see,' said Chadwick. The decision didn't surprise him after the time he had spent with the Mad Hatters. Soon he would be talking to them again anyway. He opened the door and went into the hall. 'Many thanks, Miss Hutchison.'

'No problem.'

'I must say you seem to be one of the most sensible people I've talked to since all this began.'

Tania gave him an enigmatic smile. 'Don't count on it,' she said. 'Appearances can be deceptive.'

Thursday, 18 September 1969

Perhaps it was the spices he had smelt in Portobello Road that sparked it – they say smell is closest to memory – or maybe it was even going to see the *Battle of Britain* after his visit to Tania Hutchison that brought it all back, but Chadwick awoke in his hotel bed at three a.m. in a cold sweat. He couldn't say that it was a dream because it had actually happened, but he had buried it so deeply in his subconscious that when it rose up, as it did from time to time, it did so in a jumble of images so vivid they were almost surreal.

Buried under two bodies, mouth and nose full of sand on Gold Beach, the air all smoke and fire, bullets cracking and thudding into the sand nearby, blood seeping through his uniform, the man on top of him whimpering as he died, crying for his mother. Charging the bunkers with Taffy in Burma. Taffy wounded, his guts poking out, stumbling forward into the gunfire, diving into the bunker of Japanese soldiers, knowing he was going to die and pulling the pin on his hand grenade. Bits of people raining down on Chadwick: an eyeball, brain, blood and tissue.

And so it went on, a series of fragmented nightmare images from the Burmese jungle and the Normandy beaches. He not only saw and heard but *smelt* it all again in his dream, the gunfire, smoke, heat, tasted the sand in his mouth.

He feared that there would be no more sleep tonight, so he sat up, took the glass of water he had left on his bedside table and drank it, then went to refill it. Still hours to go until dawn. And these were the worst hours, the hours when his fears got the better of him. The only solution was to get up and do something to take his mind off it. He wasn't going to go walking around King's Cross at this hour in the morning, so he turned on the bedside light, took Alistair MacLean's *Force Ten from Navarone* out of his overnight bag and settled back on the pillows to read. By the time the pale glow of sunrise started spreading over the city from the east, his book had fallen on to his chest and he was snoring quietly in a dreamless sleep.

II

In a village like Lyndgarth, Banks knew, the best way to find out about any resident was to ask at the local pub or post office. In the case of Vic Greaves, it was Jean Murray, in the post office-cum-newsagent, who directed him towards the last cottage on the left on Darlington Road, telling him that 'Mr Jones' had been there for a few years now, was definitely a bit strange, not quite right in the head, but that he seemed harmless enough, and he always paid his paper bill on time. He was a bit of a recluse, she added, and he didn't like visitors. She had no idea what he did with his time, but there had been no complaints about him. Her daughter, Susan, added that he had few visitors, but she had seen a couple of cars come and go. She couldn't describe them.

Banks left his car parked on the cobbles by the village green. It was another miserable day, with wind and rain from the east, and the flagstone roofs of the houses looked as dark green as moss-pools. Bare tree branches waved beyond the TV aerials, and beyond them lay the washed-out backdrop of a dishwater-grey sky.

At the top right of the village green between the old Burgundy Hotel and the dark, squat Methodist chapel, a narrow lane led down towards a wooded beck. On each side there was a terrace of one-up-one-down limestone cottages that had once housed farm labourers. Banks stood for a moment in front of the end one on the left and listened. He could hear no sign of life, see no lights. The downstairs curtains were closed, but the upstairs ones were open, as were the windows.

Finally he knocked on the door.

Nothing happened, so he knocked again, harder this time.

When it seemed that no one was going to answer, the door opened and a figure stood there, looking anxious. It was hard to say whether it was Vic Greaves or not, as Banks only had the old group photographs to go by, when Greaves had been a promising twenty-something rock star. Now he must be in his late fifties, Banks thought, but he looked much older. Round-shouldered with a sagging stomach the size of a football, he wore a black T-shirt with a silver Harley Davidson on the front, baggy jeans and no shoes or socks. His eyes were bruised and hollow, his dry skin pale and lined. He was either bald or shaved his head regularly, which accentuated the boniness of his cheeks and the hollowness of his eyes. He looked ill to Banks, and light years from the pretty young boy all the girls had adored, who had set the Mad Hatters' career in motion.

'I'm looking for Vic Greaves,' Banks said.

'He's not here today,' the man said, his expression un-changing.

'Are you sure?' Banks asked.

This seemed to puzzle the man and cause him some distress. 'He might have been. He might have been, if he hadn't been trying to go home. But his car's broken down. The wheels won't work.'

'Pardon?'

Suddenly the man smiled, revealing stained, crooked teeth, with the odd gap here and there, and said, 'He's nothing to do with me.' Then he turned and walked back inside the house, leaving the door wide open. Puzzled, Banks followed him. The door led straight into the front room, the same as it did in Banks's own cottage. Because the curtains were closed, downstairs was in semi-darkness, but even in the poor light Banks could see that the room was cluttered with piles of books, newspapers and magazines. There was a slight odour of sour milk about the place, and of cheese that had been left out of the fridge too long, but a better smell mingled with it: olive oil, garlic and herbs.

Banks followed the man through to the back, which was the kitchen, where a bit more light filtered in through the grimy windows and past half-open floral curtains. Inside, the place was spotlessly clean and neat, all the pots and pans gleaming on wall hooks, dishes and cups sparkling in glass-fronted cupboards. Whatever Greaves's problem was – and Banks believed he was Greaves – it didn't stop him taking care of his home better than most bachelors Banks had known. The man stood with his back to Banks, stirring a pot on the gas range.

'Are you Vic Greaves?' Banks asked.

No answer.

'Look,' said Banks, 'I'm a police officer. DCI Banks. Alan, my name is Alan. I need to talk to you. Are you Vic Greaves?'

The man half turned. 'Alan?' he said, peering curiously at Banks. 'I don't know who you are. I don't know any Alans. I *don't* know you, do I?'

'I just told you. I'm a police officer. No, you don't know me.'

'They weren't really meant to grow so high, you know,' the man said, turning back to his pot. 'Sometimes the rain does good things.'

'What?'

'The hillsides drink it.'

Banks tried to position himself so that he could see the man's face. When the man half turned again and saw him, he looked surprised. 'What are you doing here?' he asked, as if he had genuinely forgotten Banks's presence.

'I told you. I'm a policeman. I want to ask you some

questions about Nick Barber. He did come and talk to you, didn't he? Do you remember?'

The man shook his head, and his face turned sad for a moment. 'Vic's gone down to the woods today,' he said.

'Vic Greaves is in the woods?' Banks asked. 'Who are you?'

'No,' he said. 'He had to get some stuff, you know, he needed it for the stew.'

'You went to the woods earlier?'

'He sometimes walks there on nice days. It's peaceful. He likes to listen to the birds and look at the leaves and the mushrooms.'

'Do you live here alone?'

He sighed. 'I'm just passing through.'

'Tell me about Nick Barber.'

He stopped stirring and faced Banks, his expression still blank, unreadable. 'Someone came here.'

'That's right. His name was Nick Barber. When did he come? Do you remember?'

The man said nothing, just stared at Banks in a disturbing way. Banks was beginning to feel thoroughly unnerved. Was Greaves off his face on drugs or something? Was he likely to turn violent? If so, there was a handy rack of kitchen knives within his reach. 'Look,' he said, 'Nick Barber is dead. Somebody killed him. Can you remember anything about what he said?'

'Vic's gone down to the woods today,' he said again.

'Yes, but this man, Nick Barber. What did he ask you about? Was it about Robin Merchant's death? Was it about Swainsview Lodge?'

The man put his hands over his ears and hung his head. 'Vic can't hear this,' he said. 'Vic *won't* hear this.'

'Think. Surely you can remember? Do you remember Swainsview Lodge?'

But Greaves was counting now. 'One, two, three, four, five . . .'

Banks tried to talk, but the counting got louder. In the end, he gave up, turned away and left. He would have to come back. There had to be a way of getting some answers from Vic Greaves.

On his way out of the village, Banks passed a sleek silver Merc, but thought nothing of it. All the way back to the station he thought about the strange experience he had had, and even Pink Floyd's 'I Remember A Day' on the stereo could not dispel his gloom.

'Kev. What have you dug up?' Annie Cabbot asked, early that afternoon, when a dusty and clearly disgruntled DS Templeton trudged over to her desk and flopped down on the visitor's chair.

Templeton sighed. 'We ought to do something about that basement,' he said. 'It's a bloody health hazard.' He brushed some dust off his sixty-quid Topman distressed jeans and plonked a collection of files on the desk. 'It's all here, ma'am,' he said. 'What there is of it, anyway.'

'Kev, I've told you before not to call me "ma'am". I know that Detective Superintendent Gervaise insists on it, but that's her prerogative. A simple "Guv" will suffice, if you must.'

'Right, Guv.'

'Give me a quick run-down.'

'Top and bottom of it is,' said Templeton, 'that there was no full investigation, as such. The coroner returned a verdict of accidental death, and that was the end of it.'

'No reservations?'

'Not so far as I can tell, Guv.'

'Who was in the house at the time?'

'It's all in that file, there,' Templeton tapped a thick buff folder, 'for what it's worth. Statements and everything. Basically, there were the band members, their manager, Lord Jessop, and various assorted girlfriends, groupies and hangers-on. They're all named on the list, and they were all questioned.'

Annie scanned the list quickly and put it aside. Nothing, or no one, she hadn't expected, though most of the names meant little to her.

'It happened after a private party to celebrate the success of their second album, which was called – get this – *He Whose Face Gives No Light Shall Never Become A Star.*'

'That's Blake,' Annie said. 'William Blake. My dad used to quote him all the time.'

'Sounds like a right load of bollocks to me,' Templeton said. 'Anyway, the album was recorded at Swainsview Lodge over the winter of 1969–70. Lord Jessop had let them convert an old banquet room he didn't use first into a rehearsal space, and then into a private recording studio. Quite a lot of bands used it over the next few years.'

'So what happened on the night of the party?'

'Everybody swore Merchant was fine when things wound up around two or three o'clock, but the next morning the gardener found him floating on his back, naked in the pool. The post-mortem found a drug called Mandrax in his system.'

'What's that?'

'Search me. Some kind of tranquilliser?'

'Was there enough to kill him?'

'Not according to the pathologist. But he'd been drinking, too, and that enhances the effects, and the dangers. Probably been smoking dope and dropping acid, as well, but they didn't have toxicology tests for them back then.'

'So what was the cause of death?'

'Officially he slipped on the side of the swimming-pool, fell into the shallow end, smashed his head on the bottom and drowned. The Mandrax might have slowed his reactions. There was water in his lungs.'

'What about the blow to the head? Any way it could have been blunt-object trauma?'

'Showed impact with a large flat area rather than a blunt object.'

'Like the bottom of a swimming-pool?'

'Exactly, Guv.'

'What did the party guests say?'

'What you'd expect. Everyone swore they were asleep at the time, and nobody heard anything. To be honest, they probably wouldn't have noticed if they were all full of drugs and he just fell into the pool. Not much to hear. He was already unconscious from hitting his head.'

'Any speculation as to why he was naked?'

'No,' said Templeton, 'but it was par for the course back then, wasn't it? Hippies and all that stuff. Free love. Orgies and whatnot. Any excuse to get their kit off.'

'Who carried out the investigation?'

'Detective Chief Inspector Cecil Grant was SIO – he's dead now – but a DS Keith Enderby did most of the legwork and digging around.'

'Summer 1970,' said Annie. 'He'll be retired by now, most likely, but he might still be around somewhere.'

'I'll check with Human Resources.'

'Kev, did you ever get the impression, reading through the stuff, that anyone put the kibosh on the investigation because a famous rock band and a peer of the realm were involved?'

Templeton scratched his brow. 'Well, now you come to mention it, it did cross my mind. But if you look at the facts, there was no evidence to say that it happened any other way. DS Enderby seems to have done a decent enough job under the circumstances. On the other hand, they all closed ranks and presented a united front. I don't believe for a minute that everyone went to sleep at two or three in the morning and heard nothing more. I'll bet you there were people up and about, on the prowl, though perhaps they were in no state to distinguish reality from fantasy. Someone could easily have been lying to protect someone else. Maybe two or even more were in it together. Conspiracy theory. The other thing, of course, is that there was no motive.'

'No strife within the band?'

'Not that anyone was able to put their finger on at the time. Again, though, they weren't likely to tell the investigating officers about it if there was, were they?'

'No, but there might have been rumours in the music press. These people lived a great deal of their lives in the public eye.'

'Well, if there was anything, it was a well-kept secret,' said Templeton. 'I've checked some of the stuff online and at that time they were a successful group, definitely going places. Maybe if someone dug around a bit now, asked the right questions . . . I don't know . . . it might be different.'

'Why don't you see if you can track down this Enderby, and I'll have a chat with DCI Banks?'

'Yes, Guv,' said Templeton, standing up. 'Want me to leave the files?'

'Might as well,' said Annie. 'I'll have a look at them.'

Thursday, 18 September 1969

Rick Hayes's Soho office was located above a trattoria in Frith Street, not too far from Ronnie Scott's and any number of sleazy sex shops and strip clubs. Refreshed by an espresso from the Bar Italia across the street, Chadwick climbed the shabby staircase and knocked at the glass pane on the door labelled HAYES CONCERT PROMOTIONS. A voice called out for him to come in, and he entered to see Hayes sitting behind a littered desk, hand over the mouthpiece of his telephone.

'Inspector. What a surprise,' Hayes said. 'Sit down. Can

you hang on a moment? I've been trying to get hold of this bloke for ever.'

Chadwick waited, but instead of sitting, he wandered round the office, a practice that he found usually made people nervous. Framed signed photos of Hayes with various famous rock stars hung on the walls, unfamiliar names, for the most part: Jimi Hendrix, Pete Townsend, Eric Clapton. Filing cabinets stuffed with folders. He was opening drawers in a cabinet near the window when his snooping obviously worried Hayes enough to make him end his phone call prematurely.

'What are you doing?' he asked.

'Just having a look round.'

'Those are private files.'

'Yes?' Chadwick sat down. 'Well, I'm a great believer in not wasting time sitting around doing nothing, so I thought I'd use a bit of initiative.'

'Have you got a search warrant?'

'Not yet. Why? Do I need one?'

'To look at those files you do.'

'Oh, I shouldn't think there's anything there of interest to me. The reason I'm here is that you've been lying to me since the moment we met, and I want to know why. I also want to know what you have to do with the murder of Linda Lofthouse.'

'Linda Lofthouse?'

'Don't play games with me, laddie,' Chadwick snarled, his Glaswegian accent getting stronger the more angry he became. 'You'll only lose. That's the victim's name.'

'How was I to know?'

'It's been in the papers.'

'Don't read them.'

'I know, they're full of establishment lies. I don't care whether you read them or not. You saw the body at Brimleigh. You were there at the scene even before I arrived.'

'So?'

'You were in a perfect position to mislead us all, to tamper with evidence. She was right there, lying dead at your feet, and you told me you hadn't seen her before.'

'I told you later that I might have seen her backstage. There were a lot of people around and I was very busy.'

'So you said. Later.'

'Well?'

'There were two important things I didn't know then, things you could have told me but didn't.'

'You've lost me. What are you talking about?'

Chadwick counted them off on his fingers. 'First, that the victim's name was Linda Lofthouse and, second, that you knew her a lot better than you let on.'

Hayes picked up a rubber band from his desk and started wrapping it round his nicotine-stained fingers. He hadn't shaved in a couple of days, and his lank hair needed a wash. He was wearing jeans and a collarless red shirt made of some flimsy material. 'I've told you everything I know,' he said.

'Bollocks. You've told me bugger all. I've had to piece it all together from conversations with other people. You could have saved me a lot of trouble.'

'It's not my job to save the fuzz trouble.'

'Enough of that phoney hippie nonsense. It doesn't suit you. You're a businessman, a filthy capitalist lackey, just like the rest, no matter how you dress and how infrequently you wash. You knew Linda Lofthouse through Dennis Nokes, the house on Bayswater Terrace, Leeds, and through her cousin Vic Greaves of the Mad Hatters. You also knew Linda's friend Tania Hutchison, the girl she was with at Brimleigh, but you didn't bother to tell us that, either, did you?'

Hayes's jaw dropped. 'Who told you all this?'

'That doesn't matter. Is it true?'

'What if it is?'

'Then you've been withholding important information in a murder investigation, and that, laddie, is a crime.'

'I didn't think we were living in a police state yet.'

'Believe me, if we were, you'd know the difference. When did you first meet Linda Lofthouse?'

Hayes glowered at Chadwick, still playing with the rubber band. 'At Dennis's place,' he said.

'When?'

'I don't know, man. A while back.'

'Weeks? Months? Years?'

'Look, Dennis is an old mate. Whenever I'm in the area I drop by and see him.'

'And one time you did this, you met Linda?'

'That's right. She was staying at Dennis's.'

'*With* Dennis?'

'No. Linda was untouchable.'

So, it looked as if Nokes had told the truth about that, at least. 'This would have been the winter of 1967, early 1968, right?'

'If you say so.'

'How often have you seen her since?'

'Just a couple of times, you know.'

'No, I don't. Enlighten me.'

'I've done some concerts with the Hatters, and she was at one of them. I met her at Dennis's again, too, but I didn't, like, *know* her or anything. I mean, we weren't close. We were just around the same scene sometimes, like lots of other people were.'

'So why did you lie about knowing her, if it was all so innocent?'

'I don't know, man. I didn't want to get involved. You guys would probably take one look at me and think I did it. Besides, every minute I was standing around in that field I was losing money. You don't know what this business is like, how hard it is just to break even sometimes.'

'So you lied because you thought that if you told the truth I'd keep you from your work and you'd lose money?'

'That's right. Surely you can understand that?'

'Oh, I can understand it well enough,' said Chadwick. 'You're speaking my language now. Concern over money is a lot more common than you think.'

'Then . . . ?'

'What were you doing after you introduced Led Zeppelin on Sunday night?'

'Listening to their set whenever I could. They were incredible. Blew me away.'

'Where were you listening?'

'Around. I still had things to do. We were looking to pack up and get out of there as soon as possible after the show, so I couldn't waste time. As it turned out—'

'But where did you go to listen to them? The press enclosure was roped off in front of the stage. Apparently that was the best place to watch from. Did you go there?'

'No. Like I said, I didn't have time to stand there and watch. I had other things to do. It was pandemonium around there, man. We had people falling off the stage stoned and people trying to sneak in the front and back. Managers wanted paying, there were cars blocking other cars, limos turning up for people, pieces of equipment to be accounted for. I tell you, man, I didn't have time to kill anyone, even if I wanted to. Which I didn't. I mean, what possible motive could I have for killing Linda? She was a great bird. I liked her.' He lit a cigarette.

'I notice you're left-handed,' Chadwick said.

'Yeah. So?'

'The killer was left-handed.'

'Lots of people are.'

'Do you own a flick-knife?'

'No, man. They're illegal.'

'Well, I'm glad you know the law.'

'Look, are we finished, because I've got a lot of phone calls to make?'

'We're finished when I say we are.'

Hayes bristled but said nothing.

'I hope you realise the extent of the trouble you're in,' Chadwick went on.

'Look, I did what anybody would do. You've got to be crazy these days to give the fuzz an inch, especially if you're a bit different.'

'In your case, it didn't work, did it? I found out anyway. All we need now is one person, just one person, who saw you leaving the backstage area for the woods while Led Zeppelin were playing. Are you so sure of yourself that no one saw you? After all, we've discovered all your other little lies. Why not this one?'

'I did not leave the enclosure, and I didn't see Linda leave, either.'

'We're re-interviewing all the security personnel and everyone else we can think of who was there. Are you certain that's the story you want to stick to?'

'I did not leave the enclosure. I did not go into those woods.'

'What did you do with the knife?'

'I can't believe this! I never had a knife.'

Chadwick spread his hands on the table, the gesture of a reasonable man laying out his cards. 'Look, Mr Hayes, I'm not persecuting you because you're different. In fact, I don't believe you're that much different from most of the petty villains I come into contact with. You just wear a different uniform. Why don't you make it easy on us all and tell me how it happened?'

'I want my solicitor.'

'What about Tania Hutchison? Did you try it on with her, too?'

'I'm not saying another word.'

'But it was Linda you really wanted, wasn't it? Linda, who seemed so unattainable. "Untouchable". Isn't that the word you used? She was so beautiful. Thought you weren't good enough for her, did she? Even your money and your famous contacts didn't impress her, did they? So, how did it happen? She wandered off into the woods. You did your MC duties, and when everyone was enthralled and deafened by Led Zeppelin, you followed Linda into the woods. She rejected you again, and this time was once too many. She had her period. Did she tell you that? Did you think it was just an excuse? Well, you were wrong. It was true. Maybe you were high? Maybe you'd been taking drugs? You could probably plead that you weren't responsible for your actions. But she turned her back on you for the last time. You grabbed her from behind and stabbed her. Then, when you realised what you'd done, you knew you had to throw us off the scent. It was a clumsy attempt, but the best you could come up with under pressure. You walked to the edge of the field, were lucky enough to steal a sleeping-bag without being seen, and the body was still undiscovered when you got back to it. You shoved her into the sleeping bag – very carelessly, I might add, and that was my first indication she hadn't been killed in it – and you carried her to the field. While everyone's attention was riveted on the stage, in the dark, you set the sleeping-bag down at the very edge of the crowd and hurried back to your duties. I don't suppose it took long. Was there a lot of blood to wash off your hands? I don't think so. You rubbed them on the leaves then rinsed them in the beck. Did you get any on your clothes? Well, we can always check. Where did you hide the knife?'

As Chadwick talked, Hayes turned paler. 'It's one thing accusing me of all this,' he said, 'but it will be quite another proving it.'

'All we need is one witness who saw you leave the enclosure at the relevant time.'

'And the non-existent knife.'

That was clever of him, Chadwick thought. The knife would help a lot, especially if it had Hayes's fingerprints and Linda Lofthouse's blood on it. But cases had proceeded and been won on less. Hayes might get a haircut and wear a suit for the jury, but people could still see through him.

Chadwick leaned forward and picked up Hayes's telephone. 'I'm going to call a contact at West End Central,' he said, 'and in no time we'll have search warrants for your office, your house and anywhere else you've spent more than ten minutes over the past two weeks. If there are any traces of Linda's blood, believe me, we'll find them.'

'Go ahead,' said Hayes, with less confidence than he was aiming for. 'And as soon as you've done that, I'll have my solicitor down here and sue you for wrongful arrest.'

'I haven't arrested you,' said Chadwick, dialling. 'Yet.'

'Yes, I know what Mandrax is. Or was,' said Banks to Annie, over an off-duty pint in the Queen's Arms early that evening.

It was dark outside, and the pub was noisy with the after-work crowd, along with those who never worked and had been there all day, mostly loud kids with foul mouths telling fart jokes over the pool table in the back. A big mistake that table was, Banks had told Cyril, the landlord, but he had replied that he had to move with the times, or the younger crowd would all go to the Duck and Drake or the Red Lion. Good riddance, Banks thought. Still, it wasn't *his* livelihood.

The mix of accents said a lot about the changing dales: Banks could discern London, Newcastle and Belfast mixed in with the locals. The yob factor was getting stronger in Eastvale, too. Everyone had noticed, and it had become a matter of concern, written up in the newspaper, argued over by members of the council and local MPs. That was why Neighbourhood Policing had been set up and Gavin Rickerd transferred, to keep tabs on known trouble-makers and share that intelligence with other communities.

Even the police station's location right on the edge of the market square didn't seem to make any difference to the drunken louts who ran wild after closing-time every Saturday night, leaving a trail of detritus and destruction in their wake on the ancient cobbles, not to mention the occasional bleeding human being. Town-centre shopkeepers and pub landlords scrubbing away the vomit and sweeping up broken glass on a Sunday morning was a common sight for the Eastvale churchgoers.

'Mandrax was a powerful sedative,' Banks said. 'A sleeping tablet, known affectionately as "mandies". Been off the market since the seventies.'

'If they were sleeping pills,' Annie asked, 'why didn't they just put people to sleep?'

Banks took a swig of Black Sheep, the only pint he was allowing himself before the drive home to Gratly. 'That's what they were supposed to do. The thing was, if you mixed them with booze and rode out the first waves of tiredness, they gave you a nice, mellow buzz. They were also especially good for sex. I expect that was why Robin Merchant was naked.'

'Were they?'

'What?'

'Good for sex?'

'I don't know. I only took two once and I didn't have a girlfriend at the time. I fell asleep.'

Annie patted his arm. 'Poor Alan. So, was Merchant on his way towards an assignation or was he just taking a post-coital stroll?'

'What did the files say?' Banks asked.

'They were remarkably silent on the subject. No one

admitted to sleeping with him. Of course, if he'd been in the water all night, it would have been difficult for the pathologist to tell whether he'd had sex or not.'

'Who was his girlfriend at the time?'

'No one in particular,' said Annie. 'No information on Robin Merchant's sexual habits or preferences made it to the official case notes.'

'This Enderby character might remember something, if and when Templeton tracks him down.'

'Maybe he was gay?' Annie suggested. 'Him and Lord Jessop in the sack together? I could see why they might want to suppress that.'

'There's no evidence to suggest that Lord Jessop was gay,' said Banks. 'Apparently he liked the ladies. For a while, at any rate.'

'What happened?'

'He became a heroin addict, though he functioned well enough for years. Many addicts do, if they can get a regular and reliable supply. But heroin doesn't do a lot for your sex drive. In the end he got Aids from an infected needle.'

'You'd think he could afford clean needles, wouldn't you, him being a lord and all?'

'He was broke by then,' Banks said. 'Apparently, he was rather a tragic figure towards the end. He died alone. All his friends had deserted him, including his rock-star pals. He'd spent his inheritance, sold off most of his land. Nobody wanted to buy Swainsview Lodge, and he had no heirs. He'd sold everything else he had.'

'Is that where he died, Swainsview?'

'Ironically enough, yes,' said Banks. 'That place has a sad history.'

They both paused to take in the implications of that, then Annie said, 'So they caused disorientation and tiredness, these mandies?'

'Yes. If Robin Merchant had been taking mandies and drinking, he could easily have lost his footing. I suppose when he hit his head on the bottom of the shallow end he'd already be feeling the effects of the drug and might have drowned. It's like Jimi Hendrix, in a way, choking on his own vomit because he had so much Vesperax in his system that he couldn't wake up and stop it happening. Usually the body's pretty good at self-preservation, gag reflexes and such, but certain drugs can inhibit or depress those functions.'

Across the room, a white ball cracked into a triangle of reds, breaking the frame and launching a new game. Someone started arguing loudly and drunkenly about the rules.

'What happened to Mandrax?' Annie asked.

'I don't know the exact details, but they took it off the market in the late seventies. People soon replaced it with Mogadon, which they called "moggies". Same sort of thing, but a tranquilliser, not a sedative, and probably not as harmful.'

Annie sipped some beer. 'But someone *could* have pushed him, couldn't they?'

'Of course they could. Even if we could find a motive, though, we might have a devil of a job proving it after all this time. And, strictly speaking, it's not our job.'

'It is if it's linked to Nick Barber's murder.'

'True enough. Anyway, I can't see Vic Greaves being much help.'

'That really upset you, didn't it, talking to him?'

'I suppose it did,' said Banks, toying with his beer mat. 'It's not as if he was one of my idols or anything, but to see him in that state, to see that emptiness in his eyes up close.' Banks gave an involuntary shudder.

'Was it drugs? Was he really an acid casualty?'

'That's what everyone said at the time. You know, there was even a kind of heroic stature about it. He was put on a pedestal for being mad. People thought there was something cool about it. He attracted a cult following, a lot of weirdoes. They still hound him.' Banks shook his head. 'What a time. The way they used to glorify tramps and call madmen visionaries.'

'You think there was something else to it?'

'I don't know how much LSD he took. Probably buckets full of the stuff. I've heard he's done a few stints in psychiatric establishments over the years, along with group therapy and any other kind of therapy that happened to be fashionable at the time, but as far as I know there's still no official diagnosis. No one seemed to know exactly what his problem was, let alone cured him. Acid casualty, psychotic, schizophrenic, paranoid schizophrenic. Take your pick. None of it really matters in the long run. He's Vic Greaves and his head's fucked. It must be hell inside there.'

Brian and Emilia were in the entertainment room watching *La Dolce Vita* on the plasma screen when Banks got home. They were on the sofa, Brian sitting up with his feet on the pouffe, his arm round Emilia, who leaned against him, head on his chest, face hidden by a cascade of hair. She was wearing what looked like one of Brian's shirts. It wasn't tucked in at the waist because she wasn't wearing anything to tuck it into. They certainly looked as if they'd made themselves at home during the couple of days they'd been around, and Banks realised sadly that he had been so busy he had hardly seen them. A tantalising smell drifted through from the kitchen.

'Oh, hi, Dad,' said Brian, putting the DVD on pause. 'Got your note. We were out walking round Relton way.'

'Not a very nice day for it, I'm afraid,' said Banks, flopping into one of the armchairs.

'We got soaked,' said Emilia.

'It happens,' said Banks. 'Hope it didn't put you off?'

'Oh, no, Mr Banks. It's beautiful up here. I mean, even

when it's grey and rainy it's got a sort of romantic, primitive beauty, hasn't it? Like *Wuthering Heights.*'

'I suppose so,' said Banks. He gestured towards the screen. 'And call me Alan, please. Didn't know you were Fellini fans. It's one of your uncle Roy's. I've been trying to watch them all. Bergman. Truffaut. Chabrol. Kurasawa. I'm getting quite used to the subtitles now, but I still have a bit of trouble following what's going on half the time.'

Brian laughed. 'I heard someone talking about *La Dolce Vita* a while ago, how great it was, and there it was, right in front of me. Emmy here's an actress.'

'I thought I'd seen you somewhere before,' Banks said. 'You've done TV, right?'

Emilia blushed. 'A little. I've had small parts in *Spooks*, *Hustle* and *Bad Girls*, and I've done quite a bit of theatre, too. No movies yet.' She stood up. 'Please excuse me a moment.'

'Of course.'

'What's that smell?' Banks asked Brian, when she had left the room.

'Emilia's making us dinner.'

'I thought we'd get a takeaway tonight.'

'This'll be better, Dad, believe me. You took us out on Sunday. Emilia wants to repay you. She's a gourmet cook. Leg of lamb with garlic and rosemary. Potatoes dauphinois.' He put his fingers to his lips and made a kissing sound. 'Fantastic.'

'Well,' said Banks, 'I've never been one to turn down a gourmet meal, but she doesn't have to feel obliged.'

'She *likes* doing it.'

'Then I'd better open a nice bottle of wine.'

Banks walked to the kitchen and opened a bottle of Peter Lehmann Australian shiraz, which he thought would go well with the lamb. When Emilia came in, she was wearing jeans, with the shirt tucked in at the waist and her long hair tied back in a simple ponytail. She smiled at him, cheeks glowing, and bent to open the oven. The smell was even stronger.

'Wonderful,' said Banks.

'It won't be long now,' said Emilia. 'The lamb and potatoes are almost done. I'm just going to make a salad. Pear and blue cheese. That's OK, isn't it? Brian said you like blue cheese.'

'It's fine,' said Banks. 'Sounds delicious, in fact. Thank you.'

Emilia flashed him a shy smile, and he guessed she was a little embarrassed because he'd caught her with her trousers down, so to speak.

Banks poured himself a glass of shiraz, offered one to Emilia, who said she'd wait until later, then went back to sit with Brian, who had now turned off the DVD and was playing the first Mad Hatters CD, which Banks had bought at the HMV on Oxford Street, along with their second and third albums.

'What do you think of it?' he asked Brian.

'It must have been quite something in its time,' Brian said. 'I like the guitar and keyboards mix they've got. That sounds quite original. Really spacey. It's good. Especially for a début. Better than I remember. I mean, I haven't listened to them in years.'

'Me neither,' said Banks. 'I met Vic Greaves today. At least, I think I did.'

'Vic Greaves? Jesus, Dad. He's a legend. What was he like?'

'Strange. He spoke in non-sequiturs. Referred to himself in the third person a lot.' Banks shrugged. 'I don't know. Everyone says he took too much LSD.'

Brian seemed deep in thought for a few moments. Then he said, 'Acid casualties. Makes it sound like war, doesn't it? But things like that happened. It's not as if he was the only one.'

'I know that,' said Banks, finding himself start to wonder about Brian. He was living the rock-star life, too, as Vic

Greaves had. What did he get up to? How much did he know about drugs?

'Dinner's ready,' Emilia called.

Banks and Brian got up and went into the kitchen, where Emilia had lit candles and presented the salad beautifully. They talked about Brian's music and Emilia's acting ambitions as they ate, a pleasant relief for Banks after his distressing encounter with Vic Greaves. This time, Banks actually got as far as dessert – raspberry crème brûlée – before the phone rang. Cursing, he excused himself.

'Sir?'

'Yes.'

'Winsome here. Sorry to bother you, Guv, but it's Jean Murray. You know, from the post office in Lyndgarth. She rang about five minutes ago about Vic Greaves. Said she was out walking her dog and heard all sorts of shenanigans up at the house. Lights going on and off, people shouting and running around and breaking things. I thought I should tell you.'

'You did right,' said Banks. 'Did you send a car?'

'Not yet.'

'Good. Don't. Is more than one person involved?'

'Sounds like it to me.'

'Thanks, Winsome,' said Banks. 'I'll be there as soon as I can.'

He thanked Emilia for a wonderful dinner, made his apologies and left, saying he wasn't sure how late he would be back. He didn't think Brian minded too much, the way he was looking at Emilia and holding her hand in the candlelight.

12

Friday, 19 September 1969

Detective Chief Superintendent McCullen called a meeting for Friday afternoon in the incident room at Brotherton House. The town-hall dome looked dark and forbidding against the iron-grey sky, and only a few shoppers were walking up the Headrow towards Lewis's and Schofield's, struggling with their umbrellas. Chadwick was feeling a little better after a decent and nightmare-free sleep in his own bed, helped along considerably by the news that Leeds United had beaten SK Lyn Oslo 10–0 in the first round of the European Cup.

Photos were pinned to the boards at the front of the room – the victim, the scene – and those present sat in chairs at the various scattered desks. Occasionally a telephone rang and a telex machine clattered in the distance. Present were McCullen, Chadwick, Enderby, Bradley, Dr O'Neill and Charlie Green, a civilian liaison officer from the forensic laboratory in Wetherby, along with a number of uniformed and plainclothes constables who had been involved in the Lofthouse case. McCullen hosted the proceedings, calling first on Dr O'Neill to summarise the pathology findings, which he did most succinctly. Next came Charlie Green.

'I've been in meetings with our various departments this morning,' he said, 'so I think I can give you a reasonable précis of what we've discovered so far. Which isn't very much. Blood analysis determines that the victim's blood is group A, a characteristic she shares with about forty-three per cent of the population. As far as Toxicology has been able to gather so far, there is no evidence to suggest the presence of illegal substances. I must inform you at this point, though, that we have no test for LSD, a fairly common drug among . . . well, the type of people we're dealing with. It disappears from the system very quickly.'

'As you all know, the areas around where the body was found, and where the victim was stabbed, have both been searched exhaustively by our search teams and by specially trained police dogs. They turned up a small amount of blood at the scene, some on the ground and more on some nearby leaves. The blood matches the victim's group and we submit that the killer used the leaves to wipe her blood from his hands and perhaps from the murder weapon, a narrow, single-edged blade, the kind you often find on a flick-knife. There are no footprints in the woods, and the footprints found near the sleeping-bag were so muddled as to be useless.

'Upon examination, the sleeping-bag yielded traces of the victim's blood, along with hair and . . . er . . . bodily fluids that contain the respective blood types of Ian Tilbrook and June Betts, neither group A, by the way, who claimed the sleeping-bag was stolen from them while they sought out a better viewing position on the field.'

'In all this, then,' said McCullen, 'there are no traces of the killer? No blood? No hair?'

'We still have unidentified hairs, some taken from the tree-trunk near which the girl was killed,' said Green. 'As you know, hair comparison is weak, to say the least, and it often doesn't stand up in court.'

'But you do have hairs, and they might belong to the killer?'

'Yes. We also have some fibres, again some from the tree and some from the victim's dress, but they're common blue denim, which I'm sure just about everyone was wearing, and black cotton, which is also common. There's a chance we might be able to make a match if we had the clothes, but I'm afraid these fibres aren't going to lead us to anything you can't get at Lewis's or Marks and Spencer's.'

'Is there anything else?'

'Just one more thing, really.'

McCullen raised his eyebrows. 'Do tell.'

'We found stains on the back of the girl's dress,' Green said, hardly able to stop the smile spreading across his large mouth. 'They turned out to be semen, a secretor, type A blood, same as the victim. Hardly conclusive, of course, but certainly interesting.'

McCullen turned back to Dr O'Neill. 'Doctor,' he said, 'do we have any evidence of recent sexual activity on the part of the girl?'

'As I said to DI Chadwick at the post-mortem, the victim was menstruating at the time she was killed. Now, that doesn't rule out sexual activity, of course, but vaginal and anal swabs reveal absolutely no sign of it, and the tissue shows no sign of tearing or bruising.'

'Was she on the pill?' McCullen asked.

'We did find evidence of oral contraception, yes.'

'So perhaps,' Chadwick said, 'our killer got his pleasure by ejaculating *on* to the victim, not into her.'

'Or perhaps he couldn't help himself, and it happened as he was stabbing her. Was there a great deal of semen, Mr Green?'

'No,' said Green. 'Minute traces. As much as might have seeped through a person's underpants and jeans, say.'

'So what do we know about our killer in total, Mr Green?' he asked.

'That he's between five foot ten and six feet tall, left-handed, wore blue denim jeans and a black cotton shirt or T-shirt, he's a secretor, and his blood type is A.'

'Thank you.' McCullen turned to Enderby. 'I understand you've got something for us, Sergeant?'

'It's not much, sir,' said Enderby, 'but DI Chadwick asked me to track down the girl who was doing the body-painting backstage at Brimleigh. It seems there's some question about the flower painted on the victim's face, whether it was pre- or post-mortem.'

'And?'

'Robin Merchant, one of the members of the Mad Hatters, told DI Chadwick that he saw her with a painted flower on her face late that evening. Her friend, Tania Hutchison, can't remember. Hayes was also uncertain. If she did have one, we were wondering if the killer did it for some reason, sir.'

'Did he?'

'I'm afraid we still don't know for certain. The body-painter was a bit . . . well, not so much stupid as sort of lost in her own world. She couldn't remember who she painted and who she didn't. I showed her the victim's photograph, and she thought she recognised her. Then I showed her the design, and she said it could have been one of hers but she didn't usually paint cornflowers.'

'Wonderful,' said McCullen. 'Do any of these people have the brains they were born with, I wonder?'

'I know, sir,' said Enderby, with a grin. 'It's very frustrating. Should I continue my enquiries?'

McCullen looked at Chadwick. 'Stan? You're in charge.'

'I'm not sure if it's relevant,' Chadwick said. 'I simply thought that the drawing of such a flower by the killer indicated a certain type of mentality.'

'A nutcase, you mean?' said McCullen.

'To put it bluntly, yes,' said Chadwick. 'And while I'm not saying our killer didn't do it, I'm beginning to think that if he did, it's another clumsy attempt at sleight-of-hand, like moving the body.'

'Explain.'

Chadwick took Green's place at the front by the boards. 'Yesterday in London, with the permission of the local police at West End Central, I questioned Rick Hayes, the festival promoter. He's lied to me on a couple of occasions, and when I confronted him with this, he admitted to knowing the victim previous to the festival. He denies any sexual involvement – and I must add that a couple of other people I have spoken with regard this as highly unlikely, too – but he did know her. He's also the kind of man who asks just about every girl he meets to hop into bed with him, so I'm thinking there's a chance that if he was attracted to Linda and she rejected him . . . well, I think you can see in which direction my thoughts are leading me.'

'What about his alibi?' McCullen asked.

'Shaky, to say the least. He was definitely onstage at one o'clock to introduce the last group. After that, who knows? He claims he was in the backstage enclosure paying people – I gather a lot of this sort of thing operates on a cash-in-hand basis, probably to avoid income tax – and seeing to various problems that came up. We can re-interview everyone who was there, but I don't think that'll get us anywhere. The point is that things were so chaotic backstage when Led Zeppelin were playing that Hayes could easily have followed Linda out of the compound, stayed away for long enough to kill her and get back without being missed. Don't forget, it was dark as well as noisy, and most people were at the front of the stage watching the band. The drugs they take also make them rather narcissistic and inward-looking. Not a very observant lot, by and large.'

'Have we enough to hold him?'

'I'm not sure,' said Chadwick. 'With West End Central's help we searched his Soho office and his flat in Kensington and turned up nothing.'

'Is he left-handed?'

'Yes.'

'The right height?'

'Five foot eleven.'

'So it's all circumstantial?'

'We've had worse cases, but there's nothing to link him directly to the murder, without the weapon, except that he knew the victim, he fancied her, he had a bit of a temper, and his alibi's weak. He's not a nutcase, so if he did paint the flower on her check, he did it to make us *think* it was the work of a nutcase.'

'I see your point,' said McCullen. 'He still sounds like the best bet we've got so far. He could have ditched the knife anywhere. Talk to the kid who found the body again, ask him at what point Hayes turned up and what sort of state he was in. And organise another search of the woods.'

'Yes, sir,' said Chadwick. 'What do we do about him in the meantime?'

'We've got enough to hold him, haven't we? Let's bring him back up here and treat him to a bit of Yorkshire hospitality. Arrange it with West End Central. I'm sure there must be someone down there looking for a chance to come up and watch tomorrow's game.'

'Which game would that be, sir?'

McCullen looked at him as if were mad and said, 'Which game? There is only one game, as far as I know.'

Chadwick knew he meant the Yorkshire Challenge Cup at Headingley, knew McCullen was a rugby man, so he was teasing. The others knew it, too, and they were grinning behind cupped hands.

'Sorry, sir,' said Chadwick. 'I thought you meant Leeds and Chelsea.'

McCullen grunted. 'Football?' he said, with scorn. 'Nothing

but a bunch of sissies. Now, enough of your cheek and get on with it.'

'Yes, sir,' said Chadwick.

The end cottage was quiet when Banks walked up to the door at around nine o'clock. He had called on Jean and Susan Murray, who shared the flat above the post office, just to let them know that he was there and they weren't to worry. Jean Murray's account of events in person was no more coherent than what Winsome had repeated on the phone. Noise. Lights. Things breaking. A domestic tiff, Banks would have guessed, except that he was certain Vic Greaves had been alone when he left, and he wasn't in any shape to argue coherently with anyone. Banks had also considered calling in Annie, but there was no point in dragging her all the way from Harkside for what might turn out to be nothing.

He had parked his car by the green again, next to a silver Merc, because it wouldn't fit up the lane. He looked at the Merc again and remembered it was the same one he had seen when he left Lyndgarth in the late afternoon. Wind thrashed the bare branches in the street-lights, casting eerie shadows over the cottage and the road. The air smelt of rain that hadn't started falling yet.

The front curtains were closed, but Banks could see a faint light shining inside. He walked down the path and knocked on the door. This time, it was answered quickly. The man who stood there, framed by the light, had a red complexion, and his thinning grey hair was pulled back in a ponytail, which made his face seem bulbous and belligerent, as if Banks were seeing it through a fisheye lens. He was wearing a leather jacket and jeans. 'What the fuck do you want?' he said. 'Are you the bastard who came round earlier upsetting Vic? Can't you sick bastards leave him alone? Can't you see he's ill?'

'He did look rather ill to me,' said Banks, reaching inside his pocket for his warrant card. He handed it over, and the man examined it, then passed it back.

'I'm sorry,' he said, running his hand over the top of his head. 'Excuse me. Come in. I'm just used to being protective. Vic's in a hell of a state.'

Banks followed him in. 'You're right, though,' he said. 'It was me who was here earlier, and he did get upset. I'm sorry if I'm to blame.'

'You weren't to know.'

'Who are you, by the way?'

The man stuck out his hand. 'Name's Chris. Chris Adams.'

Banks shook. Adams had a firm grasp, although his palm was slightly sweaty.

'The Mad Hatters' manager?'

'For my sins. You understand the situation, then? Sit down, sit down.'

Banks sat on a cracked vinyl armchair of some indeterminate yellow-brown colour. Adams sat at an angle to him. All around them were stacks of papers and magazines. The room was dimly lit by two table-lamps, with pink and green shades. There didn't seem to be any heat, and it was chilly in the cottage. Banks kept his coat on. 'I wouldn't say I understand the situation,' he said. 'I know Vic Greaves is living here, and that's about all.'

'He's resting at the moment. Don't worry, he'll be OK,' said Adams.

'You take care of him?'

'I try to drop by as often as I can when I'm not in London or LA. I live just outside Newcastle, near Alnwick, so it's not too long a journey.'

'I thought you were all living in America?'

'That's just the band, most of them, anyway. I wouldn't live there if you paid me a fortune in gold bullion. Right now, there's plenty to do at this end, organising the forthcoming tour. But you don't want to know about my problems. What exactly can Vic do for you?'

Now that he was here, Banks wasn't entirely sure. He hadn't had time to plan an interview, hadn't even expected to see Chris Adams this evening: he had come in response to Jean Murray's call. Perhaps that was the best place to start.

'I'm sorry I upset Mr Greaves earlier,' he began, 'but I had a phone call a short while ago from someone in the village complaining about shouting and things breaking.'

Adams nodded. 'That would have been Vic. When I got here it must have been shortly after you left. I found him rolled up in a ball on the floor counting. He does that when he feels threatened. I suppose it's like sheep turning their backs on danger and hoping it will go away.'

'I thought maybe he was on drugs or something.'

Adams shook his head. 'Vic hasn't touched drugs – at least non-prescription drugs – in thirty years or more.'

'And the noise, the breakages?'

'I got him to sleep for a while, then, when he woke after dark, he got disoriented and frightened. He remembered your visit and got hysterical, had one of his tantrums and smashed a couple of plates. It happens from time to time. Nothing serious. I managed to calm him down eventually, and he's sleeping again now. Small village. Word gets round.'

'Indeed,' said Banks. 'I've heard stories, of course, but I had no idea he was so fragile.'

Adams rubbed at his lined forehead, as if scratching an itch. 'He can function well enough on his own,' he said, 'as you've no doubt seen, but he finds interaction difficult, especially with strangers and people he doesn't trust. He tends to get angry, or just to shut down. It can be very distressing, not only for him but for whoever is trying to talk to him, as you no doubt found out, too.'

'Has he been getting any professional help?'

'Doctors? Oh, yes, he's seen many doctors over the years. None of them has been able to do much except prescribe more and more drugs, and Vic doesn't like to take them. He says they make him feel dead inside.'

'How does he get in touch with you?'

'Pardon?'

'If he needs you or wants to see you. Has he got a phone?'

'No. Having a telephone would only upset him.' Adams shrugged. 'People would find out his number. Crazy fans. That's what I thought you were, at first. He gets enough letters as it is. Like I said, I drop by whenever I can. And he knows he can always get in touch with me. I mean, he knows how to use a phone, he's not an idiot, and sometimes he'll phone from the box by the green.'

'Can he get around?'

'He doesn't drive, if that's what you mean. He does have a bicycle.'

A bicycle wasn't much good for many of these steep country roads, Banks thought, unless you were especially fit, and Greaves didn't look it. But Fordham, he reminded himself, was only about a mile away, and you didn't need a car, or even a bicycle, to cover that sort of distance.

'Look, what's going on?' Adams asked. 'I don't even know what you're doing here. Why do you want to know about Vic?'

'I'm investigating a murder,' said Banks, eyes on Adams to judge his reaction. There wasn't one, which was odd in itself. 'Ever heard of a man called Nicholas Barber?'

'Nick Barber? Sure. If it's the same man, he's a freelance music journalist. Been writing about the Hatters on and off for the past five years or so. Nice bloke.'

'That's the one.'

'Is he dead, then?'

'He was murdered in a cottage a little over a mile from here.'

'When was this?'

'Just last week.'

'And you think . . . ?'

'I happen to know that Barber was working on a feature about the Mad Hatters for *MOJO* magazine. He found Greaves up here and came to talk to him, but Greaves freaked out and sent him packing. He was planning on coming back, but before he could, he was killed and all his work notes were stolen.'

'Of course he'd get nothing out of Vic. He doesn't like talking about the old days. They're painful for him to remember if, indeed, he *can* remember much about them.'

'Makes him angry, does it? Gives him a tantrum?'

Adams leaned forward, face thrust out aggressively. 'Now, wait a minute. You surely can't be thinking . . .' Then he leaned back. 'You've got it all wrong. Vic's a gentle soul. He's got his problems, sure, but he wouldn't harm a fly. He's no more capable of—'

'Your confidence in him is admirable, but he certainly strikes me as being capable of irrational or violent behaviour.'

'But why would he hurt Nick Barber?'

'You've said it yourself. He's not good at interaction, especially with strangers or people he doesn't trust, people he perceives as a threat. Maybe Barber was after information that was painful for Vic to remember, something he'd buried long ago.'

Adams relaxed and sat back in his chair. The vinyl squeaked. 'That's a bit fanciful, if you don't mind my saying so. Why would Vic perceive Nick Barber as a threat? He was just another fucking music journalist, for crying out loud.'

'That's what I'm trying to find out,' said Banks.

'Well, good luck to you, but I honestly can't see you getting anywhere. I think you're barking up the wrong tree on this one. And, besides, I'd guess there were plenty of heavy people more interested in Nick Barber than Vic.'

'What do you mean?'

Adams gave a twisted smile, put his finger to one nostril and sniffed through the other. 'Had quite a habit, so I heard. They can be unforgiving, some of those coke-dealers.'

Banks made a note to check into that area of Barber's life, but he wasn't going to be deflected so easily. 'Did he talk to you?'

'Who?'

'Nick Barber. He was doing a feature on the Hatters reunion, after all. It would only have been natural.'

'No, he didn't.'

'I suppose he hadn't got round to it,' Banks said. 'Early days. Were you present when Robin Merchant drowned in the swimming-pool at Swainsview Lodge?'

Adams looked surprised at the change of direction. He took a packet of Benson & Hedges from his jacket pocket and lit one, not offering the packet to Banks, who was grateful; he might have accepted. Adams inhaled noisily, and the smoke curled in the dim, chilly light of the pink- and green-shaded table-lamps. 'I wasn't present at the drowning, but I was in the Lodge, yeah, asleep, like everybody else.'

'Like everybody else said they were.'

'And like the police and the coroner believed.'

'We've had a lot of success lately with cold cases.'

'It's not a cold case. It's an over-and-done-with case, dead and buried. History.'

'I'm not too sure about that,' said Banks. 'Did you drop by to see Vic last week at all?'

'I was in London most of last week for meetings with promoters. I called in to see him on my way back up north.'

'What day would that be?'

'I'd have to check my calendar. Why? Is it important?'

'Would you check, please?'

Adams paused a moment, obviously not used to being given

orders, then pulled a PDA from his inside pocket. 'Isn't it wonderful, modern technology?' he said, tapping it with the stylus.

'Indeed,' said Banks. 'It's one of the reasons we've had such a high success rate with cold cases. New technology. Computers. DNA. Magic.' Banks wasn't too sure about it himself, though. He was still trying to master a laptop computer and an iPod; he hadn't got round to PDAs yet.

Adams shot him an angry glance. 'Are we talking about last week?' he asked.

'Yes.'

'Then I would have seen him on Wednesday, on my way back from London. I'd been down there since the previous weekend.'

'Wednesday. Was there anything odd or different about his behaviour, anything he said?'

'No, not that I noticed. He was quite docile. He was reading a book when I arrived. He reads a lot, mostly non-fiction.' Adams gestured to the magazines, books and papers. 'As you can see, he doesn't like to throw anything away.'

'He didn't tell you about anything unusual or frightening happening, about Nick Barber or anyone else coming to see him?'

'No.'

According to John Butler at *MOJO*, Nick Barber had tracked down Vic Greaves to this cottage and paid him a visit, but Butler hadn't known the actual day this had happened. Vic had freaked out, refused to talk, become angry and upset, and Barber had said he was going to try again. The phone call to Butler had been made on Friday morning, probably from the telephone box by the church.

If Vic Greaves *hadn't* told Adams about his meeting with Barber, it must have happened as late in the week as Thursday, perhaps, and Barber might have tried again on Friday, the day of his murder. Kelly Soames said he had been in bed with her between two and four, but that still left him virtually all day. Unless, of course, either Kelly Soames or Chris Adams was lying, in which case all bets were off. And of the two, Banks felt that while Kelly Soames would lie to protect herself from her father, Adams might have any number of less forgivable reasons for doing it.

'Where were you on Friday?' Banks asked.

'Home. All weekend.'

'Any witnesses?'

'Sorry. I'm afraid my wife was away, visiting her mother.'

'Can you give me the names and addresses of some of the people you met with in London, and the hotel you were staying at?' Banks asked.

'Am I hearing you right? Are you asking me for an alibi now?'

'Process of elimination,' said Banks. 'The more people we can rule out straight away, the easier our job is.'

'Bollocks,' said Adams. 'You don't believe me. Why don't you just come out and admit it?'

'Look,' said Banks, 'I'm not in the business of believing the first thing I'm told by anybody. I'd be a bloody useless detective if I were. It's a job, nothing personal. I want to get the facts straight before I come to any conclusions.'

'Yeah, yeah,' said Adams, tapping his way through the PalmPilot and giving Banks some names and numbers. 'And I was staying at the Montcalm. They'll remember me. I always stay there when I'm in town. I've got a suite. OK?'

'Appreciate it,' said Banks.

They heard a bang from upstairs. Adams cursed and headed out. While he was gone, Banks took as good a look as he could round the room. Some of the newspapers were ten years old or more, the same with the magazines, which meant Greaves must have brought them with him when he moved in.

The books were mostly biography or history. One thing he did find of interest: on the table, half hidden under the lamp, was a business card that had Nick Barber's Chiswick address printed on it and his Fordham address scribbled on the other side. Had Barber left this for Vic Greaves when he paid his visit? It should be possible to check it against a sample of his handwriting.

Adams came back. 'Nothing,' he said. 'His book slipped off the bed to the floor. He's still out.'

'Are you staying here overnight?' Banks asked.

'No. Vic'll sleep right through till morning now, and by then he'll have forgotten whatever upset him today. One of the marvels of his condition. Every day is a new adventure. Besides, it won't take me too long to drive home, and I have a lovely young wife waiting for me there.'

Banks wished he had someone living with him, but even if he had, he realised, it wouldn't be possible with Brian and Emilia around. How ironic, he thought. They could do whatever they wanted, but he didn't feel he could spend the night with a woman in his own house while they were there. Chance would be a fine thing. Banks felt nervous of going home, fearing what he might disturb. He'd phone them on his way, when he got within mobile range, to warn them, give them time to get dressed, or whatever.

He showed Adams the card. 'I found this pushed under the lamp over there,' he said. 'Only the edge was showing. Did you put it there?'

'Never seen it before,' said Adams.

'It's Nick Barber's card.'

'So what? That doesn't prove anything.'

'It proves he was here at least once.'

'But you already know that.'

'It also has his Fordham address written on it, so anyone who saw it here would know where he was staying when he was killed. Nice meeting you, Mr Adams. Have a safe drive home. I'm sure we'll be talking again soon.'

Saturday, 20 September 1969

While Chadwick was cheering on Leeds United to a 2–0 victory over Chelsea at Elland Road that Saturday afternoon, Yvonne walked to Springfield Mount to meet Steve and the others. Judy was going to make a macrobiotic meal, then they'd smoke a joint or two and take the bus into town. There was a bunch of stuff happening at the Adelphi that night: poets, a blues band, a jazz trio.

She was surprised, and more than a little put out, when McGarrity opened the door, but she asked for Steve, and he stood aside to let her in. The place was unusually quiet. No music or conversation. Yvonne went into the front room, sat on the sofa and lit a cigarette, glancing at the Goya print, which always mesmerised her. A moment later McGarrity strolled through the door with a joint in his hand and said, 'He's not here. Will I do?'

'What?'

McGarrity put a record on and sat in the armchair opposite her. He had that sort of fixed, crooked smile on his face, cynical and mocking, that always made her feel nervous and ill at ease in his presence. His pale skin was pockmarked, as if he'd scratched it when he had chickenpox as a child, the way her mother said would happen to her, and his dark hair was greasy and matted, flopping over his forehead and almost covering one dark brown eye. 'Steve. He's out. They're all out.'

'Where are they?'

'Town Street, shopping.'

'When will they be back?'

'I don't know.'

'Maybe I should come back later.'

'No. Don't go so soon. Here.' He handed her the joint.

Yvonne hesitated, then put her cigarette in the ashtray, accepted it and took a couple of drags. A joint was a joint, after all. It tasted good. Quality stuff. She recognised the music now: The Grateful Dead, 'China Cat Sunflower'. Nice. She still felt uncomfortable with the way he was looking at her, though, and she remembered the other night at the Grove, when he'd touched her and whispered her name. At least he didn't have his knife in his hand today. He seemed normal enough. Still, she felt edgy. She shifted on the sofa and said, 'Thank you. I should go now.'

'Why are you being so rude? You'll share a joint with me, but why don't you want to stay and talk to me?' He handed her the joint again and she took another couple of drags, hoping it would set her at ease, calm her down. What was it about him that disturbed her so? The smile? The sense that behind it lay only darkness?

'What do you want to talk about?' she said, handing the joint back to him and picking up her cigarette again.

'That's better. I don't know. Let's talk about that girl who got killed last week.'

Yvonne remembered McGarrity's knife, and that he had been wandering the crowds at Brimleigh during the festival. A terrible thought leaped into her mind. Surely he couldn't have . . . ? She began to feel real fear now, a physical sensation like insects crawling over her skin. She looked at *The Sleep of Reason* and thought she could see the bats flying round the man's head, biting at his neck with vampire teeth. The cat at his feet licked its lips. Yvonne felt an electric tingling in her arms and in the backs of her legs. Insects and ee-leck-triss-ittee. God, that hash was strong. And the song had changed. It wasn't 'China Cat Sunflower' any more, but 'What's Become of the Baby?', a creepy sound montage of disembodied voices and electronic effects. 'Linda?' she heard herself say, in a strange, distant voice that might have been someone else's. 'What about her?'

'You met her. I know you did. Wasn't she pretty? Sad, isn't it? But it's an absurd and arbitrary world,' he said. 'That sort of thing could happen to anyone. Anywhere. Any time. The pretty and the plain alike. "As flies to wanton boys are we to the gods. They kill us for their sport." Not with a bang but a whimper. One day you'll understand. Have you read about those people in Los Angeles? The rich people who got butchered? One of them was pregnant, you know. They cut her baby out of her womb. The newspapers are saying they were killed by people like us because they were rich piggies. Wouldn't you like to do something like that, little Von? Kill the piggies?'

'No. I don't want to hurt anyone,' Yvonne blurted out. 'I believe in love.'

'His scythe cuts down the innocent and the guilty alike. And the dead shall rise incorruptible.'

Yvonne put her hands over her ears. Her head was spinning. 'Stop it!'

'Why?'

'Because you're making me nervous.'

'Why do I make you nervous?'

'I don't know, but you do.'

'Is it exciting?'

'What?'

He leaned forward. She could see the decay on his front teeth, bared in that arrogant, superior smile. 'Being nervous. Does it make you excited?'

'No, it makes me nervous and you excited.'

McGarrity laughed. 'You're not as stupid as you look, are you, little Von? Even when you're stoned. And here was me thinking the only reason Steve wanted you was for your cunt. But it is a pretty little cunt, isn't it?'

Yvonne felt herself flushing to the roots of her being with anger and embarrassment. McGarrity was looking at her curiously, as if she were some unusual specimen of plant life. The owls in the Goya print seemed to be whispering in the sleeper's ear just as the song's eerie voices were whispering in her head.

'You don't need to show me it,' he said. 'I've already seen it.'

'What do you mean?'

'I've watched you. With Steve.'

Yvonne's jaw dropped. She stubbed out her cigarette so hard the sparks burned her fingers and tried to stand up. It wasn't easy. Somehow or other, she couldn't believe how, she found herself sitting down again, and McGarrity was beside her, grasping her arm. Hard. His face was so close to hers she could smell smoke and stale cheese on his breath. He let go of her arm and started rolling a cigarette. She thought she should make a run for it, but she felt too heavy to move. The joint, she thought. Opiated hash. It always did that to her, gave her a heavy, drifting, dreamy feeling. But this time the dream was turning into a nightmare.

He reached forward and touched her cheek with his finger, just as he had done at the Grove. It felt like a slug. 'Yvonne,' he whispered, 'what harm can it do? We believe in free love, don't we? After all, it's not as if you're the only one, you know.'

Her chest tightened. 'What do you mean?'

'Steve. Do you think you're the only pretty girl who comes round here to take her clothes off for him?'

Yvonne desperately wanted to get away from McGarrity's cloying and overbearing presence, but even more desperately she wanted to know if he was telling the truth. 'I don't believe you,' she said.

'Yvonne, Fridays and Saturdays. You're just his weekend hippie. Tuesdays and Wednesdays it's the lovely Denise. Let me see now, who's Monday, Thursday and Sunday? Is it the same one all three days, or is it three different ones?'

He was looking at her with that mocking smile.

'Stop it!' she said. 'I won't believe you. I want to go home.' She tried to rise again and was a little more successful this time. She was still dizzy, though, and soon fell back.

McGarrity stood up and started pacing up and down, muttering to himself. She didn't know if it was T. S. Eliot or the Book of Revelation. She could see the bulge at the front of his jeans, and knew he was getting more excited every second. She didn't trust him, knew he had that knife somewhere. Unless . . . Christ, he'd probably had his way with Linda, killed her and got rid of the knife. That was why he didn't have it. Yvonne's mind was spinning. Why didn't Steve and the others come home? What were they doing? Had he killed them all? Was that it? Were they all lying upstairs in their rooms in pools of blood with flies buzzing around? The ideas flashed and cracked electrically in her brain, bouncing around her mind like the thunderstorm in the painting.

Yvonne sensed that now was the time, while he was distracted. She went through it quickly in her head first, visualising herself doing it. She would have to be fast, and that would be the hardest part. She was still disoriented because of the hash he had drugged her with. She would have only one chance. Get to the door. Get outside fast. How did it open? Yale lock. In or out? In. So twist to the left, pull and run. There would be people out there, in the street, in the park. It was still light outside. She could make it. Twist to the left, pull and run.

When McGarrity was at the far end of the room, by the window, his back turned to her, Yvonne summoned all her energy and made a dash for the door. She didn't know if he was after her or not. She bounced off the walls down the hallway, reached the door, twisted the Yale and pulled. It opened. Daylight flooded her like warm honey. She stumbled a bit on the top step but ran down the garden path and out of the gate as fast as she could. She didn't look round, didn't listen for his footsteps following her. She didn't know where she was running. All she knew was that she had to run, run, run for her life.

13

Detective Superintendent Gervaise had called another progress meeting in the incident room, as the boardroom had now become known, for early Wednesday morning. The team lounged at the polished table sipping coffee from Styrofoam cups and chatting about last night's television, or Boro's prospects for the weekend's football. The corkboards had acquired more crime-scene photographs, and the names and details of various people connected with the victim were scrawled across the whiteboard.

Annie Cabbot sat next to Winsome and DC Galway, on loan from Harrogate CID, and tried to digest what Banks had told her over an early breakfast in the Golden Grill. The presence in the area of two people connected with the Mad Hatters, the band on whom Nick Barber had been writing a major feature, seemed too much of a coincidence for her, too. She knew far less about the group and its history than Banks did, but she could see there were a few skeletons in those closets worth shaking up a bit.

Detective Superintendent Gervaise clicked in on her shiny black heels, smoothed her navy pinstripe skirt and sat down at the head of the table, gracing everyone with a warm smile. A chorus of 'Good morning, ma'am' rose from the assembled officers.

She turned first to Stefan Nowak and asked if there was anything more from Forensics.

'Not really,' said Stefan. 'Naturally, there are numerous fibres and hairs remaining to be analysed. The place was supposed to be thoroughly cleaned after each set of guests, but nobody's that thorough. We've got a list of the last ten renters from the owner, so we'll check against their samples first. It was a busy summer. Some of them live as far afield as Germany and Norway. It could take a long time.'

'Prints?'

'The poker was wiped clean, and there are nothing but blurs round the door and conservatory entrance. Naturally, we've found almost as many fingerprints as we have other trace evidence, and it'll all have to be sifted, compared to existing records. As I said, it will take time.'

'What about DNA?'

'Well, we did find traces of semen on the bedsheets, but the DNA matches that of the victim. We're trying to separate out any traces of female secretion, but no luck so far. Apparently, he used condoms and flushed them down the toilet.' He glanced towards Annie for confirmation. She nodded.

'We know who this . . . companion was, don't we, DI Cabbot?'

'Yes,' said Annie. 'Unless there was someone else, which I'd say he hardly had time for, Kelly Soames admits to sleeping with the victim on two occasions: Wednesday evening, which was her night off, and Friday afternoon, between the hours of two and four, when she rearranged a dental appointment so she could visit his cottage.'

'Resourceful girl,' Superintendent Gervaise reflected. 'And Dr Glendenning estimates time of death between six and eight on Friday?'

'He says he can't be any more precise than that,' replied Stefan.

'Not earlier?'

'No, ma'am.'

'All right,' said Superintendent Gervaise. 'Let's move on. Anything from the house-to-house?'

'Nothing positive, ma'am,' said Winsome. 'It was a miserable night even before the blackout, and most people shut their curtains tight and stayed in.'

'Except the killer.'

'Yes, ma'am. In addition to the couple in the Cross Keys and the New Zealander in the youth hostel who thought she saw a light-coloured car heading up the hill, away from Moorview Cottage between seven thirty and seven forty-five, we have one sighting of a dark-coloured four-by-four going up the same lane at about six twenty, before the power cut, and a white van at about eight o'clock, while the electricity was off. According to our witnesses, though, neither of these stopped by the cottage.'

'Not very promising, is it?' said Gervaise.

'Well, one could have stopped further up the lane and walked back. There are plenty of passing places.'

'I suppose so,' Superintendent Gervaise conceded, but it was clear her heart wasn't in it.

'Oh,' Winsome added, 'someone says he saw a figure running across a field just after dark, before the lights went out.'

'Any description?'

'No, ma'am. He was closing his curtains, and he thought he saw this dark figure. He assumed it was someone jogging and ignored it.'

'Fat, thin, tall, short, child, man, woman?'

'Sorry, ma'am. Just a dark figure.'

'Which direction was the figure running?' Banks asked.

Winsome turned to face him. 'The short cut from Fordham to Lyndgarth, sir, across the fields and by the river. It's a popular jogging route.'

'Yes, but probably not after dark. Not in that sort of weather.'

'You'd be surprised, DCI Banks,' said Superintendent

Gervaise. 'Some people take their exercise very seriously indeed. Do you know how many calories there are in a pint of beer?'

Everyone laughed. Banks wasn't convinced. Vic Greaves didn't drive, so Adams had said, but it wasn't very far from his cottage to Fordham, and that would have been the best route to take. It cut the journey almost in half. He made a note to get Winsome to talk to this witness again, or to do it himself.

'What about this Jack Tanner character?' Gervaise asked. 'He sounded like a possible.'

'His alibi holds water,' said Templeton. 'We've talked to six members of his darts team and every one swears he was in the King's Head playing darts from about six o'clock until ten.'

'And I don't suppose he was drinking Britvic Orange, either,' said Gervaise. 'Maybe we ought to get Traffic to keep an eye on Mr Tanner.'

Everyone laughed.

'So do we have *any* promising lines of inquiry yet?' Gervaise asked.

'Chris Adams suggested that Nick Barber had a cocaine problem,' Banks said. 'I'm not convinced, but I've put in a request for the Met Drugs Squad to look into it. But there's something else.' He told her about Vic Greaves's breakdown, the drowning death of Robin Merchant at Swainsview Lodge thirty-five years ago, and the feature Nick Barber had been writing for *MOJO*.

'It's a bit far-fetched, isn't?' said Gervaise, when he had finished. 'I've always been a bit suspicious of events from so far in the past reaching forward into the present. Sounds like the stuff of television. I'm more inclined towards the most obvious solution – someone closer to hand, a jilted lover, cheated business partner, whatever. In this case, perhaps some disgruntled drug-dealer. Besides, I take it this Merchant business was settled at the time?'

'After a fashion,' said Banks.

'What are you suggesting?'

'DS Templeton dug up the paperwork, and it looks to have been a rather cursory investigation,' Banks said. 'After all, a major rock star and a peer of the realm were involved.'

'Meaning?'

Christ, Banks thought, do I have to spell it out for you? 'Ma'am, I should imagine nobody wanted a scandal that might in any way touch the establishment and make it to the House,' he said. 'There'd been enough of that sort of thing over the previous few years with Profumo, Kim Philby and the rest. As it was, the tabloids no doubt had a field day. Sex and drugs orgies at Lord Jessop's country manor. A deeper investigation might have unearthed things nobody wanted brought to the surface.'

'Oh, for heaven's sake, Banks, this is paranoid conspiracy rubbish,' said Superintendent Gervaise. 'Honestly, I'd have thought better of you.'

'Well,' Banks went on, unfazed, 'the victim's personal belongings are all missing, including his laptop and mobile, and he was definitely silenced for good.'

'We do know that he had a laptop and mobile?'

'The girl, Kelly Soames, says she saw them when she visited him, ma'am,' said Annie.

Gervaise frowned as if she had a bad taste in her mouth and tapped her pen on the blank pad in front of her. 'People have been killed or beaten up for a mobile phone or less. I'm still not convinced about this girl, DI Cabbot. She could be lying. Talk to her again, see if her story's consistent.'

'Surely you don't really believe she might have killed him?' Annie said.

'All I'm saying is that it's possible.'

'But she was working in the pub at the time. There are plenty of witnesses to vouch for her.'

'Except when she was supposed to be going to the dentist's on Friday afternoon, but was in bed with a man she'd only just met, a man who was found dead not long after. The girl can obviously lie with the best of them. All I'm saying is it's suspicious, DI Cabbot. And the MO fits. Crime of passion. Maybe he slighted her, asked her to do something she found repugnant. Or she found out he had another girlfriend. Perhaps she left the pub for a few moments later, in the dark. It wouldn't have taken long.'

'That would involve some premeditation, not a crime of passion, ma'am,' said Annie, 'and the odds are that she would also have got some blood on her.'

'Perhaps this sense of being wronged built up in her until she snapped when the lights went out and seized her opportunity before they got organised with candles. I don't know. All I'm saying is that it's possible, and that it makes a good deal more sense than any conspiracy rooted deep in the past. Either way, push her a bit harder, DI Cabbot. Do I make myself clear? And, DS Nowak?'

'Yes, ma'am.'

'Have a word with the pathologist, Dr Glendenning. See if you can push him a bit on time of death, find out if there's any possibility that the victim could have been killed around four rather than between six and eight.'

'Yes, ma'am.' Stefan gave Annie a quick glance. They both knew Dr Glendenning could not be pushed on anything.

'And let's have the girl's father in,' Superintendent Gervaise went on. 'He disappeared for long enough around the time of the murder. If he found out that this Barber character was having casual sex with his daughter, he might have taken the law into his own hands.'

'Ma'am?' said Annie.

'What, DI Cabbot?'

'It's just that I sort of promised – I mean, I indicated to the girl, to Kelly, that is, that we had no need to tell her father about what happened. Apparently he's a bit of a disciplinarian, and it could go badly for her.'

'All the more reason to have a close look at him. It might already have gone badly for Nicholas Barber. Had you thought of that?'

'No, ma'am, you don't understand. It's her I'm worried about. Kelly. He'll hit the roof.'

Superintendent Gervaise regarded Annie coldly. 'I understand perfectly well what you're saying, DI Cabbot. It serves her right for jumping into bed with every man she sees, then, doesn't it?'

'With all due respect, there's no evidence to suggest that she does anything of the kind. She happened to like Nick Barber.'

Superintendent Gervaise glared at Annie. 'I'm not going to argue sexual mores, especially with you, DI Cabbot. Ask around. Find out. The girl must have had other partners. Find them. And find out if anyone's ever paid her for it.'

'But, ma'am,' Annie protested, 'that's an insult. Kelly Soames isn't a prostitute, and this case isn't about her sex life.'

'It is if I say it is.'

'I talked to Calvin Soames,' Banks cut in.

Superintendent Gervaise looked at him. 'And?'

'In my opinion he didn't know what was going on between the victim and his daughter.'

'In your opinion?'

'Yes,' said Banks.

'He couldn't have been hiding it?'

'He could, I suppose,' Banks admitted, 'but if we're assuming that he did it out of anger or righteous indignation, he would have been far more likely to wear his heart on his sleeve. He would have been angry when I was questioning his daughter about Barber, but he wasn't.'

'Did you suggest they had slept together?'

'No,' said Banks. 'I merely asked her about her dealings with Barber as a customer in the Cross Keys. While her father was watching us, I was watching him, and I believe that if he'd known there was more to it than that, it would have shown in his expression, his behaviour, or in something he said. In my opinion, he's not the sort of man accustomed to being sly.'

'And it didn't?'

'No.'

'Very well. I'd be more convinced, however, if I could witness his reaction to being told what his daughter had been up to.'

'But, ma'am—'

'That's enough, DI Cabbot. I want you to pursue this line of inquiry until I'm satisfied there either is or isn't something to it.'

'It'll be too late for Kelly Soames then,' Annie muttered, under her breath.

'DS Templeton?' said Banks.

Templeton sat up. 'Sir?'

'Did you manage to locate Detective Sergeant Enderby?'

Templeton shifted uneasily in his chair. 'Er . . . yes, sir, I did.' He looked at Superintendent Gervaise while he was speaking.

'What is this?' she asked.

'Well, ma'am,' Templeton said, 'DCI Banks asked me to track down the detective who investigated the Robin Merchant drowning.'

'This is the drug addict who fell into the swimming-pool thirty-five years ago?'

'Yes, ma'am, though I'm not certain that he was an addict. Not technically speaking.'

Superintendent Gervaise sighed theatrically and ran a hand over her layered blonde hair. 'Very well, DCI Banks. I see you're hell-bent and determined on following this up, so I'll give you the benefit of the doubt. I'll bear with you for the moment and assume there might be something in it. But DI Cabbot sticks with the Soameses. OK?'

'Fine,' said Banks. He turned to Templeton. 'Well, then, Kev. Where is he?'

Templeton glanced at Superintendent Gervaise again before answering. 'Er . . . he's in Whitby, sir.'

'That's nice and handy, then, isn't it?' Banks said. 'I quite fancy a day at the seaside.'

The sun was out again when Banks began his descent from the North York moors down into Whitby. It was a sight that always stirred him, even in the most gloomy weather, but today the sky was milky blue, and the sun shone on the ruined abbey high on the hill and sparkled like diamonds on the North Sea beyond the dark pincers of the harbour walls.

Retired Detective Inspector Keith Enderby lived in West Cliff, where the houses straggled east off the A174 towards Sandsend. At least his fifties pebbledash semi had a sea view, even if it was only a few square feet between the houses opposite. Other than that, it was an unremarkable house on an unremarkable estate, Banks thought, as he pulled up behind the grey Mondeo parked at the front. 'Mondeo Man'. A journalistically contrived representative of a certain kind of middle-class Briton. Was that what Enderby had become?

On the phone, Enderby had indicated that he was keen enough to talk about the Robin Merchant case, and in person he welcomed Banks into his home with a smile and handshake, introduced his wife Rita, a small, quiet woman with a halo of pinkish-grey hair. Rita offered tea or coffee and Banks went for tea. It came with the requisite plate of chocolate digestives, arrowroots and KitKats, from which Banks was urged to help himself. He did. After a few pleasantries, at a nod from her husband, Rita made herself scarce, muttering something about errands in town, and drove off in the grey Mondeo. 'Mondeo Woman', then, Banks thought. Enderby said something about what a wonderful woman she was. Banks agreed. It seemed the polite thing to do.

'Nice place to retire to,' Banks said. 'How long have you been here?'

'Going on for ten years now,' Enderby said. 'I put in my twenty-five years and a few more besides. Finished up as a DI in South Yorkshire Police, Doncaster, but Rita always dreamed of living by the seaside and we used to come here for our holidays.'

'And you?'

'Well, the Costa del Sol would have suited me just fine, but we couldn't afford it. Besides, Rita won't leave the country. Foreigners begin at Calais and all that. She doesn't even have a passport. Can you believe it?'

'You probably wouldn't have liked it there,' Banks said. 'Too many villains.'

'Whitby's all right,' said Enderby, 'and not short of a villain or two either. I could do without all those bloody Goths, mind you.'

Banks knew that Whitby's close association with Bram Stoker's *Dracula* made the place a point of pilgrimage for Goths, but as far as he knew they were harmless enough kids, caused no trouble, and if they wanted to wear black all the time and drink a little of one another's blood now and then, it was fine with him. The sun flashed on the square of sea through the houses opposite. 'I appreciate your agreeing to talk to me,' Banks said.

'No problem. I just don't know that I can add much you don't already know. It was all in the case files.'

'If you're anything like me,' Banks said, 'you often have a feeling, call it gut instinct or whatever, that you don't think belongs in the files. Or a personal impression, something interesting but that seems irrelevant to the actual case.'

'It was a long time ago,' Enderby said. 'I probably wouldn't remember anything like that now.'

'You'd be surprised,' said Banks. 'It was a high-profile case, I should imagine. Interesting times back then, too. Rubbing shoulders with rock stars and aristos and all that.'

'Oh, it was interesting all right. Pink Floyd. The Who. I met them all. More tea?'

Banks held out his cup while Enderby poured. His gold wedding band was embedded deeply in his pudgy finger, surrounded by tufts of hair. 'You'd have been how old then?' Banks asked.

'In 1970? Just turned thirty that May.'

That would be about right, Banks guessed. Enderby looked to be in his mid-sixties now, with the comfortable paunch of a man who enjoys his inactivity and a head bereft of even a hint of a hair. He made up for the lack with a grey scrubbing-brush moustache. A delicate pink pattern of broken blood vessels mapped his cheeks and nose, but Banks put it down to blood pressure rather than drink. Enderby didn't talk or act like a boozer, and his breath didn't smell of Trebor extra-strong mints.

'So what was it like working on that case?' Banks asked. 'What do you remember most about the Robin Merchant investigation?'

Enderby screwed up his eyes and gazed out of the window. 'It must have been about ten o'clock by the time we got to the scene,' he said. 'It was a beautiful morning, I do remember that. Clear. Warm. Birds singing. And there he was, floating in the pool.'

'What was your first impression?'

Enderby thought for a moment, then gave a brief, barking laugh and put his cup down on the saucer. 'Do you know what it was?' he said. 'You'll never believe this. He was on his back, naked, you know, and I remember thinking he'd got such a little prick for a famous rock star. All the stuff we heard back then about groupies and orgies. The *News of the World* and all that. We assumed they were all hung like horses. It seemed so incongruous, him floating there all shrivelled, like a shrimp or a seahorse or something. It was the water, of course. No matter how warm the day was, the water was still cold.'

'That'll do it every time. Were the others up and around when you arrived?'

'You must be joking. The uniforms were rousing them. If it hadn't been for Merchant's drowning and our arrival they'd probably have slept until well into the afternoon. They looked in pretty bad shape, too, some of them. Hung-over and worse.'

'So who phoned it in?'

'The gardener, when he arrived for work.'

'Was he a suspect?'

'Nah, not really.'

'Many hangers-on and groupies around?'

'It's hard to say. According to their statements, everyone was a close friend of the band. No one *admitted* to being a groupie or a hanger-on. Most of the guys in the band were just with their regular girlfriends.'

'What about Robin Merchant? Was he with anyone that night?'

'There was a girl asleep in his bed,' said Enderby.

'Girlfriend?'

'Groupie.'

'According to what I've read,' Banks said, 'the thinking at the time was that Merchant had taken some Mandrax and was wandering around the pool naked when he fell in at the shallow end, hit his head on the bottom and drowned. Is that right?'

'Yes,' said Enderby. 'That was what it looked like, and that was what the pathologist confirmed. There was also a broken glass on the edge of the pool with Merchant's fingerprints on it. He'd been drinking. Vodka.'

'Did you consider other possible scenarios?'

'Such as?'

'That it wasn't accidental.'

'Somebody pushed him?'

'It would be a natural assumption. You know what suspicious minds we coppers have.'

'True enough,' Enderby agreed. 'I must admit, it crossed my mind, but I soon ruled it out.'

'Why?'

'Nobody had any motive.'

'Not according to what they *told* you.'

'We dug a bit deeper than that. Give us some credit. We might not have had the resources you've got today, but we did our best.'

'There was no friction within the band?'

'As far as I know there's always friction in bands. Put a group of people together with egos that big and there has to be. Stands to reason.'

Banks laughed. Then he thought of Brian and wondered if the Blue Lamps were due for a split before too long. Brian hadn't said anything, but Banks sensed something different about him, a certain lack of excitement and commitment, perhaps, and his turning up like that, out of the blue, was unusual. He seemed weary. And what about Emilia? Was she the Yoko Ono figure? Still, if Brian wanted to talk, he would get round to it in his own time. There was no use in pushing him: he'd always been that way. 'Anything in particular?' he asked Enderby.

'Let's see. They were all worried about Vic Greaves's drug intake, for a start. His performances were getting more and more erratic, and his behaviour was unreliable. Apparently, he'd missed a concert engagement not that long back, and the rest of them were still a bit pissed off with him for leaving them in the lurch.'

'Did Greaves have an alibi?'

Enderby scratched the side of his nose. 'As a matter of fact, he did,' he said. 'Two, actually.'

'Two?'

Enderby grinned. 'Greaves and Merchant were the only two band members who didn't have regular girlfriends. That night, Greaves happened to be in bed with two groupies.'

'Lucky devil,' said Banks. 'I'd never have thought he had it in him.' He remembered the bald, bloated figure with the hollow eyes he had seen in Lyndgarth.

'According to them, he didn't,' said Enderby. 'Apparently he was too far gone to get it up. Bloody waste, if you ask me. They were lovely-looking girls.' He smiled at the memory. 'Not wearing very much, either, when I interviewed them. That's one of the little things you don't forget in a hurry. Not so little, either, if you catch my drift.'

'Could Greaves not have sneaked away for a while during the night? They must have both slept, or passed out, at some time.'

'Look, when you get right down to it, any of them could have done it. At least, anyone who could still walk in a straight line. We didn't really set great store by the alibis, as such. For a start, hardly any of them could remember much about the previous evening, or even what time they finally went to bed. They might have been wandering about all night, for all I know, and not even noticed Merchant in the swimming-pool.'

'So what made you rule out murder so quickly?'

'I told you. No real motive. No evidence that he'd been pushed.'

'But Merchant could have got into an argument with some-one, gone a bit over the top.'

'Oh, he *could* have, yes. But no one says he did, so what are we supposed to do? Jump to conclusions and pick someone? Anyone?'

'What about an intruder?'

'Couldn't be ruled out either. It was easy enough to get into the grounds. But, again, there was no evidence of an intruder, and nothing was stolen. Besides, Merchant's injuries were consistent with falling into a swimming-pool and drowning, which was what happened. Look, if you ask me, at worst it could have been a bit of stoned and drunken larking around that went wrong. I'm not saying that was what happened, because there's no proof, but if they were all stoned or pissed, which they were, and they started running around the pool playing tag or what-have-you, and someone tagged Merchant just a bit too hard and he ended up in the pool dead . . . Well, what would you do?'

'First off,' said Banks, 'I'd try to get him out. There was no way I could be sure he was dead. Then I'd probably try artificial respiration, or the kiss of life or whatever it was back then, while someone called an ambulance.'

'Aye,' said Enderby. 'And if you'd had as much drugs in your system as they had, you'd probably have stood there for half an hour twiddling your thumbs before doing anything, and then the first thing you'd have done is get rid of your stash.'

'Did the Drugs Squad search the premises? There was no mention in the file.'

'Between you and me, we searched the place. Oh, we found a bit of marijuana, a few tabs of LSD, some mandies. But nothing hard.'

'What happened?'

'We decided, in the light of everything else – like a body to deal with – that we wouldn't bring charges. We just disposed of the stuff. I mean, what were we to do, arrest them all for possession?'

Disposed of? Banks doubted that. Consumed or sold, more likely. But there was no sense in opening that can of worms. 'Did you get any sense that they'd cooked up a story between them?'

'No. As I said, half of them couldn't even remember the party. It was all pretty fragmented and inconclusive.'

'Lord Jessop was present, right?'

'Right. Probably about the most coherent of the lot. That was before he got into the hard stuff.'

'And the most influential?'

'I can see where you're going with this. Of course nobody wanted a scandal. It was bad enough as it was. Maybe that was why we didn't bring drugs charges. There'd been enough of that over the past two or three years with the Stones bust, and it was all beginning to seem pretty ridiculous. Especially after *The Times* ran that editorial about breaking a butterfly on a wheel. Within hours we had them all banging at the door and jumping over the walls. The *News of the World*, the *People*, the *Daily Mirror*, you name them. So even if someone else had been involved in a bit of horseplay, the thinking went, it had still been an accident, and there was no point in inviting scandal. As we couldn't *prove* that anyone else had been involved and no one was admitting to it, that was the end of it. Tea's done. Fancy another pot?'

'No, thank you,' said Banks. 'If there's nothing more you can tell me, I'd better be off.'

'Sorry to disappoint you.'

'It wasn't disappointing.'

'Look, you never did tell me what it was all about. Remember, we're in the same job, or used to be.'

Banks was so used to not giving out any more information than he needed to that he sometimes forgot to say why he was asking about something. 'We found a writer by the name of Nick Barber dead. You might have read about it.'

'Sounds vaguely familiar,' said Enderby. 'I try to keep up.'

'What you won't have read about is that he was working on a story about the Mad Hatters, on Vic Greaves and the band's early days in particular.'

'Interesting,' said Enderby. 'But I still don't see why you're asking about Robin Merchant's death.'

'It was just something Barber said to a girlfriend,' Banks said. 'He mentioned something about a juicy story with a murder.'

'Now you've got me interested,' said Enderby. 'A murder, you say?'

'That's right. I suppose it was just journalistic licence, trying to impress his girlfriend.'

'Not necessarily,' said Enderby.

'What do you mean?'

'Well, I'm pretty sure that Robin Merchant's death was accidental, but that wasn't the first time I was out at Swainsview Lodge in connection with a suspicious death.'

'Really?' said Banks. 'Do tell.'

Enderby stood up. 'Look, the sun's well over the yard arm. How about we head down to my local and I'll tell you over a pint?'

'I'm driving,' said Banks.

'That's all right,' said Enderby. 'You can buy me one and watch me drink it.'

'What took you out there?' Banks asked.

'A murder,' said Enderby, eyes glittering. 'A real one that time.'

Saturday, 20 September 1969

'She won't come out of her room,' Janet Chadwick said, as she sat with her husband eating tea on Saturday evening, football results on the telly. Chadwick was filling in his pools coupon, but it was soon clear that the £230,000 jackpot was going to elude him this week, just as it had every other week.

Chadwick ate some toad-in-the-hole, after dipping it liberally in the gravy. 'What's wrong with her now?'

'She won't say. She came dashing in late this afternoon and went straight upstairs. I called to her, knocked on her door, but she wouldn't answer.'

'Did you go in?'

'No. She has to be allowed some privacy, Stan. She's sixteen.'

'I know. I know. But this is unusual, missing her tea like this. And it's Saturday. Doesn't she usually go out Saturday night?'

'Yes.'

'I'll have a word with her after tea.'

'Be careful with her, Stan. You know how on edge she seems these days.'

Chadwick touched his wife's wrist. 'I'll be careful. I'm not really the terrible child-gobbling monster you think I am.'

Janet laughed. 'I don't think you're a monster. She's just at a difficult age. A father doesn't always understand as much as a mother does.'

'I'll tread gently, don't worry.'

They finished their tea in silence, and while Janet went to wash the dishes, Chadwick went upstairs to try to talk to Yvonne. He tapped at her door but got no answer. He tapped again, a little louder, but all he heard was a muffled 'Go away'. There wasn't even any music playing. Yvonne must have had her transistor radio turned off. Another unusual sign.

Chadwick reckoned he had two choices: leave Yvonne to her own devices, or simply walk in. Janet would favour the former, *laissez-faire* approach, no doubt, but Chadwick was in a mood to take the bull by the horns. He'd had enough of Yvonne's sneaking around, stopping out all night, her secrets and lies and prima-donna behaviour. Now was the time to see what was at the bottom of it. Taking a deep breath, he opened the door and walked in.

The outrage he expected didn't come. The curtains were closed, the lights off, giving the room a dim, twilit appearance. It even disguised the untidy mess of clothes and magazines on the floor and bed. At first, Chadwick couldn't see Yvonne. Then he realised she was on her bed, under the eiderdown. When his eyes adjusted, he could also see that she was shaking. Concerned, he perched on the edge of the bed and said softly, 'Yvonne . . . Yvonne, sweetheart. What's wrong? What is it?'

She didn't react at first, and he sat patiently waiting, remembering when she was a little girl and came to him when she had nightmares. 'It's all right,' he said, 'you can tell me. I won't be angry with you. I promise.'

Her hand snaked out from under the eiderdown and sought his. He held it. Still she said nothing, then she slowly slid the cover off her face, and he could see even in the weak light that she had been crying. She was still shaking, too.

'What is it, love?' he asked. 'What's happened?'

'It was horrible,' she said. '*He* was horrible.'

Chadwick felt his neck muscles tense. 'What? Has somebody done something to you?'

'He's ruined everything.'

'What do you mean? You'd better tell me from the start, Yvonne. I want to understand, honestly I do.'

Yvonne stared at him, as if trying to come to a decision. He knew he came across as strict and straight and unbending, but he really did want to know what was upsetting her, and not with a view to punishment this time. Whatever she thought, and however difficult it was, he really did love his daughter. One by one, the terrible possibilities crowded in on him. Had she found out she was pregnant? Was that it? Like Linda Lofthouse when she was Yvonne's age? Or had someone assaulted her?

'What is it?' he asked. 'Did somebody hurt you?'

Yvonne shook her head. 'Not like you think.' Then she launched herself into his arms and he could feel her tears on his neck and hear her talking into his shoulder. 'I was so scared, Daddy, the things he was saying. I really thought he was going to do something terrible to me. I know he had a knife somewhere. If I hadn't run away . . .' She collapsed into sobs. Chadwick digested what she had said, trying to keep his fatherly anger at bay, and gently disentangled himself. Yvonne lay back on her pillows and rubbed her eyes with the backs of her hands. She looked like a little girl. Chadwick handed her the box of tissues from the dresser top.

'Start at the beginning,' he said. 'Slowly.'

'I was at the Brimleigh festival, Dad. I want you to know that before I start. I'm sorry for lying.'

'I knew that.'

'But, Dad? . . . How?'

'Call it a father's instinct.' *Or a copper's instinct,* he thought. 'Go on.'

'I've been hanging around with some people. You wouldn't like them. That's why . . . why I didn't tell you. But they're people like me, Dad. We're into the same music and ideas and beliefs about society. They're different. They're not boring, not like the kids at school. They read poetry and write and play music.'

'Students?'

'Some of them.'

'So they're older than you?'

'What does age matter?'

'Never mind. Go on.'

Yvonne looked a little uncertain now, and Chadwick saw that he would have to keep his editorial comments to a bare minimum if he hoped to get the truth from his daughter. 'Everything was fine, really it was. And then . . .' She started trembling again, got herself under control and went on. 'There's this man called McGarrity. He's older than the others and he acts really weird. He always scared me.'

'In what way?'

'He's got this horrible, twisted sort of smile that makes you feel like an insect, and he keeps quoting things, T. S. Eliot, the Bible, other stuff. Sometimes he just paces up and down with his knife.'

'What knife?'

'He's got this knife, and he keeps just, you know, tapping it against his palm as he walks.'

'What kind of knife is it?'

'A flick-knife with a tortoiseshell handle.'

'Which palm does he tap it against?'

Yvonne frowned, and Chadwick realised again that he had to be careful. It could wait. 'Sorry,' he said. 'It doesn't matter. Go on.'

'They say, Steve says, he's a bit weird because he had electric-shock treatment. They say he used to be a great blues harmonica player, but since the shocks he can't play any more. But I don't know . . . He just seems weird to me.'

'Is this the man who bothered you?'

'Yes. I went over there this afternoon to see Steve – he's my boyfriend – but he wasn't in and only McGarrity was there. I wanted to go but he insisted I stay.'

'Did he force you?'

'Well, I wouldn't say he forced me, but I was uncomfortable. I was hoping Steve and the others would get back soon, that's all.'

'Was he on drugs?'

Yvonne looked away and nodded.

'OK. Go on.'

'He said some terrible things.'

'About what?'

'About the girl who was killed. About those dead people in Los Angeles. About me.'

'What did he say about you?'

Yvonne looked down. 'He was rude. I don't want to repeat it.'

'All right. Stay calm. Did he touch you?'

'He grabbed my arm and he touched my face. He was so frightening. I was terrified he was going to do something.'

Chadwick felt his teeth grinding. 'What happened?'

'I waited until he had his back turned to me and I ran away.'

'Good girl. Did he come after you?'

'I don't think so. I didn't look.'

'OK. You're doing fine, Yvonne. You're safe now.'

'But, Dad, what if he . . .'

'What if he what? Was he at Brimleigh?'

'Yes.'

'With you?'

'No, he was wandering around the field.'

'Did you see him go in the woods?'

'No. But it was dark most of the time. I wouldn't have seen.'

'Where did it happen this afternoon?'

'Just down the road, Springfield Mount. Look, Dad, they're all right, really, the others, Steve. It's just him. There's something wrong with him, I'm sure of it.'

'Did he know Linda Lofthouse?'

'Linda? I don't . . . Yes, yes, he did.'

Chadwick's ears pricked up at the familiarity with which Yvonne mentioned Linda's name. 'How do you know? It's all right, Yvonne, you can tell me the truth. I'm not going to be angry with you.'

'Promise?'

'Cross my heart and hope to die.'

Yvonne smiled. It was an old ritual. 'It was at another house, on Bayswater Terrace,' she said. 'There's three places people, like, gather to listen to music and stuff. Springfield Mount and Carberry Place are the other two. Anyway, some time during the summer I was with Steve, and Linda was there. McGarrity too. They didn't know one another, they weren't close or anything, but he *had* met her.'

Chadwick paused a moment to take it all in. Bayswater Terrace. Dennis, Julie and the rest. So Yvonne was part of *that* crowd. *His own daughter.* He held himself in check, remembering he'd promised not to be angry. Besides, the poor girl had been through a trauma, and it had taken a lot for her to open up; the last thing she needed now was a lecture from her father. But it was hard to keep his rage inside. He felt so wound up, so tight, that his chest ached.

'You met Linda, too?' he asked.

'Yes.' Tears filled Yvonne's eyes. 'Once. We didn't talk much, really. She just said she liked my dress and my hair, and we talked about what a drag school can be. She was so nice, Dad, how could anyone do that to her?'

'I don't know, sweetheart,' Chadwick said, stroking his daughter's silky blonde hair. 'I don't know.'

'Do you think it was him? McGarrity?'

'I don't know that, either, but I'm going to have to have a talk with him.'

'Don't be too hard on Steve or the others, Dad. Please. They're all right. Really they are. It's only McGarrity who's weird.'

'I understand,' said Chadwick, and paused. 'How do you feel now about getting up and having something to eat?'

'I'm not hungry.'

'Well, at least come downstairs and see your mother. She's worried sick about you.'

'OK,' said Yvonne. 'But give me a few minutes to get changed and wash my face.'

'Right you are, sweetheart.' Chadwick kissed the top of her head, left the room and headed for the telephone, jaw set hard. Later tonight, someone was going to be very sorry he had ever been born.

14

Annie Cabbot tried to control her temper as she waited to knock and enter Detective Superintendent Gervaise's office after Banks had left for Whitby. It was difficult. She had sensed from the start that Gervaise didn't like her, and had sussed her as another ambitious woman who had got where she was the hard way and was damned if she was going to give any other woman anything less than her worst. So much for female solidarity.

Annie took several deep, calming breaths, the way she did when she was meditating or practising yoga. It didn't work. She knocked anyway and entered, even before the slightly puzzled voice called, 'Enter.'

'I'd like a word, ma'am,' said Annie.

'DI Cabbot. Please, sit down.'

Annie sat. She remembered how she had always felt slightly awed and nervous when Detective Superintendent Gristhorpe had called her into this office, but now she felt nothing of the kind.

'What can I help you with?'

'You were seriously out of order back there,' Annie said. 'At the morning briefing.'

'I was?' Gervaise feigned surprise. At least, Annie believed it was feigned.

'You have no right to make public comments about my private life.'

Superintendent Gervaise held up her hand. 'Now, let's wait

a moment before we go any further. Exactly what did I say to upset you so much?'

'You know damn well what it was. Ma'am.'

'We don't seem to be getting off on the right foot here, do we?'

'You said you had no desire to argue sexual mores, *especially* with me.'

'Those meetings aren't a forum for argument, DI Cabbot. They're called to bring everyone up to date and set the scene for more actions and lines of inquiry. You know that.'

'Yet you deliberately insulted me in front of my colleagues.'

Superintendent Gervaise regarded her as she might a particularly troublesome schoolgirl. 'Well, since we're on the subject,' she said, 'you do have something of a chequered history with us, don't you?'

Annie said nothing.

'Let me remind you. You'd not been in North Yorkshire five minutes before you were jumping into bed with DCI Banks. And let me also remind you that fraternising between fellow officers is seriously frowned upon, and liaisons between a DS, as you were then, and a DCI, are particularly fraught with danger, as I'm sure you found out. He was your superior officer. What were you thinking of?'

Annie felt her heart beating hard in her chest. 'My private life is my affair.'

'You're not a stupid woman,' Superintendent Gervaise went on. 'I know that. We all make mistakes, and they're rarely fatal.' She paused. 'But your last one was, wasn't it? Your last mistake almost cost DCI Banks his life.'

'We weren't involved in anything then,' Annie said, aware as she spoke of how weak her response sounded.

'I know that.' Gervaise shook her head. 'DI Cabbot, I'm not entirely certain how you've managed to last here so long, let alone why you were promoted to DI so quickly. Things must have been very easy-going around here. Or perhaps DCI Banks had a certain amount of influence with the ACC?'

Annie felt as if her heart was about to explode at the slur, but a dreadful calm flooded her, disconcerting at first, like a sort of cooling numbness in her blood, a falling away of feeling. Then it warmed a little, transformed into a calm, altered state. *It didn't matter.* Whatever Superintendent Gervaise thought, said or did, *it didn't matter.* Annie cared about her career, but there were some things she wouldn't take, not for anything, not from anyone, and that knowledge made her feel free. She almost smiled. Gervaise must have sensed some change in the air, because there was a new edge to her voice when she noticed she wasn't getting the desired response from Annie.

'Anyway, in case you haven't noticed it, things have changed now. I won't countenance romantic relationships among my officers. They're distracting and sow the seeds for all kinds of mistakes and future difficulties, as you have discovered. And in the future, I would strongly suggest that you think again before continuing your relationship with DCI Banks.'

Did Gervaise really believe that Annie and Banks had got back together? Why? Had someone told her? A few moments ago Annie would have leaped out of her seat at such words and throttled Gervaise, but now she took it in calmly. The superintendent had also known about Banks having a pint in the Cross Keys on the night of the murder. Who had told her? Was there a spy in their midst? Annie didn't react.

'DI Cabbot?'

'Sorry,' said Annie. 'I was miles away.'

'That's irresponsible of you. You barge in here telling me I'm not doing my job properly, and the minute you realise you're in the wrong, you start daydreaming.'

'It wasn't that,' Annie said. 'Are we finished here?'

'Not until I say so.'

'Ma'am.'

'This other business. Kelly Soames.'

'It's not other business,' said Annie. 'It's all connected.'

'What do you mean?'

'I defended Kelly Soames's sexual mores so you attacked mine. It's connected.'

'I thought we'd left that behind.'

'Look, you want me to subject the poor girl to the ordeal of her father finding out she'd had a sexual relationship with Nick Barber, and I said I'd given her some assurances that wouldn't happen.'

'Those assurances weren't yours to give.'

'I'm aware of that. Even so, you can hardly attack me for wanting to stand by my word.'

'Admirable as that may seem, it's not workable here. This job isn't about saving your conscience and keeping your promises. I want that girl confronted with what happened in the presence of her father, and if you won't do it I'll find someone who will.'

'What is it with you? Are you a sadist or something?'

Gervaise's lips narrowed in a nasty smile. 'I'm a professional detective just doing her job,' she said. 'Which is something you should take a little more seriously. Sympathy for victims is all very well, in its place, but remember that Nicholas Barber is the victim here, not Kelly Soames.'

'Not yet,' said Annie.

'Insubordination will get you nowhere.'

'No, but it feels good.' Annie stood up to leave. 'There's obviously no further point talking to you, so if you're thinking of taking action against me, do it. I don't care. Either shit or get off the pot.'

Gervaise's face fell. 'What did you say?'

Annie walked towards the door. 'You heard me,' she said.

'Right,' said Superintendent Gervaise. 'I want you on statement-reading as of now. And send in DS Templeton.'

'Yes, ma'am,' said Annie, and shut the door softly behind her as she left. *Templeton.* Now, that made sense.

Sunday, 21 September 1969

Chadwick went with the Springfield Mount team because that was the house where Yvonne had been accosted by McGarrity. Two other teams, also with search warrants, carried out simultaneous raids on Bayswater Terrace and Carberry Place. They waited until well after midnight, by which time Yvonne was fast asleep in bed. As any prior announcement of their presence was likely to result in drugs being flushed down the toilet, they were authorised to enter by force.

The streets were deserted, most of the houses in darkness apart from the lonely light of an insomniac here and there, or a student burning the midnight oil; a sheen of rain reflected the amber streetlights on the pavements and tarmac. Directly across from Springfield Mount a small, triangular park was locked up for the night, wedged between two merging main roads. At the end of the street, across the road, loomed the local grammar school, all in darkness now, with its bell-tower and high windows.

The unmarked police car pulled up behind a patrol car. There were five officers altogether: Chadwick, Bradley and three uniforms, one of whom would guard the back. Geoff Broome was leading the Carberry team, and his colleague, Martin Young, the raid on Bayswater Terrace. They didn't expect any resistance or problems, except perhaps from McGarrity, if he had his knife.

Chadwick could hear music coming from the front room, and candlelight flickered behind the curtains. Good. Someone was at home. Surprise was of the essence now. When everyone was in position, Chadwick gave a nod to the uniform with the battering-ram and one smash was enough to break the lock and send the door banging back on its hinges.

As arranged, the two uniformed constables dashed upstairs to secure the upper level and Chadwick and Bradley entered the front room. The officer on guard at the back would take care of the kitchen.

In the living room, Chadwick found three people lying on the floor in advanced stages of intoxication – marijuana, judging by the smell that even two smouldering joss-sticks couldn't mask. Candles flickered, and dreadful, wailing electric-guitar music came from the record-player, a kangaroo with a pain in its testicles, by the sound of it, Chadwick thought.

It didn't look as if their arrival had interrupted any deep conversation, or any conversation at all for that matter: they all seemed beyond speech, and one only managed a quick 'What the hell?' before Chadwick announced who he was and told them the police were there to search the premises for drugs and for a knife that may have been used in the committing of a murder. Bradley switched on the electric light and turned off the music.

Things didn't look so bad, Chadwick saw with surprise, not what he had expected, just three scruffy long-haired kids lounging around stoned, listening to what passed for music. There was no orgy; nobody was crawling around naked and drooling on the floor or committing outrageous sex acts. Then he saw the LP cover leaning against the wall. It showed a girl with long wavy red hair and full red lips. She was naked from the belly-button up, and couldn't have been more than eleven or twelve. In her hands, she cradled a chrome model aeroplane. What kind of perverts was he dealing with? Chadwick wondered. And one had been seeing his daughter. This was where Yvonne would have been tonight, had McGarrity not scared her off. This was what she would have been doing. She had been here before, done this, and that set his teeth on edge.

Bradley took their names: Steve Morrison, Todd Crowley and Jacqueline McNeil. They all seemed docile and sheepish enough. Chadwick took Morrison aside to a corner of the room and gripped the front of his shirt in his fist. 'Whatever comes of this,' he hissed, 'I want you to stop seeing my daughter. Understand?'

Steve turned pale. 'Who? Who am I supposed to be seeing?'

'Her name's Yvonne – Yvonne Chadwick.'

'Shit, I didn't know she—'

'Just stay away from her. OK?'

Steve nodded, and Chadwick let him go. 'Right,' he said, turning to the others. 'Where's McGarrity?'

'Dunno,' said Todd Crowley. 'He was here earlier. Maybe he's upstairs.'

'What were you doing?'

'Nothing. Just listening to music.'

Chadwick gestured towards the LP cover. 'Where did you get that filth?'

'What?'

'The naked child. You realise we could probably prosecute you under the Obscene Publications Act, don't you?'

'That's art, man,' Crowley protested. 'You can buy it at any record shop. Obscenity's in the eye of the beholder.'

There were greasy fish-and-chip wrappers and newspaper on the floor beside empty beer bottles. Bradley went to the ashtray and extracted the remains of a number of hand-rolled cigarettes he identified by their smell as having been a mix of tobacco and hash. That, in itself, was enough to charge them with possession.

What the hell did Yvonne see in this dump? Chadwick wondered. Why did she come here? Was her life at home so bad? Was she so desperate to get away from him and Janet? But there was no point trying to work it out. As Enderby had said, it was probably down to freedom.

Chadwick heard a brief scuffle and a bang upstairs, followed by a series of loud thumps, getting closer. When he went to the foot of the stairs, he saw the two uniformed constables, one without his hat, holding the arms of a man who was struggling to get up.

'He didn't want to come with us, sir,' one of the officers said.

It looked as if they had held his arms and dragged him down the stairs backwards, which shouldn't have done much damage to anything except his dignity and maybe his tailbone. Chadwick watched as the unruly black-clad figure with the lank dark hair and pockmarked face got to his feet and dusted himself off, the superior smirk already back in place, if indeed it had ever been gone.

'Well, well, well,' he said, 'Mr McGarrity, I assume. I've been wanting a word with you.'

Enderby's local, two streets down, was like his house: comfortable and unremarkable. It was a relatively new building, late sixties from its low, squat shape and the large picture windows facing the sea. The advantages, from Banks's point of view, were that it was practically empty at that time in the afternoon, and they sold cask-conditioned Tetley's. One pint wouldn't do him any harm, he decided, as he bought the drinks at the bar and carried them over.

Enderby looked at him. 'Thought your resolve might weaken.'

'It often does,' Banks admitted. 'Nice view.'

Enderby took a sip of beer. 'Mmm.'

The window looked out over the glittering North Sea, dotted here and there with fishing-boats and trawlers. Whitby was still a thriving fishing town, Banks reminded himself, even if the whaling industry it had grown from was long extinct. Captain Cook had had his seafaring start in Whitby, and his statue stood on West Cliff, close to the jawbone of a whale.

'When did this real murder happen?' Banks asked.

'September the year before. 1969. By Christ, Banks, you're taking me on a hell of a trip down Memory Lane today. I haven't thought about that business in years.'

Banks knew all about trips down Memory Lane: not so long ago he had looked into the disappearance of an old schoolfriend, whose body was found buried in a field outside Peterborough. Sometimes, as he got older, it seemed that the past was always overwhelming the present.

'Who was the victim?'

'A woman, young girl, really, called Linda Lofthouse. Lovely girl. Funny, I can still picture her there, half covered by the sleeping-bag. That white dress with the flowers embroidered on the front. She had a flower painted on her face, too. A cornflower. She looked so peaceful. She was dead, of course. Someone had grabbed her from behind and stabbed her so viciously he cut off a piece of her heart.' He gave a little shudder. 'Someone's just walked over my grave.'

'How was Swainsview Lodge involved in all this?'

'I'm getting to that. The murder took place at a rock festival in Brimleigh Glen. The body was found on the field by one of the volunteers cleaning up after it was all over. The evidence showed that she was killed in Brimleigh Woods nearby and then moved. It was only made to look as if she was killed on the field.'

'I know Brimleigh Glen,' said Banks. He had taken his wife Sandra and the children, Brian and Tracy, on picnics there shortly after they had moved to Eastvale. 'But I know nothing about any festival.'

'Probably before your time here,' said Enderby. 'First weekend of September 1969. Not so long after Woodstock and the Isle of Wight. It wasn't one of the really big ones. It was overshadowed by the others. And it was also the only one they ever held there.'

'Who played?'

'The biggest names were Led Zeppelin, Pink Floyd and Fleetwood Mac. The others? Maybe you remember Family, the Incredible String Band, Roy Harper, Blodwyn Pig, Colosseum, the Liverpool Scene, Edgar Broughton and the rest. The usual late-sixties festival line-up.'

Banks knew all those names, even had a number of their CDs, or used to have. He would have to work harder at building up his collection again instead of just buying new stuff or recent reissues. He should make a note whenever he missed something he had once had. 'How were the Mad Hatters involved?' he asked.

'They were one of the two local bands to play there, along with Jan Dukes de Grey. The Hatters were just getting big at the time, in late 1969, and it was a pivotal gig for them.'

'You've followed their career since then?' said Banks.

Enderby raised his glass. 'Of course. I was more into blues back then – still am, really – but I got all their records. I met them, got a signed album. It was a big thrill. Even if I didn't get to keep it.' He smiled at a distant memory.

'Why not?'

'DI Chadwick took it for his daughter. Good Lord, Chiller Chadwick. I haven't thought of him in years. What a cold, hard bastard he was to work for. Tough Scot, ex-army, hard as nails. Old school, stickler for detail. Always perfectly turned out. You could see your reflection in his brogues, that sort of thing. I'm afraid I was a bit of a rebel back then. Let my hair grow down to my collar. He didn't like it one bit. Good detective, though. I learned a lot from Chiller Chadwick. And he did apologise about the LP, I'll give him that.'

'What happened to him?'

'No idea. Retired, I suppose. Maybe dead now. He was quite a few years older than me. Fought in the war. And he was with West Yorkshire, see. Leeds. They didn't reckon we'd got anyone bright enough up here to solve a murder, and they might have been right. Anyway, I heard there was some sort of trouble with his daughter, and it affected his health.'

'What sort of trouble?'

'I don't know. She went to stay with relatives. I never met her. I think perhaps she was a bit of a wild child, though, and he wouldn't stand for that, wouldn't Chiller. You know what some of the kids were like back then, smoking marijuana, dropping acid, sleeping around. Anyway, whatever it was, he kept it under his hat. You should talk to his driver, if he's still around.'

'Who's that?'

'Lad called Bradley. Simon Bradley. He was a DC then, Chiller's driver. But now, who knows? Probably a chief constable.'

'Why do you say that?'

'Bit of an arse-licker. They always get ahead, don't they?'

'What was Chadwick's first name?'

'Stanley.'

Banks thought that Templeton or Winsome ought to be able to track down Simon Bradley easily enough, and if Leeds was involved, he might be able to enlist the help of DI Ken Blackstone to find out about Chadwick. He offered Enderby another drink, which Enderby accepted. Banks's pint glass, fortunately, was still half full.

'I take it this murder was solved?' Banks asked, when he returned with the drink.

'Oh, yes. We got him, all right.'

'So, back to how the Mad Hatters and Swainsview Lodge were involved.'

'Oh, yes, forgot about that, didn't I? Well, Vic Greaves was the victim's cousin, see, and he'd arranged for her and her friend to get backstage passes for the festival. During Led Zeppelin's performance on the last night, this cousin, Linda

Lofthouse, decided to take a walk in the woods by herself. That's where she was killed.'

'Any sexual motive?'

'She wasn't raped, if that's what you mean. They did find some semen on the back of her dress, though, so what he did obviously gave him some sort of thrill. Secretor. Mind you, it was a common enough blood group – A, if I remember correctly, same as the victim's. We didn't have DNA and all that fancy forensic technology back then, so we had to rely on good old-fashioned police work.'

'Did you recover the murder weapon?'

'Eventually. Complete with traces of group A blood and the killer's fingerprints.'

'Very handy. I suppose he could have argued that it was his own blood. It was *his* knife, after all.'

'He could have, but he didn't. Our Forensics blokes were good. They also found traces of white fibre and a strand of dyed cotton wedged between the blade and the handle. These were eventually linked to the victim's dress. There was no doubt about it. The dye on its own was enough.'

'Seems pretty much cut and dried, then.'

'It was. I told you. Anyway, a week or so later, the Mad Hatters were up at Swainsview rehearsing for a tour, so that was the first time I went there and met them.'

'Tell me a bit more about the personalities involved.'

'Well, Vic Greaves was mad as a hatter, no doubt about it. When we tried to talk to him at Swainsview Lodge he was practically incoherent. You know, he'd keep going, like, "If you go down to the woods today . . ." Remember? "The Teddy Bears' Picnic"?'

Banks did remember. He had even heard another version of it recently when Vic Greaves said to him, 'Vic's gone down to the woods today.' Coincidence? He would have to find out. Greaves hadn't been coherent during the rest of their chat in

Lyndgarth the other day, either. 'Was he on drugs at the time?' Banks asked.

'He was on something, that's for certain. Most of the people around him said he took LSD like it was Smarties. Maybe he did.'

'What about the rest of them?'

'The others weren't too bad. Adrian Pritchard, the drummer, was a bit of a wild man, you know, wrecking hotel rooms on tour, getting into fights and that sort of thing, but he settled down. Reg Cooper, of course, well, he was the quiet one. He became one of the best, most respected guitarists in the business. Great songwriter, too. Along with Terry Watson, the rhythm guitarist and lead singer, he pushed the band in a more pop direction. Robin Merchant always seemed the brightest of the bunch to me, though. He was educated, well read, articulate, but a bit weird in his tastes, you know, he was into all that occult stuff, magic, tarot, astrology, Aleister Crowley, Carlos Castaneda – but lots of them were, back then.'

'What about Chris Adams?'

'Seemed a nice enough bloke on both occasions I met him. A bit straighter than the rest, maybe, but still one of the "beautiful people", if you catch my drift.'

'Did they all take drugs?'

'They all smoked a lot of dope and did acid. Robin Merchant obviously got into mandies in a big way, and later Reg Cooper and Terry Watson had their problems with heroin and coke, but they're clean now, as far as I know, have been for years. I'm not sure about Chris. I don't think he was as much into it as the rest of them. Probably had to keep his wits about him for all the organising managers have to do.'

'I suppose so,' said Banks. 'Are you still in touch?'

'Good Lord, no. They wouldn't know me from Adam. The bumbling, awestruck young detective who came round asking bothersome questions? They didn't even remember me from the first time when I went there over Robin Merchant's death. But I tried to keep up with their careers, you know. You do when you've actually met someone as famous as that, don't you? I got to meet Pink Floyd, you know. And the Nice. Roy Harper, too. Now, *he* was stoned. They live in Los Angeles these days, most of the Mad Hatters. Except Tania, I think.'

'Tania Hutchison? The singer they brought in after Merchant died and Vic Greaves drifted off?'

'Yes. Beautiful girl. Absolutely stunning.'

Banks remembered lusting after Tania Hutchison when he'd watched her on *The Old Grey Whistle Test* in the early seventies. Every young male did. 'I seem to remember reading that she lives in Oxfordshire, somewhere like that,' Banks said.

'Yes, the proverbial country manor. Well, she can afford it.'

'You actually met her? I thought she came on the scene much later, after all that mess with Merchant and Greaves.'

'Sort of. See, she was the manager's girlfriend at the time. Chris Adams. She was with him when we went to investigate Robin Merchant's drowning. They were in bed together. I interviewed her the next morning. She wasn't looking her best, of course, a bit the worse for wear, but she still put the rest to shame.'

'So Chris Adams and Tania provided one another with alibis?'

'Yes.'

'And you had no reason to disbelieve them?'

'Like I said before, I had no real reason to disbelieve any of them.'

'How long had she known Adams and the group?'

'I can't say for certain, but she'd been around for a while before Merchant died,' Enderby said. 'I know she was at the Brimleigh festival with Linda Lofthouse. They were friends. I reckon that was where Adams met her. She and Linda lived in

London, Notting Hill. Practically flatmates. And they played and sang together in local clubs. Folk sort of stuff.'

'Interesting,' said Banks. 'I'll have to have a look into this Linda Lofthouse business.'

'Well, it was a murder but there's no mystery about it.'

'Oh, I don't know,' said Banks. 'And there's still the little matter of who killed Nick Barber, and why.'

Sunday, 21 September 1969

Chadwick could tell right from the start that McGarrity was not like the others, who had been bound over quickly to appear before the magistrate first thing Monday morning and released on police bail. No, McGarrity was another kettle of fish entirely.

For a start, like Rick Hayes, he was older than the rest. Probably in his early to mid-thirties, Chadwick estimated. He also had the unmistakable shiftiness of a habitual criminal and a pallor that, experience had taught Chadwick, came only from spending time in prison. There was something sly about him behind the smirk, and a deadness in his eyes that gave off danger signals. Just the kind of nutter to kill Linda Lofthouse, Chadwick reckoned. Now all he needed was a confession, and evidence.

They were sitting in a stark, windowless room, redolent of other men's sweat and fear, the ceiling filmed brownish-yellow from years of cigarette smoke. On the scarred wooden desk between them sat a battered and smudged green tin ashtray bearing the Tetley's name and logo. DC Bradley sat in a corner to the left of, and behind, McGarrity, taking notes. Chadwick intended to conduct this preliminary interview himself, but if he met stubborn opposition, he would bring in someone else later to help him chip away at the suspect's resistance. It had worked before and it would work again, he was certain, even with as slippery-looking a customer as McGarrity.

'Name?' he asked finally.

'Patrick McGarrity.'

'Date of birth?'

'The sixth of January 1936. I'm Capricorn.'

'Good for you. Ever been in prison, Patrick?'

McGarrity stared at him.

'Not to worry,' said Chadwick. 'We'll find out one way or another. Do you know why you're here?'

'Because you bastards smashed the door down in the middle of the night and brought me.'

'Good guess. I suppose you know we found drugs in the house?'

McGarrity shrugged. 'Nothing to do with me.'

'As a matter of fact,' Chadwick went on, 'they do have something to do with you. My officers found a significant amount of cannabis resin in the same room where they found you asleep. Over two ounces, in fact. Easily enough to sustain a dealing charge.'

'That wasn't mine. It wasn't even my room. I was just crashing there for the night.'

'What's your address?'

'I'm a free spirit. I go where I choose.'

'No fixed abode, then. Place of employment?'

McGarrity emitted a harsh laugh.

'Unemployed. Do you claim benefits?'

Silence.

'I'll take it that you do, then. Otherwise there might be charges under the Vagrancy Act.'

McGarrity leaned back in his chair and crossed his legs. His clothes were old and worn, like a tramp's, Chadwick noticed, not the bright peacock fashions the others favoured. And everything he wore was black, or close to it.

'Look,' McGarrity said, 'why don't you just cut the crap and get it over with? If you're going to charge me and put me in a cell, do it.'

'All in good time, Patrick. All in good time. Back to the cannabis. Where did it come from?'

'Ask your pig friends. They must have planted it.'

'Nobody planted anything. Where did it come from?'

'I don't know.'

'OK. Tell me about this afternoon.'

'What about it?'

'What did you do?'

'I don't remember. Not much. Read a book. Went for a walk.'

'Do you remember receiving a visitor?'

'Can't say as I do.'

'A young woman.'

'No.'

Chadwick's muscles were aching from keeping the rage inside. He felt like flinging himself across the table and strangling McGarrity with his bare hands. 'A woman you terrorised and assaulted?'

'I didn't do any such thing.'

'You deny the young woman was in the house?'

'I don't remember seeing anyone.'

Chadwick stood up so quickly he knocked over his chair. 'I've had enough of this, Constable,' he said to Bradley. 'Take him down and lock him up.' He glared at McGarrity for a second and said, 'We'll talk again, and the next time it won't be so polite.' Outside in the corridor, he leaned against the wall and took several deep breaths. His heart was beating like a steam piston inside his chest, and his skin was burning. Slowly, as he mopped his brow, the rage subsided. He straightened his tie and jacket and walked back to his office.

15

Detective Sergeant Kevin Templeton relished his latest assignment, and even more that Winsome was to accompany him as an observer. Even though he had got nowhere with her, not for lack of trying, he still found her incredibly attractive, and the sight of her thighs under the taut material of her pinstripe trousers still brought him out in a sweat. He'd always thought of himself as a breast man, but Winsome had soon put the lie to that. He tried not to make his glances obvious as she drove out of town and on to the main Lyndgarth Road. The farmhouse was at the end of a long, muddy track, and no matter how close to the door they parked, there was no way to avoid getting their shoes muddy.

'Christ, it bloody stinks here, dunnit?' Templeton moaned.

'It's a farmyard,' said Winsome.

'Yeah, I know that. Look, let me do the questioning, right? And you keep a close eye on the father, OK?' Templeton hopped on one leg by the doorway, trying to wipe some of the mud off his best Converse trainers.

'There's a shoe-scraper,' said Winsome.

'What?'

She pointed. 'That thing with the raised metal edge by the door. It's for scraping the mud off the soles of your shoes.'

'Well, you live and learn,' said Templeton, and had a go at it. 'Whatever will they think of next?'

'They thought of it a long time ago,' said Winsome.

'I know that. I was being sarcastic.'

'Yes, Sarge.'

Nearby, a dog was growling and barking fit to kill, but luckily it was chained up to a post.

Templeton shot Winsome a glance. 'No need for you to be sarcastic as well. Don't think I didn't catch your tone. Are you OK with the way the super wants us to play it?'

'I'm fine.'

Templeton's eyes narrowed. 'Am I to take it you don't—'

But before he could finish, the door opened and Calvin Soames stood there. 'Police, isn't it?' he said. 'What do you want this time?'

'Just come to clear a couple of things up, Mr Soames,' said Templeton, bringing out his best smile and offering his hand. Soames ignored it. 'Is your daughter at home?'

Soames grunted.

'All right if we come in?'

'Wipe your feet.' And with that he turned back into the gloom and left them to their own devices.

After wiping their feet on a bristly mat, they followed him into the inner recesses of the house and heard him call, 'Kelly! It's for you.'

The girl came downstairs, and her face registered disappointment when she saw Templeton and Winsome standing there in the hallway. 'You'd better come through,' she said, leading them into the kitchen, which was marginally brighter and smelt of bleach and overripe bananas. A black and white cat stirred lazily, jumped off its chair and sidled out of the room.

They all sat on sturdy hard-backed chairs round the table. Calvin Soames muttered something about work and headed out, but Templeton called him back. 'This concerns you, too, Mr Soames,' he said. 'Please sit down.'

Soames let a moment pass, then sat.

'What's this all about?' asked Kelly. 'I've told you everything already.'

'Well, that's just it, you see,' said Templeton. 'Being the untrusting detectives that we are, we don't take anything at face value, or on first account. It's like first impressions, see, they can so often be wrong. Any chance of a cup of tea?'

'I'll put the kettle on,' said Kelly.

She was definitely fit, Templeton thought, as he watched her move towards the range with just the barest swing of her hips, encased in tight jeans. Her waist was slender as a wand and she wore a jet belly-piercing, which made a nice contrast to her pale skin. The blonde hair was tied back, but a few tresses had escaped and framed her pale, oval face. Her breasts moved tantalisingly under the short yellow T-shirt, and Templeton guessed that she wasn't wearing a bra. Lucky bugger, that Barber, he thought. If the last thing on earth he'd done was shag Kelly Soames, it can't have been such a bad way to go. He began to wonder if, perhaps when they'd got this business over and done with, he might be in with a chance himself.

When the tea was served, Winsome took out her notebook and Templeton sat back in his chair. 'Right,' he said. 'Now, you, Mr Soames, returned here at about seven o'clock on Friday evening. Am I right?'

'That's right.'

'To check if you'd turned off the gas ring?'

'It's sometimes on so low,' he answered, 'that a puff of air would blow it out. A couple of times I've come home and smelt gas. I thought it best to check, as I don't live far from the Cross Keys.'

'About a five-minute drive each way, is that right?'

'About that, aye.'

'And you, Miss Soames, you were working at the Cross Keys all evening, right?'

Kelly chewed her thumbnail and nodded.

'How long have you been working there?'

'About two years now. There's not much else to do round here.'

'Ever thought of moving to the big city?'

Kelly looked at her father and said, 'No.'

'Nice place to work, is it, the Cross Keys?'

'It's all right.'

'Good spot to meet lads?'

'I don't know what you mean.'

'Oh, come on, Kelly. You're a barmaid. You must meet lots of lads, get chatted up a lot, nice-looking girl like you.'

She blushed at that, and the ghost of a smile crossed her face, Templeton noticed. Maybe he was in with a chance after all. As Calvin Soames looked on, the frown deepened on his forehead in a series of lines down to the bridge of his nose.

'Do they tell you their troubles?' Templeton went on. 'How their wives don't understand them and they're wasted on the jobs they're doing?'

Kelly shrugged. 'Sometimes,' she said. 'When it's quiet.'

'What do you do for fun?'

'Dunno. Go out with my mates, I suppose.'

'But where do you go? There's not a lot for a young girl to do round here, is there? It can't be very exciting.'

'There's Eastvale.'

'Oh, yes. I'm sure you enjoy a Saturday night out in East-vale with the lads, listening to dirty jokes, getting bladdered and puking your guts up with the rest of them around the market cross. No, I mean, a girl like you, there must be something better, something more. Surely?'

'There's dances sometimes, and bands,' Kelly said.

'Who do you like?'

'Dunno.'

'Come on, you must have a favourite.'

She shifted in her chair. 'I dunno, really. Keane. Maybe.'

'Ah, Keane.'

'You know them?'

'I've heard them,' said Templeton. 'Nick Barber was really into bands, wasn't he?'

Kelly seemed to tense up again. 'He said he liked music,' she said.

'Didn't he say he could get you into all the best concerts in London?'

'I don't think so. I've never been to London.'

Templeton felt Winsome's gaze boring into the side of his head. Her legs were crossed, and one was twitching. She clearly didn't like the way he was drawing the interview out, postponing the moment of glory. But he was enjoying himself. He closed in for the kill.

'Did Nick Barber promise to take you there?'

'No.' Kelly shook her head, panic showing on her face. 'Why would he do that?'

'Gratitude, perhaps?'

Calvin Soames's face darkened. 'What are you saying, man?'

Templeton ignored him. 'Well, Kelly?'

'I don't know what you're on about. I only talked to him at the bar when he ordered his drink. He was nice, polite. That's all.'

'Oh, come off it, Kelly,' said Templeton. 'We happen to know that you slept with him on two occasions.'

'What—' Calvin Soames tried to get to his feet but Templeton gently pushed him back down. 'Please stay where you are, Mr Soames.'

'What's all this about?' Soames demanded. 'What's going on?'

'Wednesday evening and Friday afternoon,' Templeton went on. 'A bit of afternoon delight. Beats the dentist's any day, I'd say.'

Kelly was crying now and her father was fast turning purple

with fury. 'Is this true, Kelly?' he asked. 'Is what he's saying true?'

Kelly buried her face in her hands. 'I feel sick,' she said, between her fingers.

'Is this true?' her father demanded.

'Yes! All right, damn you, yes!' she said, glaring at Templeton. Then she turned to her father. 'He fucked me, Daddy. I let him fuck me. I *liked* it.'

'You whoring slut!' Soames raised his hand to slap her but Winsome grabbed it first. 'Not a good idea, Mr Soames,' she said.

Templeton looked at Soames. 'Are you telling me you didn't already know this, Mr Soames?' he said.

Soames bared his teeth. 'If I'd've known I'd've—'

'You'd have what?' Templeton asked, shoving his face close to Soames's. 'Beaten up your daughter? Killed Nick Barber?'

'What?'

'You heard me. Is that what you did? You found out what Kelly had been doing, and you waited until she was back working behind the bar, then you made an excuse to leave the pub for a few minutes. You went to see Barber. What happened? Did he laugh at you? Did he tell you how good she was? Or did he say she meant nothing to him, just another shag? Was the bed still warm from their lovemaking? You hit him over the head with a poker. Maybe you didn't mean to kill him. Maybe something snapped inside you. It happens. But there he was, dead on the floor. Is that how it happened, Calvin? If you tell us now it'll go better for you. I'm sure a judge and jury will understand a father's righteous anger.'

Kelly lurched to the sink and made it just in time. Winsome held her shoulders as she heaved.

'Well?' said Templeton. 'Am I right?'

Soames deflated into a sad, defeated old man, all the anger drained out of him. 'No,' he said, without inflection. 'I didn't kill anyone. I had no idea . . .' He looked at Kelly bent over the sink, tears in his eyes. 'Not till now. She's no better than her mother was,' he added bitterly.

Nobody said anything for a while. Kelly finished vomiting and Winsome poured her a glass of water. They sat down at the table again. Her father wouldn't look at her. Finally Templeton got to his feet. 'Well, Mr Soames,' he said, 'if you change your mind, you know where to get in touch with us. And in the meantime, as they say in the movies, don't leave town.' He pointed at Kelly. 'Nor you, young lady.'

But nobody was looking at him, or paying attention. They were all lost in their own worlds of misery, pain and betrayal. That would pass, though, Templeton knew, and he'd see Kelly Soames again under better circumstances, he was certain of it.

Outside at the car, dodging the puddles and mud as best he could, Templeton turned to Winsome, rubbed his hands together and said, 'Well, I think that went pretty well. What do you think, Winsome? Do you think he knew?'

Banks had a great deal of information to digest, he thought, as he parked down by the Co-op at the inner harbour and walked towards the shops and restaurants of West Cliff. He passed a reconstruction of the yellow and black HMS *Grand Turk*, used in the *Hornblower* TV series, and stood for a moment admiring the sails and rigging. What a hell of a life it must have been at sea back then, he thought. Maybe not so bad if you were an officer, but for the common sailor, the bad, maggot-infested food, the floggings, the terrible wounds of battle, butchery thinly disguised as surgery. Of course, he'd got most of his ideas from *Hornblower* and *Master and Commander*, but they seemed pretty accurate to him, and if they weren't, how would he know?

Thinking back on what Keith Enderby had just told him, he

realised he would have been living in Notting Hill at around the same time as Linda Lofthouse and Tania Hutchison. He was sure he would remember seeing someone as beautiful as Tania, even though she wasn't famous then, but he couldn't. There had been a lot of beautiful young women in colourful clothes around at the time, and he had met his fair share of them.

But Tania and Linda would have moved in very different circles. For a start Banks hadn't known anyone in a band; he had paid for all his concert tickets, like everyone else he knew. He also lacked the musical talent to perform in local clubs, although he often went to listen to those who did. But most of all, perhaps, he had always felt like an outsider, had felt, somehow, merely on the fringes of it all. He never wore his hair too long, couldn't get much beyond wearing a flowered shirt or tie, let alone kaftans and beads, couldn't bring himself to join the political demonstrations, and when he found himself involved in any sort of counterculture conversation, he thought it all sounded simplistic, childish and boring.

Banks leaned on the railing and watched the fishing-boats bobbing at anchor in the harbour. Then he walked to a café he remembered that served excellent fish and chips, one thing you could usually rely on in Whitby. It was almost empty and he went in, ordered a pot of tea, with jumbo haddock and chips, with bread and butter for chip butties, from a bored young waitress in a black apron and white blouse.

He sat down at the window, which looked out over the harbour to the old part of town, with its 199 steps leading up to the ruined abbey and St Mary's Church, where the salt wind had robbed the tombstones of their names. A group of young Goths walked by the sheds where the fishing-boats unloaded and sold their catch, all black clothes, white faces and intricate silver jewellery.

From what Banks had read about them, and the music he

had heard, they seemed obsessed with death and suicide, as well as with the undead and the 'dark side' in general, but they were passive and pacifist and concerned with social matters, such as racism and war. Banks liked Joy Division, and he had heard them described as the archetypal Goth band. On balance, he thought, Goths were no weirder than the hippies had been, with their fascination for the occult, poetry and drug-induced enlightenment.

1969 was a period of great transition for Banks. After leaving school with a couple of decent A levels, he was living in a bedsit in Notting Hill and taking a course in business studies in London. He hadn't felt much in common with his fellow students, though, so he had tended to fall in with a crowd from the art college, two of whom lived together in the same building as him, and they formed his real introduction, rather late in the day, to that strange blend of existentialism, communalism, hedonism and narcissism that was his take on late-sixties culture. They shared joints with him and Jem from across the hall, went to concerts and poetry readings, discussed squatters' rights, Vietnam and *Oz*, and played 'Alice's Restaurant' over and over again.

Banks had no idea what to do with his life. His parents had made it clear that they wanted him to have a crack at a white-collar career, rather than ending up in the brick factory, or the sheet-metal factory like his father, so business studies seemed like a logical step. And he did so much need to escape the stifling provinciality of Peterborough.

He loved the music and had hitch-hiked with his first real girlfriend Kay Summerville to the Blind Faith concert in London's Hyde Park during the summer of that year, when he was still living at home in Peterborough, and to the Rolling Stones concert in memory of Brian Jones, at which Mick Jagger freed all the caged butterflies that hadn't already died from the heat. He also remembered Dylan at the Isle of Wight, coming on late and singing 'She Belongs To Me' and 'To Ramona', two of Banks's favourites.

But in Peterborough, he had been fairly isolated from the trendy fashions, causes and ideologies of the times, embarrassingly ignorant of what was really happening out there. For all the hyped-up change and revolution of the decade, Engelbert Humperdinck's 'Release Me' prevented 'Strawberry Fields Forever' reaching number one and if you'd grown up in Peterborough, you could see why.

That first college year, he remembered following with horror the saga of the Manson family, eventually arrested for the murders of Sharon Tate, Leno LaBianca and others. It had all passed into the history books now, of course, but then, as the story unfolded day by day in the newspapers and on television and the horrors came to light, it had a powerful impact, not least because the Manson 'family' seemed a bit like hippies and quoted the Beatles and revolutionary slogans. And then there were the girls, Manson's 'love slaves', with strange names like Patricia Krenwinkel, Squeaky Fromme and Leslie Van Houten. The way they dressed and wore their hair, they might have been living in Notting Hill. The famous photo of the bearded, staring Manson had given Banks almost as many nightmares as the one of Christine Keeler sitting naked on a chair had prompted wet dreams.

Altamont had taken place late in 1969, too, he remembered. There, someone had been stabbed by a Hell's Angel during the Stones' performance. There were other things he vaguely remembered – the police charging a house in Piccadilly to evict squatters, rioting in Northern Ireland, stories of women and children murdered by American troops in My Lai, violent anti-war protests, four students shot by the National Guard at Kent State University in Ohio.

Maybe it was hindsight, but things had seemed to be taking a turn for the worse back then, falling apart, or perhaps it had been happening for a while and he had only just noticed because he was in the thick of it. The change in political climate might have passed him by if he'd stayed in Peterborough. Perhaps the business career would have worked out if he hadn't been caught up in the tail end of the sixties in Notting Hill. As it was, by the end of his first year he had lost all interest in cost accounting, industrial psychology and mercantile law.

But he had no memory of hearing about the murder of a girl at a festival in Yorkshire. Back then, the rest of the country was of little interest to those at the centre of things in London, and local police forces worked far more independently of one another than they did today. He wondered if Enderby was right about Linda Lofthouse's murder being the one Nick Barber had referred to. Banks had been so certain he had meant Robin Merchant, and he still wasn't ruling that possibility out. But the news about Linda Lofthouse had brought a whole new complexion to things, even if her murder had been solved. Was the killer still in jail? If not, could he somehow be involved in Nick Barber's death? The more Banks thought about it, no matter what Catherine Gervaise said, the more he thought he was right, and that Barber had died for digging up the past, a past that someone wanted to remain buried.

Banks noticed a few clouds drift in from the east as he ate his haddock and chips, and by the time he had finished it was starting to drizzle. He paid, left a small tip and headed for his car. Before he set off, he phoned Ken Blackstone in Leeds and asked him to find out what he could about Stanley Chadwick and the Linda Lofthouse investigation.

Sunday, 21 September 1969

Steve answered the door late that Sunday afternoon, and when he saw Yvonne standing there, he turned away and walked down the hall. 'I never thought I'd see you again,' he said. 'You've got a bloody nerve showing up here.'

Yvonne followed him into the living room. 'But, Steve, it wasn't my fault. It was McGarrity. He tried to force himself on me. He's dangerous. You've got to believe me. I didn't know what to do.'

Steve turned to face her. 'So you went straight to Daddy.'

'I was upset.'

'You never told me your father was a pig.'

'You never asked. Besides, what does it matter?'

'What does it matter? He violated our space. Him and the others. We got busted. That's what matters. Now we're going to have to go to court tomorrow morning. I'll get a fine at least. And if my parents find out, they'll stop my allowance. That's all down to you.'

'But it wasn't my fault, Steve. I'm sorry, really I am. I didn't know they were going to bust you.' Yvonne moved towards him and reached out to touch him.

He jerked away and sat down in the armchair. 'Oh, come off it. You must have known damn well we'd be sitting around here smoking a few joints and listening to music. It's not as if you haven't done it with us often enough.'

Yvonne knelt at his feet. 'But I never sent them here. Honestly. I thought they'd just arrest McGarrity. You know I'd never do anything to get you into trouble.'

'Then you're more stupid than I thought you were. Look, I'm sorry, but I don't want you coming round here any more. Whether you wanted to or not, you've brought nothing but trouble. Who knows who might follow you?'

Yvonne's heart pounded in her chest. She still had one card to play. 'McGarrity told me you've been seeing someone else.'

Steve laughed. 'If only you could hear yourself.'

'Is it true?'

'What if I have?'

'I thought we . . . I mean . . . I didn't . . .'

'Oh, Yvonne, for God's sake, grow up. You sound like such a child sometimes. We can both see whoever we want. I thought that was clear from the start.'

'But I don't want to see anyone else. I want to see you.'

'What you're really saying is that you don't want me to see anyone else. You can't own someone, Yvonne. You can't control their affections.'

'But it's true.'

Steve turned away his face. 'Well, I don't want to see you. That's just not on any more.'

'But—'

'I mean it. And you won't be welcome at Bayswater Terrace or Carberry Place, either. They got raided as well, in case you didn't know. People got busted, and they're not happy with you. Word gets round, you know. It's still a small scene.'

'So what should I have done? Tell me!'

'You shouldn't have done anything. You should have kept your stupid mouth shut. You should have known bringing the pigs in would only mean trouble for us.'

'But he's my *father*. I had to tell someone. I was so upset, Steve, I was shaking like a leaf. McGarrity—'

'I've told you before, he's harmless.'

'That's not the way he seemed to me.'

'You were stoned, the way I hear it. Maybe your imagination was running away with you. Maybe you even wanted him to touch you. Maybe you should run away with your imagination instead.'

'I don't know what you're talking about.'

Steve sighed. 'I can't trust you any more, Yvonne. *We* can't trust you any more.'

'But I love you, Steve.'

'No, you don't. Don't be stupid. That's not real love you're talking about, that's just romantic schoolgirl crap. It's possessive love, all jealousy and control, all the negative emotions. You're not mature enough to know what real love is.'

Yvonne flinched at his words. She felt herself turn cold all over, as if she had been hit by a bucket of water. 'And you are?'

He stood up. 'This is a waste of time. Look, I'm not arguing with you any more. Why don't you just go? And don't come back.'

'But, Steve—'

Steve pointed to the door and raised his voice. 'Just go. And don't send your father and his piggy friends round here again or you might find yourself in serious trouble.'

Yvonne got slowly to her feet. She had never known Steve to look or sound so cruel. 'What do you mean?' she asked.

'Never mind. Fuck off.'

Yvonne looked at him. He was bristling with anger. There was clearly going to be no more talking to him. Not this afternoon, maybe not ever. As tears started to burn down her cheeks, she turned away from him abruptly and left.

'It's not so much what he said or did, Guv,' said Winsome, 'it was the pleasure he took in doing it.'

Annie nodded. She was treating Winsome to an after-work drink in the Black Lion, off an alley behind the market square, away from the prying eyes and ears of Western Area Headquarters. Winsome was visibly upset, and Annie wanted to get to the bottom of it. 'Kev can be insensitive at times,' she said.

'*Insensitive?*' Winsome took a gulp of her vodka and tonic. '*Insensitive?* It was more like bloody sadistic. I'm sorry, Guv, but I'm still shaking. See?'

She stuck her hand out. Annie could see it was trembling slightly. 'Calm down,' she said. 'Another drink? You're not driving, are you?'

'No. I can walk home from here. I'll have the same again, thanks.'

Annie went to the bar and got the drinks. There was nobody else in the place except the barmaid and a couple of her friends at the far end. One was playing the machines, and the other was sitting down, watching over two toddlers, cigarette in one hand, drink in the other. Every time one of the little boys started to cry or make any sort of noise, she told him to shut up. Time after time. Cry. 'Shut up'. Cry. 'Shut up'. The kids shouldn't be there, but Annie wasn't interested in enforcing the licensing laws. There was a tape of old music playing loudly – 'House of the Rising Sun', 'The Young Ones', 'Say A Little Prayer For Me', 'I Remember You' – the sort of stuff Banks would remember, competing with the TV blaring out *Murder She Wrote* on one of the Sky channels. But the noise certainly drowned anything Annie and Winsome were talking about.

Annie was going to get a Britvic Orange for herself, as she had to get back to Harkside, but she was still furious after her session with Superintendent Gervaise, feeling far from calm, and she needed another bloody stiff drink herself, so she ordered a large vodka with her orange juice. If she had too much, she'd leave the car and get one of the PCs to drive her home, or pick up a taxi if the worst came to the worst. It couldn't cost all that much. She had been thinking of moving to Eastvale recently, as it would be convenient for the job, but house prices there had gone through the roof, and she didn't want to give up her little cottage, even though it was now worth nearly twice what she had paid for it.

Winsome thanked Annie for the drink. 'That poor girl,' she said.

'Look, Winsome, I know how you feel. I feel just as bad. I'm sure Kelly thinks I'm the one who betrayed her trust. But DS Templeton was only doing his job. Superintendent Gervaise had asked him to check the girl's story against her father's and that was the way he did it. It might seem harsh to you, but it worked, didn't it?'

'I can't believe you're defending them,' Winsome said. She took a gulp of vodka then put the drink on the table. 'You weren't there or you'd know what I'm talking about. No. I'm not working with him again. You can transfer me. Do what you want. But I won't work with that bastard again.' She folded her arms.

Annie sipped her drink and sighed. She had been foreseeing problems ever since Kevin Templeton got his promotion. He had passed his sergeant's board ages ago, but he didn't want to go back to uniform and he didn't want to transfer, so it had been a while before his opportunity came up. Then he had nipped a possible serial killer's career in the bud and become the golden boy. Annie had always found him a bit too full of himself, and she had worried what a little power might do to his already skewed personality. And if he thought she hadn't noticed the way he had practically drooled down the front of her blouse the other day, he was seriously deluding himself. The thing was, though, he got the job done, as he had now. Banks did, too, but he managed to do it without treading on everyone's toes – only the brass's, usually – but Templeton was one of the new breed: he didn't care. And here was Annie defending him when she knew damn well that Winsome, who had also passed her boards with flying colours and didn't want to leave Eastvale, would have been a much better person for the job. Where is positive discrimination when you really need it? she wondered. Obviously not in Yorkshire.

'I shouldn't have made a promise I couldn't possibly keep,' Annie said. 'The blame's entirely mine. I should have done it myself.' She knew that she had deliberately *not* made any such promise to Kelly Soames, but she felt as if she had.

'Pardon me, Guv, but like I said, you weren't there. Listen to me. He enjoyed it. Enjoyed every minute of it. The humiliation. Taunting her. He drew it out to get more pleasure from it. And in the end he didn't even know what he'd done wrong. I don't know if that's the worst part of it.'

'OK, Winsome, I'll admit DS Templeton has a few problems.'

'A few problems? The man's a sadist. And you know what?'

'What?'

Winsome shifted in her chair. 'Don't laugh, but there was something . . . sexual about it.'

'Sexual?'

'Yes. I can't explain it, but it was like he was getting off on his power over her.'

'Are you certain?'

'I don't know. Maybe it was just me, reading things wrongly. It wouldn't be the first time. But there was something really creepy about the whole thing, even when the girl was being sick—'

'Kelly was physically sick?'

'Yes. I thought I'd told you that.'

'No. How did it happen?'

'She was just sick.'

'What did DS Templeton do?'

'Just carried on as if everything was normal.'

'Have you told anyone else what happened?'

'No, Guv. I'd tell Superintendent Gervaise if I thought it would do any good, but she thinks the sun shines out of Kevin Templeton's arse.'

'She does, does she?' That didn't surprise Annie. Just the mention of Gervaise made her bristle. The sanctimonious cow, putting Annie on statement-reading, a DC's job at best, and making jibes about her private life.

'Anyway,' Winsome went on, 'I don't have to put up with it. There's nothing in the book says I have to put up with behaviour like that.'

'That's true,' said Annie. 'But life doesn't always go by the book.'

'It does when you agree with what the book says.'

Annie laughed. 'So what do you want to do about it?'

'Dunno,' said Winsome. 'Nothing I can do, I suppose. 'Cept I don't want to be near the creep any more, and if he ever tries anything I'll beat seven shades of shit out of him.'

Annie laughed. The phrase sounded odd coming from Winsome with her Jamaican lilt. 'You can't avoid him all the time,' she said. 'I mean, I can do my best to make sure you're not paired up or anything, but Superintendent Gervaise can overrule that if she wants, and she interferes with our jobs a bit more than Superintendent Gristhorpe did.'

'I liked Mr Gristhorpe,' said Winsome. 'He was old-fashioned, like my father, and he could be a bit frightening sometimes, but he was fair and he didn't play favourites.'

Well, Annie thought, that wasn't strictly true. Banks had certainly been a favourite of Gristhorpe's, but in general Winsome was right. There was a difference between having favourites and playing them. Gristhorpe hadn't set out to build a little empire, pick his teams and set people against one another the way Gervaise was doing. Nor did he interfere in people's private lives. He must have known about her and Banks, but he hadn't said anything – at least, not to her. He might have warned Banks off, she supposed, but if he had, it hadn't affected their relationship either on or off the job.

'Well, Gristhorpe's gone and Gervaise is here,' said Annie, 'and for better or worse we've got to live with it.' She looked at her watch. She still had half her drink left. 'Look, I'd better go, Winsome. I'm not over the limit yet, but I will be if I have any more.'

'You can stay at mine, if you like.' Winsome looked away. 'I'm sorry, Guv, I don't mean to be presumptuous. I mean, you being an inspector and all, my boss, but I've got a spare room. It's just that it helps talking about it, that's all. And I don't know about you, but I feel like getting rat-arsed.'

Annie thought for a moment. 'What the hell?' she said, finishing her drink. 'I'll get another round.'

'No, you stay there. It's my shout.'

Annie sat and watched her walk to the bar, a tall, graceful, long-legged beauty about whom she knew . . . well, not very much. But, then, she didn't really know very much about anyone, when it came down to it, she realised, not even Banks. And as she watched, she smiled to herself. Wouldn't it be funny, she thought, if she did stay at Winsome's and Superintendent Gervaise found out? What would the sad cow make of that?

Monday, 22 September 1969

'But we've got no real evidence, Stan,' Detective Chief Superintendent McCullen argued, on Monday morning. They were in his office and rain spattered the windows, blurring the view.

Chadwick ran his hand over his hair. He'd thought this out in advance – hadn't done anything else but think it over, all night. He didn't want Yvonne involved; that was the main problem. He had seen the bruise on her arm McGarrity had caused, and it was enough to bring assault charges, but once he went that route he wouldn't be able to do anything for Yvonne. She was upset enough as it was, and he didn't want to drag her through court. If truth be told, he didn't want his name tainted by his daughter's folly, either. He thought he could make a decent case without her, and he laid it out carefully for McCullen.

'First off, he's got form,' he said.

McCullen raised an eyebrow. 'Oh?'

'The most recent's for possession of a controlled substance, namely LSD. November 1967.'

'Only possession?'

'They think he dumped his stash down the toilet when he

heard them coming. Unfortunately he still had two doses in his pocket.'

'You said most recent?'

'Yes. The other's a bit more interesting. March 1958.'

'How old was he then?'

'Twenty-two.'

'And?'

'Assault causing bodily harm. He stabbed a student in the shoulder during a town-and-gown altercation in Oxford, which apparently is where he comes from. Unfortunately the student happened to be the son of a local Member of Parliament.'

'Ouch,' said McCullen, a sly smile touching his lips.

'It didn't help that McGarrity was a teddy-boy. Apparently the judge didn't like teds. Threw the book at him. He was a Brasenose man, too, same as the student. Gave McGarrity eighteen months. If the wound had been more serious, and if it hadn't been inflicted defensively during a scuffle – apparently the gown lot were carrying cricket bats, among other weapons – he'd have got five years or more. Another interesting point,' Chadwick went on, 'is that the weapon used was a flick-knife.'

'The same weapon used on the girl?'

'Same *kind* of weapon.'

'Go on.'

'There's not much more,' Chadwick said. 'We spent yesterday interviewing the people at the three houses who knew McGarrity. He definitely knew the victim.'

'How well?'

'There's no evidence of any sort of relationship, and from what I've found out about Linda Lofthouse I very much doubt that there was one. But he knew her.'

'Anything else?'

'Everyone said he was an odd duck. They often didn't

understand what he was talking about, and he had a habit of playing with a flick-knife.'

'What kind of flick-knife?'

'Just a flick-knife, with a tortoiseshell handle.'

'Why did they put up with him?'

'If you ask me, sir, it's down to drugs. Our lads found five ounces of cannabis resin hidden in the gas meter at Carberry Place. Apparently the lock was broken. We think it belonged to McGarrity.'

'Defrauding the gas company too, I'll bet?'

Chadwick smiled. 'Same shilling, again and again. The Drugs Squad think he's a mid-level dealer, buys a few ounces now and then and splits them up into quid deals. Probably what he used the knife for.'

'So the kids tolerate him?'

'Yes, sir. He was also at the festival, and according to the people he went with he spent most of the time roaming the crowd on his own. No one can say where he was when the incident occurred.'

McCullen tapped his pipe on the ashtray, then said, 'The knife?'

'No sign of it yet, sir.'

'Pity.'

'Yes. I suppose it might be a coincidence that McGarrity simply lost his knife around the same time a young woman was stabbed with a similar weapon, but we've gone to court with less before.'

'Aye. And lost from time to time.'

'Well, the judge has bound him over on the dealing charge. No fixed abode, so no bail. He's all ours.'

'Then get cracking and build up a murder case if you think you've got one. But don't get tunnel vision here, Stan. Don't forget that other bloke you fancied for it.'

'Rick Hayes? We're still looking into him.'

'Good. And, Stan?'

'Yes, sir?'

'Find the knife. It would really help.'

Some people, Banks realised, never travel far from where they grow up, and Simon Bradley was one of them. He had, he said, transferred several times during his career, to Suffolk, Cumbria and Nottingham, but he had ended up back in Leeds, and when he had retired in 2000 at the age of fifty-six and the rank of superintendent, Traffic, he and his wife had settled in a nice detached stone-built house just off Shaw Lane in Headingley. It was, he told Banks, only a stone's throw from where he grew up in more lowly Meanwood. Beyond the high green gate was a well-tended garden, which, Bradley said, was his wife's pride and joy. Bradley's pride and joy, it turned out, was a small library of floor-to-ceiling shelves, where he kept his collection of first-edition crime and thriller fiction, primarily Dick Francis, Ian Fleming, Len Deighton, Ruth Rendell, P. D. James and Colin Dexter. It was there that he sat with Banks over coffee and talked about his early days at Brotherton House. In the peaceful, book-lined room, Banks found it hard to believe that Hyde Park was just down the road, where one of that summer's suicide-bombers had lived.

'I was young,' Bradley said, 'twenty-five in 1969, but I was never really one of that generation.' He laughed. 'I suppose it would have been difficult, wouldn't it, to be a hippie and a copper at the same time? Sort of like being on both sides at once.'

'I'm a few years behind you,' said Banks, 'but I did like the music. Still do.'

'Really? Dreadful racket,' said Bradley. 'I've always been more of a classical man myself: Mozart, Beethoven, Bach.'

'I like them, too,' said Banks, 'but sometimes you can't beat a bit of Jimi Hendrix.'

'Each to his own. I suppose I always associated the music too closely with the lifestyle and the things that went on back then,' Bradley said, with distaste. 'A soundtrack for the drugs, long hair, promiscuity. I was something of a young fogey, a *square*, I suppose, and now I've grown up into an old fogey. I went to church every Sunday, kept my hair cut short and believed in waiting until you were married to have sex. Still do, much to my son's chagrin. Very unfashionable.'

Bradley was almost ten years older than Banks, and he was in good physical shape. There was no extra flab on him the way there had been on Enderby, and he still had a fine head of hair. He was wearing white trousers and a shirt with a grey V-neck pullover, a bit like a cricketer, Banks thought, or the way cricketers used to look before they became walking multi-coloured advertisements for everything from mobile phones to trainers.

'Did you get on well with DI Chadwick?' Banks asked, remembering Enderby's description of 'Chiller' as cold and hard.

'After a fashion,' said Bradley. 'DI Chadwick wasn't an easy man to get close to. He'd had certain . . . experiences . . . during the war, and he tended towards long silences you didn't dare interrupt. He never spoke about it – the war – but you knew it was there, defining him in a way, as it did many of that generation. But, yes, I suppose I got along with him as well as anyone.'

'Do you remember the Linda Lofthouse case?'

'As if it were yesterday. Bound to happen eventually.'

'What was?'

'What happened to her. Linda Lofthouse. Bound to. I mean, all those people rolling in the mud on LSD and God knows what. Bound to revert to their primitive nature at some point, weren't they? Strip away that thin but essential veneer of civilisation and convention, of obedience and order, and what do you get? The beast within, Mr Banks, the beast within. Someone was bound to get hurt. Stands to reason. I'm only surprised there wasn't more of it.'

'But what do you think it was about Linda Lofthouse that got her killed?'

'At first, when I saw her there in the sleeping-bag, you know, with her dress bunched up, I must confess I thought it was probably a sex murder. She had that look about her, you know?'

'What look?'

'A lot of young girls had it then. As if she'd invite you into her sleeping-bag as soon as look at you.'

'But she was dead.'

'Well, yes, of course. I know that.' Bradley gave a nervous laugh. 'I mean, I'm not a necrophiliac or anything. I'm just telling you the first impression I had of her. Turned out it wasn't a sex crime after all, but some madman. As I said, bound to happen when you encourage deviant behaviour. She'd had an illegitimate baby, you know.'

'Linda Lofthouse?'

'Yes. She was on the pill when we found her, like most of them, of course, but not when she was fifteen. Gave it up for adoption in 1967.'

'Did anyone find out what became of the child?'

'It didn't concern us. We tracked down the father, a kid called Donald Hughes, garage mechanic, and he gave us a couple of ideas as to the sort of life Linda was leading and where she was living it, but he had an alibi, and he had no motive. He'd moved on. Got a proper job, wanted nothing to do with Linda and her corrupt hippie lifestyle. That was why they'd split up in the first place. If she hadn't been seduced by it, the baby might have grown up with a proper mother and father.'

The child's identity might be an issue now, Banks thought.

A child born in the late sixties would be in his late thirties now, and if he had discovered what had happened to his birth mother . . . Nick Barber was thirty-eight, but he was the victim. Banks was confusing too many crimes: Lofthouse, Merchant, Barber. He had to get himself in focus. At least the connection between Barber and Lofthouse was something he could check into and not come away looking too much of a fool if he was wrong.

'What was the motive?'

'We never found out. He was a nutcase.'

'That being the technical term for a psychopath back then?'

'It's what we used to call them,' Bradley said, 'but I suppose psychopath or sociopath – I never did know the difference – would be more politically correct.'

'He confessed to the murder?'

'As good as.'

'What do you mean?'

'He didn't deny it when faced with the evidence.'

'The knife, right?'

'With his fingerprints and Linda Lofthouse's blood on it.'

'How did this person – what's his name, by the way?'

'McGarrity. Patrick McGarrity.'

'How did McGarrity first come to your attention?'

'We found out that the victim was known at various houses around the city where students and dropouts lived and sold drugs. McGarrity frequented the same places, was a drug-dealer, in fact, which was what we first arrested him for after a raid.'

'And then DI Chadwick became suspicious?'

'Well, yes. We heard that McGarrity was a bit of a nutcase, and even the people whose houses he went to were a bit frightened of him. There was a lot of tolerance for weird types back then, especially if they provided people with drugs, which is why I say I'm surprised these things didn't happen more often. This McGarrity clearly had severe mental problems. Dropped on the head at birth, for all I know. He was older than the rest, for a start, and he also had a criminal record and a history of violence. He had a habit of playing with this flick-knife. It used to make people nervous, which was no doubt the effect he wanted. There was also some talk about him terrorising a young girl. He was a thoroughly unpleasant character.'

'Did this other young girl come forward?'

'No. It was just something that came up during questioning. McGarrity denied it. We got him on the other charges, though, and that gave us all we needed.'

'You met him?'

'I sat in on some of the interviews. Look, I don't know why you want to know all this now. There's no doubt he did it.'

'I'm not doubting it,' said Banks, 'just trying to find a reason for Nick Barber's murder.'

'Well, it's got nothing to do with McGarrity.'

'Nick Barber was writing about the Mad Hatters,' Banks went on, 'and Vic Greaves was Linda Lofthouse's cousin.'

'The one that went bonkers?'

'If you care to put it that way, yes,' said Banks.

'How else would you put it? Anyway, I'm afraid I never met them. DI Chadwick did most of the North Riding of the investigation with a DS Enderby. I do believe they interviewed the band.'

'Yes, I've talked to Keith Enderby.'

Bradley sniffed. 'Bit of a scruff, and not entirely reliable, in my opinion. Rather more like the types we were dealing with, if you know what I mean.'

'DS Enderby was a hippie?'

'Well, not as such, but he wore his hair a bit long, and on occasion he wore flowered shirts and ties. I even saw him in sandals once.'

'With socks?'

'No.'

'Well, thank the Lord for that,' said Banks.

'Look, I know you're being sarcastic,' said Bradley, with a smug smile. 'It's OK. But the fact remains that Enderby was a slacker, and he had no respect for the uniform.'

Banks could have kicked himself for letting out the sarcasm, but Bradley's holier-than-thou sanctimony was getting up his nose. He felt like saying that Enderby had described Bradley as an arse-licker, but he wanted results not confrontation. Time to hold back and stick to relevant points, he told himself.

'You say you think this writer was killed because he was working on a story about the Mad Hatters, but do you have any reason for assuming that?' Bradley asked.

'Well,' said Banks, 'we do know about the story he was working on, that he mentioned to a girlfriend that it might involve a murder, and we know that Vic Greaves now lives very close to the cottage in which Nick Barber was killed. Unfortunately, all Barber's notes were missing, along with his mobile and laptop, so we were unable to find out more. That in itself is suspicious, though, that his personal effects and notes were taken.'

'It's not much, though, is it? I imagine robbery's as common around your patch as it is everywhere, these days.'

'We try to keep an open mind,' said Banks. 'There could be other possibilities. Did you have any other suspects?'

'Yes. There was a fellow called Rick Hayes. He was the festival promoter. He had the freedom of the backstage area and he couldn't account for himself during the period we think the girl was killed. He was also left-handed, as was McGarrity.'

'Those were the only two?'

'Yes'

'So it was the knife that clinched it?'

'We knew we had the right man – you must have had that feeling at times – but we couldn't prove it at first. We were able to hold him on a drugs charge, and while we were holding him we turned up the murder weapon.'

'How long after you first questioned him?'

'It was October, about two weeks or so.'

'Where was it?'

'In one of the houses.'

'I assume those places were searched as soon as you had McGarrity in custody?'

'Yes.'

'But you didn't turn up the knife then?'

'You have to understand,' said Bradley, 'there were several people living in each of those houses at any one time. They were terribly insanitary and overcrowded. People slept on the floors and in all kinds of unlikely combinations. There was all sorts of stuff around. We didn't know what belonged to whom, they were all so casual in their attitude towards property and ownership.'

'So how did you find out in the end?'

'We just kept looking. Finally, we found it hidden inside a sofa cushion. A couple of the people who lived there said they'd seen McGarrity with such a knife – it had a tortoiseshell handle – and we were fortunate enough to find his prints on it. He'd wiped the blade, of course, but the lab still found blood and fibre where it joined the handle. The blood matched Linda Lofthouse's type. Simple as that.'

'Did the knife match the wounds?'

'According to the pathologist it could have.'

'Only *could* have?'

'He was in court. You know what those barristers are like. Could have been her blood, could have been the knife. A blade consistent with the kind of blade . . . blah blah blah. It was enough for the jury.'

'The pathologist didn't try to match the knife with the wound physically, on the body?'

'He couldn't. The body had been buried by then, and even if it had been necessary to exhume it, the flesh would have been too decomposed to give an accurate reproduction. You know that.'

'And McGarrity didn't deny killing her?'

'That's right. I was there when DI Chadwick presented him with the evidence and he had this strange smile on his face, and he said, "It looks like you've got me, then."'

'Those were his exact words – "It looks like you've got me, then"?'

Bradley frowned with annoyance. 'It was over thirty years ago. I can't promise those were the exact words, but it was something like that. You'll find it in the files and the court transcripts. But he was sneering at us, being sarcastic.'

'I'll be looking at the transcripts later,' said Banks. 'I don't suppose you had anything to do with the investigation into Robin Merchant's death?'

'Who?'

'He was another member of the Mad Hatters. He drowned about nine months after the Linda Lofthouse murder.'

Bradley shook his head. 'No. Sorry.'

'Mr Enderby was able to tell me a bit about it. He was one of the investigating officers. I was just wondering. I understand DI Chadwick had a daughter?'

'Yes. I only ever saw her the once. Pretty young thing. Yvonne, I think she was called.'

'Wasn't there some trouble with her?'

'DI Chadwick didn't confide in me about his family life.'

Banks felt a faint warning signal. Bradley's answer had come a split second too soon and sounded a little too pat to be quite believable. The clipped tones also told Banks that perhaps he wasn't being entirely truthful. But why would he lie about Chadwick's daughter? To protect Chadwick's family and reputation, most likely. So if Enderby was right and this

Yvonne had been in trouble, or *was* trouble, it might be worth finding out exactly what kind of trouble he was talking about. 'Do you know where Yvonne Chadwick is now?' he asked.

'I'm afraid not. Grown-up and married, I should imagine.'

'What about DI Chadwick?'

'Haven't seen hide nor hair of him for years, not since the trial. I should imagine he's dead by now. I mean, he was in his late forties back then and he wasn't in the best of health. The trial took its toll. But I transferred to Suffolk in 1971, and I lost touch. No doubt Records will be able to tell you. More coffee?'

'Thanks.' Banks held out his mug and gazed at the spines of the books. Nice hobby, he thought, collecting first editions. Maybe he'd look into it. Graham Greene, perhaps, or Georges Simenon. There were plenty of those to spend a lifetime or more collecting. 'So, even after confessing, McGarrity pleaded not guilty?'

'Yes. It was a foolish move. He wanted to conduct his own defence, too, but the judge wasn't having any of it. As it was he kept getting up in court and interrupting, causing a fuss, making accusations that he'd been framed. I mean, the nerve of him, after he'd as good as admitted it. Things didn't go well for him at all. We got the similar fact evidence about the previous stabbing in. The bailiffs had to remove him from the court at least twice.'

'He said he'd been framed?'

'Well, they all do, don't they?'

'Was he more specific about it?'

'No. Couldn't be, really, could he, seeing as it was all a pack of lies? Besides, he was gibbering. There's no doubt about it, Patrick McGarrity was guilty as sin.'

'Perhaps I should have a chat with him.'

'That would be rather difficult,' said Bradley. 'He's dead. He was stabbed in jail back in 1974. Something to do with drugs.'

16

'Is it just me, or do I sense a bit of an atmosphere around here?' Banks asked Annie in the corridor on Thursday morning.

'Atmosphere would be an understatement,' said Annie. Her head still hurt, despite the paracetamol she had taken before leaving Winsome's flat that morning. Luckily, she always carried a change of clothes in the boot of her car. Not because she was promiscuous or anything, but because once, years ago, a mere DC, when she had done a similar thing, got drunk and stayed with a friend after a break-up with a boyfriend, someone in the station had noticed and she had been the butt of unfunny sexist jokes for days. And after that, her DS had come on to her in the lift after work one day.

'You look like shit,' said Banks.

'Thank you.'

'Want to tell me about it?'

Annie looked up and down the corridor to make sure no one was lurking. Great, she thought, she was getting paranoid in her own station, now. 'Think we can sneak over the road to the Golden Grill without setting too many tongues wagging?'

'Of course,' said Banks. He looked as if he was wondering what the hell she was talking about.

The day was overcast and chilly and most of the people window-shopping on Market Street wore sweaters under their windcheaters or anoraks. They passed a couple of serious ramblers, kitted out in all the new fancy gear, each carrying the two long pointed sticks, like ski poles. Well, Annie supposed, they might be of some use climbing up Fremlington Edge, but not on the cobbled streets of Eastvale.

Their regular waitress greeted them and soon they were sitting over hot coffee and toasted teacakes, looking through the misted window at the streams of people outside. Annie felt a sudden rush of nausea when she took her first sip of black coffee, but it soon waned. It was always there, though, a low-level sensation in the background.

Annie and Winsome had certainly made a night of it, shared more confidences than Annie could ever have imagined. It made her realise, when she thought about it in the cold hangover dawn, that she didn't really have any friends, anyone to talk to like that, be silly or do girly things with. She had always thought it was a function of her job, but perhaps it was a function of her personality. Banks was the same, but at least he had his kids. She had her father, Ray, down in St Ives, of course, but they rarely saw one another, and it wasn't the same; for all his eccentricities and willingness to act as a friend and confidant, he was still her father.

'So what were you up to last night that's left you looking like death warmed up? Feeling like it, too, by the look of you.'

Annie pulled a face. 'You know how I love it when you compliment me.'

Banks touched her hand, a shadow of concern passing over his face. 'Seriously.'

'If you must know, I got pissed with Winsome.'

'You did what?'

'I told you.'

'But Winsome? I didn't think she even drank.'

'Me, neither. But it's official now. She can drink me under the table.'

'That's no mean feat.'

'My point exactly.'

'How was it?'

'Well, a bit awkward at first, with the rank thing, but I've never held that in very great esteem.'

'I know. You respect the person, not the rank.'

'Exactly. Anyway, by the end of the evening we'd got beyond that, and we had quite a giggle. It was "Annie" and "Winsome" – she hates Winnie. She's got a wicked sense of humour when she lets her hair down, has Winsome.'

'What were you talking about?'

'Mind your own business. It was girl-talk.'

'Men, then.'

'Such an ego. What makes you think we'd waste a perfectly good bottle of Marks and Spencer's plonk talking about you lot?'

'That puts me in my place. How was it when you met up at work this morning? A bit embarrassing?'

'Well, it'll be "Winsome" and "Guv" in the workplace, but we had a bit of a giggle over it all.'

'So what started it?'

Annie felt another wave of nausea. She let it go, the way she did thoughts in meditation, and it seemed to work, at least for the moment. 'DS Templeton,' she said finally.

'Kev Templeton? Was this about the promotion? Because—'

'No, it wasn't about the promotion. And keep your voice down. Of course Winsome's pissed off about that. Who wouldn't be? We know she was the right person for the job, but we also know the right person doesn't always get the job, even if she is a black female. I know you white males always like to complain when a job goes elsewhere for what you see as political reasons, but it's not always the case, you know.'

'So what, then?'

Annie explained how Templeton had behaved with Kelly Soames.

'It sounds a bit harsh,' he said, when she had finished. 'But I don't suppose he was to know the girl would be physically sick.'

'He enjoyed it. That was the point,' said Annie.

'So Winsome thought?'

'Yes. Don't tell me you're going to go all male and start defending the indefensible here, because if you are, I'm off. I'm not in the mood for an all-lads-together rally.'

'Christ, Annie, you ought to know me better than that. And there's only one lad here, as far as I can see.'

'Well . . . you know what I mean.' Annie ran her hand through her tousled hair. 'Shit, I'm hung-over and I'm having a bad-hair day, too.'

'Your hair looks fine.'

'You don't mean it, but thank you. Anyway, that's the story. Oh, and Superintendent Bloody Gervaise had a go at me yesterday in her office.'

'What were you doing there?'

'I went to complain about the personal remarks she made about me during the briefing. At the very least I expected an apology.'

'And you got?'

'A bollocking, more personal remarks, and an assignment to statement-reading.'

'That's steep.'

'Very. And she warned me off you.'

'What?'

'It's true.' Annie looked down into her coffee. 'She seems to think we're an item again.'

'Where could she possibly have got that idea from?'

'I don't know.' Annie paused. 'Templeton's in thick with her.'

'So?'

Annie leaned forward and rested her hands on the table. 'She knew about the pint you had at the Cross Keys, that first night, when we went to the scene of Barber's murder. And Templeton was there, too. He knew about that. But this. . . . Look, tell me if I'm being paranoid, Alan, but don't you think it's a bit suspicious? I think Kev Templeton might be behind it.'

'But why would he think we were an item, as you put it?'

'He knows that we were involved before, and we turned up at Moorview Cottage together. We also stayed overnight in London. He's putting two and two together and coming up with five.'

Banks seemed to mull over what Annie had said. 'So what's he up to? Ingratiating himself with the new super?'

'It looks that way,' said Annie. 'Kev's smart, and he's also ambitious. He thinks the rest of us are plods. He's a sergeant already, and he'll pass his inspector's boards first chance he gets, too, but he's also smart enough to know he needs more than good exam results to get ahead in this job. It helps to have recommendations from above. We know our Madam Gervaise thinks she's cut out for great things, chief constable at the very least, so a bit of coat-tail riding wouldn't do Templeton any harm. At least, that's my guess.'

'Sounds right to me,' said Banks. 'And I don't like what you told me earlier, about the Soames interview. Sometimes we have to do unpleasant things like that – though I believe in this case it could have been avoided – but we don't have to take pleasure in them.'

'Winsome thinks he's a racist, too. She's overheard him make the odd comment about "darkies" and "Pakis" when he thinks she's not listening.'

'That would hardly make him unique in the force, sadly,' said Banks. 'Look, I'll have a word with him.'

'Fat lot of good that will do.'

'Well, we can't go to Superintendent Gervaise, that's for certain. Red Ron would probably listen, but that's too much like telling tales out of school for me. Not my style. No, if anything's to be done about Kev Templeton, I'll do it myself.'

'And what might you do?'

'Like I said, I'll have a word, see if I can talk some sense into him. On the other hand, it might be even better if I tipped the wink to Gervaise that we're on to him. She'll drop him like the proverbial hot potato. It's no bloody good having a spy who blows his cover on his first assignment, is it? And gets the wrong end of the stick, into the bargain.'

'Good point.'

'Look, I have to go to Leeds to see Ken Blackstone later today. Want to come?'

'No, thanks.' Annie made a grim face. 'Statements to read. And the way I feel today, if I'm doing a menial job, I might even knock off early, go home and have a long hot bath and an early night.'

They paid and left the Golden Grill, then walked across the road to the station in the light drizzle. At the front desk, the PC on Reception called Annie over. 'Got a message for you, Miss,' he said, 'from Lyndgarth. Local copper's just called in to say all hell's broke loose up at the Soames farm. Old man Soames went berserk, apparently.'

'We're on our way,' said Annie. She looked at Banks.

'Ken Blackstone can wait,' he said. 'We'd better put our wellies on.'

Annie drove, and Banks tried to find out what he could over his mobile, but coverage was patchy and in the end he gave up.

'That bastard Templeton,' Annie cursed, as she turned on to the Lyndgarth road by the Cross Keys in Fordham, visions of flaying Templeton alive and dipping him in a vat of boiling oil flitting through her mind. 'I'll have him for this. He's not getting away with it.'

'Calm down, Annie,' Banks said. 'Let's find out what happened first.'

'Whatever it is, he's behind it. It's down to him.'

'If that's the case, you might have to join the queue,' said Banks.

Annie shot him a puzzled glance. 'What do you mean?'

'If you were thinking clearly right now, one of the things that might cross your mind—'

'Oh, don't be so bloody patronising,' Annie snapped. 'Get on with it.'

'One of the things that might cross your mind is that if something has happened as a direct result of DS Templeton's actions, the first person to distance herself will be Detective Superintendent Gervaise.'

Annie turned into the drive of the Soames farm. She could see the patrol car up ahead, parked outside the house. 'But she told him to do it,' Annie said.

Banks just smiled. 'That was when it seemed like a good idea.'

Annie pulled up to a sharp halt, sending gobbets of mud flying, and they got out and walked over to the uniformed officer. The door to the farmhouse was open, and Annie could hear the sound of a police radio from inside.

'PC Cotter, sir,' said the officer on the door. 'My partner PC Watkins is inside.'

'What happened?' Banks asked.

'It's not entirely clear yet,' said Cotter, 'but we had a memo from Eastvale Major Crimes asking us to report anything to do with the Soameses.'

'We're glad you were so prompt,' Annie cut in. 'Is anybody hurt?'

Cotter looked at her. 'Yes, ma'am,' he said. 'Young girl. The daughter. She rang the station, and we could hear cursing and things breaking in the background. She was frightened. Told us to come as soon as we could. We did, but by the time we got here . . . Well, you can see for yourselves.'

Annie was first inside the farmhouse, and she gave a curt nod to PC Watkins, who was standing in the living room scratching his head at the sight. The room was a wreck. Broken glass littered the floor, one of the chairs had been smashed into the table and splintered, a window was broken and lamps knocked over. The small bookcase had been pulled away from the wall, and its contents joined the broken glass on the floor.

'The kitchen's just as bad,' said PC Watkins, 'but that seems to be the extent of the damage. Everything's fine upstairs.'

'Where's Soames?' Annie asked.

'We don't know, ma'am. He was gone when we arrived.'

'What about his daughter, Kelly?'

'Eastvale General, ma'am. We radioed ahead to A and E.'

'How bad is she?'

PC Watkins looked away. 'Don't know, ma'am. Hard to say.' He gestured back into the room. 'Lot of blood.'

Annie hadn't noticed it before, but now she could see dark stains on the carpet and on a broken chair leg. *Kelly*. Oh, Jesus Christ.

'OK,' said Banks, stepping forward. 'I want you and your partner to organise a search for Calvin Soames. He can't have gone far. Get some help from the uniformed branch in East-vale if you need it.'

'Yes, sir.'

Banks turned to Annie. 'Come on,' he said. 'There's nothing more we can do here. Let's pay a visit to Eastvale General.'

Annie didn't need asking twice. When they got back into the car she thumped the steering-wheel with both fists and strained to hold back tears of anger. Her head was still throbbing from the previous night's excess. She felt Banks's hand rest on her shoulder, and her resolve not to cry strengthened. 'I'm all right,' she said, after a few moments, gently shaking him off. 'Just needed to let off a bit of steam, that's all. And there was me thinking I'd go home early and have a nice bath.'

'You OK to drive?'

'I'm fine. Really.' To demonstrate, Annie started the car, set off slowly down the long bumpy drive and didn't start speeding until she hit the main road.

Tuesday, 23 September 1969

'Yes, what is it?' Chadwick said, when Karen stuck her head round his office door. 'I told you I didn't want to be disturbed.'

'Urgent phone call. Your wife.'

Chadwick picked up the phone.

'Darling, I'm so glad you're there,' Janet said. 'I was worried I wouldn't be able to reach you. I don't know what to do.'

Chadwick could sense the alarm in her voice. 'What is it?'

'It's Yvonne. The school have rung wanting to know where she is. They said they'd tried to reach me earlier, but I was out shopping. You know what a busybody that headmistress is.'

'She's not at school?'

'No. And she's not here either. I checked her room, just in case.'

'Did you notice anything unusual?'

'No. Same mess as ever.'

Chadwick had left for the station before his daughter had woken up that morning. 'How did she seem at breakfast?' he asked.

'Quiet.'

'But she left for school as usual?'

'So I thought. I mean, she took her satchel and she was wearing her mac. It's not like her, Stan. You know it's not.'

'It's probably nothing,' Chadwick said, trying to ignore the fear crawling in the pit of his stomach. McGarrity was in jail, but what if one of the others had decided to take revenge for the Drugs Squad raids? He had probably been foolish to identify himself to Yvonne's boyfriend, but how else was he supposed to make his point? 'Look, I'll come straight home. You stay there in case she turns up.'

'Should I call the hospitals?'

'You might as well,' said Chadwick. 'And have a good look round her room. See if there's anything missing. Clothes and things.' That would give Janet something to do until he got there. 'I'm on my way. I'll be there as quick as I can.'

Eastvale General Infirmary was the biggest hospital for some distance, and as a consequence the staff there were over-worked and its facilities were strained to the limit. Just down King Street, behind the police station, it was a Victorian pile with high, draughty corridors and large wards with big sash windows, no doubt to let in the winter chill for the TB patients it had once housed.

A and E wasn't terribly busy, as it was only Thursday lunchtime, and they found Kelly Soames easily enough with the help of one of the admissions nurses. The curtains were drawn round her bed, but more, the nurse said, to give her privacy than for any more serious reason. When they went through and sat by her, Annie was relieved to see, and hear, that most of the damage was superficial. The blood had come almost entirely from a head wound, by far the most serious of her cuts and abrasions, but even this had only caused concussion. Her face was bruised, her lip split, and there was a stitched cut over her eye, but there were no broken bones or internal injuries.

Annie felt an immense relief that didn't diminish her anger against Kevin Templeton and Calvin Soames. It could have been so much worse. She held Kelly's hand and said, 'I'm sorry. I honestly didn't know anything like this was going to happen.'

Kelly said nothing, just continued to stare at the ceiling.

'Can you tell us what happened?' Banks asked.

'Isn't it obvious?' Kelly said. Her speech was a little slurred from the painkillers she had been given, and from the split lip, but she made herself clear enough.

'I'd rather hear it from you,' Banks said.

Annie continued to hold Kelly's hand. 'Tell us,' she said. 'Where is he, Kelly?'

'I don't know,' Kelly said. 'Honestly. The last thing I remember is feeling like my head was exploding.'

'It was a chair leg,' Banks said. 'Someone hit you with a chair leg. Was it your father?'

'Who else would it be?'

'What happened?'

Kelly took some of the water Annie offered and flinched when the flexi-straw touched the cut on her lip. She put the glass aside and spoke listlessly. 'He'd been drinking. Not like usual, just a couple of pints before dinner, but real drinking, like he used to. Whisky. He started at breakfast. I told him not to, but he ignored me. I caught the bus into Eastvale and did some shopping, and when I got back he was still drinking. I could tell he was really drunk by then. The bottle was almost empty, and he was red in the face, muttering to himself. I was worried about him. And scared. As soon as I opened my mouth, he went berserk. Asked me who I thought I was to tell him what to do. To be honest, I really thought he believed I was Mother, the way he was talking to me. Then he got really abusive – just shouting at first, not violent or anything. That was when I phoned the local police station. But as soon as he saw me on the phone, that was it. He went mad. He started hitting me, slapping and pushing then he punched me. After that, he started breaking things, smashing the furniture. It was all I could do to put my hands in front of my face to protect myself.'

'He didn't interfere with you in any way?' Annie asked.

'No. He wouldn't do anything like that. But the names he was calling me . . . I won't repeat them. They were the same ones he used to call Mother when they fought.'

'What happened to her?' Annie asked.

'She died in hospital. There was something wrong with her insides – I don't know what it was – and at first the doctors didn't diagnose it in time, then they thought it was something else. When they finally did get round to operating, it was too late. She never woke up. Dad said something about the anaesthetic being wrong, but I don't know. We never got to the bottom of it and he's never been able to let it go.'

'And your father's been over-possessive ever since?'

'He's only got me to take care of him. He can't take care of himself.' Kelly sipped some more water and coughed, dribbling it down her chin. Annie took a tissue from the table and wiped it away. 'Thanks,' said Kelly. 'Where's Dad? What's going to happen to him?'

'We don't know yet,' said Annie, glancing at Banks. 'We'll find him, though. Then we'll see.'

'I don't want anything to happen to him,' Kelly said. 'I know he's done wrong, but I don't want anything to happen to him.'

Annie held her hand. It was the old, old story, the abused defending her abuser. 'We'll see,' she said. 'Just get some rest for now.'

Back at the station, Banks found Detective Superintendent Gervaise in her office and told her about Kelly Soames. He also hinted that he knew Templeton had been passing her information and warned her not to put too much trust in its accuracy. It was worth it to see the expression on her face.

After that, he tried to put Kelly Soames and her problems

out of his mind for a while and focus on the Nick Barber investigation again before setting off to visit Ken Blackstone in Leeds. A couple of DCs had read through the boxes of Barber's papers sent up from his London flat and found they consisted entirely of old articles, photographs and business correspondence – none of it relating to his Yorkshire trip. He had clearly brought all of his current work with him, and now it was gone. Banks found a Brahms cello sonata on the radio and settled down to have another look through the old *MOJO* magazines that John Butler had given to him in London.

It didn't take him long to figure out that Nick Barber knew his stuff. In addition to some pieces on the Mad Hatters, there were also articles on Shelagh MacDonald, JoAnn Kelly, Comus and Bridget St John. His interest in the Hatters went back about five years, as Banks had been told, although he'd been into music since he was a teenager.

Childhood. Banks remembered the frisson of possibility he had experienced when Simon Bradley had talked about Linda Lofthouse's unwanted pregnancy.

It shouldn't be too hard to find out whether he was right, he decided, picking up the phone and looking up the Barbers' number in the case file.

When he got Louise Barber on the phone, Banks told her who he was and said, 'I know this is probably an odd question, and it's not meant to be in any way disturbing or upsetting, but was Nick adopted?'

There was a short pause followed by a sob. 'Yes,' she said. 'We adopted him when he was only days old. We raised him as if he were our own and that's how we always think of him.'

'I'm sure you did,' said Banks. 'Believe me, there's no hint of criticism here. I wouldn't expect it to enter your head at such a time, and, from all I've found out, Nick led a healthy and happy life with many advantages he probably wouldn't have had otherwise. It's just that . . . well, did he know? Did you tell him?'

'Yes,' said Louise Barber. 'We told him a long time ago, as soon as we thought he'd be able to absorb it.'

'And what did he do?'

'Then? Nothing. He said that as far as he was concerned, we were his parents and that was all there was to it.'

'Did he ever get curious about his birth mother?'

'It's funny, but he did, yes.'

'When was this?'

'Five or six years ago.'

'Any particular reason?'

'He told us he didn't want us to think there was a problem, or that it was anything to do with us, but a friend of his who was also adopted had told him it was important to find out. He said something about it making him whole, complete.'

'Did he find her?'

'He didn't talk to us about it much after that. We found it all a bit upsetting, and Nicholas was careful not to hurt us. He told us he'd found out who she was, but we have no idea if he traced her or met her.'

'Did he tell you her name?'

'Yes – Linda Lofthouse. But that's all I know. We asked him not to talk to us about her again.'

'The name is enough,' said Banks. 'Thank you very much, Mrs Barber, and I do apologise for bringing up difficult memories.'

'I suppose it can't be helped. Surely this can't have anything to do with . . . with what happened to Nicholas?'

'We don't know. Right now, it's just another piece of information to add to the puzzle. Goodbye.'

'Goodbye.'

Banks hung up and thought. So Nick Barber *was* Linda Lofthouse's son. He must have found out that his mother had been murdered a couple of years after he was born, and that she was Vic Greaves's cousin, which no doubt fuelled his interest in the Mad Hatters, already present to some extent because of his interest in the music of the period.

But the knowledge raised a number of new questions for Banks. Had Barber accepted the standard version of her murder? Did he believe that Patrick McGarrity had killed her? Or had he found out something else? If he had stumbled across something that indicated McGarrity was innocent, or had not acted alone, he might easily have blundered into a situation without knowing how dangerous it was. But it all depended on whether or not Chadwick had been right about McGarrity. It was time to head for Leeds and have a chat with Ken Blackstone.

Banks made it to Leeds in little over an hour, coming off New York Road at Eastgate and heading for Millgarth, the Leeds Police Headquarters at about half past three on Thursday afternoon. Like many things, he supposed, this business could have been conducted over the telephone, but he preferred personal contact, if possible. Somehow, little nuances and vague impressions didn't quite make it over the phone lines.

Ken Blackstone was waiting in his office, a tiny space partitioned at the end of a room full of busy detectives, nattily dressed as ever in his best Next pinstripe, dazzling white shirt and maroon and grey striped tie, held in place by a silver pin in the shape of a fountain pen. With his wispy grey hair curling over his ears and his gold-framed reading-glasses, he looked more like a university professor than a police officer. He and Banks had known one another for years, and Banks thought Ken was the closest he had to a friend, next to Dirty Dick Burgess, but Burgess was in London.

'First off,' said Blackstone, 'I thought you might like to see this.' He slid a photograph across his desk and Banks turned it to face him. It showed the head and shoulders of a man in his early forties, perhaps, neat black hair plastered flat with

Brylcreem, hard, angled face, straight nose and square jaw
with a slight dimple. But it was the eyes that caught Banks's
attention. They gave nothing away except, perhaps, a slight
hint of dark shadows in their depths. If eyes were supposed to
be the windows to the soul, these were the blackout curtains.
This was a hard, haunted, uncompromising man, Banks
thought. And a moral one. He didn't know why, and realised
he was being a bit fanciful, but he sensed a hint of hard religion
in the man's background. Hardly surprising, as there had been
plenty of that around in both Scotland and Yorkshire over the
years. 'Interesting,' Banks said, passing it back. 'Stanley
Chadwick, I assume?'

Blackstone nodded. 'Taken on his promotion to detective
inspector in October 1965.' He glanced at his watch. 'Look,
it's a bit noisy and stuffy in here. Fancy heading out for a
coffee?'

'I'm all coffeed out,' said Banks, 'but maybe we can have a
late lunch? I haven't eaten since this morning.'

'Fine with me. I'm not hungry, but I'll join you.'

They left Millgarth and walked on to Eastgate. It had turned
into a fine day, with that mix of cloud and sun you got so often
in Yorkshire, when it wasn't raining, and just chilly enough for
a raincoat or light overcoat.

'Did you manage to find out anything?' Banks asked.

'I've done a bit of digging,' said Blackstone, 'and it looks like
pretty solid investigating on the surface of it.'

'Only on the surface?'

'I haven't dug *that* deeply yet. And remember, it was
essentially a *North* Yorkshire case, so most of the paperwork's
up there.'

'I've seen it,' he said. 'I was just wondering about the West
Yorkshire angle, and about Chadwick himself.'

'DI Chadwick was on loan to the North Yorkshire Constabulary. From what I can glean, he'd had a few successes

here since his promotion and was a bit of a golden boy at the time.'

'I heard he was tough, and he certainly looks that way.'

'I never knew him personally, but I managed to turn up a couple of retired officers who did. He was a hard man, by all accounts, but fair and honest, and he got results. He had a strong Scottish Presbyterian background, but one of his old colleagues told me he thought he'd lost his faith during the war. Hardly bloody surprising when you consider the poor sod saw action in Burma *and* was part of the D-Day invasion.'

'Where is he now?'

They waited until the lights changed, then crossed Vicar Lane. 'Dead,' Blackstone said finally. 'According to our personnel records, Stanley Chadwick died in March 1973.'

'So young?' said Banks. 'That must have been a hell of a shock for all concerned. He would only have been in his early fifties.'

'Apparently his health had been in decline for a couple of years,' Blackstone said. 'He'd had a lot of sick time and, performance-wise, there were rumours that he was dragging his feet. He retired due to ill-health in late 1972.'

'That seems a rather sudden decline,' Banks said. 'Any speculation as to what it was?'

'Well, it wasn't murder, if that's what you're thinking. He had a history of heart problems, hereditary apparently, which had gone untreated, perhaps even unnoticed. He died in his sleep of a heart-attack. But you have to remember, this is just from the files and the memory of a couple of old men I managed to track down. And some of the information is impossible to locate. We moved here from Brotherton House in 1976, which was well before my time, and inevitably stuff went missing in the move, so your guess is as good as mine as to the rest.'

Simon Bradley had told Banks he'd heard Chadwick wasn't

in good health, but Banks hadn't realised things were that bad.
Could there have been anything suspicious about his death?
First Linda Lofthouse, then Robin Merchant, then Stanley
Chadwick? Banks couldn't imagine what linked them. Chad-
wick had investigated the Lofthouse case, but had had nothing
to do with Merchant's drowning. He had, however, met the
Mad Hatters at Swainsview Lodge, and Vic Greaves was
Linda Lofthouse's cousin. He was missing something. Maybe
Chadwick's daughter Yvonne would help, if he could find her.

They turned down Briggate, a pedestrian precinct. There
were plenty of shoppers in evidence, many of them young
people, teenage girls pushing prams, the boys with them
looking too young and inexperienced to be fathers. Many
of the girls looked too young to be mothers, too, but Banks
knew damn well they weren't merely helping out their big
sisters. Teenage pregnancies and sexually transmitted diseases
were at appallingly high rates.

Because he still had Linda Lofthouse and Nick Barber on
his mind, Banks thought back to the sixties, to what the media
had dubbed the 'sexual revolution'. True, the pill had made it
possible for women to have sex without fear of pregnancy, but
it had also left them with little or no excuse *not* to have sex. In
the name of liberation, women were expected to sleep around:
they had the freedom to do so, the reasoning went, so they
should, and there was subtle and not-so-subtle cultural and
peer pressure on them to do so. After all, the worst anyone
could get was crabs or a dose of clap, so sex was relatively fear-
free.

But there were plenty of unwanted pregnancies back then,
too, Banks remembered, as not all girls were on the pill, or
willing to have abortions, certainly in the provinces. Linda
Lofthouse had been one of them, and Norma Coulton, just
down the street from where Banks lived, another. Banks
remembered the gossip and the dirty looks she got after she'd

walked into the newsagent's. He wondered what had happened to her and her child. At least he knew what had happened to Linda Lofthouse's son: he had met the same fate as his mother.

'Any idea what happened to Chadwick's family?' he asked.

'According to what I could find out, he had a wife called Janet and a daughter called Yvonne. Both survived him, but nobody's kept tabs on them. I don't suppose it would be too difficult to track them down. Pensions or Human Resources might be able to help.'

'Do what you can,' said Banks. 'I appreciate it. And I'll put Winsome on to it at our end. She's good at that sort of thing. The daughter may have married, changed her name, of course, but we'll give it a try – electoral rolls, DVLA, PNC and the rest. Who knows? we might get lucky before we have to resort to more time-consuming methods.'

They passed a thin, bearded young man selling the *Big Issue* at the entrance to Thornton's Arcade. Blackstone bought a copy, folded it and slipped it into his inside pocket. Two young policemen passed them, both wearing black helmets and bulletproof vests and carrying Heckler & Koch carbines.

'It's a fact of the times here, I'm afraid,' said Blackstone.

Banks nodded. What bothered him most was that the officers looked only about fifteen.

'Sorry I'm not being a lot of help,' Blackstone went on.

'Nonsense,' said Banks. 'You're helping me fill in the picture, and that's all I need right now. I know I'll have to read the files and the trial transcripts soon, but I keep putting it off because those things bore me so much.'

'You can do that in my office after we've had a bite to eat. I have to go out. I know what you mean, though. I'd rather curl up with a good Flashman or Sharpe, myself.' Blackstone stopped at the end of an alley. 'Let's try the Ship this time. Whitelocks is always too damned crowded, these days, and they've changed the menu. It's getting too trendy. And some-how I don't see you sitting out in the Victoria Quarter at the Harvey Nichols café eating a garlic and Brie frittata.'

'Oh, I don't know,' said Banks. 'You'd be surprised. I scrub up quite nicely, and I don't mind a bit of foreign grub every now and then. But the Ship sounds fine.'

They ordered pints of Tetley's, and Banks chose a giant Yorkshire pudding filled with sausages and gravy and sat down in the dim brass and dark wood interior. Blackstone stuck with his beer.

Banks told Blackstone about their troublesome new super-intendent and that Templeton might be bringing in too many apples for the teacher. Then he chatted about Brian and his new girlfriend Emilia turning up. When his food came, they got back to Stanley Chadwick and Linda Lofthouse.

'Do you think I'm tilting at windmills, Ken?' Banks asked.

'It wouldn't be the first time, but I don't have enough to go on to advise you on that score. Usually your windmills turn out to be all too human. Explain your reasoning.'

Banks sipped some beer, trying to order his thoughts. It was a useful, if difficult, exercise. 'There isn't much, really,' he said. 'Superintendent Gervaise thinks the past is over and the guilty have been punished, but I'm not so sure. It's not that I think Vic Greaves is a killer because he has mental problems. Christ, it might even be Chris Adams, for all I know. He doesn't live that far away. Or even Tania Hutchison. It's not as if Oxfordshire's on the moon either. I just think that if Nick Barber was as good and as thorough a music journalist as everyone says he was, he might have struck a nerve, and Vic Greaves is one of the few people he had tried to speak to about the story. I've also discovered that Nick was Linda Lofthouse's son, adopted at birth by the Barbers, and that he found out who his birth mother was about five years ago. Barber was a journalist, and I think he simply tried to find out as much about her and her times as he could because he was already interested in the music and the period. One thing he found out was that Vic Greaves was her cousin. Greaves also lived only walking distance away from Barber's rented cottage, and someone saw a figure running around at the time of the murder. The only things I can find in the past that cast any sort of suspicions on Greaves and the others are the murder of Linda Lofthouse, because she was backstage at the Brimleigh festival with Tania Hutchison, and she was Greaves's cousin, and the drowning of the Mad Hatters' bassist, Robin Merchant, when Greaves, Adams and Tania Hutchison were all present at Swainsview Lodge. And they're both closed cases.'

'Linda Lofthouse's murderer was caught, and Merchant's drowning was ruled death by misadventure, right?'

'Right. And Linda's killer was stabbed in jail, so it's not as if we can ask him to clear anything up for us. Sounds as if he was deranged in the first place.'

'But ruling out the angry-husband or passing-tramp theory, that's the default line of inquiry?'

'Pretty much so. Chris Adams said Barber had a coke habit, but we can't find any evidence of that. If he did, it obviously wasn't big-time.'

'Have you got Barber's phone records yet?'

'We're working on it, but we don't expect too much there.'

'Why not?'

'There was no landline at the cottage where he was staying, and he was out of mobile range. If he needed to phone anyone he'd have had to use the public telephone box, either in Fordham or in Eastvale.'

'What about Internet access? You'd think a savvy music journalist would be all wired up for that sort of thing, wouldn't you?'

'Not if he didn't have a phone line, or wireless access. Blackberry or Bluetooth, or whatever it is.'

'Aren't there any Internet cafés in Eastvale?'

Banks glanced at Blackstone, ate another mouthful of sausage and washed it down with a swig of beer. 'Good point, Ken. Apart from the library, which is as slow as a horse and cart, there's a computer shop in the market square, Eastvale Computes. I suppose we could check there. Problem is, the owner's only got two computers available to the public, and I should imagine the histories get wiped pretty often. If Nick Barber used either of them, it'd have been a couple of weeks ago, and all traces would be gone by now. It's worth a try, though.'

'So, what next?'

'Well,' said Banks, 'there are a few more people to talk to, starting with Tania Hutchison and Chadwick's daughter, Yvonne, when we find her, but for the moment, I've got a CD collection with a lot of holes in it, and Borders is beckoning just up Briggate.'

Annie got Banks's phone call from Blackstone's office in Leeds late that afternoon and welcomed the break from the dull routine of statement-reading. Kelly Soames was holding her own and would most likely be discharged the following day. They still hadn't found her father.

Before Annie left the squad room, Winsome came up trumps with Nick Barber's mobile service, but the results were disappointing. He had made no calls since arriving at the cottage because he had no coverage there. He could, of course, have used his mobile in Eastvale but, according to the records, he hadn't. If he had been up to anything at all, he had kept it very much to himself. That wouldn't be surprising, Annie thought. She had known a few journalists in her time, and had found that, on the whole, they were a secretive lot; they had to be – theirs was very much a first-come, first-served kind of business.

Templeton had just got back from Fordham, and Annie noticed him watching closely as she leaned over Winsome's shoulder to read the notes. She whispered in Winsome's ear, then let her hand rest casually on her shoulder. She could see the prurient curiosity in Templeton's gaze now. Enough rope, she thought. And if he knew that she had stayed at Winsome's the other night, who could guess what wild tales he might take to Superintendent Gervaise? Since talking to Banks, Annie's anger had diminished, although she still blamed Templeton for what had happened. She knew there was no point in confronting him: he just wouldn't get it. Banks was right. Let him crucify himself: he was already well on the way.

Annie picked up a folder from her desk, plucked her suede jacket from the hanger by the door, said she'd be back in a while, and walked down the stairs with a smile on her face.

A cool wind gusted across the market square and the sky was quickly filling with dirty clouds, like ink spilled on a sheet of paper. Luckily, Annie didn't have far to go, she thought, as she pulled the collar of her jacket round her throat and crossed the busy square. People leaned into the wind as they walked, hair flying, plastic bags from Somerfield's and Boots fluttering as if they were filled with birds. The Darlington bus stood at its stop by the market cross, but nobody seemed to be getting on or off.

Eastvale Computes had been open a couple of years now, and the owner, Barry Gilchrist, was the sort of chap who loved a technical challenge. As a consequence, people came in to chat about their computer problems, and Barry usually ended up solving them for free. Whether he ever sold any computers or not, Annie had no idea, but she doubted it, with Aldi, and even Woolworths, offering much lower prices.

Barry was one of those ageless young lads in glasses who looked like Harry Potter. Annie had been in the shop fairly often, and she was on friendly enough terms with him; she had even bought CD-Roms and printer cartridges from him in an effort to give some support to local business. She got the impression that he rather fancied her because he got all tongue-tied when he spoke to her and found it hard to look her in the eye. He wasn't offensive, though, like Templeton, and she was surprised to find that she felt more maternal towards him than anything else. She hadn't thought she was old enough for that sort of thing, but now she supposed she might, at a pinch, be of an age with his mother if he was as young as he seemed. It was a sobering thought.

'Oh, hello,' he said, blushing, as he looked up from a monitor behind the counter. 'What can I do for you today?'

'It's official business,' Annie said, smiling. Judging by the expression that crossed his face and the way he surreptitiously hit a few keys, Annie wondered if he'd been looking at Internet porn. She didn't have him down as that type, but you never could tell, especially with computer geeks. 'You might be able to help us,' she added.

'Oh, I see.' He straightened his glasses. 'Well, of course . . . er . . . whatever I can do. Computer problems at the station?'

'Nothing like that. It's Internet access I'm interested in.'

'But I thought . . .'

'Not for me. A customer you might have had a couple of weeks ago.'

'Ah. Well, I don't get very many, especially at this time of year. Tourists come in, of course, to check their email, but most of the locals either have their own computers, or they're not interested.' Not to be interested, the way Barry Gilchrist said it, sounded infinitely sad.

Annie took a photograph from the folder she had brought and handed it to him. 'This man,' she said. 'We know he was in Eastvale on Wednesday two weeks ago. We were wondering if he came in here and asked to use your Internet access.'

'Yes,' said Barry Gilchrist, turning a little pale. 'I remember him. The journalist. That's the man who was murdered, isn't it? I saw it on the news.'

'What day of the week did he come in?'

'Not Wednesday. I think it was Friday morning.'

The day he died, Annie thought. 'Did he tell you he was a journalist or did you hear it?'

'He told me. Said he needed a few minutes to do a spot of research, that there was no access where he was staying.'

'How long was he on?'

'About fifteen minutes. I didn't bother charging him.'

'Now comes the tricky part,' said Annie. 'I don't suppose there'd still be any traces of where he went online?'

Gilchrist shook his head. 'I'm sorry, no. I mean, I said I don't get a lot of customers this time of year, but I do get some, so I have to keep the histories and temporary Internet files clean.'

'They say you can never quite get rid of everything on a computer. Do you think our technical unit could get anything if we took them in?'

Gilchrist swallowed. 'Took the computers away?'

'Yes. I hardly have to remind you this is a murder investigation, do I?'

'No. And I'm very sorry. He seemed a nice enough bloke. Said he had wireless access on his laptop but there were no signals in these parts. I could sympathise with that. It took me long enough to get broadband.'

'So, would they?'

'Sorry, what?'

'If they took the computers apart would they find anything?'

'Oh, they don't need to do that,' he said.

'Why's that?' Annie asked.

'Because I know the site he visited. One of them, at any rate. The first.'

'Do tell.'

'I wasn't spying or anything. I mean, there's no privacy, anyway, as you can see – the computers are in a public area. Anyone could walk in and see what site someone was visiting.'

'True,' said Annie. 'So he was making no efforts to hide his tracks? He didn't erase the history himself, for example?'

'He couldn't do that. That power's limited to the administrator, and that's me. Providing access is one thing, but I don't want people messing with the programs.'

'Fair enough. So what was he doing?'

'He was at the Mad Hatters' website. I could tell because it plays a little bit of that hit song of theirs when it starts up. What's it called? "Love Got In The Way"?'

Annie knew the song. It had been a huge hit about eight years ago. 'Are you sure?' she asked.

'Yes. I had to go round the front to check the printer cartridge stock, and I could see it over his shoulder, photos of the band, biographies, discographies, that sort of thing.'

Annie knew Banks would be as disappointed as she was with this. What could be more natural for a music journalist writing about the Mad Hatters than to visit their website? 'Was that all?'

'I think so. I heard the music when he started, and he finished a short while after I'd checked the stock. He could have followed any number of links in between, but if he did, he went back to the main site.' Gilchrist pushed his glasses back up the bridge of his nose with his forefinger. 'Does that help?'

Annie smiled at him. 'Every little bit helps,' she said.

'There's one more thing.'

'Yes?'

'Well, he was carrying a paperback book with him, as if he'd been sitting and having a read in a café or something. I saw him writing something in the back of it with a pencil. I couldn't see what it was.'

'Interesting,' said Annie, remembering the Ian McEwan

book Banks had found at Moorview Cottage. He had said something about some pencilled numbers in the back. Maybe she should have a look. She thanked Gilchrist for his time and headed out into the wind.

17

Because of roadworks and poor weather on the M1, it took Banks almost three hours to drive to Tania Hutchison's house on Friday morning, and when he got to her village, he was so thoroughly pissed off with driving that the beautiful rolling country of the English heartland was lost on him.

He had spent the latter part of Thursday afternoon, and a good part of the evening, reading over the files on the Linda Lofthouse investigation and the Patrick McGarrity trial transcripts, all to little avail, so he had not been in the best of moods when he got up that morning. Brian was still in bed, but Emilia had been pottering about. She had made him a pot of coffee and some delicious scrambled eggs. He was getting used to having her around.

Tania's house, perched on the edge of a tiny village, wasn't especially large, but it was built of golden Cotswold stone, with a thatched roof, and must have cost her a pretty penny. The thing that surprised Banks most was that he could drive right up to her front gate: there was no security, no high wall or fence, merely a privet hedge. He had rung earlier to let her know he was coming, to get directions and make sure she would be in, but had told her nothing about the reason for his visit.

Tania greeted him at the door, and although no one else was present, Banks knew he would have been able to pick her out easily in a crowd. It wasn't that she looked like a rock star or anything, whatever a rock star looked like. She was more petite than he had imagined from seeing her on stage and television, and she certainly looked older now, but it wasn't so much the familiarity of her looks as a certain presence. Charisma, Banks supposed. It wasn't something he came across often in his line of work. For a moment, Banks felt absurdly embarrassed, remembering the teenage crush he had had on her. He wondered if she could tell from his behaviour.

Her clothes were of the casual-expensive kind, understated designer jeans and a loose cable-knit sweater; she was barefoot, toenails painted red, and her dark hair, in the past so long and glossy, was now cut short and threaded with grey. There were lines round her eyes and mouth, but otherwise her complexion seemed flawless and smooth. She wore little makeup, just enough to accentuate the full lips and watchful green eyes, and she moved with natural grace as Banks followed her through a broad arched hallway into a large living room, where a lacquered grand piano stood by the French windows, and the floor was covered with a lush Persian carpet.

The other thing Banks noticed was a heavy glass ashtray, and Tania wasted no time in lighting a cigarette once she had curled up in an armchair and gestured for Banks to sit opposite her. She held it in the V of her index and second fingers and took short, frequent drags. He felt like smoking with her, but suppressed the urge. There was a fragility and a wariness about her, as well as charisma, as if she'd been hurt or betrayed so many times that once more would cause her world to crumble. Her name had been romantically linked with a number of famous rock stars and actors, and with equally famous break-ups, but now, Banks had read recently, she lived alone with her two cats, and she liked it that way. The cats, one marmalade and one tabby, were in evidence, but neither showed much interest in Banks.

As he made himself comfortable, Banks had to remind himself that Tania was a suspect, and he had to put out of his mind the vivid sexual fantasies he had once entertained about her and stop acting like a tongue-tied adolescent. She had been at Brimleigh with Linda Lofthouse and had later been a member of the Mad Hatters. She had also been present at Swainsview Lodge on the night Robin Merchant drowned. She had no motive for either crime, as far as Banks knew, but motives sometimes had a habit of emerging later, once the means and the opportunity were firmly nailed in place.

'You weren't very forthcoming over the telephone, you know,' she said, a touch of reproach in her husky voice. Banks could still hear hints of a North American accent, although he knew she had been in England since her student days.

'It's about Nick Barber's murder,' he said, watching for a reaction.

'Nick Barber? The writer? Good Lord. I hadn't heard.' She turned pale.

'What is it?'

'I spoke to him a couple of weeks ago. He wanted to talk to me. He was doing a piece on the Mad Hatters.'

'Did you agree to talk to him?'

'Nick was one of the few music journos you could trust not to distort everything. Oh, Christ, this is terrible.' She put her hand to her mouth. If she was acting, Banks thought, then she was damned good. But she was a performer by trade, he reminded himself. As if sensing her grief, one of the cats made its way over slowly and, with a scowl at Banks, leaped on to her lap. She stroked it absently and it purred.

'I'm sorry,' he said. 'I didn't realise you were close, or I would have broken the news a bit more tactfully. I assumed you knew.'

'We weren't close,' she said. 'I just knew him in passing, that's all. I've met him once or twice. And I liked his work. It's a hell of a shock. He was planning to come by and talk to me about my early days with the band.'

'When was this?' Banks asked.

'We didn't have a firm date. He phoned two, maybe three weeks ago and said he'd get in touch with me again soon. He never did.'

'Did he say anything else?'

'No. He said he was ringing from a public telephone, and his phone card ran out. What happened? Why would anyone murder Nick Barber?'

The public phone box call explained why they hadn't seen Tania's number on Barber's mobile or landline phone records, Banks thought. 'I think it might be something to do with the story he was working on,' he said.

'The story? But how could it be?'

'I don't know yet, but we haven't been able to find any other lines of inquiry.' Banks told her a little about Barber's movements in Yorkshire, in particular his unsatisfactory meeting with Vic Greaves.

'Poor Vic,' she said. 'How is he?'

Banks didn't know how to answer that. He'd thought Greaves was clearly off his rocker, if not clinically insane, but he seemed to function well enough, with a little help from Chris Adams, and he was certainly high on Banks's list of suspects. 'Same as usual, I suppose,' he said, though he didn't know what was usual for Vic Greaves.

'Vic was one of the sensitive ones,' Tania said. 'Much too fragile for the life he led and the risks he took.'

'What do you mean?'

Tania stubbed out her cigarette before answering. 'There are people in the business whose minds and bodies can take an awful lot of substance abuse – Iggy Pop and Keith Richards come to mind, for example – and there are those who go on the ride with them and fall off. Vic was one who fell off.'

'Because he was sensitive?'

She nodded. 'Some people could eat acid as if it were candy and have nothing but a good time, like watching their favourite cartoons over and over again. Others saw the devil, the jaws of hell or the Four Horsemen of the Apocalypse and the horrors beyond the grave. Vic was one of the latter. He had Hammer-horror trips, and the visions unhinged him.'

'So LSD caused his breakdown?'

'It certainly contributed to it. But I'm not saying something wouldn't have happened anyway. Certainly the emotions and some of the images were in his mind already. Acid merely released them. But maybe he should have kept the cork in the bottle.'

'Why did he keep taking it?'

Tania shrugged. 'There's really no answer to that. Acid certainly isn't addictive in the way heroin and coke are. Not all his trips were bad. I think maybe he was trying to get through hell to something better. Maybe he thought if he kept trying, then one day he would find the peace he was looking for.'

'But he didn't?'

'You've seen him yourself. You should know.'

'Who was he riding with?'

'There wasn't any particular person. It was meant as a sort of metaphor for the whole scene back then. The doors of perception and all that. Vic was a poet and he loved and wanted all that mystical, decadent glamour. He admired Jim Morrison, even met him at the Isle of Wight.' She smiled to herself. 'Apparently, it didn't go well. The Lizard King was in a bad mood, and he didn't want to know poor Vic, let alone read his poetry. Told him to fuck off. That hurt.'

'Too bad,' said Banks. 'What about the rest of the band's drug intake?'

'None of them was as sensitive as Vic, and none of them did as much acid.'

'Robin Merchant?'

'Hardly. I'd have put him down as one of the survivors if it hadn't been for the accident.'

'What about Chris Adams?'

'Chris?' A flicker of a smile crossed her face. 'Chris was probably the straightest of the lot. Still is.'

'Why do you think he takes such good care of Vic? Guilt?'

'Over what?'

'I don't know,' Banks said. 'Responsibility for the break-down, something like that?'

'No,' Tania said, shaking her head vigorously. 'Far from it. Chris was always trying to get Vic off acid, helping him through bad trips.'

'Then why?'

Tania paused. It was quiet outside, and Banks couldn't even hear any birds singing. 'If you ask me,' she said, 'I'd say it was because he loved him. Not in any homosexual sense, you understand – Chris isn't like that, or Vic, for that matter – but as a brother. Don't forget, they grew up together, knew each other as kids on a working-class estate. They shared dreams. If Chris had had any musical talent, he'd have been in the band, but he was the first to admit he couldn't even manage the basic three rock chords, and he certainly couldn't carry the simplest melody. But he did have good business sense and vision, and that was what shaped the band after the tragedies. It was all very well to tune in, turn on, drop out and say, "Whatever, man," but someone had to handle the day-to-day mechanics of making a living, and if someone trustworthy like Chris didn't do it, you could bet your life that there were any number of unscrupulous bastards waiting in the wings ready to exploit someone else's talent.'

'Interesting,' said Banks. 'So in some ways Chris Adams was the driving force behind the Mad Hatters?'

'He held things together, yes. And he helped us with a new direction when both Robin and Vic were gone.'

'Was it Chris who invited you to join the band?'

Tania twisted a silver ring on her finger. 'Yes. It's no secret. We were going out together at the time. I met him at Brimleigh. I'd seen him a couple of times before, when my friend Linda got me into Mad Hatters events, but we hadn't really talked like we did at Brimleigh. I had a boyfriend then, a student in Paris, but we soon drifted apart, and Chris was in London a lot. He'd phone me and finally I agreed to have dinner with him.'

'Brimleigh's something else I want to talk to you about,' said Banks. 'If you can cast your mind back that far.'

Tania gave him an enigmatic smile. 'There's nothing wrong with *my* mind,' she said, 'but if you're going to send me leafing through my back pages, I think we're going to need some coffee, don't you?' She dumped the cat unceremoniously on the floor and headed into the kitchen. The animal hissed at Banks and slunk away. Banks was surprised that Tania had no one to make the coffee for her, no housekeeper or butler but, then, Tania Hutchison was full of surprises.

While she was gone, he gazed round the room. There was nothing to distinguish it particularly, except a few modernist paintings on the walls, originals by the look of them, and an old stone fireplace that would probably make it very cosy on a winter evening. There was no music playing and no evidence of a stereo or CDs. Neither was there a television.

Tania returned shortly with a cafetière, mugs, milk and sugar on a tray, which she set on the low wicker coffee-table. 'We'll give it a few minutes, shall we? You do like your coffee strong?'

'Yes,' said Banks.

'Excellent.' Tania lit another cigarette and leaned back.

'Can we talk about Brimleigh?'

'Naturally. But as I remember it, the man who killed Linda was caught and put in jail.'

'That's true,' said Banks. 'Where he has since died.'

'Then . . . ?'

'I just want to get a few things clear, that's all. Did you know the man, Patrick McGarrity?'

'No. I'd met him on a couple of occasions, when I accompanied Linda to her friends' houses in Leeds, but I never spoke with him. He seemed an odious sort of character, pacing around with that silly smile on his face, as if he was enjoying some sort of private joke at everyone else's expense. Gave me the creeps. I suppose they only put up with him because of the drugs.'

'You knew about that?'

'That he was a dealer? It was pretty obvious. But he could only have been small-time. Even most dealers had more class than him, and they didn't smell as bad.'

'Did you see him at Brimleigh?'

'No, but we were backstage.'

'All the time?'

'Unless we went out front to the press enclosure to see the bands – and, of course, when Linda took her walk in the woods. But we were never with the general audience, no.'

'I've read through the files and trial transcripts,' said Banks, 'and apparently you weren't worried about her.'

'No. We both knew we might go our separate ways. She knew I was heading off to Paris the next day, and she told me she'd probably stay with friends in Leeds, so I had no cause to worry. The last thing you expected at a festival back then was a murder. This was before Altamont, remember, coming hot on the heels of successes at Woodstock and the Isle of Wight. Everyone was high on rock festivals. The bigger the better.'

'I appreciate that,' said Banks. 'Did you see her talking to anyone in particular?'

'Not really. I mean, we talked to a lot of people. There was a party atmosphere, and it was a big thrill to be hanging out with the stars.' She gave Banks a coy smile. 'I was still an impressionable young girl back then, you know. Anyway, Linda spent a bit of time with the Hatters, but she would, wouldn't she? It was Vic who got us the passes in the first place, and he was her cousin, even if they weren't especially close.'

'Did anyone show unusual interest in her?'

'No. People chatted her up, if that's what you mean. Linda was a very attractive girl.'

'But she didn't go off with anyone?'

'Not that I knew of.' Tania leaned forward and pressed the plunger on the cafetière, then carefully poured two mugs. She added milk and sugar to her own, then offered them to Banks, who declined. 'Linda was in a very spiritual phase then, into yoga and meditation, Tibetan Buddhism. She wasn't into drugs and I don't think she was into men all that much.'

'Did you see her leave the enclosure?'

'Not as such, no, but she told me she was going for a walk. I was heading to the front to see Led Zeppelin, and she said she needed a bit of space, she'd catch up with me later.'

'So where was Linda when you last saw her?'

'Backstage.'

'Was she with anyone?'

'A group of people.'

'Including?'

'I can't really remember that far back. Some of the Hatters were there.'

'Vic Greaves?'

'Vic was around, but he took some acid after the show and . . . who knows where he was? Most people went round to the front. It was a real crush in there, I do remember that. I couldn't say for certain who was there and who wasn't.'

'So you didn't see Linda head for the woods?'

'No. Look, you're not saying Vic might have done this, are you? Because I don't believe that. Whatever his problems, Vic was always a gentle soul. Still is, only he's a bit disturbed. They caught the killer fair and square. They found his knife with Linda's blood on it. I'd seen McGarrity with that knife myself at Bayswater Terrace.'

'I know,' said Banks. 'But he maintained at the trial that he was framed, that the knife was planted.'

Tania snorted. 'He would, wouldn't he? You of all people should know that.'

Banks had read all about McGarrity's bumbling efforts to defend himself in court, and he had no doubt that the man had been his own worst enemy. But if Vic Greaves had killed his cousin Linda, it made much more sense of later events, including Nick Barber's murder. Greaves certainly had a violent streak, as he had made evident at the cottage after Banks's visit. Perhaps, Banks thought, Greaves wasn't quite as crazy as he made himself out to be. But he couldn't tell Tania this. She was partisan: she would stick by her friends. He sipped some coffee. It was strong and full of flavour. 'Delicious,' he said.

She inclined her head at the compliment. 'Blue Mountain. Jamaica.'

'Did you know that Linda had an illegitimate child?'

'Yes. She told me she gave him up for adoption. She was only sixteen at the time.'

'And that child was Nick Barber?'

'He . . . What? My God! No, I didn't know that. How . . . That's an incredible coincidence.'

'Not really,' said Banks. 'Plenty of people are adopted. Maybe Nick came by his love of music through Linda's genes, I don't know that, but the knowledge did give him a particular interest in the Mad Hatters when he found out his birth mother was related to one of them. Then, when he found out she had been murdered, I should imagine his journalistic curiosity got him sniffing around that, too.'

'You don't think it was anything to do with what happened to him, do you?'

'Only in that it set him on the course that led to his death. He probably wouldn't have been writing that story and found out what he did – if, indeed, that's what happened – if his mother hadn't been Linda Lofthouse. But there again, maybe he would. He was already a Mad Hatters fan. I just find it a curious detail, that's all. You were at Swainsview Lodge the night Robin Merchant died, weren't you?'

'Yes,' said Tania. Banks couldn't be certain, but he thought he detected a certain reticence, or tightness, slip into her tone.

'What was he like?'

'Robin? Of all of them, he was probably the brightest and the most intellectual. The weirdest, too.'

'What do you mean?'

'He always seemed remote, unreachable, to me. You couldn't touch him. You didn't know where he was, what he was thinking. Yet on the surface he was always friendly and pleasant enough. He was well educated and well read, but musically a bit plodding.'

'What was he like with the girls?'

'Oh, they all fancied Robin. He was so pretty with that mass of dark curls, but I'm not sure . . . I don't think he cared that much for anyone, underneath it all. I didn't know him long, but he never had any sort of relationship during that time. It was all rather mechanical for him. He took what he was offered, then cast them aside. He was more into metaphysical and occult things.'

'Black magic?'

'Tarot cards, astrology, eastern philosophy, the cabbala, that sort of thing. A lot of people were into it back then.'

'As they are again now,' said Banks, thinking of Madonna and all the other stars who had discovered the cabbala of late, not to mention Scientology, which had also been a powerful presence in the late sixties. If you wait, everything comes round again.

'I suppose so,' Tania said. 'Anyway, Robin was usually immersed in some book or other. He didn't say much. As I said, I didn't really know him. Nobody did. His life outside the band was a mystery to all of us. If he had one.'

'Did Linda like him?'

'She said he was cute, yeah, but like I said, she was into other things at the time. Men weren't high on her list of priorities.'

'But she wasn't off them completely?'

'Oh, no. I'm sure she'd have been interested if the right person had come along. She was just tired of the attitude some of the guys had. *Free love.* What they thought it meant was that they could screw any woman they wanted.'

'What about relations between Robin and Vic Greaves?'

'Nothing unusual, really. Robin seemed upset sometimes that Vic got more of his songs performed, but Vic was the better songwriter. Robin's lyrics were too arcane, too dark.'

'That's all?'

'Yes, as far as I know. It was nothing more serious. Mostly they got along just fine.'

'And the rest of the band?'

'Same. There were disagreements, of course, as there always are when groups of people spend too much time cooped up together, but they weren't at each other's throats all the time, if that's what you mean. I'd say, as things go in this business, as a group they were a pretty well-behaved bunch of kids, and I've seen some bad behaviour in my time.'

'And after you joined?'

'Everyone treated me with respect. They still do.'

'What were the other members like as individuals?'

'Well, Vic was the sensitive poet, and Robin, as I said, the intellectual and the mystic. Reg was the angry one. The working-class boy made good with a bloody great chip on his shoulder. He's over it now, more or less – I think a few million quid might have had a bit to do with that – but it was what drove him back then. Terry was the quiet one. He had a rough background. Apparently his father died when he was a kid and his mother was really weird. I think she ended up in an institution. He was troubled, but he never talked about it. He seems a bit better adjusted, these days. At least, he manages to smile and speak a civil word now and then. And Adrian, well, he was the joker, the fun-lover. Still is. Laugh a minute, Adrian.'

'And you?'

Tania raised her delicately arched eyebrows. 'Me? I'm the enigmatic one.'

Banks smiled. 'What about your relationship with Chris Adams?'

'It faded over time. It's hard to keep a relationship going, the punishing schedule we had those first two or three years. We were touring or recording constantly. But we're still friends, have been ever since.'

'The night Robin Merchant drowned,' Banks said, 'did you really expect the police to believe that you were all sound asleep in bed?'

She seemed taken aback by the question, but she answered, without much hesitation, 'They did, didn't they? Death by misadventure.'

'But you weren't all asleep all the time, were you?' Banks pressed, shooting in the dark, hoping for a hit.

Tania looked at him, her green eyes disconcerting. He could tell she was trying to weigh him up, figure out what he knew and how he might have found out. 'It's a long time ago,' she said. 'I can't remember.'

'Come off it, Tania,' Banks said. 'Why did you all lie?'

'For God's sake, nobody lied.' She shook her head, puffing on her third cigarette. 'Oh, what the hell? It was a lot easier that way. None of us killed Robin. We knew that. Why would we? If we'd said we were all up and about, they'd only have asked more stupid questions, and we were all a bit the worse for wear. We just wanted to be left alone.'

'So what really happened?'

'I honestly don't know. I was drunk.'

'Drugs?'

'Some of the others. I stuck to vodka. Believe it or not, I never did anything else, except for a few tokes once in a while. Anyway, it was a big house. People were all over the place. You couldn't possibly keep track of one another even if you wanted to.'

'Were people out by the swimming-pool?'

'I don't know. I wasn't. If anybody saw Robin in there, they knew it was too late to do anything for him.'

'So you left him until the gardener came the next morning?'

'You're putting words into my mouth. I'm not saying that's what happened. I didn't see him there, and I don't know for a fact that anyone else did.'

'But someone *could* have?'

'Of course someone could have, but what use is "could have", especially now?'

'And someone could have pushed him in.'

'Oh, for Christ's sake, why would anyone do that?'

'I don't know. Maybe things weren't as peachy as you say they were.'

Tania sat forward. 'Look, I've had enough of this. You come into my house and call me a liar to my face—'

'I'm not the one calling you a liar. You've already admitted you lied to the police in 1970. Why should I believe you now?'

'Because I'm telling the truth. I can't think of any reason on earth why any of us would have wanted Robin dead.'

'I'm just trying to find the connection between then and now.'

'Well, maybe there isn't one. Have you thought of that?'

'Yes. But put yourself in my position. I have one definite murder in September 1969, and although the killer was apparently caught and jailed, there's still room for doubt in my mind. We have another death in June 1970, easily explained as an accident at the time, but now that you tell me people were up and about most of the night, maybe there's some doubt about that too. And the common factor to all of these is the Mad Hatters. And Nick Barber was going to write their story, specifically Vic Greaves's story, and he made reference to a murder.'

Tania drew on her cigarette, thought for a moment. 'Look,' she said, 'I know when you put it like that it sounds suspicious, but they're all just coincidences. I was at that party when Robin died, and to my recollection there were no arguments. Everyone just had a good time and that was that. We all went off to bed – I was with Chris at the time – but it was hard to sleep, a hot night, and maybe people got the munchies, whatever, and wandered around, went to raid the fridge. I mean, I heard people around the place on and off. Voices. Laughter. Vic was tripping, as usual. Maybe some of the group even swapped partners. It happened.'

'You weren't asleep the whole time?'

'Of course not.'

'And Chris Adams was with you all night?'

'Yes.'

'Come on, Tania.'

'Well, I . . . I mean, maybe not every minute of the night.'

'So you woke up and he wasn't there?'

'It wasn't like that. For crying out loud, are you trying to blame Chris now? What is it with you?'

'Believe it or not,' said Banks, 'I'm trying to get at the truth. Maybe it was a lark. Maybe someone was playing around with Robin beside the pool and he slipped and fell. An accident.'

'In that case, why does it matter now? Even if Robin wasn't the only one by the pool at the time, if it was an accident anyway, why does it matter?'

'Because if someone feels threatened by the truth, and if Nick Barber was close to it, then . . .' Banks spread his hands.

'Couldn't there be some other explanation?'

'Like what?'

'I don't know. Robbery?'

'Well, Nick's laptop and his mobile were stolen, but that just supports the theory that someone didn't want people to know what he was doing.'

'His girlfriend or something, then. A jealous lover. Aren't most people killed by someone they know, someone close to them?'

'True enough,' said Banks, 'and it's an area we've been looking into, along with a drug connection, but we've had no luck there yet.'

'I just don't see how the past could have had anything to do with it. It's over. Judgements were handed down.'

'If there's one thing I've learned in all my years as a detective,' Banks said, 'it's that the past is never over, no matter what has been handed down.'

Banks was on his way back from visiting Tania Hutchison when two uniformed constables brought Calvin Soames into Western Area Headquarters in Eastvale. Annie Cabbot told them to put him into an empty interview room and let him wait there a while.

'Where did you find him?' she asked one of the PCs.

'Daleside above Helmthorpe, ma'am,' he said. 'He was hiding in an old shepherd's shelter. Must have been there all night. Shivering, he was.'

'Is he OK?'

'He seems all right. It might be a good idea to get a doctor to check him out, though, just to be on the safe side.'

'Thanks,' said Annie. 'I'll put in a call to Dr Burns. In the meantime, I think I'll have a little chat with Mr Soames myself.'

Annie called Winsome over and noticed Templeton looking at them anxiously from behind his desk. 'What is it, Kev?' she called. 'Sudden attack of conscience? Bit late for that, isn't it?' She immediately regretted her outburst, which had no effect on Templeton: he just shrugged and got back to his paperwork. Annie could have throttled him, but that way he'd win.

Calvin Soames looked wet, cold and miserable. And old. At least there was some heat in the otherwise bleak interview room, and the constable had had the foresight to give him a grey blanket, which he wore over his shoulders like a robe.

'Well, Calvin,' said Annie, after dealing with the preliminaries, and making it clear on the tape that Soames had refused the services of a duty solicitor, 'what have you been up to?'

Soames said nothing. He just stared at a fixed point ahead of him, a nerve at the side of his jaw twitching.

'What's wrong?' Annie said. 'Cat got your tongue?'

Still Soames said nothing.

Annie leaned back in her chair, hands resting on the desk. 'You'll have to talk eventually,' she said. 'We already know what happened.'

'Then you don't need me to tell you, do you?'

'We need to hear it in your own words.'

'I hit her. Something snapped and I hit her. That's all you need to know.'

'Why did you hit Kelly?'

'You know what she did.'

'She slept with a man she liked. Is that so terrible?'

'That's not what he said.'

Annie looked puzzled. 'What who said?'

Soames looked at Winsome. 'You know who,' he said.

'He means Kev Templeton, Guv,' Winsome said.

Annie had worked that out for herself. 'What did DS Templeton say?' she asked.

'I won't repeat the words he used,' Soames said. 'Vile, terrible things. Disgusting things.'

So Templeton's inflammatory language had set Soames off on his rampage, Annie thought, as if she needed more evidence of his culpability. Even so, she cursed him again under her breath. 'What about the drink?'

Soames scratched his head. 'I won't say I'm proud of that,' he said. 'I used to be a hard-drinking man, but I got it under control, down to a couple of pints for the sake of being sociable. I let myself . . .' He stopped and put his head into his hands. Annie wasn't certain what the next words were, but she thought she heard him say, 'Her mother.'

'Mr Soames,' she said gently, 'Calvin, would you speak clearly, please?'

Soames wiped his eyes with the backs of his hands. 'I said she was just like her mother.'

'What was her mother like?'

'A good-for-nothing slut.'

'Kelly said she thought you were talking to her as if she were her mother. Is that true?'

'I don't know. I just saw red. I don't know what I was saying. Her mother was younger than me. Pretty. The farm . . . wasn't her sort of life. She liked the town, parties and dances. There were men. More than one. She didn't care whether I knew about them or not. She flaunted it, laughed at me.'

'Then she died.'

'Yes.'

'That must have torn you apart,' said Annie.

Soames gave her a sharp glance.

'I mean, she caused you so much pain. But there she was, dying, thanks to medical incompetence. You must have felt for her despite how she hurt you.'

'It was God's judgement.'

'How did Kelly react to all this?'

'I tried to keep it from her,' he said, 'but she's turned out to be the same.'

'That's not true,' Annie said. She was aware that the tape was running and she was exceeding her role as interviewer, but she couldn't help it. Let Superintendent Gervaise give her another bollocking, if that was what it came to. 'Just because Kelly slept with someone, it doesn't mean she was a slut or any other of those words men like to call women. You should be talking to your daughter, not beating her with a chair-leg.'

'I'm not proud of what I did,' said Soames. 'I'll face the consequences.'

'Damn right, you will,' said Annie. 'And so will Kelly, unfortunately.'

'What do you mean?'

'She's lying in a hospital bed because of you, and do you know what? She's worried about *you* – about what will happen to you.'

'I sinned. I'll take my punishment.'

'And what about Kelly?'

'She'll be better off without me.'

'Oh, stop feeling sorry for yourself.' Annie didn't trust herself to continue the interview. She shoved a statement sheet over to him and stood up. 'Look, write down in your own words exactly what happened, what you can remember of it, then DC Jackman here will see that it's typed up for you to sign. In the meantime, the police surgeon will be coming in to look you over, just routine. Anything else you want to say?'

'Kelly? How is she?'

'Recovering,' said Annie, her hand on the doorknob. 'It's nice of you to ask.'

18

As Banks sifted through the files on his desk on Saturday morning, he noticed the extra photocopy he had made of the list of numbers at the back of Nick Barber's book. It reminded him that he hadn't heard back from DC Gavin Rickerd yet, so he picked up the phone. Rickerd answered on the third ring.

'Anything on those numbers I gave you yet?' Banks asked.

'Sorry, sir,' said Rickerd. 'We've been snowed under. I haven't had a lot of time to work on it.'

'Any ideas at all?'

'It might be some kind of code, but without a key it'll be difficult to crack.'

'I don't think we have any keys,' said Banks.

'Well, sir . . .'

'Look, keep trying, will you? If I come up with anything that I think might help you I'll let you know.'

'OK, sir.'

'Thanks, Gavin.'

As Banks put down the phone, Annie came in to tell him that after fairly exhaustive inquiries made by the Metropolitan Police, there was no evidence to suggest that Nick Barber had been involved with the cocaine business.

'That's interesting,' said Banks, 'seeing as it was Chris Adams who suggested we look there.'

'A bit of nifty misdirection?'

'Looks like it. I want another word with Adams anyway.

Maybe I can intimidate him with the old wasting-police-time routine.'

'Maybe,' said Annie.

'Any news on Kelly Soames?'

'She was discharged from hospital this morning. She's staying with an aunt here in Eastvale for the time being.'

'Calvin Soames can't just walk away, Annie, no matter how contrite he is. You know that.'

'You don't think I want him to get off scot-free, do you? But it's Kelly I'm concenred about at the moment,' she said.

'Kelly's young. She'll get over it. I doubt that any magistrate or jury is going to put Calvin away, should he even see the inside of a courtroom.'

'He'll plead guilty. He wants to be punished.'

'I'll bet you Kelly won't go into the witness box, and we won't have much of a case without her testimony.'

'What's that?' Annie pointed at the list on Banks's desk.

'He realised that she hadn't been with him when he'd found it, and he hadn't looked at it since he gave the copy to Rickerd. 'Some figures Nick Barber had scribbled in the back of his book.'

Annie peered at it. 'Of course. The Kelly Soames business put it right out of my mind, but I was meaning to ask you about that. Barry Gilchrist in the computer shop mentioned that he saw Nick Barber writing in the back of a book while he was on the web. I wonder what it is.'

'Does it mean anything to you?' Banks asked.

'No.' Annie laughed. 'But it does remind me of something.'

'Oh? What?'

'Never mind.'

'Seriously. It could be important.'

'Just something I used to do when I was younger, that's all.'

Banks could hardly keep the exasperation out of his voice. 'What?'

Annie gave him a look. He could see that she was blushing. 'You know,' she said. 'Ring dates?'

'What dates?'

'For crying out loud.' Annie glanced over her shoulder and lowered her voice. She still sounded as if she were shouting at him. 'Are you thick or something?'

'I'm trying not to be, but you've lost me.'

'My period, idiot. I used to ring the day of the month my period was due. It's something a lot of girls do. I know this isn't exactly the same, not the same time between the dates – if that's what the numbers are – for a start, but it's the same idea.'

'Well, pardon me, but not being a girl and not having periods—'

'Don't be sarcastic. Maybe it's family birthdays or lottery numbers or whatever, but it amounts to the same thing. I've told you what you want to know. It reminds *me* of when I used to ring dates on the calendar to mark the start of my period. OK?'

Banks held his hands up 'OK?' he said. 'I surrender.'

Annie snorted, turned away abruptly and left the room. Still feeling the disturbed air buffeting in her wake, Banks sat and gazed at the numbers.

6 8 9 21 22 25
1 2 3 16 17 18 22 23
10 (12) 13
8 9 10 11 12 15 16 17 19 22 23 25 26 30
17 18 (19)
2 5 6 7 8 11 13 14 16 18 (19) 21 22 23

Six rows. Many numbers duplicated, and no list going beyond 30. A calendar of some kind, then? Ringed dates? But why were they ringed and, perhaps even more to the point, which months, which year did they refer to? And why were some days missing? It should be possible to find out, Banks thought, perhaps with the help of a computer, then he realised that each group was not even necessarily from the same month, or the same year. They could be strings of days taken over a period of, say, thirty years. His spirits fell, and he cursed Nick Barber under his breath for not being clearer with his notes: this might be the clue he was looking for, perhaps the only one Nick had left, and he felt about as far from understanding it now as he ever had.

Annie had got over her irritation with Banks by mid-afternoon when he poked his head round the squad-room door to tell her that Ken Blackstone had discovered the whereabouts of Yvonne Chadwick, DI Stanley Chadwick's daughter, and would she like to accompany him to the interview? She didn't need asking twice – bugger Superintendent Gervaise, she thought, grabbing her jacket and briefcase. She noticed Kev Templeton give her an evil eye as she left the room. Maybe he was already getting the cold shoulder from Madam Gervaise, now that what had happened to Kelly Soames had made the local news.

Banks was quiet as Annie drove the unmarked car she had signed out of the police garage. She kept snatching sideways glances at him and realised he was thinking. Well, that was a good sign. She drove on. 'I checked the Mad Hatters' website, by the way,' she said.

'And?'

'Definite possibilities for the numbers in the back of the book. There are links to other fan sites with tour dates and all sorts of esoteric information. I'll need a lot more time to follow up on it all.'

'Maybe when we get back.'

'Sounds good.'

Yvonne Chadwick, or Reeves, as she was now called, lived on the outskirts of Durham, which wasn't too far up the A1 from Eastvale. The road was busy with lorries, as usual, and on a couple of occasions the inevitable roadworks cancelled out a lane or two and slowed traffic to a crawl. Annie glimpsed Durham Castle high on its hill and followed the directions Banks had written down for her.

The house was a semi with a bay window in a pleasant, leafy neighbourhood where you wouldn't be afraid to let your children play in the street. Yvonne Reeves turned out to be a rather plump, nervous woman of about fifty, who favoured a grey peasant skirt and a shapeless maroon jumper. If she dressed up a bit, Annie thought, she would be much more attractive. She wore her long, greying hair tied back in a ponytail. The interior of the house was clean and tidy. Bookcases lined the walls, mostly philosophy and law, with a sprinkling of literature. The living room was a little cramped, but comfortable once they had wedged themselves into the leather armchairs. There wasn't much natural light, and the room smelt of dark chocolate and old books.

'This is all very intriguing,' said Yvonne. Her voice still bore the traces of her Yorkshire roots, though the rough edges had been flattened over the years. 'But I've no idea why you think I might be able to help you. What's it all about?'

'Have you heard about the death of a music journalist called Nick Barber?' Banks asked.

'I saw something in the paper,' Yvonne said. 'Wasn't he murdered somewhere in Yorkshire?'

'Near Lyndgarth,' said Banks.

'I still don't understand.'

'Nick Barber was working on a story about a group called the Mad Hatters. Do you remember them?'

'Good Lord. Of course I do.'

'In September 1969, there was a pop festival at Brimleigh Glen. Remember? You would have been about fifteen.'

Yvonne clapped her hands together. 'Sixteen. I was there! I wasn't supposed to be, but I was. My father was terribly strict. He would never have let me go if I'd told him.'

'You might also remember then that a young girl was found dead when the festival was over. Her name was Linda Lofthouse.'

'Of course I remember. It was my father's case. He solved it.'

'Yes. A man called McGarrity.'

Annie noticed Yvonne give a little shiver at the name, and an expression of distaste flitted across her features. 'Do you know him?' she asked, before the moment was lost.

Yvonne flushed. 'McGarrity? How could I?'

She was a poor liar, Annie thought. 'I don't know. You seemed to react to the name, that's all.'

'Dad told me about him, of course. He sounded like a terrible person.'

'Yvonne, I get the feeling there's a bit more to it than that.' Annie persisted. 'It was a long time ago, but if you know anything that might help us, you should tell us.'

'How could knowing about back then possibly help you now?'

'Because,' said Banks, 'we think the cases might be linked. Nick Barber was Linda Lofthouse's son. She gave him up for adoption, but he found out who his mother was and what happened to her. That gave him a special interest in the Mad Hatters and the McGarrity case. We think that Nick had stumbled across something to do with his mother's murder, and that he was killed for it. Which means that we have to look very closely at what happened at Brimleigh and afterwards. Someone who worked on the case with your father let slip that McGarrity had possibly terrorised another girl, but that never came up at the trial, or in the case notes. We also heard that

Mr Chadwick had a bit of trouble with his daughter, that she
was perhaps running with a wild crowd, but we couldn't get
anything more specific than that. It might be nothing, and I
might be wrong, but you are that daughter, and if you do know
something, anything at all, please tell us and let us be the
judges.'

Yvonne said nothing for a few moments. Annie could hear a
radio in the back of the house, probably the kitchen, talking,
not music. Yvonne chewed her lip and stared over their heads
at one of the bookcases.

'Yvonne,' Annie said, 'if there's anything we don't know
about, you should tell us. It can't possibly harm you, not now.'

'But it was all so long ago,' Yvonne said. 'God, I was such an
idiot. An arrogant, selfish, stupid idiot.'

'That would describe quite a lot of sixteen-year-olds,' Annie
said.

It broke the ice a little, and Yvonne managed a polite laugh.
'I suppose so,' she said. Then she sighed. 'I used to run with a
wild crowd, it's true,' she said. 'Well, not really wild, but
different. Hippies, you'd call them. The kind of people my
father hated. He'd go on about why he fought the war for lazy,
cowardly sods like that. But they were harmless, really. Well,
most of them.'

'And McGarrity?'

'McGarrity was a sort of hanger-on, older, not really part of
the crowd, but they couldn't summon the energy or find a
reason to kick him out, so he drifted from place to place,
sleeping on floors and in empty beds. Nobody really liked him.
He was weird.'

'And he had a knife.'

'Yes. A flick-knife with a tortoiseshell handle. Nasty thing.
Of course, he said he'd lost it, but . . .'

'But the police found it in one of the houses,' said Banks.
'Your father found it.'

'Yes.' Yvonne squinted at Banks. 'You seem to know plenty about this already.'

'It's my job. I read the trial transcripts, but they didn't tell me about the girl he terrorised, the one your father asked him about during the interrogation.'

'I suppose not.'

'It was you, wasn't it?'

'Me?'

'You knew McGarrity. Something happened. How else could you explain your father's zeal in pursuing him or his reticence to pursue the issue? He abandoned all his other leads and concentrated on McGarrity. Now I'd say that was a little personal, wouldn't you?'

'OK, I told him,' Yvonne said. 'McGarrity frightened me. We were alone together in the front room at Springfield Mount, and he frightened me.'

'What did he do?'

'It wasn't so much what he did, just the way he talked and looked at me, although he grabbed me.'

'He grabbed you?'

'My arm. Just a bruise. And he touched my cheek. It made me cringe. Mostly it was the things he said, though. He wanted to talk about Linda, and when that got him all excited, he started going on about those murders in Los Angeles. We didn't know who did it then – Manson and his family – but we knew the people had been butchered and someone had written PIGGIES on the walls in blood. He found all that exciting. And he said . . . he . . .'

'Go on, Yvonne,' Annie urged her.

Yvonne looked at her as she answered. 'He said he'd . . . watched me with my boyfriend, and that now it was his turn.'

'So he threatened to rape you?' Annie said.

'That's what I thought. That's what I was scared of.'

'Did he have his knife?' Banks asked.

'I didn't see it.'

'What did he say about Linda Lofthouse?'

'Just how pretty she was, and how it was sad that she'd had to die, but that it was an absurd and arbitrary world.'

'Is that all?'

'Then he talked about the Manson murders and asked me if I'd like to do something like that.'

'What happened next?'

'I made a break for it and ran for my life. He was pacing, spouting gibberish.'

'And then what?'

'I told my father. He was furious.'

'I can understand that,' said Banks. 'I have a daughter, and I'd feel exactly the same. What happened next.'

'The police raided Springfield Mount and a couple of other hippie pads that night. They gave everyone a hard time, brought some drugs charges against them, but it was McGarrity they really wanted. He'd been at the festival, you see, at Brimleigh, and plenty of people had seen him wandering around near the edge of the woods with his flick-knife.'

'Did you think he did it?'

'I don't know. I suppose so. I never really questioned it.'

'Yet he went on to deny it, said he was framed.'

'Yes, but all criminals do that, don't they? That's what my father told me.'

'It's pretty common,' said Banks.

'So there. Look, what is this all about? He's not due to be released, is he?'

'You need have no worries on that score. He died in prison.'

'Oh. Well, I can't say I'm heartbroken.'

'What happened after the arrest and everything?'

Yvonne shook her head slowly. 'I can't believe what an absolute idiot I was. My father let my boyfriend at Springfield Mount know that he was my father and told him to stay away from me. Steve, his name was. What an awful self-obsessed little prick. But good-looking, as I remember.'

'I've known one or two like that,' said Annie.

Banks glanced at her, as if to say, 'We'll get back to that later.'

'Anyway,' Yvonne went on, 'it was the usual story. I thought he loved me, but he just wanted me out of the way. It was so embarrassing. You know, it's funny, but the thing I remember most about the room is the Goya print on the wall. *El sueno de la razon produce monstruos.* "The Sleep of Reason Produces Monsters". The one of the sleeping man surrounded by owls, bats and cats. It used to scare me and fascinate me at the same time.'

'Did you go there again, after the raid?'

'Yes. The next day. Steve didn't want to know me. None of them did. He spread the word that I was a copper's daughter, and I was ostracised by the lot of them.' She snorted. 'Nobody wants to share a joint with a copper's daughter.'

'What did you do?'

'I was really hurt. I ran away from home. Took all the money I could and went to London. I had one address there, Lizzie, a girl who'd stayed at Springfield Mount once. She was nice and let me sleep in a sleeping-bag on her floor. But it wasn't very clean. There were mice, and they kept trying to get into the sleeping-bag, so I had to hold it tight round my neck, and I couldn't really get any sleep.' She gave a little shiver. 'And there were even more weird people about than there had been in Leeds. I was very depressed, and I started to get frightened of my own shadow. Lizzie got really fed up with me. She talked about negative energy and stuff like that. I was feeling lost, really out of place, like I didn't belong anywhere and nobody loved me. Typical adolescent *Angst*, I can see now, but at the time . . .'

'So what did you do?'

'I went home.' She gave a harsh laugh. 'Two weeks. That was the sum of my life's big adventure.'

'And how did your parents react?'

'Relief. And anger. I hadn't rung them, you see. That was cruel of me. If my daughter did that I'd be beside myself, but that's how selfish and upset I was. My father, being a policeman, always thought the worst. He had visions of me lying dead somewhere. He even told me he'd thought something had happened to me, and that maybe it had something to do with McGarrity or the others taking revenge on me for shopping them. But he couldn't do anything official because he didn't want people to know. It must have torn him apart. He took his duty as a policeman so seriously.'

'Didn't want people to know what?'

'About me and those hippies.'

'What was your father like during the investigation and trial?'

'He was working very hard, very long hours. I remember that. And he was very tense, tightly wound. He started getting chest pains, I remember, but it was a long time before he would go to the doctor. We didn't talk much. He was under a lot of strain. I think he was doing it for me. He thought he'd lost me, and he was taking it out on McGarrity and everyone else involved. It wasn't a comfortable time in the house, not for any of us.'

'But better than mice in the sleeping-bag?' Annie said.

Yvonne smiled. 'Yes, better than that. But we were all glad when it was over and McGarrity was convicted. It seemed to take for ever, like a big black cloud over our heads. I don't think the trial started until the following April. It went on for about four weeks and things were pretty tense. Anyway, in the meantime, I went back to school, got on with my A levels, then went to university in Hull. This would be the early seventies. There were still a lot of long-hairs about, but I kept my distance. I'd learned my lesson. I applied myself to my studies, and in the end I became a teacher and married a university professor. He teaches here, at Durham. We have two children, a boy and a girl, both married now. And that's the story of my life.'

'Did you ever hear your father express any doubt about McGarrity's guilt?' Banks asked.

'Not that I can remember. It was as if he was on a crusade. I can't imagine what he would have done if McGarrity had got off. It doesn't bear thinking about. As it was, the whole thing ruined his health.'

'And your mother?'

'Mum stood by him. She was a brick. She was devastated when he died, of course. We both were. But eventually she remarried and lived quite happily. She died in 1999. We were close right until the end. She only lived a short drive away, and she loved her grandchildren.'

'That's nice,' said Annie. 'We've nearly finished now. The only other thing we want to ask you about is the death of Robin Merchant.'

'The Hatters' bass player! God, I was absolutely gutted. Robin was *so* cool. They were one of my favourite bands, back when I used to listen to pop music, and we'd sort of claimed them as our own, too. You know they were from Leeds?'

'Yes,' said Annie.

'Anyway, what about him?'

'Did your father say anything about it?'

'I don't think so. Why would he . . . ? Oh, yes. My God, this *is* taking me back. He talked to them during the McGarrity thing, and he got me an LP signed by all of them. I think I've still got it somewhere.'

'Must be worth a bob or two now,' said Banks.

'Oh, I'd never sell it.'

'Still . . . did he say anything?'

'About Robin Merchant? No. Well, it was nothing to do with him, was it? That was the next summer, after McGarrity had been sent to jail, and my dad's heart was showing the strain even more. We never really talked about those sorts of things – you know, the music and hippie stuff – not after I came back from London. I mean, I was done with that scene, and my dad was grateful for that, so he didn't go on at me about it any more. Mostly I threw myself into my A levels.'

'Does this mean anything to you?' Banks brought out a photocopy of the ringed numbers from the back page of Nick Barber's book.

Yvonne frowned at it. 'I'm afraid not,' she said. 'I didn't say I was a maths teacher.'

'We think it might be dates,' Banks explained. 'Most likely dates connected with the Mad Hatters tour schedule or something similar. But we've no idea which months or years.'

'Leaves it pretty wide open, doesn't it, then?'

Annie looked at Banks and shrugged. 'Well, that,' Banks said, 'is just about it, unless DI Cabbot has any more questions for you.'

'No,' said Annie, standing and leaning forward to shake Yvonne's hand. 'Thanks for your time.'

'You're welcome. I'm only sorry I couldn't be any more help.'

'What do you think about what Yvonne told us?' Annie asked Banks, over an after-work drink with cheese-and-pickle sandwiches in the Queen's Arms. The bar was half empty and the pool table, happily, not in use. A couple of late-season tourists sat at the next table poring over Ordnance Survey maps and speaking German.

'I think what she said should make us perhaps just a little more suspicious of Stanley Chadwick and his motives,' said Banks.

'Chadwick? What do you mean?'

'If he really thought his daughter had been terrorised and threatened with rape, and he was on a personal crusade . . . who knows what he might have done? I try to imagine how I would behave if anything like that ever happened to Tracy and, I tell you, I can really frighten myself. Yvonne told us that McGarrity talked to her about Linda Lofthouse. Admittedly she didn't say he'd given her any information only the killer could have known, but we both know that sort of thing mostly happens on TV. But what he *did* say sounded damn suspicious to me. Imagine how it sounded to her father, at his wits' end trying to catch a killer and worried about his daughter hanging around with hippies. Then he finds out this weirdo who terrorised her had a flick-knife and was seen wandering around with it at Brimleigh festival. Imagine he puts the two together, and suddenly the light goes on. Yvonne told us he didn't really look at anyone else for the crime after that. Rick Hayes went right out of the picture. It was McGarrity all the way, and only McGarrity.'

'But the evidence says McGarrity did it.'

'No, it doesn't. Everyone knew that McGarrity carried a flick-knife with a tortoiseshell handle, including Stanley Chadwick. It wouldn't have been that hard for him to get hold of one like it. Don't forget, Yvonne says she didn't see the knife when McGarrity terrorised her.'

'Because he'd already hidden it.'

'Or lost it, as he said.'

'I don't believe this,' said Annie. 'You'd take the word of a convicted killer over a detective inspector with an unimpeachable reputation?'

'I'm just thinking out loud, for God's sake, trying to get a handle on Nick Barber's murder.'

'And have you?'

Banks sipped some Black Sheep. 'I'm not sure yet. But I do

believe that Chadwick *could* have obtained such a knife, tricked McGarrity into handling it, and got access to Linda Lofthouse's clothing and blood samples. It might be a lot tougher now, but not necessarily back then, before PACE. Someone in Chadwick's position would probably have had free run of the place. And I think he might have been driven to do it because of what had happened to his daughter. Remember, this was a man on a mission, convinced he was right but unable to prove it by legitimate means. We've all been there. So in this case, because it's personal, and because of suspicious and disturbing things his daughter has told him about McGarrity that he can't use without bringing her into it and losing all credibility, he goes the extra mile and fabricates the vital bit of evidence he needs. Remember, apart from the knife there's no case. It falls apart. And there's another thing.'

'What?'

'Chadwick's health. He was basically a decent, God-fearing, law-abiding copper with a strong Presbyterian background, probably deeply repressed because of his war experiences, and angry with what he saw around him, the disrespect of the young, the hedonism, the drugs.'

'Turned psychoanalyst now, have you?'

'You don't need to be a psychoanalyst to know that if Chadwick really did fabricate a case against McGarrity, even for the best of reasons, it would tear a man like him apart. As Yvonne said, he was a dedicated copper. The law and basic human decency meant everything to him. He might have lost his faith during the war, but you can't change your nature that easily.'

Annie put her glass to her cheek. 'But McGarrity was seen near the murder scene, he was known to be seriously weird, he had a flick-knife, he was left-handed, and he had met the victim. Why do you insist on believing that he didn't do it, and that a good copper turned bad?'

'I'm not insisting. I'm just trying it out for size. We'd never prove it now, anyway.'

'Except by proving that someone else killed Linda Lofthouse.'

'Well, there is that.'

'Who do you think?'

'My money's on Vic Greaves.'

'Why? Because he was mentally unstable?'

'That's part of it, yes. He had a habit of not knowing what he was doing and he had dark visions on his acid trips. Remember, he took acid that night at Brimleigh, as well as on the night of Robin Merchant's death. It doesn't take a great stretch of the imagination to guess that maybe he heard voices telling him to do things. But Linda Lofthouse was his cousin, so if you work on the theory that most people are killed by someone they know, particularly a family member, it makes even more sense.'

'You don't think he killed Robin Merchant, too, do you?'

'It's not beyond the bounds of possibility. Maybe Merchant knew, or guessed.'

'But Greaves had no history of violence. Not to mention no motive.'

'OK, I'll give you all that. But it doesn't mean he couldn't have flipped. Drugs do very strange things to people.'

'What about Nick Barber?'

'He found out.'

'How?'

'I haven't got that far yet.'

'Well,' said Annie, 'I still think Stanley Chadwick got it right and Patrick McGarrity did it.'

'Even so, Rick Hayes might be worth another look, too, if we can find him.'

'If you insist.' Annie finished her Britvic Orange. 'That's my good deed for the day,' she said.

'What are you up to tomorrow?' Banks asked.

'Browsing websites, most likely. Why?'

'I just thought you might like to take an hour or two off and come out for Sunday lunch with me and meet Emilia.'

'Emilia?'

'Brian's girlfriend. Didn't I tell you? She's an actress. Been on telly.'

'Really?'

'*Bad Girls*, among others.'

'One of my favourites. All right, sounds good.'

'Let's keep our fingers crossed that nothing interrupts us like it did the other night.'

For once, it wasn't long after dark when Banks got home, having checked back at the station after his drink with Annie and finding things ticking along nicely. Brian and Emilia were out somewhere, which allowed him a few delicious moments alone to listen to a recent CD purchase of Susan Graham singing French songs and enjoy a glass of Roy's Amarone. When Brian and Emilia finally got back, the CD was almost over, and the glass half empty. Banks went into the kitchen to greet them.

'Dad,' said Brian, putting packages on the table, 'we went to York for the day. We didn't know if you were going to be here so we picked up an Indian takeaway. There's plenty if you want to share.'

'No, thanks,' said Banks, trying not to imagine what seismic reactions might occur in his stomach when curry met Amarone. 'I'm not really hungry. I had a sandwich earlier. How did you enjoy York?'

'Great,' said Emilia. 'We did all the tourist stuff – toured the minster, visited Jorvik. We even went to the train museum.'

'You took her there?' Banks said to Brian.

'Don't blame me. It was her idea.'

'It's true,' Emilia said, taking Brian's hand. 'I love trains. I had to drag him.'

They both laughed. Banks remembered taking Brian to the National Railway Museum, or York Railway Museum as it was then known, on a day trip from London when he was about seven. He had loved climbing all over the immaculate steam engines and playing at being the driver.

Brian and Emilia ate their curry in the kitchen while Banks sat sipping his wine and chatting with them about their day. When they had finished, Brian tidied up – an oddity in itself – then said, 'Oh, I forgot. I bought you a present, Dad.'

'Me?' said Banks. 'You shouldn't have.'

'It's not much.' Brian took an HMV bag from his backpack. 'Sorry I haven't had a chance to wrap it.'

Banks slipped a DVD out of the bag: *The Mad Hatters' Story*. Judging by the account on the back of the box, it contained footage from every stage of the band's career, including the earliest line-up with Vic Greaves and Robin Merchant. 'Should be interesting,' Banks said. 'Do you want to watch it with me?'

'I wouldn't mind.'

'Emilia?'

Emilia took a book out of her shoulder-bag, *Reading Lolita in Tehran*. 'Not me,' she said, with a smile. 'I'm tired. It's been a long day. I think I'll go to bed and read for a while, leave you boys together.' She kissed Brian, then turned to Banks and said, 'Good night.'

'Good night,' Banks said. 'Before you go, would the two of you like to come out for Sunday lunch with Annie and me tomorrow? If we can get away, that is.'

Brian raised his eyebrows and looked at Emilia, who nodded. 'Sure,' he said, then added, with the weight of many broken engagements, '*if* you can get away.'

'I promise. You are staying a while longer, aren't you?'

'If that's OK,' said Brian.

'Of course it is.'

'If we're not cramping your style.'

Banks felt himself blush. 'No. Why should you . . . ? I mean . . .'

Emilia said good night again, smiled and went upstairs. 'She seems a nice girl,' he said to Brian, when she was out of earshot.

Brian grinned. 'She is.'

'Is it . . . ?'

'Serious?'

'Well, yes, I suppose that's what I meant.'

'Too early to say, but I like her enough that I'd hurt if she left me, as the song says.'

'Which song?'

'Ours, idiot. The last single.'

'Ouch. I don't buy singles.'

'I know that, Dad. I was teasing. And it wasn't for sale on a CD. You had to download it from iTunes.'

'Hey, wait a minute. I know how to do that now. I've got an iPod. I'm not a complete Luddite, you know.'

Brian laughed and grabbed a can of lager from the fridge. Banks refilled his glass and the two of them went into the entertainment room.

The DVD started with manager Chris Adams giving a potted history, then segued into a documentary made up of old concert footage and interviews. Banks found it amusing and interesting to see the band members of thirty-five years ago in their bell-bottoms and floppy hats sounding pretentious and innocent at the same time as they spoke about 'peace and love, man'. Vic Greaves, looking wasted as usual in a 1968 interview, went off at a tangent punctuated with long pauses every time the interviewer asked him a question about his songs. There was something icily detached and slightly more cynical about Robin Merchant, and his cool, practical intelligence often provided a welcome antidote to the vapid musings of the others.

But it was the concert footage that proved most interesting. There was nothing from Brimleigh, unfortunately, except a few stills of the band relaxing with joints backstage, but there were some excellent late-sixties films of the band performing at such diverse places as the refectory at Leeds University, Bristol's Colston Hall and the Paradiso, in Amsterdam. At one of the gigs, an outrageously stoned and enthusiastic MC yelled in a thick Cockney accent, 'And now, ladies and gentlemen, let's 'ave a 'uge 'and for the 'ATTERS!'

The music sounded wonderfully fresh, and Vic Greaves's innocent pastoral lyrics had a haunting, timeless sadness, meshing with his delicate, spacy keyboards work and Terry Watson's subtle riffs. Like many bass-players, Robin Merchant stood and played expressionlessly, but well, and like many drummers, Adrian Pritchard thrashed around at his kit like a maniac. Keith Moon and John Bonham were clearly big influences there.

There was something a bit odd about the line-up, but Banks was half watching and half talking to Brian, and the next thing he knew, both Vic Greaves and Robin Merchant were gone and the lovely, if rather nervous, Tania Hutchison was making her début with the band at London's Royal Festival Hall in early 1972. Banks thought about his meeting with her the other day. She was still a good-looking woman, and he might have fancied his chances, but he thought he had alienated her with his probing questions. That seemed to be the story of his life, alienating women he fancied.

The documentary went on to portray the band's upward trajectory until their official retirement in 1994, with clips from the few reunion concerts they had performed since then, along with interviews from an older, chain-smoking, short-haired Tania, and a completely bald, bloated and ill-looking Adrian Pritchard. Reg Cooper and Terry Watson must have declined to be interviewed because they appeared only in the concert footage.

When the film came to a sequence about disagreements within the band, Banks noticed Brian tense a little. Since the investigation had taken him further into the world of rock than he had ever been before, he had thought a lot about Brian and the life he was living. Not just drugs, but all the trappings and problems that fame brought with it. He thought of the great stars who had destroyed themselves at an early age through self-indulgence or despair: Kurt Cobain, Jimi Hendrix, Tim Buckley, Janis Joplin, Nick Drake, Ian Curtis, Jim Morrison . . . The list went on. Brian seemed all right, but he was hardly likely to tell his father if he had a drug problem, for example.

'Anything wrong?' Banks asked.

'Wrong? No. Why? What could be wrong?'

'I don't know. It's just that you haven't talked about the band much.'

'That's because there's not much to say.'

'So things are going fine?'

Brian paused. 'Well . . .'

'What is it?'

Brian turned to face his father, who turned down the DVD volume a notch or two. 'Denny's getting weird, that's all. If it gets much worse, we might have to get rid of him.'

Denny, Banks knew, was the band's other guitarist-vocalist, and Brian's songwriting partner.

'Get rid of him?'

'I don't mean kill him. Honestly, Dad, sometimes I wonder about the effect your job has on you.'

So do I, Banks thought. But he also thought about killing off disruptive band members – Robin Merchant, for example – and how easy it would have been: just a gentle nudge in the direction of the swimming-pool. Vic Greaves had been disruptive, too, but he had made his own voluntary exit. 'Weird? How?' he asked.

'Ego, mostly. He's getting into really off-the-wall musical influences, like acid Celtic punk, and he's trying to import it into our sound. If you challenge him on it, he gets all huffy and goes on about how it's *his* band, *he* brought us together and all that shit.'

'What do the others have to say about him?'

'Everybody's sort of retreated into their own world. We're not communicating very well. We're going through the motions. There's no talking to Denny. We can't write together any more.'

'What happens if he goes?'

Brian gestured towards the video. 'We get someone else. But we're not going pop.'

'You're doing fine as you are, aren't you?'

'We are. I know. We're selling more and more. People *love* our sound. It's got an edge, but it's accessible. That's the problem. Denny wants to change it, and thinks he's got a right to do so.'

'What about your manager?'

'Geoff? Denny keeps sucking up to him.'

Banks immediately thought of Kev Templeton. 'And how is Geoff dealing with that?'

Brian scratched his chin. 'Come to think of it,' he said, 'he's getting sick of it. I think at first he liked it that someone in the band was giving him a lot of attention, not to mention telling tales out of school, but I don't know if you've ever noticed this, and it's a weird thing, but eventually people get fed up with toadies.'

From the mouths of babes, Banks thought, as a lightbulb went on in his brain. Though Brian was hardly a baby. It was as he had suspected. Templeton was digging his own grave.

Nobody needed to do anything. Sometimes the best thing to do is nothing. Annie ought to appreciate that, too, Banks thought, with her interest in Taoism and Zen. 'Have drugs got anything to do with it?' he asked.

Brian looked at him. 'Drugs? No. If you mean have I ever done any drugs, then the answer's yes. I've smoked dope and taken E. I took speed once, but when I came down I was depressed for a week, so I've never touched it since. Nothing stronger. And, as it happens, I still prefer lager. OK?'

'OK,' said Banks. 'It's good of you to be so frank, but I was thinking more about the others.'

Brian smiled. 'Now I see how you trick confessions out of people. Anyway, the answer's still no. Believe it or not, we're a pretty straight band.'

'So, what next?' Banks asked.

Brian shrugged. 'Dunno. Geoff said we all needed to take a breather, we'd been working so hard in the studio and on tour. When we get back . . . we'll see. Either Denny will have changed his ideas or he won't.'

'What do you predict?'

'That he won't.'

'And then?'

'He'll have to go.'

'Does that worry you?'

'A bit. Not too much, though. I mean, *they* did all right, didn't they?' The Mad Hatters were performing their jaunty, rocking 1983 number-one hit, 'Young At Heart'. 'The band will survive. It's more the lack of communication that upsets me. Denny was a mate, and now I can't talk to him.'

'Losing friends is always sad,' said Banks, aware of how pathetic and pointless that observation was. 'It's just one of those things, though. When you first get together with some-one it's a great adventure, finding out stuff you've got in common. You know, places you love, music, books. Then the more you get to know them, the more you start to see other things.'

'Yeah, like a whingeing, lying, manipulative bastard,' said Brian. He laughed and shook his empty can. 'Want another glass of plonk?' he asked Banks, whose glass was also empty.

'Sure, why not?' said Banks, and watched the lovely Tania sway in pastel blue diaphanous robes that flowed round her like water while Brian got the drinks.

'There is one thing I'd like to know,' he said, after a sip of Amarone. *Plonk*, indeed!

'What's that?' Brian asked.

'Just what the hell does acid Celtic punk sound like?'

19

Annie jotted something down, then turned back to the computer monitor and scrolled. It was Monday morning. On Sunday, most of the team had taken a well-deserved day off, their first since Nick Barber's murder almost two weeks ago. Annie had spent the morning doing household chores, the afternoon on the Mad Hatters website and the evening enjoying that long bath and the trashy magazines she had been promising herself. At lunchtime she had gone out with Banks, Brian and Emilia to the Bridge in Grinton. Emilia had been charming, and Annie had been secretly awestruck to meet an up-and-coming actress. More so than by meeting Banks's rock-star son, whom she had met before, though Brian had also, in his way, been charming and far less full of himself than she remembered from previous occasions. He seemed to have matured and become comfortable with his success, no longer the young tearaway with something to prove.

The coffee at her right hand was lukewarm, and she made a face when she took a sip. There was plenty of activity around her in the squad room, but she was still on the web, oblivious to most of it as she zoomed in on the mystery of the numbers in the back of Nick Barber's book.

It wasn't such an esoteric solution after all, she saw, with a sense of disappointment. It didn't suddenly make everything clear and solve the case, and it was nothing she wouldn't have expected him to make a note of anyway.

She hadn't found everything she wanted at the official Mad

Hatters website, but she had found links there that took her to more obscure fan sites, as Nick Barber must have done in Eastvale Computes. But all the owner had heard was the snatch of song that played when he accessed the official site. Now she negotiated her way through bright orange and red Gothic print, black backgrounds with stylised logos and flashing arrows. All signs that some young web designer was eager to show off and lacked restraint. Before long, her eyes were starting to buzz and felt as if they had been massaged with sandpaper.

Once she had the final string jotted down, she printed the whole document, bookmarked the website and closed the browser. Then she rubbed her eyes and went in search of a cup of coffee, only to find that it was her turn to make a fresh pot. When she finally got back to her desk, it was close to lunchtime and she felt like a break from the office.

'I was just thinking about you,' she said, when Banks popped his head round the door and asked how she was getting on. 'I'm feeling cooped up here. Why don't you take me to that new bistro by the castle and we go over what I've found so far?'

'What?' said Banks. 'Lunch together two days in a row? People will talk.'

'A working lunch,' Annie said.

'OK. Sounds good to me.'

With Templeton's deepening frown following them, Annie picked up her papers and they walked out into the cobbled market square. It was a fine day for the time of year, scrubbed blue sky and just a hint of chill in the wind. A couple of coachloads of tourists from Teesside were disembarking by the market cross and making a beeline for the nearest pub. The church clock struck twelve as Banks and Annie crossed the square and took the narrow lane that wound up to the castle. The bistro was down a small flight of stone stairs about half-way up the hill. It had been open about three months and had garnered some good local reviews. Because it was early, only two tables were occupied, and the owner welcomed them, giving them the pick of the rest. They chose a corner, with their backs to the whitewashed walls. That way nobody could look over their shoulders. Little light got through the half-window, and all you could see were legs and feet walking by, but the muted wall lighting was good enough to read by.

They both decided on sparkling mineral water, partly because Annie rarely drank at lunch-time and Banks said he was beginning to find that even one glass of wine so early in the day made him drowsy. He went for a steak sandwich and *frites*, and Annie the cheese omelette and green salad. The food ordered and fizzy water poured, they began to go over the results of her morning's work. Soft music played in the background. Eastvale's idea of Parisian chic: Charles Aznavour, Edith Piaf, Françoise Hardy. But it was so quiet as to be unobtrusive. Banks broke off a chunk of baguette, buttered it and looked at Annie's notes.

'Put simply,' she said, 'it's the Mad Hatters' tour dates from October 1969 to May 1970.'

'But that's eight months, and there are only six rows.'

'They didn't tour in December or February,' Annie said. She showed Banks the printout from the website. 'I got this all from a site run by what must be their most devoted fan. The trivia some of these people put out there is amazing. Anyway, it must have been a godsend to a writer like Nick Barber.'

'But is it all accurate?'

'I'm sure there are errors,' Annie said. 'After all, these websites are unedited, and it's easy to make a mistake. But on the whole I'd say it's probably pretty close.'

'So the Mad Hatters were on tour the sixth, eighth, ninth, twenty-first, twenty-second and twenty-fifth of October? That's how it goes?'

'Yes,' said Annie. She handed him the printout. 'And these were the places they played.'

'The Dome, Brighton, the Locarno Ballroom, Sunderland, the Guildhall, Portsmouth. They got around.'

'They certainly did.'

'And the ringed dates?'

'Just three, as you can see,' said Annie. 'The twelfth of January, the nineteenth of April and the nineteenth of May. All in 1970.'

'Any significance in those two nineteenths?'

'I haven't figured out the significance of any of the ringed dates yet.'

'Maybe it was one of his girlfriend's periods.'

Annie gave him a sharp nudge in the ribs. 'Don't be rude. Anyway, periods don't come that irregularly. Not usually, at any rate.'

'So you did consider it?'

Annie ignored him and prepared to move on as their food arrived. They took a short pause to arrange papers, plates, knives and forks. Then she carried on: 'The first gap is three months, and the second is one.'

'Drug scores?'

'Perhaps.'

'What about the venues?'

Annie consulted her notes. 'On the twelfth of January, they were playing at the Top Rank Suite in Cardiff, on the nineteenth of April, they were at the Dome in Brighton, and on the nineteenth of May, they were at the Van Dyke Club in Plymouth.'

'You can't get much more diverse than that,' said Banks. 'OK. Now we need to find out if there's any significance to those dates and places.'

The owner came over to see if everything was all right. They assured him it was, and he scooted off. That kind of solicitude wouldn't last long in Yorkshire, Annie thought, finding herself wondering if his French accent was as false as his hairpiece. 'I'll enlist Winsome's aid after lunch,' she said. 'You?'

'It's time I paid Vic Greaves another visit,' said Banks. 'See if I can get any sense out of him. I was thinking of taking Jenny Fuller along, but she's off on the lecture circuit, and there's no one else around I can really trust for that sort of thing.'

'Be careful,' said Annie. 'Remember what happened to Nick Barber when he got too interested in Greaves.'

'Don't worry. I will.'

'And good luck,' Annie added. 'By the sound of him, you'll need it.'

Banks cut off a lump of glutinous brown gristle from his steak and put it on the side of his plate. The sight of it made Annie feel vaguely queasy and glad to be a vegetarian. 'You know,' Banks said, 'I still can't decide whether Greaves is truly bonkers or just a genuine English eccentric.'

'Maybe there isn't much difference,' Annie said. 'Have you thought of that?'

There were plenty of cars parked on Lyndgarth's village green early on Monday afternoon, and several groups of walkers in serious gear had assembled nearby for briefings. Banks found a spot to park near the post office and headed up the lane to Vic Greaves's cottage. He was hoping that the man might be a bit more coherent this time and had a number of questions prepared to jog the ex-keyboard-player's memory if he needed to. Since his last visit, he had come to believe that Stanley Chadwick had been seriously misguided about Patrick McGarrity's guilt, for personal reasons, and he now knew that not only had Greaves been Linda Lofthouse's cousin, but that Nick Barber was her son, which meant that Greaves and Barber were also related in some complicated way that Banks couldn't quite figure out. But, most important, it meant *connections* between the different cases, and connections always excited Banks.

He walked up the short path and knocked on the door. The front curtains were closed. No answer. He remembered the last time, how it had taken Greaves a while to answer, so he knocked again. When he still got no answer, he walked round to the back, where there was a small cobbled yard and a storage shed. He peered through the grimy kitchen window and saw that things were in pretty much the same spotless order as they had been when he had first visited Greaves.

Curious, Banks tried the back door. It opened.

He was treading on dangerous ground now, he knew, entering a suspect's premises alone, without a search warrant. But he thought that, if he had to, he could justify his actions. Vic Greaves was mentally unstable, and Banks feared that he might have come to some harm, or harmed himself in some way. Even so, he hoped he didn't stumble across the one piece of vital evidence that linked Greaves inextricably with Barber's murder, or with Linda Lofthouse's, or he might have a hard time getting it admitted in court. What he would do, he decided, was not touch anything and return with full authorisation if he had to.

As he entered, Banks felt a shiver of fear run down his spine. Annie had been right in her warning. If he indicated that he was at all close to the truth, Greaves might lash out, as Banks thought he had done at Nick Barber. He might already know who was at his door, might be lying in wait, armed and ready to attack. Banks moved cautiously through the dim kitchen. At least all of the knives were in their slots in the wooden block where Greaves kept them. Banks stood still in the doorway that led through to the living-room and listened. Nothing but the wind whipping the tree branches and the distant sounds of a car starting and a dog barking.

From what he could make out in the pale light that filtered

through the curtains, the living room was just as it had been, too, with newspapers and magazines piled everywhere. Banks stood at the bottom of the stairs and called Greaves's name again. Still no answer.

Tense and alert, he started to walk up the stairs. They creaked as he moved. Every once in a while he would pause, but still he heard nothing. He stood on the upstairs landing and listened again. Nothing. It was a small cottage, and in addition to the toilet and bathroom there were only two bedrooms. Banks checked the first and found it almost as full of newspapers and magazines as the living room. Then he went into the second, which was obviously Greaves's bedroom.

In one corner lay a mattress heaped with sheets and blankets. It reminded Banks of nothing so much as a nest. Carefully, he poked around with his toe in the sheets, but no one was there, either hiding or dead. Although the sheets were piled in an untidy mess, they were clean and smelt of apples. There was nothing else in the room except a wardrobe and a dresser full of old but clean and neatly folded clothes.

After a cursory glance at the toilet and bathroom, which told him nothing, Banks went back downstairs into the living room. It was an ideal opportunity for him to poke around, but it didn't seem as if Greaves had anything worth poking around for. There were no mementoes, no Mad Hatters memorabilia, no photos or keepsakes. In fact, as far as Banks could tell, the cottage contained nothing but a few basic toiletries, clothes, kitchenware and newspapers.

Idly, he started looking at some of the papers on the top of the pile: *Northern Echo* and *Darlington & Stockton Times*, along with the *Yorkshire Evening Post* dating back about three years, as far as he could tell. The magazines covered just about everything from computing, though Greaves had no computer as far as Banks had seen, to coin-collecting. There were none on rock music, or music of any kind. Many of the magazines still had free gifts stuck to their covers, and some hadn't even been removed from their Cellophane wrapping.

Finding nothing of interest among the papers, Banks headed for the shed in the backyard. It had a padlock, but it was open, hanging loosely on the hasp. Banks opened the door. He expected more newspapers, at the very least, but the shed was empty. It had no particular smell, except soil and wood. Spiders went about their webs in the corners and one particularly large specimen scuttled across the window. Banks shuddered. He had hated spiders ever since he had found one under his pillow when he was about five.

Banks closed the door behind him and left it as it was. There was one thing, he guessed, that should have been there but wasn't: Vic Greaves's bicycle. So, had Greaves gone for a ride, or had he gone somewhere specific?

Banks went back to his car and took out his mobile. The signal was poor, but at least there was one. Chris Adams answered almost immediately.

'Mr Adams,' said Banks. 'Where are you?'

'At home. Why?'

'Do you have any idea where Vic Greaves is?'

'I'm not his keeper, you know.'

'No, but you're the closest he's got to one.'

'Sorry, no. I don't know. Why?'

'I've just been to see him and his bike's not there.'

'He does go out from time to time.'

'Anywhere in particular?'

'He just rides. I don't know where he goes. Look, are you telling me there's some reason to be worried?'

'Not at all. I'm just trying to find him to ask him a few more questions.'

'What about?'

'Things seem to be coming to a head. I think we're almost there.'

'You know who killed Nick Barber?'

'Not yet, but I'm getting close.'

'And Vic knows this?'

'I don't know what he knows. I'll bet he can be remarkably perceptive at times, though.'

'You never know with Vic, what goes in, what goes straight through.'

'Any idea where he might be?'

'No. I told you. He goes for bike rides from time to time. Helps keep him in shape.'

'If you hear from him, please let me know.'

'OK.'

'One more thing, Mr Adams.'

'Yes?'

'The night Robin Merchant drowned. Were you up and around at the time?'

'Who told you that?'

'Were you?'

'Of course not. I was fast asleep.'

'You and I both know that's a load of bollocks, Mr Adams, and the police probably knew it even then. They just didn't have any evidence to suggest Robin Merchant might have been murdered, or that his death might have been caused by someone else in some way.'

'This is absurd. Is it Tania? Have you been talking to Tania?'

'Why would that make a difference?'

'Because she was pissed. If you've talked to her, she's no doubt told you we were what they call an item at the time. Her drug of choice was alcohol. Vodka mostly. She was probably so drunk she didn't know her arse from her elbows.'

'So you weren't up and about?'

'Of course not. Besides, Tania's got it in for me. We haven't been on the best of terms these past few years.'

That wasn't exactly what Tania had told him, Banks remembered. Who was lying? 'Oh. Why's that?'

'A mixture of business and personal matters. And none of your business, really. Now, look, this connection's getting worse and worse. I'm going to hang up.'

'I'd like to talk to you again. Can you come into the station?'

'I'll be passing nearby on my way to London next week. I'll try to drop in if I have time.'

'Try to make time. And ring first.'

'I will if I remember. Goodbye, Mr Banks.'

As Banks was putting his mobile away, he noticed he had voicemail waiting. Curious, he pressed the button and, after the usual introduction, heard Annie's voice: 'I hope things are going well with Vic Greaves,' she said. 'Winsome and I seem to be making progress here and we'd like to have a chat with you about the possibilities we've raised. Can you come back to the station as soon as you have a moment? It could be important. Cheers.'

Well, Banks thought, turning his car towards Eastvale and slipping in a Roy Harper CD, *Flashes from the Archives of Oblivion*, at least someone was making progress.

Winsome said she didn't need to use the online computer any more, so they adjourned to the privacy of Banks's office. The market square was busy with tourists and shoppers going into and coming out of the narrow streets that radiated from it. The day was warming up, so Banks opened his window about six inches to let in some fresh air. The noise of the cars, snatches of music, laughter and conversation all sounded distant and muffled. A whiff of diesel fumes from the revving coaches drifted in.

'You've been busy, by the look of it,' Banks said, as Winsome dropped a pile of paper on his desk.

'Yes, sir,' she said. 'I've been on the telephone or the Internet for over three hours now, and I think you'll find the results very interesting.'

'Go ahead.'

They sat in a semi-circle around Banks's desk so they could all see. 'Well,' Winsome began, pulling out the first sheet, 'let's start with the twelfth of January 1969, Top Rank Suite, Cardiff.'

'What happened there?' Banks asked.

'Nothing. At least not at the Top Rank Suite.'

'Where, then?'

'Hold your horses a minute,' said Annie. 'Let Winsome tell it her own way.'

'I spoke with the archivist at one of the big newspapers there,' Winsome went on, 'the *South Wales Echo*, and he seemed surprised that somebody else was asking him about that particular date.'

'Somebody else?'

'Exactly,' Winsome went on. 'It seems that Nick Barber did quite a bit of background work *before* he went up to Yorkshire, specifically into the Mad Hatters' tour dates between the Brimleigh festival and Robin Merchant's death.'

'Which makes me wonder why he needed to check the websites at Eastvale Computes and jot what he found down in the back of his book,' said Annie.

'John Butler, the editor at *MOJO*, told me that Barber was meticulous about checking his facts,' said Banks. 'He checked everything at least twice before he went after a story. I should imagine he was getting it right, preparing for another chat with Vic Greaves.'

'Makes sense,' said Annie. 'Go on, Winsome.'

'Well, sometimes he had to contact the local papers to see if they kept back issues, but generaly he didn't need to. Most of what he wanted is available at the British Library Newspapers

Catalogue, and he could read the papers on microfilm at the library's Newspaper Reading Room. His London phone records, by the way, show quite a few calls to the library, as well as to the local newspapers concerned, in Plymouth, Cardiff and Brighton.'

'What did he discover?'

'In the first place,' Winsome went on, 'I should guess that he was simply looking for reviews of Mad Hatters' performances. Maybe a few quotes from the time to spice up his article. As you said, sir, he was thorough. And it looks as if he was also trying to get a broader context of the times – little local snippets about what was going on that day in Bristol or Plymouth, what was of interest to the people there, that sort of thing. Background.'

'Nothing unusual in that, either,' Banks said. 'He was a music journalist. I imagine he was also scrounging around for any old photos or live bootleg recordings he could find.'

'Yes, sir,' Winsome said. 'Obviously he couldn't research every gig – they played over a hundred towns and cities during that period – but he did cover a fair bit of ground in the reading room. I've spoken to the librarian he dealt with and she was able to give me a list of what he did get round to and fax me prints from the microfilm reader of the newspapers for the three dates in question. She was very helpful. Sounded quite excited to be part of a police investigation. Actually, it was the issues on the days *after* the gigs that interested Barber, of course.'

'Because that was when the reviews appeared,' said Banks.

'Exactly. Well,' Winsome went on, 'there's nothing especially interesting in the reviews. Apparently, they were in good form that night, even Vic Greaves. It's another item of news that I suspect was more interesting to Nick Barber.' She picked a sheet from her pile and turned it round so that Banks could read it. 'I'm sorry about the quality, sir,' she said, 'but it was the best she could do at short notice.'

The print was tiny and Banks had to take out his reading-glasses. The story was about a young woman called Gwyneth Harris, who was found dead in Bute Park, near the city centre of Cardiff, at six o'clock in the morning of 13 January, by an elderly man walking his dog. Apparently, Gwyneth had been held from behind and stabbed five times in the heart with a blade resembling that of a flick-knife. There were no more details.

'Jesus Christ,' said Banks. 'Linda Lofthouse.'

'There's more,' said Annic, nodding to Winsome, who slipped out another sheet.

'Monday, the twentieth of April 1970. The *Brighton & Hove Gazette*, the day after the Mad Hatters played at the Dome there. Not very well, apparently. The reviewer mentioned that Greaves in particular seemed barely conscious, and at one point Reg Cooper had to go over to him and direct his fingers to the right keys for the chords. But there's a piece about a young girl called Anita Higgins, found dead on a stretch of beach not far from the West Pier.'

'Stabbed?' said Banks.

'Yes, sir. This time from the front.'

'And I suppose the same thing happened at the third circled gig?'

'*Western Evening Herald*, Wednesday, the twentieth of May 1970, a review of the Mad Hatters' gig and an item about Elizabeth Tregowan, aged seventeen, found dead in Hoe Park, Plymouth. She was strangled.'

'So if it was the same person,' said Banks, 'he was getting bolder, more daring, more personal. The first two he didn't want to see him, the third he stabbed from the front and the last he strangled. Is that all?'

'Yes, sir,' said Winsome. 'There may be more, but these are the only three Nick Barber got round to uncovering. It must have been enough for him.'

'It's enough for anyone,' said Banks. 'If you count Linda Lofthouse at Brimleigh, that's four girls murdered within close proximity to a Mad Hatters' gig. Were any of them at the concerts? Had they any connection with the group?'

'We don't know yet,' Annie said. 'Winsome thought it best to bring you up to date as soon as possible on this, and we've still got a lot of legwork to do. We need follow-up stories, if any are available, and we need to get on to the local forces, see what they've got in their archives. You know we never give everything out to the newspapers.'

'There's one more thing,' Winsome said. 'It might be of interest, I don't know, but the Mad Hatters were on tour in France for most of August 1969.'

'So?' said Banks.

'The flick-knife,' said Winsome. 'They're illegal here, but you can get them easily enough in France. And I don't think they had metal detectors all over the place back then.'

'Right,' said Banks. 'Excellent work. So, where does this lead us? Before he left for Yorkshire, Nick Barber found out about a trail of bodies after Mad Hatters' gigs in the late sixties and early seventies, starting with that of his birth mother. Clearly the local forces at the time had no communication about these killings, which isn't surprising. Even as late as the eighties lack of inter-force communications botched the Yorkshire Ripper investigation. Stanley Chadwick thought he'd got his man, for good reason, so he had no further interest in the case. He also had problems of his own to deal with. Yvonne. Besides, one of the victims was strangled, not stabbed. Different MO. Even if Chadwick had come across the story, which is unlikely, it wouldn't have meant anything to him. And who'd be looking at the Mad Hatters as a common denominator?'

'Clearly Nick Barber was,' said Annie. 'Before his second interview with Vic Greaves, on the day of his murder, Friday, he went to Eastvale Computes in the morning to verify his dates, and he made a note of what he found – what he already knew – in the back of a book he was carrying. We already know from the landlord of the Cross Keys that Barber was in the habit of carrying a book with him when he went for a drink or a meal.'

'Lucky for us he was so thorough,' said Banks, 'since all his other research material was stolen.'

'So you think Vic Greaves is the killer?' Annie said.

'I don't know. When you put it like that, it sounds absurd, doesn't it?'

'Well, somebody killed those girls,' Annie argued, 'and Vic Greaves was definitely around for each one.'

'Why did he stop?' Banks asked.

'We don't know that he did,' Annie answered. 'Though I'd guess he became too disorganised to function. Obviously Chris Adams has been shielding him, protecting him.'

'You think Adams knows the truth?'

'Probably,' Annie said.

'Why would he shield Greaves?'

'They're old friends. Isn't that what you said Tania Hutchison told you? They grew up together.'

'What about Robin Merchant?'

'He might have found out.'

'So you think Greaves killed him, too?'

'It wouldn't have been difficult. Just a little nudge.'

'Trouble is,' said Banks, 'we're not likely to get much sense out of Greaves.'

'At least we can try.'

'Yes.' Banks stood up and grabbed his jacket. 'Great work, Winsome. Carry on with the follow-up. Get all you can from the locals.'

'Where are you going?'

'I think I know where Vic Greaves is,' said Banks. 'I'm going to have a word with him.'

'Don't you think you should take back-up, sir?' said Winsome. 'I mean, if he really is the one, he could be dangerous if you corner him.'

'No,' said Banks, remembering that Annie had given him the same warning. 'That's one thing that'll likely lose him to us for good. He can't handle social interaction, and he's especially afraid of strangers. I can only imagine how he'll react if a few carloads of coppers turn up. At least he's seen me before. I don't think I've got anything to fear from him.'

'I hope you're right,' said Annie.

So did Banks as he started the Porsche and negotiated his way out of Eastvale towards Lyndgarth. He recalled the fear he had felt searching Greaves's cottage and it made his mouth dry. People as disturbed as Vic Greaves could sometimes summon up amazing, almost superhuman, strength. At least Banks had told Annie and Winsome where he was going before he set off and asked them to give him a twenty-minute start before they sent in a patrol car as back-up. He couldn't be certain that Greaves was where he thought he was, he realised, as he crossed the bridge over the Swain and headed for Lyndgarth, but he had a damned good idea.

The estate agent had told him that someone had been seen in the vicinity of Swainsview Lodge, and Greaves had turned uncommunicative at the mention of the place. It must have had strong associations for him from a particular period of his life, and it would be natural enough for him to gravitate there in times of stress or confusion. Or so Banks hoped, as he parked on the bleak daleside and the wind whipped at his face when he opened the car door.

The door through which he had previously entered was securely locked, and Banks was certain nobody could get in that way. An unpaved lane ran down the hill by the side of the lodge to the riverside hamlet of Brayke, and at the top of the lane a side entrance led to two large garages, both also locked. A fairly high drystone wall ran down the hill parallel to the lane, but it would be easy enough for anyone to climb, Banks thought, especially in one section, which had lost a few stones. You might not be able to get into the house without breaking a window but anyone could gain access to the grounds.

Banks's first clue was a bicycle partially hidden in the ditch and covered with a blue plastic sheet held down by two stones, flapping in the wind. Clearly Greaves couldn't get himself *and* his bicycle over the wall.

Convinced that he was right now, Banks hopped the wall and found himself in the garden beyond the swimming-pool, where the vast, neglected lawn started its long slope down to the river. He moved up to the edge of the pool, the familiar dark, cracked stone covered with moss and lichen, and the pool itself, choked with weeds, littered with broken glass and empty Carlsberg tins.

He called Vic Greaves's name, but the wind blew it back. There were shadows everywhere and Banks found himself jumping at each one, a heavy knot at the centre of his chest. He was in the open, he realised, and wished he could be more certain of his assessment that Vic Greaves was harmless.

An empty Coke tin skittered out of the grass on to the patio and Banks turned, tense, ready to defend himself.

When he reached the side of the pool closest to the house, he thought he could see something sticking out from behind one of the pillars under the upper terrace, close to where the French windows from the studio opened into the courtyard. The area was in the shadows, so it was hard to be sure, but he thought it was the lower half of a leg, with the trouser tucked into a boot, which when he got closer, turned out to be a bicycle clip.

'Hello, Vic,' he said. 'Aren't you going to come out?'

After what seemed like a long time, the leg moved and Vic Greaves's shiny bald head appeared from behind the pillar.

'You remember me, don't you?' Banks said. 'There's no need to be afraid. I came to see you at the cottage.'

Still Vic didn't respond or move. He just kept looking at Banks.

'Come on out, Vic,' Banks said. 'I just want to ask you a few questions, that's all.'

'Vic's not here,' the small voice said finally.

'Yes, he is,' said Banks.

Vic held his ground. Banks circled a little, so he could at least get a better view. 'All right,' he said. 'If you want to stay there, I'll talk to you from here. OK?'

The wind was howling in the recess made by the overhanging terrace, but Banks could just about make out Greaves's agreement. He was sitting with his back to the wall, hunched over, arms hugging his knees to his chest.

'I'll do the talking,' said Banks, 'and you can tell me whether I'm right or wrong. OK?'

Greaves studied him with serious, narrowed eyes and said nothing.

'It goes back a long time,' Banks began, 'to 1969, when the Mad Hatters played the Brimleigh festival. There was a girl backstage called Linda Lofthouse. Your cousin. She got a backstage pass because of you. She was with her best friend, Tania Hutchison, who became a member of the band about a year later. But that's getting ahead. Are you with me so far?'

Greaves still didn't say anything, but Banks could swear he detected a flicker of interest in his expression.

'Cut forward to late on that last night of the festival. Led Zeppelin were playing and Linda needed a little space to clear her head so she went for a walk in the woods. Someone followed her. Was that you, Vic?'

Greaves shook his head.

'Are you sure?' Banks persisted. 'Maybe you were tripping, maybe you didn't know what you were doing, but something happened, didn't it? Something changed that night, something snapped in you, and you killed her. Perhaps you didn't grasp what you'd done – perhaps it was like looking down on someone else doing it, but you did it, didn't you, Vic?'

Greaves found his voice. 'No,' he said. 'No, he's wrong. Vic's a good boy.' His words were almost blown into silence by the wind.

'Tell me how I'm wrong, Vic,' Banks went on. 'Tell me what I'm wrong about. I want to know.'

'Can't,' said Greaves. 'Can't tell.'

'Yes, you can. Am I wrong about how it happened? What about Cardiff? What about Brighton? And Plymouth? Were there any others?'

Greaves just shook his head from side to side, muttering something Banks couldn't hear for the wind.

'I'm trying to help you,' said Banks, 'but I can't if you don't tell me the truth.'

'There is no truth,' said Greaves.

'There must be. Who killed those girls? Who killed Nick Barber? Did he find out? Is that why? Did he confront you with the evidence?'

'Why don't you leave him alone?' said a deep voice behind Banks. 'You can tell he doesn't know what's going on.'

Banks turned and saw Chris Adams standing by the pool, ponytail blowing in the wind, bulbous face red, pot-belly sagging over his jeans. Banks walked over to him. 'I think he does,' he said. 'But as you're here, why don't you tell me? I think you know as much about it as he does.'

'It was all over and done with years ago,' said Adams.

'You may wish it was, but it isn't. That's what Nick Barber found out about, isn't it? So Vic here killed him.'

'No, that's not what happened.'

'What about the girl in Cardiff? The one in Plymouth? What about them?'

Adams paled. 'You know?'

'It wasn't that hard once we started following in Nick Barber's footsteps. He was thorough, and even his killer didn't manage to obliterate everything he'd found out. Why have you been protecting Vic Greaves all these years?'

'Look at him, Mr Banks,' said Adams. 'What would you do? He's my oldest friend. We grew up together, for crying out loud. He's like a baby.'

'He's a killer. That means he could kill again. You weren't able to supervise him twenty-four hours a day. I imagine you only came down here because I phoned you and told you things were coming to a head, that I was close to finding out who killed Nick Barber. You guessed where Vic was. He's been here before, hasn't he? And told you about it, too, I'll bet.'

'The place does seem to attract him,' said Adams, calmly. 'But you're wrong about the rest. Vic's no killer.'

At first, Banks thought Adams was blowing smoke, but something snagged at his mind, a little thing, and it pulled until it brought a number of other little things tumbling into the open with it. As the wind howled round his head, Banks found himself rearranging the pieces inside and putting them together in a different pattern, one he could have kicked himself for not seeing sooner. He still wasn't sure about everything yet, but it was all starting to add up. Was Greaves left-handed? He tried to remember from their meeting which hand Greaves had used to stir the stew, but he couldn't.

He was certain of one thing, though: when he was watching the Mad Hatters DVD the previous evening with Brian, he had noticed that Robin Merchant played his bass left-handed, like Paul McCartney. He had simply registered it unconsciously at the time, not really made anything of it, or tried to link it to the case. But now, as he thought about it, he realised that the last killing they knew of was on 19 May, about a month before Robin Merchant's drowning. Unless there were later incidents that Barber hadn't uncovered, the timing worked. He glanced at his watch. He had been at Swainsview Lodge for only ten minutes.

'Robin Merchant,' he said.

'Bravo,' said Adams. 'Robin Merchant was one sick puppy, as they say. Oh, he was glib and charming enough on the surface, but beyond that it was a case of Jekyll and Hyde. His mind was polluted by all that Aleister Crowley stuff he immersed himself in. Have you heard about Crowley?'

'I know the name,' said Banks.

'He was a drug-addict and womaniser, the self-proclaimed "wickedest man in the world". The Great Beast. His motto was "Do what thou wilt shall be the whole of the law." Robin Merchant took him literally. Do you know, Robin even tried to justify his "sacrifices", as he called them to me? He had no conscience, even before he got involved in drugs and black magic and all that shit. It just made him worse, made him think he was more god-like, or more devil-like, I should say. But he hid it so well. He got obsessed with those Los Angeles murders, too, the ritualistic elements. He thought he saw some sort of occult significance in them. I don't know if you remember, but they finally caught Manson that October, and Robin started to identify with him and his power trip. He saw himself as some sort of messenger of darkness. He didn't murder rich piggies, though. He murdered beauty and purity. The flower was his signature.'

'What happened?'

'Why should I tell you?'

'Because you know I'll find out.'

Adams sighed and stared across the pool as if he were staring across almost forty years of bad history. He reached into his pockets for a cigarette, dipped his head and cupped his hand to light it against the wind. 'I saw him,' he said finally.

'The fifth time, in Winchester. You don't know about that one, do you?'

'No,' said Banks.

'That's because I saved her life.' Adams spoke without any hint of vanity or self-satisfaction, as if he were stating a mere fact. 'I had my suspicions about Robin, and I was the only one who ever bothered to read the newspapers back then. I saw our reviews, and I read the stories about those girls. At first I thought nothing of it. It's hard to believe that the person sitting next to you on the tour bus is a killer. But I should have known. It all kept adding up. Things he said, the way he talked about people. Then I remembered Brimleigh. The first. I still couldn't be certain it was Robin, couldn't accept it, I suppose, but I didn't know where he was at the time.

'Anyway, at Winchester – this would be June, just a week or so before his death – I followed him after the show. A girl was taking a short-cut through a cemetery, of all places, the fool, and that was where he pounced. I was just behind him. I shouted something. It was dark, and I don't know if he recognised me, but he growled at me like some sort of wild animal, then belted off like nobody's business. The girl was all right. I made sure she got home OK without letting on who I was. I don't know if she reported the incident or not, but I heard no more of it. Now the problem became what to do about Robin. I talked to him. He didn't deny it. That was when he gave me all that Aleister Crowley and Charles Manson crap, trying to justify himself and his actions. I couldn't let him go on killing people, but at the same time, a trial, conviction . . . It was unthinkable. I mean, back then, a rock band could get away with most things, but murder . . . especially that kind of murder. We'd have been tarnished for ever, especially in the wake of the Manson family trial. We'd never have survived. The band would never have survived. Vic. I couldn't allow that to happen to the others after all the hard work they'd put in. Fortunately the problem took care of itself.'

'No,' said Banks. 'You killed Robin Merchant. You weren't in bed with Tania Hutchison that night. You went to confront him, here, by the pool. I'm not sure whether you intended to kill him, but you saw something unstoppable in him, and you felt you had no other choice. It worked perfectly. So easy.' He glanced over to the terrace. Vic Greaves was still there, apparently listening. 'But someone saw you, didn't he, Chris? Vic saw you.' Fifteen minutes had passed now since Banks arrived.

'I'm not admitting to killing anybody,' said Adams. 'You think what you like. You can't prove a thing.'

'And you killed Nick Barber,' Banks went on. 'It was your silver Mercedes that the tourist couple and the girl in the youth hostel saw that night. The running figure was just a jogger. It was foolish of me to think that Vic could have done anything like that. Everyone was right about him. He might be a bit off in the head, but he's a gentle soul at heart. Vic was upset, and he told you in that roundabout way of his that a music journalist had come pestering him with questions about the past, about Brimleigh, Linda Lofthouse and the other murders. Cardiff. Brighton. Plymouth. Questions to which only you and Vic knew the answers. The journalist said he was going to come back. He'd left his card. You didn't think Vic could take the strain of another interview. You thought he would soon break down and tell all, given what he'd witnessed all those years ago, so you killed Barber. You couldn't kill Vic, could you, even though he was the one carrying the secret, the most obvious victim? Did you know that Linda Lofthouse was Nick Barber's birth mother?'

Adams put his fist to his chest and seemed to stagger back a pace or two as if he had been hit. 'My God, no!' he said. 'I'm not admitting to anything,' he went on. 'I talked to Robin, yes, made sure that he knew I knew, and that I was watching him. That's all. The rest was an accident.'

'You killed him to make certain. You knew he wouldn't stop, that there would be more victims. And you knew he'd get caught eventually and bring it all tumbling down.'

'The world's a safer place without him, and that's a fact. But I'm still not admitting anything. I'm guilty of no crime. There's nothing you can do to me. Anyway, it would have been very easy just to reach out and . . .' Adams reached out his arm to demonstrate and let his hand fall on Banks's shoulder. Then he smiled sadly. '. . . and just give a little push.' Almost twenty minutes now. The cavalry would arrive in moments.

But he didn't push. Banks, who had tensed ready for a struggle, felt the hand relax on his shoulder, and he knew that Adams was about to turn away, that he had reached the end of his resources. Killing Nick Barber and seizing his notes was one thing, but killing a copper in cold blood was quite another.

It all happened at once. Before Banks could move or say anything, he heard footsteps running down the lane, and someone shouted his name. Then he heard a terrible scream from his left and a dark, powerful figure came hurtling forward, crashing right into Adams and toppling them both into the deep end of the empty pool. The cavalry had arrived, but they were too late.

By the time Annie and Winsome arrived on the scene, the ambulances had been and gone. It was getting dark, and the wind was howling through the trees, the nooks and crannies of Swainsview Lodge fit to wake the dead. The SOCOs had lit the scene with bright arc-lamps and were still strutting about in their white boiler-suits like spacemen on a mission. There were spatters of blood at the bottom of the pool mixed with the other detritus. Annie saw Banks standing alone, head bowed, by the poolside and walked over to him, touching him gently on the shoulder. 'OK?' she said.

'Fine.'

'I heard what happened.'

'Greaves thought Adams was going to do to me what he saw him do to Robin Merchant all those years ago. Then the uniforms came dashing down the lane and frightened him. It's nobody's fault. I doubt that anyone could have foreseen it and stopped him.'

'Wasn't Adams going to push you in?'

'No. He ran out of steam.'

'But you think Greaves witnessed Adams push Merchant?'

'I'm certain of it. He was on LSD at the time. That was what sent him over the edge. Can you imagine it? Adams has taken care of him ever since, protected him, as much for his own sake as anything. Persuaded him not to talk, maybe even persuaded him that it happened some other way. Greaves was so confused. He couldn't trust his own judgement. But when he saw Adams rest his hand on my shoulder by the pool . . .'

'It all came back?'

'Something like that, in whatever fragmented and chaotic way Greaves's mind works, these days. However it happened, he snapped. He'd been like a coiled spring all those years. Adams protected him from anything that was likely to push him towards snapping point. But when Barber appeared with his questions about Plymouth, Cardiff and Brighton, it was too much. Greaves had heard Adams's conversation with Merchant at the pool, so somewhere in his messed-up mind he knew what Merchant had done. But he couldn't confront it. He told Adams, who was terrified that Barber would push too hard and crack the veneer. So he killed him. Barber didn't think he had anything to fear. He knew who Adams was, thought he'd come to talk to him. He was just having a chat, turning away, reaching for his cigarettes, then Adams picked up the poker, seized the moment. Luckily for him, he still had time to gather Barber's stuff before the power cut.'

'Can we prove it?'

'I don't know. He's tired of it all, but he wouldn't admit to anything. He's not stupid. You should have seen him down there, crying like a baby, cradling Greaves's head in his lap, even though he must have been in considerable pain himself.'

'What's the extent of his injuries?'

'Dislocated shoulder, couple of broken ribs, cuts and bruises, according to the paramedics.'

'And Greaves?'

'Landed badly. Broke his neck. Died instantly.'

Annie was silent for a moment, gazing into the harshly lit swimming-pool. 'Maybe it's a blessing.'

'Maybe,' said Banks. 'God knows he was a tortured soul.'

'What now?'

'We try to get as much evidence as we can on Adams. He's not getting away with this. Not if I can help it. We'll go over the forensics, check and recheck witness statements, interview the entire village again, probe his alibi, the lot. There has to be something to link him to Barber's murder. Not Merchant's. That's too long ago, and there's no way we'll get him for that now.'

'Stefan says he's got some prints and hair from the living room that don't match anyone else's so far.'

Banks looked at her, a hint of a smile on his face. 'Then I'd say we've got him, wouldn't you? An amateur like Adams would never be able to clean up completely after himself. Besides, when the fact that Greaves is dead sinks in, we'll have a better chance of appealing to his conscience. He's got no one to protect any more.'

'What about the Mad Hatters? The past? The reputation? Aren't they supposed to be doing some reunion tour?'

'There's every chance none of it will get out, anyway. Cardiff. Brighton. Plymouth. Why should it, if Adams pleads guilty? Those cases are long over, and the killer died more than thirty-five years ago. Maybe the local forces can put a tick in a box and claim another success in their statistics of crimes solved, but that'll be about as far as it goes.'

'Until another Nick Barber comes along.'

'Perhaps,' said Banks. 'But that's none of our business.'

'Winsome talked to people in Plymouth and Cardiff, who were able to dig up the old files,' Annie said.

'And?'

'In the file, it said that each girl had a flower painted on her cheek. A cornflower.'

Banks nodded. 'Merchant's signature. Just like Linda Lofthouse.'

'They didn't release that to the general public.'

'Funny, isn't it?' said Banks. 'If they had, we might not be here now.' He turned up the collar of his jacket. His teeth were chattering.

'Cold?' Annie said.

'Getting there.'

'By the way,' she said, 'I just saw Kev Templeton come storming out of Superintendent Gervaise's office with a face like a slapped arse.'

Banks smiled. 'So there is some justice in the world.' He glanced at his watch. Seven thirty. 'I'm starving,' he said, 'and I could do with a stiff drink. How about it?'

'Sure you're up to it?'

Banks gave her an unreadable glance, his features cast into planes of light and shadow by the bright arc-lamps, his eyes a piercing blue. 'Let's go,' he said, turning away. 'I've finished here.'

Monday, 29 September 1969

The deserted stretch of canal ran by a scrapyard where the pattering rain echoed on the piles of rusty old metal. Stanley Chadwick walked along the towpath with his raincoat collar turned up. He knew that what he was about to do was wrong, that it went against everything he believed in, but he felt that it was the only way. He couldn't leave things to chance because, in his experience, chance had no history of supporting the right side without a little help. And he was right. Of that he was certain. Proving it was another matter.

Yvonne had been gone almost a week, run away from home. Janet had found some items of her favourite clothes missing, along with an old rucksack they had carried pop and sandwiches in when they went on family hikes from the Primrose Valley caravan. Chadwick was worried about his daughter, but at least he knew that no immediate harm had come to her. Not that the cities were safe for vulnerable sixteen-year-old girls, but he was certain she wasn't as foolish as some, and he hoped that she would soon come back. He couldn't make her disappearance official, set the country's police forces looking for her, so he would just have to bide his time and hope she got homesick. It tore at his heart, but he could see no other way. For the moment, he and Janet had told curious friends and neighbours that Yvonne had gone to stay with her aunt in London. She probably had gone to London, anyway, Chadwick thought. Most run-aways ended up there.

The figure approached from under the Kirkstall Viaduct, as arranged. Jack Skelgate was a small-time fence who resembled a ferret, and he had been useful to Chadwick as an informer on many occasions. Chadwick had chosen Skelgate because he had so much on him he could send him away for the next ten years, and if there was one thing that terrified Skelgate more than anything else, it was the idea of prison. Which, Chadwick had often thought, ought to have made him consider another, more honest, occupation, but some people don't make the connection. They don't get it. That's why the jails are always full. Like so many of the people Chadwick had met and interviewed over the past couple of weeks, Skelgate was as thick as two short planks, but this would play to Chadwick's advantage.

'Miserable bloody day, in't it?' said Skelgate, by way of greeting. He was always sniffing, as if he had a permanent cold.

'There was a burglary in Cross Gates the other night,' Chadwick said. 'Someone drove off with fifty canteens of cutlery. Nice ones. Silver. I wonder if any of them happened to find their way into your hands?'

'Silver cutlery, you say? Can't say as I've seen any of that in quite a while.'

'But you'd let me know if you did?'

'Of course I would, Mr Chadwick.'

'We think the Newton gang might be behind it, and you know how interested I am in putting them away.'

Skelgate cringed at the words, even though they referred to someone else. 'The Newtons, you say. Nasty lot, them.'

'They may be planning other raids. If you happen to hear anything, we could come to the usual arrangement.'

'I'll keep my ears open, Mr Chadwick.' Skelgate looked around with his ferrety eyes. Paranoia was another trait of his: he always thought someone was watching or listening in. 'Is that all, Mr Chadwick? Can I go now? Only I don't want us to be seen together. Those Newtons are a violent bunch. Think nothing of putting a man in hospital for a month, they wouldn't.'

'Just keep your eyes and ears open.' Chadwick paused, tensing as he reached the point of no return. For weeks he had been moving among people who despised everything he valued, and somewhere in the midst of it all, he had become unglued. He knew this, and he also knew there was no going back. All he wanted was for Yvonne to come home and McGarrity to go to jail for the murder of Linda Lofthouse. Then, he hoped, he might find some peace. But, deep down, he also knew that there was every chance peace would elude him for ever. His strict religious upbringing told him he would be damning himself to eternal hellfire for what he was about to do. But so be it.

He felt a sudden heaviness in his chest. Not a sharp pain or anything, just a heaviness, the way he always thought the sort of heartbreak that torch-singers described would feel. He had felt it once before, when he ran out of the landing craft on the morning of 6 June 1944, but that day he had soon forgotten it in the noise and smoke, in dodging the mortar and machine-gun fire. 'There is one more thing I'd like you to do for me,' he said.

Skelgate clearly didn't like the sound of that. He was practically bobbing up and down on the balls of his feet. 'What?' he said. 'You know I do what I can for you.'

'I want a flick-knife.' There, he'd said it.

'A flick-knife?'

'Yes. With a tortoiseshell handle.'

'But why do you want a flick-knife?'

Chadwick gave him a hard look. 'Can you get me one?'

'Of course,' said Skelgate. 'Nothing could be easier.'

'When?'

'When do you want it?'

'Soon.'

'Same place, same time tomorrow?'

'That'll do fine,' said Chadwick. 'Be here.'

'Don't worry, I will,' Skelgate said, glanced around, saw nothing to worry about, and scurried down the towpath.

Chadwick stood watching him go and wondered just what it was that had brought him to this godforsaken place on this ungodly mission. Then he turned in the other direction and walked back in the rain to his car.

ACKNOWLEDGEMENTS

I would like to thank Sheila Halladay and Dominick Abel for reading and commenting on early versions of the manuscript, and my editors Dinah Forbes, Carolyn Marino and Carolyn Mays for doing such a wonderful job on the final version. The copy editors certainly had their work cut out, too, and came through with flying colours.

They say that if you remember the 60s you weren't there. I was, so I could hardly rely entirely on memory for the sections of this book that take place in 1969. Jill Bullock, Communications Coordinator of the Alumni and Development Team at the University of Leeds, proved to be a mine of useful information. Kenneth Lee and Paul Mercs, who were both also there, shared some interesting stories with me, some of which could be repeated in the book. Among the many books I read and DVDs I watched, I would like to single out Jonathon Green's account of the period, *All Dressed Up*, and Murray Lerner's documentary on the 1970 Isle of Wight festival, *Message to Love*.

A special thanks to Andrew Male, Deputy Editor of *MOJO*, for interesting conversations and information about some of the more obscure elements of late 60s music, and for letting me be a fly on the wall in the office. Thanks also, as ever, to Philip Gormley and Claire Stevens.

I also have special thank yous for Dr Sue, of the Calgary Wordfest volunteers, for the doctors, staff and paramedics of Mineral Springs Hospital, Banff, and for Doctors Michael

Connelly and Michael Curtis, along with the nurses and staff of the cardiac unit at Foothills Hospital, Calgary, without whom PIECE OF MY HEART might have taken on a whole new meaning altogether! Also, thanks for Janet, Randy, Matthew, Jonathan and Megan for a home away from home.